BREACH OF CONTRACT

THE DATA COLLECTORS BOOK TWO

DANIELLE PALLI

DEDICATION

As always, no man (or in this case, no woman) is an island. The Data Collectors: Breach of Contract would not have been possible without the support of the following people...

Thank you to a woman of many hats, Cindy Readnower of Skinny Leopard Media, for her publishing, editing and marketing support. Thank you to Joshua Spaid for your "badassery" test reading prior to publication. Thank you to artist Joan Peters for creating another vibrant book cover. Thank you to voiceover artist Graham Mack for bringing the characters to life in the audio version (and encouraging me to be a part of the process).

And, thank you to my partner in love and life, John Palli, for his never-ending love and tech support, insightful feedback, and patience while I rambled on about the story, at length, for the past year. (You will always be my favorite "tinkerer.")

Once again, thank you to the friends and family who make up my tribe.
I am grateful.

CONTENTS

SECTION ONE

"Empathy is a heart thing, not a head thing. Everyone is affected by their environment, their internal and external ones. You put someone under stress, and they will react. It's that simple."

DRAMATIS PERSONAE

Roman Aurelius: Human male (Section 0), wavy black hair, green eyes, tall and slender.

The Baby: Born of Sabrina and Fredo (Section 3), now adopted by Hamish.

Cepheus Baruch: Royal male (Section 1, Section 3), stringy gray hair, yellow eyes, tall and lanky, shapeshifter (lizard/human).

Hysechia: Unknown origin, female (Section 1), striped black and white tiger with golden eyes, human-like features.

Petrichor Baruch: Erde-born female (Section 1), the late wife of Cepheus, long auburn hair, pale blue eyes.

Tanager Blackletter: Erde-born male (Section 1), curly blonde hair, brown eyes, average height and weight.

Bryce Cushing: Human male (Section 0), brown hair, blue eyes, medium height and build.

Clusaladek: Erde-Born male (Section 1), tall and thin, blonde hair, pale blue-gray eyes.

Commander Royce: Erde-born female (Section 1), walnut and gray hair, coal colored eyes, small and athletic frame with deep wrinkles.

Constable Melokuhle: Erie-born male (Section 1), bulky with dark skin, curly black hair and brown eyes.

Dallen: Vitruvian male (Section 2), non-shapeshifter, gold hair and blue eyes, tall with strong build.

Dr. Archibald Ennis: Human male (Section 0), bald, brown eyes, tall and thin.

Far: Macar-born male (Unsectioned by the IPP), blonde hair and green eyes, pale and thin.

Fatima Fortunata: Human female (Section 0), purple hair, gray eyes, short and Rubenesque.

Iris: Undetermined gender and species (Section 1), covered in black armor with little discernible features, average height and weight.

Lucene (Lucy) Jones: Earth-born female (Section 0), blonde or brown hair, hazel eyes, average height and weight, toned form.

Kunz Malaya: Trappist male (Section 5), monarch, blue/gray fur and matching eyes, small, bulky stature, shapeshifter (wolf/human-like).

Jasper Set: Demon male (Section 4), red eyes, bald, thin legs and barrel-like body, small wings.

Reverend Isabella Simone: Female (Section 0), spiritual advisor, white hair, violet eyes, tall and thin.

Bagheera: Male cat (Section 0), black short hair with yellow eyes, very handsome.

Fredo: Lesser Royal male (Section 3), red body and black eyes, large and thick, salamander-like with no noticeable shapeshifting abilities.

Hamish: Royal male (Section 3), brown hair and gold eyes, short and slightly overweight, shapeshifter (lizard/human-like).

Ivan (the Tinkerer): Human male (Section 0), red hair and green eyes, medium height and stocky.

Mallory: Erde-born male (Section 1), heavyset, dark hair with multi-colored eyes.

Mateo: Unknown origin (Section 1), short and heavy, little hair, long tail.

Marzipan: Unknown origin, male (Section 1), firefly and ladybug-like features, multicolored with wings.

Morphinae: Vitruvian (Section 2), shapeshifter (gender, species, coloring), Balance-Keeper, often prefers doll-like and butterfly-like forms.

Moksha: Royal (Section 3) assassin, black hair, yellow eyes, petite but athletic build.

Neroni: Erde-born female (Section 1), olive complexion, slightly heavyset, red-green hair and brown eyes.

Odessa: Vitruvian (Section 2), shapeshifter (gender, species, coloring), prefers mermaid-like form the most.

Renenet: Unknown origin, female (Section 5), red/brown fur and fire agate eyes, tall and broad, bulky stature, shapeshifter (lion/human-like).

Sabrina: Royal woman (Section 3), black hair and yellow eyes, tall with average shape, shapeshifter (lizard/human-like form).

Director Sutton: Human male (Section 0), light brown hair and hazel eyes, average height and slightly overweight.

Townspeople: Humans from other planets, Earth and beyond, includes Abe, Marcy, Mrs. Glazor and others.

Wilah: Erde-born female doctor (Section 1), tiny and thin, translucent glow.

Xeni: Unknown origin (Section 1), pink eyes, heart-shaped face, blue-black hair.

LOCALES / SPECIAL GROUPS

Achel: Main province on Erde.

The Assembly: Intergalactic gathering for the Intergalactic Peace Project (IPP).

Balance-Keepers: Special interest group in Section 2, Vitruvians. Will intervene to ensure all forces remain in balance.

Data Collectors: Specialized team from Section 1, collecting data on Earth to save species.

The Crosses: Preservation sites and residential homes on Erde comprised of four quadrants.

Erde: Planet in Section 1 known for setting up preserves to rescue and protect humans.

Erdelings: Species from the Erde planet in Section 1.

Global Environmental Agency (GEA): Earth organization for environmental concerns.

Intergalactic Peace Project (IPP): Formed to create and maintain peace among intergalactic species.

International Registry of Alien Residency (IRAR): Created by the United Commonwealth (UC) to record and track aliens living on Earth.

The Null: Crustacean-like species in Section 4 trying to destroy the universe in order to serve the mighty Segue.

Peace-Keepers: Nickname given to all inhabitants of Section 2, in particular, those living on Erde.

Planetary Defense League (PDL): Government entity on Erde for protection.

Royals: Nickname given to all inhabitants of Section 3, no specific planet-base, nomads.

Section 0: Earth and planets from common and neighboring galaxies.

Section 1: Erde and planets from common and neighboring galaxies.

Section 2: Vitruvia and planets from common and neighboring galaxies.

Section 3: Royal landscape and planets from common and neighboring galaxies. Galaxy boundaries change regularly.

Section 4: Home of the Null. Limited communication with neighboring species, located in a section of the universe with multiple black holes.

Section 5: Silva and Trappist solar system as well as planets from common and nearby galaxies.

Singulari: The Null people in Section 4. They bow to their God, Segue and refer to themselves as Singulari (which represents their religion).

United Commonwealth (UC): Earth subdivision of the IPP to keep and maintain peace.

Universal Marketplace: A place where money and goods are exchanged.

Terrestrial Academy of Research and Awareness (TARA): A major university in Achel where the Data Collectors are trained.

Vitruvia: Planet in Section 2 known for its renegade band of Balance-Keepers.

Vitruvians: Species from the Vitruvia planet in Section 2.

PRELUDE: THE STATE OF THE ASSEMBLY

Tanager Blackletter and Cepheus Baruch, professors of the Terrestrial Academy of Research and Awareness (TARA), are returning to Erde's home planet in Section 1. They are accompanied by Lucene Jones and Roman Aurelius from Earth after the Intergalactic Peace Project (IPP) banned all of Section 1, along with the Vitruvians in Section 2, and the Royals in Section 3, for allegedly breaking the rules of the IPP.

TARA sent their Data Collectors to Earth in an effort to save the human race. Still, their initiative fell under the scrutiny of some ill-intentioned people who would rather auction off Earth to the highest bidder. The Data Collectors are genetically modified Erdelings with an exceptional capacity for empathy and the ability to transmit information through thoughts and emotions instead of words.

Lucene Jones is an anomaly in that she was born of two Data Collectors and appears to have these skills naturally. The Royals discovered her through their surveillance of The Data Collectors and want her for the powers she could potentially bring to their military brigade. Meanwhile, the Vitruvians claim non-interference and yet, have made questionable alliances with a former member of the

United Commonwealth (UC) on Earth, Drake Cushing, in the hopes that they would assume control of Earth and hand-deliver Lucene. Their intentions for her were never made clear.

Now, there is to be a New Assembly, one where Erdelings and Vitruvians must form an uneasy alliance.

1

CHATROOM

SEPTEMBER. FOUR MONTHS BEFORE THE NEW ASSEMBLY.

Kudzu48: Maker197 - private chat - urgent

Maker197: I am here.

Kudzu48: Authorities closing in on all inventors. Not safe. FortuneGirl getting questioned regularly. Having more health incidents as a result.

Maker197: How can I help?

Kudzu48: Prototype vessel nearly complete. Need coordinates.

Maker197: When will you launch?

Kudzu48: One week.

Maker197: Will send support to meet you at a mid-range locale and guide you the rest of the way.

Kudzu48: May need medical.

Maker197: I understand. Coordinates incoming...

Cepheus sent Ivan the coordinates to a way station halfway between Earth and Erde, then quickly logged off and cleared the channel.

"You look worried," Tanager observed. "What happened?" Tanager paused, holding steady the chisel he was using to hand engrave a piece of wood he'd shaped into a mermaid. He sat at the other end of Cepheus's desk, on a small stool surrounded by a floor covered in blueprints, contraptions and possibly a bit of last night's dinner that had fallen there. Tanager had to shuffle the mess aside to fit in his stool.

Where Tanager's office was well-organized and minimalist, Cepheus's space was a mess, and chronically filled wall-to-wall and ceiling-to-floor with model prototypes for flying machines, automatic vegetable growers, manuals and hand tools. Tanager had simply come in to ask to borrow a chisel when he noticed his friend online and suspected he was in contact with Ivan on Earth. He decided to stick around and find out.

"The government is continuing to harass Ivan and Fatima. It is my fault." Cepheus hung his head solemnly, his eyes starting to roll back in his head as he half fell into a desk chair.

"No, no, no." Tanager leapt to his feet and grabbed his friend by the shoulders, dropping the carving and chisel on the desk in the process. "Get a hold of yourself. I can't deal with two of you having an episode on the same day."

Cepheus looked up, suddenly amused. "Get a hold of yourself," he smirked, revealing his vampire-like teeth. "*I can't deal...* You have spent much time with Lucene of late, haven't you?"

Tanager's face turned crimson. "People on the preserves talk that way, too, you know."

"I see," Cepheus acknowledged. The distraction was enough to keep him grounded.

"Tell me, how is the Earth government continuing to question Ivan and Fatima your fault?" Tanager released his friend's arms and returned to his stool, picking up the fallen carving to resume his work.

"It was I who reached out to Ivan in the first place. And..."

"Yes?"

"I gave him a bit of technology—"

"What kind of technology?"

"It was to help Earth catch up. They are still so far behind in their technological development. But it was enough to cause suspicion."

"What did you tell him?"

"You know the Vessel?"

"Of course, I know the Vessel. We recently spent seven months on the Vessel—a month more than we planned thanks to the Royals tracking us." Agitated, Tanager accidentally cut too deeply into the wood and the edge of the mermaid's tail chipped off. He flung the tool and carving back onto the desk in disgust. "Sorry," Tanager apologized. "Please continue."

Cepheus shut down his personal computer, stashing it in a desk drawer, the only one that wasn't chock full of papers and trinkets that he thought he might someday have a use for. He had to push it down a little to get the drawer to close.

"Well…that."

"You showed him how to build his own?"

"Well," Cepheus continued, "not exactly the Vessel. Most of that Ivan figured out himself when we met. But a modified, clean-air transportation system. Ever since he presented his discovery to the Global Environmental Agency, authorities have become more aggressive."

"What will they do?"

"You know the Vessel?"

"Yes," Tanager grew more impatient. "We just covered this."

"That."

"So, he is building a vessel?"

"A slightly smaller one, yes." Tanager was afraid to ask. After a long pause, Cepheus shared, "Actually, it is already built…Ivan and Fatima are coming to Erde."

"Well, you are just lovely," Fatima complimented the lavender growing outside their home, checking the soil to make sure the outdoor sprinklers did their job the night before.

"Thank ye," Ivan joked, coming up behind her from the walkway and wrapping his arms around her in an embrace. "I just shaved this morning."

"I didn't mean you, silly." She leaned back into his hug.

It had been a year since the Vessel left, carrying Roman and Lucene off to a strange new world with Cepheus and Tanager. Fatima missed her friend dearly but took solace in the fact that Ivan still had a connection with Cepheus so she could check in on Lucene. That, and she continued the meditation practice that Reverend Isabella taught her, and lovingly sent Lucene intentional mental messages each evening. On more than one occasion, she could've sworn she heard her friend whisper back, "Thank you." But that couldn't be, could it?

Life had been as challenging as it was blissful. They hid out on a remote preserve that Ivan owned, waiting it out for several months until the media coverage and questioning from the military died down. Unfortunately, as soon as Ivan resurfaced in an attempt to share some of his new ecofriendly travel knowledge with like-minded people, he was singled out—along with several other scientists and futurists—as either being of alien origin or negotiating with alien beings. In truth, it was the usual scenario, fear of the unknown and fear of intellectuals spreading bad ideas to the masses. *Or,* as Ivan reasoned, *fear of spreading good ideas to the masses and empowering individuals and small businesses.* This, he reasoned, was more likely the case.

At the same time, Fatima's heart condition worsened following Lucene's departure. Ivan chalked it up to Fatima missing her best friend and did his best to be supportive. But deep down, they both suspected it was something more. Lucene had special gifts, that much Fatima knew, but how they affected Fatima's health? Well, on that, she was still unclear.

The one positive in all this is that seven months of seclusion had a way of bringing people together, and Fatima and Ivan's relationship blossomed into something more than friendship only months after their arrival.

"I sent a wee message to Cepheus jest now," he told her.

"Was he there?"

"Aye. I told him of our plans."

Fatima began tearing up. "I can't visit my family first, can I?"

"I don't think ye should. It jest is nah safe." He hugged her harder. "But we can git a message to them once we arrive."

"In six months!" Fatima protested.

"Let's see how the travel goes. Perhaps even a month sooner… And, on the plus side, you'll git to see Lucene again. Won't that be nice?"

"Yes," Fatima nodded, wiping away a tear. "That, it will."

2

THE NULL AND JASPER

26 YEARS AGO. JUST AFTER THE CONTRACT WAS SIGNED.

The Null rarely spoke, and when they did, it typically sounded like the chirping of a spiny lobster trying to scare a predator when its resistance was low. The Null were always on the defensive, and when they were not, the group communicated in a cacophony of hissing, popping and volcano-like explosions. There was a loose hierarchy, but often one was always overtaking another. They thrived best under chaos.

An individual black hole dweller of the Null collective was unlike anything one would find anywhere else in the multiverse. A cross between an opaque sand flea and a jellyfish, they slithered across their world in a slow pace, with their frail crustacean-like spines the only thing that would help one hold its shape.

There were only two reasons for a black hole dweller to bother connecting with another black hole dweller. The first would be merely for survival. When their gelatinous bodies were connected, they moved in a blanket-like wave across their world, their venomous underbelly killing anything in its path. The second would be to destroy. The Null believed that their god, Segue, wanted this entire universe destroyed so that it could begin anew, like entropy and destruction, before order and regeneration. The collective in our universe also believed that other Null throughout the multiverse had been more successful than they had and that Segue must be angry with them. Therefore, the one agreement the black hole dwellers held dear was that they needed to destroy more quickly.

Jasper Set knew this, and he loved it. Jasper was convinced that no other demon in the multiverse loved chaos as much as he. The Null people were the epitome of chaos, of anger and fear, and of destruction. In a weird twist, he loved the Null as one might love their own parents. In fact, he was convinced that he was born out of their collective consciousness.

However, unlike his jellylike crustacean family, he was spawned from their imagination and what little they knew of the worlds they had already swallowed, in what was their ever-expanding black hole that they called "home." He had distinctly human features, if you could imagine a man walking around with skin that was so translucent that you could see all of his organs underneath. His eyes were red. His nose, toucan-like in length and form. His ears were long and pointed and rotated back and forth like that of a Great Dane following a sound. His chin was sharp enough to shuck a raw oyster. His chest was large and as round as a barrel, but his hips and legs were thin. It was difficult to imagine how he could move on those legs without the steady use of his small, bat-like wings for balance and propulsion. And yet, he flew through the air effortlessly. But when he stood, on the other hand, his back pitched forward over his feet as if balancing a plate on a stick.

Jasper traveled through the universe causing chaos for his own amusement. But he was getting bored. It was all getting too easy. Convincing the Null to leave the Royals alone until further instruction at the behest of Segue, of whom he represented; getting sentient life forms on planets to destroy each other in bloody wars in the name of religion; even causing stars to die out or grow larger, killing off planets through ice and fire. It was all him. The universe was his sandbox. But what was he to do now?

Jasper floated from galaxy to galaxy, checking in on worlds and occasionally giving one a nudge and batting them around a bit. Sometimes, he was so bored that he'd possess a human or two, but that was rare, and he often grew tired of that after only a few weeks. From his best estimation, there were only two things missing from his existence that could bring him "happiness," by his definition. One, to pierce the universe and cross the planes to the multiverse, perhaps meeting more of himself so they could compare notes. And two, to find a worthy adversary that would pose a challenge for him. Thanks to his recent contract with the Royals, he now had one such opponent in mind.

THE CONTRACT

26 YEARS AGO. BEFORE THE ORIGINAL ASSEMBLY.

"Can't you do something about this?" Sabrina barked at Hamish, overlooking what remained of a once-lush and vibrant planet. They hadn't loved it enough to give it a proper name, settling on the Training Grounds because here was where most lesser Royals were shipped to for military discipline.

Sabrina and Hamish were the sovereigns assigned to the Training Grounds and were given a small palace at the highest part of the now-desert landscape, where they could oversee much of their domain. The palace, by contrast, was filled with ornate furnishings from across the universe, exotic animals, and every manner of fruit tree and plant that they had gathered on their travels. With little regard for how these exotics would adapt in this varied climate, parts of the palace appeared almost jungle-like, with servants on constant alert so that invasive flora would not overtake the rest, and that violent fauna would not render another species extinct—possibly killing a few of the lesser Royals in the process. For all of Sabrina's complaints about the ignorance of humans about such matters, she wasn't much better.

"My dear," Hamish answered in his usual tired voice, "we have a visitor."

The visitor didn't wait to be properly escorted into the room. Instead, he swirled around Sabrina like a slow-moving tornado, eyeing her from every angle with excited curiosity.

"What are you doing? Why aren't you kneeling before your sovereign?

Jasper Set flew in so closely that his large nose poked the edge of hers. He laughed as she pulled away in disgust. "I don't kneel," he laughed. "To be clear. You ans-s-s-s-wer to me and not the other way around." He elongated the "s" with a snake-like tongue.

Sabrina was about to protest when Hamish interrupted, "My dear, this is the demon known as Jasper Set. He is of the Null people. You asked for him, remember?"

Sabrina spun in a circle one more time as she tried to follow Jasper's twirling, becoming dizzy, as her long cream-colored, Victorianesque gown tangled around her legs. It was only when Hamish reached out to grab her elbow, preventing her from tumbling over, that Jasper stopped whirling. Her eyes grew yellow.

"Careful, princes-s-s-s," Jasper warned.

Sabrina didn't like snakes any more than she liked the impertinence of someone confusing her for a princess versus the sovereign that she was. Jasper knew this, and it amused him to no end.

Sabrina's anger was eclipsed by another emotion, one that Hamish hadn't recalled ever seeing on her face before and was taken aback—fear. "Yes, of course," she acknowledged. She couldn't bring herself to bow, but Sabrina did manage to tip her head awkwardly.

Jasper crossed his arms in front of him, his right elbow resting on his lower hand while his fingers curled around his mouth as if stifling a laugh. He was hoping for more of a challenge, but quickly realized that this was not going to be the case.

"Tell me, princes-s-s-s. What is the reason that you summoned me?" Jasper already knew the answer, but he enjoyed watching others squirm in discomfort.

"Yes, well," Sabrina motioned toward Hamish's throne at the

helm of the room, even though it pained her to do so. The Royals typically bowed to no one in this universe, but she knew this demon's power and the violent nature of the Null. Unlike her people, while violent, they had a sense of self-preservation. But the Null had no concern over minor incidents such as death. In fact, it was a great honor for them to be able to die for their Segue.

She clapped her hands and a team of servants arrived with food and libation. They began laying them out on a long table opposite the thrones as a second band of servants carried in a series of pedestals which they quickly arranged, equidistant from one another, around the table.

Jasper smiled, folding his wings between his shoulder blades and hobbling on what resembled two long egret legs, slightly thicker, but not nearly supportive enough for his large torso. When he reached the thrones he grinned widely, looking directly into Sabrina's eyes as he plopped his rear-end into the cushion of her throne. She sucked in a breath, watching as he slung one leg over the arm of the chair. "Nice," he complimented. "Is this real gold?" He felt the arms of the throne. Jasper didn't need to ask. He knew the answer.

Sabrina glared at Hamish with eyes that were clearly fighting back a rare combination of rage, fear and helplessness. She folded her arms in front of her, her own fingernails digging into her biceps until they almost started to bleed.

Hamish cleared his throat, coming to his wife's rescue. "If I may, my esteemed counselor," he knelt on one knee before Jasper, bringing his eyes in direct line with Jasper's crotch, another facet of this entire scene that made Jasper's insides boil over with mirth. At that moment, he was convinced that he was the most content of all the demons in the multiverse.

Fredo watched from the doorway in obvious disgust, his wetsuit-like uniform bulging in the arms and legs as his muscles twitched involuntarily. Why Sovereign Sabrina chose this weakling of lesser Royal to join the ranks with her many years ago, he would never understand. The Training Grounds deserved a stronger male lead, such as—. He rubbed his large forehead and suppressed the thought. It wasn't his place.

"As you know," Hamish spoke quietly, "our Training Grounds are no longer adequate for our species. The climate is shifting, our population is growing, and resources are meager. We must move again."

"Oh," Jasper answered with interest. "Where to?"

"We were thinking, of, well, Earth."

"Earth?" Jasper tapped a pointed finger on his forehead. "There's something off about that equation." He snapped his fingers. "I know what it is! Earth already *has* a prime sentient species living on it, humans. Hmmm, if only there were something we could do."

Sabrina found her tongue. "We deserve that planet, not them." Hamish shot her a warning glance, and she, for once, fell silent.

"I see, and where do you suggest we place these humans?"

At the bottom of the deepest ocean, where the lot can drown, Sabrina thought. Jasper smiled at her. She turned a ghostly white as she realized that he could read her thoughts.

"It is not our concern what you do with them," Hamish responded as if he were talking about moving a piece of furniture instead of an entire species of living, breathing people. "We just need the space. You understand."

"I *do* understand," Jasper sat upright, planting his feet on the floor and tapping his fingertips together. "Up, up, up." He motioned for Hamish to stand, which he did with some effort. Jasper paused for what seemed like an eternity. "But you have a Royal army that, when combined with other military reserves from Section 3, could easily take over one measly little planet. What do you need me for?" He leaned an elbow on the arm of the throne, resting his chin on his upturned palm.

Hamish cleared his throat. "Well, there is the little matter of the Null."

"My family?" Jasper feigned surprise. "Whatever do you mean?"

Sabrina began grinding her teeth in annoyance. *Really? You really don't know what he means?* Jasper paused once again, turning a deliberate head in Sabrina's direction. "I was talking to him," he pointed at Hamish. Sabrina, once again, fell silent. It was hard enough for her to keep from running at the mouth; silencing her thoughts was near impossible.

Hamish played along. "You know, the Null seek to destroy this entire universe—the multiverse, even—if such a thing truly exists. We also know that you have the Null wrapped around your finger."

"Yes, well." Jasper rolled his eyes in fake humility, gesturing with his hands in the air as if he didn't understand it either. "My parents love me; what can I say?"

"Perhaps, your Excellence, you might consider, uh, re-directing your family, to another part of the universe for a while—a diversion of sorts."

"And thwart their holy duty of destroying the universe on behalf of the great Segue?" Jasper Set appeared shocked.

"Come now, Jasper," Hamish let his guard down and addressed Jasper informally. Jasper didn't seem to care. He was enjoying this. "You don't really believe that there's a god that wants to recycle the multiverse, do you?"

"Don't I, though?" Jasper paused before standing and only with the aid of his wings. After an eternity, he answered, "You're right, I don't." He began pacing the room, pausing at the long table filled with an assortment of meats and fish and a few leafy greens and fruit. He spotted a roach crawling across one of the pieces of meat and settled for that instead, popping it in his mouth and crunching heartily. He glanced up and smiled at Fredo happily. Fredo grimaced, but not in disgust. He also noticed the roach and had been eyeing it for himself. Jasper took a long nail and picked at his tooth to dislodge a bit of roach leg that was caught between them. "And, what's in it for me?"

"There's the girl?" Hamish offered, hesitantly.

Jasper tilted his head sideways, confused. *What girl?* He thought to himself. Sabrina noticed his expression and realized that he really didn't know. "The Earth-born Data Collector, of course." She smiled for the first time, feeling as if she had the upper hand.

"Uh, Data—what's that, now?"

Somehow, the Erdelings, Data Collectors and the entirety of Section 1 life forms had fallen outside the scope of his radar. *How was that possible?* "Surely, you've heard of the Peace-Keepers in Section 1?"

"The Peace… Bleh." He wrinkled his lips as if he just tasted something bitter. "Awful word, can't even bring myself to say it."

"Well, the Peace-Keepers," Sabrina emphasized the word, "are trying to save Earth. And, they're getting in our way." She went on to fill Jasper in on the abridged version of those living in Section 1 and the special, empathic powers of the genetically modified Data Collectors, including the story of how Lucene was a natural-born empath of two Data Collectors. Jasper listened with growing fascination. Sabrina ended with a promise of delivering said natural-born empath to him in exchange for Jasper re-directing the Null so that the Royals were no longer in the Null's impending firing line.

When she was finished, Jasper smiled. "But why, dear S-s-s-sabrina, do you think I need you to retrieve the girl? I'm all-powerful. I can just pluck her out of the air myself."

"We weren't sure of it until just this moment," Hamish put an arm around Sabrina's waist, and for once, she did not recoil from his touch. "You can try, but the fact that you didn't even know of either species' existence can only mean one thing."

"And what is that?" Jasper Set's expression grew dark. Hamish, Sabrina and their attendants all looked out the window at the storm clouds that had suddenly rolled in over their landscape.

"You can't touch goodness. They may not be perfect, mind you, but they're just good enough that you can't reach them."

"Well," Jasper frowned. "We shall s-s-s-s-ee about that." With that, he rolled himself into a swirling tornado once more before vanishing beneath their very eyes.

"Now what?" Sabrina barked.

"Now," Hamish grinned out of the corner of his mouth, "we wait."

For the next three months, Jasper Set didn't sleep. He managed to determine roughly the universal coordinates for where Section 1 resided by a process of elimination. He sailed through Section 0, felt ill at the "mostly good" Section 2, gleefully paused to cause more havoc in Section 3 and took a week touring Section 5, which had annoying pockets of impenetrable provinces which he vowed to return to once he'd gotten Section 1 all sorted out. During this time, he avoided his own stomping grounds—Section 4. The Null, he decided, would never understand. But every time he thought he'd reached Erde's atmosphere, he seemed to be transported back to where he started that day. He'd even gone so far as to seek out Data Collectors living on Earth since, he reasoned, they might be more susceptible to influence while outside of their normal environment. The most Jasper had been able to do was occasionally plant a bad headache in the brains of those he suspected were Data Collectors, mixing up their memories temporarily. But they were only the ones who'd grown fearful and had since rejected their former career, preferring to blend in as humans for the remainder of their days. He couldn't permanently injure them, or influence their behavior, or even kill them. It wasn't as if he particularly wanted to, mind you. He was just irritated that he was unable to.

Finally, he returned to the Training Grounds, demanding an impromptu meeting with the sovereigns. Hamish and Sabrina were more than happy to oblige.

"I've decided to help you," Jasper oozed graciousness.

"Well, no surprise—" Sabrina began before Hamish overtook the conversation. It was rare for him to display these moments of strength, usually spurred out of desperation for their situation as they were becoming increasingly more desperate.

"Thank you, Your Eminence," Hamish answered. Not really sure exactly what to call Jasper, his title for the demon changed regularly. Jasper found this funny and enjoyed the variety of ways in which Hamish demonstrated deference.

"I took the liberty of drawing up a little contract," Jasper flew over to the long meeting table, knocking a chair out of the way and rolling a scroll across the top of the rectangular tabletop. Hamish and Sabrina eyed the contract cautiously. "I think you will find that I'm being very generous," he gushed. "What I'm offering is 30 years of protection from the Null rolling over the Royals—to include your nomadic adventures to varied sections of the universe, providing that I can reach you, of course."

"Of course," Hamish acknowledged. It was implied that Section 1 was one of those areas where Jasper's powers could not reach.

"In return," Jasper tapped a long finger on the contract for emphasis. "I want the girl you spoke about. When can she be delivered?"

"I'm afraid that will take some time," Hamish cleared his throat, uncomfortably.

"Why?" Jasper was legitimately curious. "You offered her. Do you have the all-powerful genetic freak for me, or not?"

"It's just that," Sabrina came to her husband's aid, "we haven't been able to locate her…exactly."

"What?!" Jasper's temper was triggered once again as he smashed the table in two, the contract spilling to the floor. He grabbed it and ripped it in half. Once again, it grew dark outside as a sudden storm began rolling in.

"We can get her for you," Hamish assured him. "We just need a little time."

"How much time?" Jasper demanded.

"We don't know exactly," Hamish answered honestly, "but certainly before thirty years is up."

Jasper Set paused before a bellowing laugh erupted from the depths of his being. "You expect me to honor the entirety of your contract without having any collateral in advance, and no promise of when the result might be delivered?"

"What choice do you have?" Sabrina questioned, curtly.

"What choice?" Jasper swooped in, so that his face was right overtop of Sabrina's. Unlike last time, she was prepared and didn't move. She didn't even blink. She just stared back at him with the same intense gaze. "I could have the Null kill you and your entire race right now. Holy Segue, I could even do it myself!"

"But where is the fun in that?" Sabrina asked, coyly. She may have been temperamental and sometimes scattered, but she wasn't stupid. She'd taken the last few months to research everything she could about Jasper Set, and now she knew his weaknesses. "What we're offering you," she glanced at Hamish, who eyed her with the closest resemblance that he could to admiration, "is a challenge. You can't reach Section 1 and the Peace-Keepers yourself, and we're offering to hand deliver their most powerful to you. How you deal with her once we do, is on you…unless you feel your power wouldn't be strong enough even if we, quite literally, gave her to you?"

Jasper Set took the bait. "I agree to your terms." He waved his hand and the table reconnected itself, the contract now once again intact, overtop of it. "And, for my own self-interest, I'm going to throw in a bonus."

"What kind of bonus?" Sabrina wanted to know.

"I can toy with the Earth, sending hurricanes and tsunamis, but nothing I do seems to dramatically impact these precious Peace—" He choked back the word when he felt bile in his throat. "—these precious Data Collectors," he complained. "But," he paused for emphasis, "if I give *you* the power, Sovereign," he gestured to Sabrina, "That might be different."

Her eyes lit up, greedily. "What sort of power?" she wanted to know.

"For the next thirty years, I give you the power to control the weather on Earth. I can't touch the Erdelings who reside there, but I'm a demon. I wonder if you can. Either way," he concluded. "I am certain that you will have fun trying."

4

THE BABY

AUGUST. FIVE MONTHS BEFORE THE NEW ASSEMBLY.

"Permission to approach, my Sovereign." Fredo bowed at the door of Hamish's private office. He was half the size of his formidable former self, and the black uniform that clung to him wrinkled to match his shriveled skin, a product of losing too much weight too quickly after Hamish had nearly stabbed him to death almost one year ago.

"Granted," Hamish announced, tiredly, staring out the window of the now-barren landscape. They would need to find a new home soon; that much was certain. He was hoping it would be Earth, but now he feared that this option would be unlikely.

Fredo had come to terms with his sovereign's angry outburst, the one that caused Hamish to lash out and kill his wife, Sabrina, after no longer being able to bear witness to her cruelty, at least when it came to their son, Cepheus. In truth, he was filled with a new respect for his sovereign—Hamish was finally being true to himself and exhibited a strength Fredo did not expect. What surprised Fredo even more, however, was that Hamish had allowed the baby to live, partic-ularly since it wasn't his own.

"The baby is awake," Fredo informed him quietly, remembering that he was not permitted to say the Child's name out loud, nor refer to its gender.

"And is it in good health?" Hamish asked, without turning his gaze.

Fredo paused. "It is."

"If there is nothing else, I permit you to leave now." The baby was not his. That much he knew. He suspected it was a product of an encounter between Fredo and Sabrina, but he refused to entertain the thought past that point. All he knew was that in his estimation, Sabrina had been responsible for driving their son away from them. And now, this Child, a child that was not born out of any relationship between he and his late wife, was a suitable replacement for what he had once lost. He would not make the same mistakes that she had made.

"There is one other matter, my Sovereign…" Fredo began to step forward so that his shoulder was in line with Hamish's, before Hamish shot him a warning glance. The red salamander retreated three paces back.

"What is it?" Hamish grew impatient.

"Moksha has been found."

"Alive?"

"Unfortunately, yes."

"Well, retrieve the traitor so that she can face execution."

"It is more complicated than that," Fredo explained cautiously.

"You are boring me, Fredo. Say what it is you have come to say."

"She is living on one of the preserves on Erde."

Hamish could feel his eyes beginning to water, and he fought to keep from transitioning into his warrior-like lizard state. He took a deep breath, something he wouldn't have attempted even one month ago, but it seemed to help him maintain control. "And they accepted her?"

"It would seem so, my Sovereign."

"Can we get her back?"

"It is not advisable to do so." Fredo's shoulders sunk forward in an uncharacteristically sullen way.

"Why not?"

"We have calculated the risk, and if we are to petition to re-enter as members of the Intergalactic Peace Project, attacking the Peace-Keepers to retrieve a soldier may be…misconstrued."

"Why? We are simply rescuing one of our own. Is not a rescue mission a worthy cause of war?"

"Not in this case, my Sovereign." Fredo framed his words carefully. "It seems that she has claimed sanctuary."

"Sanctuary!" Hamish's eyes and nostrils flared, and his nails began to ooze venom. He raised an arm at Fredo, who backed away, unwilling to fight back.

"Yes, my Sovereign…sanctuary. If we were to attack, it would not be perceived as a rescue mission, but vengeance."

Hamish took another deep breath. "What is our best course of action?"

"We have an unusual suggestion."

Hamish turned and took a seat on his council throne as if he'd suddenly remembered it was his. It was Sabrina's idea to have a throne in every room in the castle, in case they had to be "sovereign-ly" at a moment's notice.

Fredo took to one knee and bowed out of habit. "Get up, you idiot." Hamish barked. It was a grim reminder of Sabrina, one that caused him a mix of emotions. *Perhaps I should do away with bowing,* Hamish thought. *I might even burn all the thrones in the castle one day.* Fredo stood.

"What is the legion's formal proposal?" he finally asked.

"We could send in Far."

"Far? That worthless scrap of an insect? He's so frail he would likely break in half during the journey. I didn't even think he was still alive."

"He is doing better…just well enough. If we could send him to claim sanctuary on the same preserve as Moksha—"

"He could find out what information she's been spouting about us." Hamish reveled at the idea. "And, perhaps collect some data of his own." He laughed at his own joke. *The Data Collectors*, he thought, *are wasting time doing things the wrong way. Leading with the heart, not the head, can only end in destruction.*

"We've also been endowing him with some…misinformation," Fredo continued. "If they think he is a refugee, they will trust him."

"How can we be certain he won't turn on us as well?"

"Our methods have come a long way, my Sovereign." Fredo's eyes lit up as if he momentarily remembered his former glory. "We've been steadily programming his thoughts for a year now. I believe he is ready."

Far was a prophesier who escaped from his home planet of Macar when its leaders became too afraid of his power. It was surprising to them, given that he was a waif-like man with pale skin and a soft voice. His skills in fortune-telling and in-body astral travel were unlike anything anyone had seen. He landed on Earth for a while, but the atmosphere was too polluted for his frail form, and he developed cancer. Somehow, he accidentally propelled himself to Section 3 and was promptly arrested by the legion. They would have killed him right away if they didn't think that he could potentially be useful. For that reason, they did what they've never done before… they actually nursed a non-Royal back to health…sort of.

"What happens when he encounters Moksha," Hamish wanted to know. "Won't she become suspicious?"

"She left before his programming began. In fact, I'm certain she would have wanted to take him with her, but he was too weak, and she couldn't wait. If anything, she will be pleased to see him."

"Then make the boy ready."

"Yes, my Sovereign." Fredo awkwardly backed slowly away from Hamish, retreating through the chamber door before pausing.

"Is there something else?"

"I was just wondering, my Sovereign—"

"What is it?" Hamish began grinding his sharp teeth so much that you could hear the crunching.

"The baby—"

"What about the baby?"

"May I…hold it?"

"Absolutely not!" Hamish spat. "I will be along in a moment to feed it."

"Yes, my Sovereign."

5

THE RETURN TO ERDE

MAY. EIGHT MONTHS BEFORE THE NEW ASSEMBLY.

"How is she?" Tanager asked, concerned, setting the Vessel on autopilot, removing his harness, and standing up for a stretch.

"She is okay. She's resting," Cepheus answered, shaking his head. "We tried to think of everything. If only we'd have had more time to prepare the Vessel before our return."

"Perhaps, but you and I made the journey without incident, and that took us a year. It's only been three months and Lucene is…not adjusting well."

"We were trained for this. She was not," Cepheus answered simply, motioning for Tanager to follow him into the meditation room. "Perhaps we can speak quietly in here."

The doors opened to reveal a mid-day landscape; the dome lights gave the illusion of a forest in the distance, complete with a slow running waterfall and a gentle stream. At the center of the room, Roman occupied one of the couches wearing his usual black jeans and a black t-shirt, now beginning to show signs of wear from constant use. His bare feet dug into the grass beneath them. He sat upright, with a blissful smile on his face and eyes closed in meditation. As soon as he heard the door open, he opened one eye. "Hello, gentleman," he said pleasantly.

"I'm sorry, Roman," Cepheus apologized. "Had we realized you were taking a moment of solitude we would have gone elsewhere."

"No apologies necessary," Roman shifted his weight slowly and stood. "I was about done anyway. And I would have put a note on the door if I required some alone time."

The notes were Lucene's idea. Cepheus and Tanager had no need for this when it was just the two of them traveling. If one entered the room while another was reading, meditating, studying or even pacing in circles for problem-solving purposes, the other just... adjusted. Neither of the men saw it as an intrusion, nor felt the deep need to be alone. For the humans, however, this was not the case, most especially with Lucene. She grew anxious if she went into the space to be alone and someone entered the room without realizing she was there. Roman, while he appreciated the solitude, was not as perturbed by four people sharing a relatively small space. If he didn't like the intrusion, he simply went someplace else. There were four quarters on the ship: the meditation area, the sleep station, the dining area, and the exercise and bathing station. And, if he really wanted an escape, the engine room was enormously large (by comparison), with plenty of little nooks and crevices to curl up and hide away.

But Lucene was hypersensitive, a trait they assumed was related to the fact that she was born of two genetically spliced Data Collectors. They were engineered for empathy, and in Lucene's case, she was born with a boatload of it as a result. Unfortunately, after two months of being on the Vessel, she complained, "I feel like a Goddamned sardine in this place!" A meeting around the dining table was held. And, as they ate smoked fish and drank a sweet wine (except for Cepheus, who was the lead on duty at the time—he settled on water), it was decided that they would put a sign on the meditation room door, or any door, for that matter, when absolute privacy was needed. Most often, Lucene would put the sign over her sleep pod, which was odd since no one would disturb someone while sleeping, except in emergencies.

All was better for a short time, but now, in month three, she seemed to be unraveling again.

"Would you gents prefer to speak privately, or can anyone join?" Roman smiled pleasantly. He was not without issue, he realized, having spent the better part of a year obsessing over the Data Collectors so much that he eventually came to believe that he actually *was* from Erde, an alien sent to research relationships among Earthlings. In reality, he was a former anthropology professor who sank into a deep depression at the loss of his love, Far, a man who *was* an alien and left to find a cure for his own life-threatening disease. It had only been two months since Roman had come to his senses, and he vacillated between feelings of excitement at his journey to a new world and grief at his deep loss, and then to hope that he would one day find his beloved again, whole and healed. Recognizing his own fragile feelings, he was naturally sympathetic to those around him and understood that Lucene had seen more than her fair share of trauma.

"Actually, this matter concerns you as well, friend. Please, join us." Tanager answered. The three men took a seat on the circular deep-seated, wood-toned couches. Roman opted to cross his legs under him. Cepheus did the same, while Tanager slouched backward, stretching his legs onto the grass in front, crossing his ankles and arms in front of him as the couch all but swallowed him.

"I suspect that when we realized that one of the Royal ships may have spotted the Vessel near the way station, forcing our diversion from our original course home, we may have…unsettled Lucene," Cepheus offered quietly.

"Well, six months being stuck together in a relatively small space is an adjustment," Roman acknowledged. "Learning that the journey is delayed by an entire month, well, I can understand how that would set off any introvert."

"And how are you adapting to this news?" Tanager asked.

"I'm an odd duck," Roman answered. Tanager took a moment to mouth the words to himself *odd duck,* making a mental note to look it up later. "I was so crazed in *finding* you, and then, in my mind, *becoming* you, that, while a little confining at times, this is the first peace I have experienced in a very long time."

"I'm happy for you, friend," Cepheus touched his arm.

"I have you to thank, Cephi," Roman replied.

Cepheus cringed at Roman's recent use of this affectionate nickname. It reminded him of home, of his late wife and children, and how Petrichor used to call him that. He pushed that memory back into the corners of his mind and locked them away, for now. Recognizing that Roman knew not of the name or the images it conjured, he tried to integrate its new reference in his mind, replacing a bad memory with a good one.

"Are you okay?" Roman stopped suddenly.

"Of course," Cepheus smiled, pulling himself back from sinking. Tanager had noticed it as well and was at the ready in the event an anti-psychotic was needed. As far as mental and emotional stability went, he seemed to be the only balanced member of the crew, a responsibility that he did not take lightly. "So, the meditation I have taught you has been helpful?" Cepheus asked.

"Enormously," Roman placed his hands on his knees, elbows jutting outward.

"What I am having trouble understanding," Tanager interjected, "is why her training isn't helping her. Cepheus, you worked with her as a small child and have been teaching her almost daily since we've been on board. But, instead of becoming calmer, Lucene actually seems more agitated."

"Do you think she needs a break from all the mindfulness training? Maybe bake a pizza, crack open a few beers and chill?" Roman offered, helpfully.

"A break, maybe," Tanager agreed. "I'm afraid we're out of any pizza-like ingredients, and the closest we have to beer is flavored club soda…and, what are we chilling?"

Roman opened his mouth to speak, "Eh, never mind."

"There's a larger concern, I'm afraid," Cepheus spoke in a hushed voice. The two men leaned forward to hear him. "I was communicating with Dr. Ennis."

"Archibald Ennis? The doctor who first tended Lucene as a child, after the lightning strike? Is he still alive?" Tanager was surprised.

"Why would you be surprised? That was 25 years ago. He was a young man at the time. You know that humans live past 40 now, right?"

"Of course, I know that." Tanager uncrossed and re-crossed his arms, sulking a little.

"Wait," Roman interjected. "I remember him from my research. Wasn't he the cardiologist who was also a self-trained medical geneticist…I mean, I don't know about his credentialing, but he definitely did his research."

"The same," Cepheus nodded. "It was Lucene's odd reaction to the lightning strike that got his attention. That was the first of many anomalies he's seen at the hospital. Since then, he's become obsessed with people who should have died but didn't or should be incapacitated from an injury but aren't. The interesting twist is that he wasn't even Lucene's doctor. He was checking on young Fatima who happened to be in the same hospital room."

"How did you come to know Dr. Ennis?" Roman wanted to know.

"Chat room," Cepheus answered. Somehow, his vampire-like, lanky form and deep voice sounded odd saying that.

"For a scholar, you spend an awful lot of time online communicating with people from other planets. First, Ivan, and now, Dr. Ennis." Tanager was perplexed by this.

"I see no problem with this," Cepheus explained. "By the time a book is printed, it is likely out-of-date. But, if I check in with the experts, be it a Makerspace forum where I meet inventors, or a medical specialty group where I connect with Dr. Ennis, I'm learning."

"But, aren't you guys more evolved than Earth? What can you learn from us?" Roman eyed him with confusion. As a former anthropology professor with keen observation skills, sometimes he still missed the obvious. It was as if he had a hyper-focused awareness, but only about specific subject matters.

"We may be technologically advanced as a whole, but I would never be so conceited as to think that we have all the answers nor that another species has nothing of value to add."

"That's very big of you," Roman answered.

Big of you? Another one for Tanager to learn.

"So, what is it that Dr. Ennis told you?" Tanager wanted to know.

"It's not good, I'm afraid." Cepheus let out a deep sigh. "I'm not sure if it's accurate or not. We won't know until we get back home and do further testing."

"What is it?" Tanager twitched.

"You know how we genetically modified the Data Collectors, including ourselves, to become empathic and be able to transmit messages across long distances without words?"

"Yes," Tanager answered impatiently. "Of course, I know that. I was there. Why are you asking rhetorical questions?"

"Well, we assumed that my being under Watch had to do with mental illness caused by my parents torturing me."

"Of course, it was."

"But what if it wasn't?"

"I don't understand."

"We also assumed that Lucene's behavior was a result of her parents dying when she was a child, being forced into the foster system, not being an Earthling, getting struck by lightning, and almost getting killed…several times."

"Did you hear yourself just now?" Tanager pointed at him for emphasis. "How could those things not be the reason for her current behavior?"

"They may be causing an exaggeration of symptoms, but —"

"But what?"

"What if her trauma…my trauma…were merely triggers for a deeper problem?"

"Such as? What deeper problem?" Tanager looked from Cepheus to Roman and back to Cepheus. Roman merely shrugged but was eager to hear his response. Roman was also wondering why they weren't just thinking at each other since it was their gift. But he then concluded to himself that they were probably speaking for his benefit. Either that or mentally transmitting messages was probably complex and took a lot of energy. He settled on it being a combination of both and thought he might ask them another time.

"According to Dr. Ennis, genetic splicing can backfire, and a traumatic event can trigger the foreign gene to mutate, potentially causing other illnesses, including…mental illness."

"What? No, I don't believe it!" Tanager shook his head feverishly. "By that logic, we should all be under Watch, but I don't have the same symptoms that you and Lucene have exhibited, and I went through the same trauma as you when—" Tanager stopped himself and winced. "I'm sorry, I didn't mean to bring it up."

"It is okay, I understand." Cepheus coughed uncomfortably, stuffing back an emotion.

Tanager was referring, of course, to the time the Royals broke into his home and killed Cepheus's entire family, and nearly killed both he and Tanager as well.

"I'm not saying it is for certain," Cepheus explained. "But it is something we must address with the terrestrial academy when we get home."

"I don't mean to throw a wrench in the works," Roman added. *Wrench in the works. I swear, these humans have a lot of idioms,* Tanager thought. "But I haven't been sliced and diced, but trauma sent me over the edge. How can he be sure it's related to genetic modification?"

"Numerous tests that he began after the assembly," Cepheus answered. "Many Data Collectors sought out Dr. Ennis for medical advice because he was among the few doctors they trusted. He's analyzed hundreds of blood and DNA samples and has recently started to notice some patterns. It may not be the case, but we have to at least consider the possibility that our process is potentially hazardous. It would be unethical not to."

"What about the students at TARA?" Roman asked. "Have any of them exhibited similar behaviors as those Data Collectors on Earth?"

"Good question," Cepheus answered. "I checked in with Dr. Wilah and my lead students, who are assuming our roles while we travel, and they've indicated that only a handful of students are exhibiting questionable behavior following a strange illness. But they assumed it was because they were physically unwell. Those students are currently being observed and are in quarantine until we can be sure that they are not contagious. But, on the whole, Erde is a peaceful planet, so the chances of a traumatic event setting them off are much rarer compared to Earth."

"Which brings us back to Lucene. What do you suggest we do about her current behavior?" Tanager picked at a stray thread on his pant knee nervously. He was worried about her.

"Yes," Lucene called from the entranceway. The men hadn't heard the door to the meditation room open. Lucene stood in her nightclothes, without concern over propriety or if any part of her pajamas were see-through. They weren't, but the top did cling rather tightly.

They just recently left the B-612 way station, scrounging what limited clothing and other supplies that they could. While Cepheus and Tanager had a limited wardrobe on board, the humans did not and procured what they could at the station. There wasn't much. Since the Royals were spotted nearby, TARA couldn't risk sending a relief vessel to bring more clothing and other provisions. They had to make do with what they already had on board and what they found on B-612.

Cepheus and Tanager drew their eyes to the floor, politely. Roman was indifferent. "So," she continued, "what *do* you suggest we do about Lucene's current behavior?"

"Ah, you are awake," Tanager stated the obvious. "How are you feeling?"

"Fine," Lucene crossed her arms in a way that suggested that she was not at all fine. "What does whatever you were talking about have to do with me?"

"I was just explaining a few things I recently learned about us and your parents. Perhaps you should sit down."

⁂

For the next month, Lucene's behaviors became increasingly worse. She vacillated between absurd delight, randomly laughing at everyday events out of context with anything remotely amusing, and extreme agitation, particularly if her personal space was surrounded by items she had arranged just so, and then someone unwittingly moved an object, such as a chair or dinner plate, without requesting permission first.

"What are you doing?" Lucene demanded one evening when Tanager took a red spoon out of a kitchen container so he could enjoy an afternoon snack. He looked down to see her sitting at the dining table with scraps of paper strewn all over it, pieces torn in odd shapes with unrecognizable symbols scratched across them. She laid her arms over them and leaned in as if she were a young child protecting her secret diary.

"I was taking a break from studying and thought I might have some leftover butternut porridge." He felt strange having to explain himself.

"Well, that's my fork," she eyeballed it. Tanager paused for a moment before slowly putting it back in its holster. He carefully reached in and pulled out a *blue* spoon that he held up carefully for approval.

"That's fine," she barked, returning her attention to the slips of paper before her. She began brushing them together as if brushing crumbs into a pile before sweeping them up and depositing them into a trash bin. The right side of her face twitched slightly in a tick that had only recently developed, and only showed up when she was particularly anxious.

He stood awkwardly in front of the cooling unit before reaching in to retrieve the leftover porridge, wondering exactly where he was going to eat it since Lucene had taken up the entire dining area with…whatever the hell it was she was working on.

"You can go now," she finally looked up, dismissing him with annoyance.

He had intended to heat up his food before eating it, but now thought better of it. He took the cold container and the approved blue spoon and made his way to the navigation room where Cepheus was finishing up routine checks. He took a seat next to his friend.

Cepheus eyed Tanager's food questioningly, and then nodded. "Lucene?" he asked.

"I'm afraid so," Tanager answered.

"Shall I go talk to her?"

"I don't think it's a good idea. She's got that twitch thing happening."

"Knock, knock," Roman tapped the wall in a jovial manner, even though there were no actual doors separating the navigation room from other areas of the Vessel. It was one central location.

"Yes, Roman. What is it?" Cepheus questioned.

"Any idea what this is?" he held up what once was a tattered fishing hat. The shiny ornamental bait that had been attached to the side was now poking through a hole at the center. It appeared as if someone had taken scissors and cut chunks off the rim. "I found it stuffed in one of the gears under the treadmill."

Tanager let out a sigh. He must have displeased Lucene…again. He had made every attempt to communicate more effectively with her, even suggesting a few "date nights" where he'd planned a special meal in the meditation room, under a starry dome with soft classical music playing. On those nights, Cepheus and Roman made themselves as scarce as possible, Roman spending extra time in the exercise area upping his strength-training routine while Cepheus took his time making the rounds in the engine room, often checking the same equipment two or three times. The plan almost always backfired, however, because there would always be something that set Lucene's mood into one of agitation. One evening, she went as far as to suggest that when they got back to Erde they should "see other people."

"My favorite hat," Tanager took it from Roman who gave him a perplexed look. *Really?* Roman didn't understand how that monstrosity could be anyone's favorite anything, but he felt bad for his friend.

The sound of a loud cackle interrupted the conversation. Lucene stood in the navigation room, barefoot, holding up a torque wrench. "Any idea how this ended up with the utensils?" She continued laughing hysterically.

Roman went to retrieve it from her, but she held it over her head. He wasn't sure whether she was trying to keep him from taking it from her, or if she were threatening to hit him with it. "No, it's mine. I found it."

"You found it in the kitchen?" Cepheus asked calmly. He was trying to connect with her empathically, but all he could sense was a turbulent swirl of emotions, and he couldn't seem to lock in on anything stable.

"Yes, but only after I was done with it in the engine room." Both Cepheus and Tanager exchanged a shared look of alarm.

"What *exactly* were you doing in the engine room?" Tanager made the mistake of gesturing with his hand as he spoke. Lucene took it as an attack and swung the wrench wildly. Roman grabbed her wrist and wrestled it from her fingers.

"Ow," she winced, rubbing her wrists. She stuck her tongue out at Roman, like a small child.

Cepheus didn't wait to witness the remainder of the scene play out. He snatched the tool from Roman and climbed through the passage to the engine room to assess the damage. "Safety measures," he spat at Tanager, who nodded at the cue.

"Can you handle this," Tanager asked Roman.

"Of course," Roman understood. They'd been through this scenario before, although this was the first time Lucene was in the engine room to their knowledge and had potentially put them in danger. Cepheus went to assess the damage, if there was any, while Tanager followed close at his heels in case there were unexpected occurrences such as a fire or a sudden lack of oxygen in the room.

"What are you supposed to handle?" Lucene let out the beginnings of a temper tantrum. "Me?"

Fortunately, this is where Roman's personality shined. He flashed a pearly white smile. "Lucene," he called her name in a sing-song voice, wagging a finger playfully at her as if she were in trouble. "What did you do?"

Lucene suddenly let out an uncontrollable giggle, like a small child, covering her mouth with her hands. Roman continued to smile, waiting patiently for her to calm down. Finally, she whispered, "Nothing," managing to get it out, breathlessly. "Hah! Did you see the look on their faces?!" She tapped Roman lightly on his chest, her eyes wild with glee. "I didn't do anything. I just wanted to see the look on their faces to think that I did."

"That was very naughty of you, Lucene," Roman played along. "But don't you think you've had enough fun for one evening?

Lucene's face dropped. "But I don't want to go to bed yet," she whined.

He wrapped an arm protectively around her. "I know, but I'll be heading to sleep myself after I let the gents in on your little joke. A good night's rest will do us all a world of good."

She grew serious. "Do you think they'll be mad?"

Roman reassured her, "I'm sure it will all be fine." He guided her to the dressing area, politely averting his eyes while he waited for her to privately shower, use the facilities, and change into a gown. While he did so, he sent a message from his watch, and a green light flashed to both Tanager and Cepheus's watch, indicating a perceived "all clear." Tanager and Cepheus continued to check all of the equipment that Lucene could have possibly tampered with, just in case, before returning to the navigation center.

"All done," Roman held out a robe for Lucene when she returned from the shower, once again wearing the same pair of tight-fitting polka dot pajamas. She smiled as she put her arms through the sleeves.

"Why can't Tanager be as nice to me as you?"

"Well, not everyone can be born with my charm and devilish good looks, now can they?" He opened the door to her sleep pod and gently nudged her back, guiding her inside.

"No," she smiled wistfully. "I guess they cannot."

Once she'd settled in for the night, Roman administered a light anti-psychotic airborne spray into her sleep pod. He also triggered the alert on the outside of her chamber that would send a signal to his watch if she got up in the middle of the night. It was his turn to keep an eye on her.

Frankly, they were all growing increasingly weary of this.

A meeting was called that night in the meditation room. It was decided that it would be in everyone's best interest if Lucene were placed in deep hibernation for the remainder of the journey. But, they decided, they had to get her to agree to it. The last thing they wanted was for her to be forced to make a decision that was against her will, out of their desperation. In a clear-minded state, she eventually agreed several days later. And, with much reluctance and sadness, Tanager set her sleep pod into a dormant state where Lucene would remain asleep until they'd reached Erde.

THE WESTERN CROSS

SEPTEMBER. FOUR MONTHS BEFORE THE NEW ASSEMBLY.

"I don't understand," Roman complained, rubbing an eye like a small child being told he had to finish his peas. "I've taught anthropology on Earth for nearly two decades. What makes you think I am incapable of teaching it at TARA?"

They arrived at the Western Cross just moments earlier. The terrain was most comparable to New Mexico and Arizona—a desert landscape, except with more pockets of running water and greenery. The air smelled of sage and fresh berries. In the distance, a small village could be spotted, adobe-like housing surrounded by red rock that was layered with vibrant white, green and earthen minerals. It was beautiful in a way that was completely different from the central city of Achel. For a moment, Roman almost forgot to be annoyed.

"It's not that you are incapable," Tanager explained gently, adjusting the fedora he'd taken to wearing after Lucene destroyed his fishing hat. "It's just that your information is a little…incomplete."

They arrived at the center of the village. There were a few residents meandering through the cobblestone streets, many of whom stopped to greet Tanager. He tipped his hat awkwardly. They snickered a little but were polite enough not to say anything. Roman couldn't help but notice that these Earthlings were a little…different.

Some looked as human as he did, while others were distinctly taller and leaner (if that were possible) by several feet. Others were much smaller and wider with heads that were disproportionately large, matched only by their even bigger eyes.

"I thought the preserves were to save members of the human race," Roman whispered, confused.

"These *are* members of the human race," Tanager explained as they made their way through town, passing a bakery, a cheese shop and a clean meat chop shop. "They're just not all from Earth."

Roman stopped walking. "Hang on," he said, motioning with one hand. Tanager paused, searching his database of Earth idioms and then nodded with a smile. "I thought Earth was it, and that that's why you were so keen on saving our population from extinction."

"Yes," Tanager acknowledged, taking a seat at an outdoor cafe and motioning for Roman to join him. "That was the original plan. I was as surprised as you were to return home to find that Earth was just one of many life-sustaining planets for the human race. Unfortunately, the people you are witnessing are facing the same perils as Earth, and they need our help." For once, Roman was speechless. "Really, Roman," Tanager chastised lightly, "Are you so self-centered as to think that you and Earthlings were our only potential concern?"

"Kinda," Roman admitted.

A large woman with curly hair that ran down to her ankles approached the table. "Tea to start?" she offered.

"Yes, thank you," Tanager answered. "And you?" he asked Roman.

"Got anything…stronger?" Roman asked.

She looked at Tanager, confused.

"Alcohol," Tanager explained. "Something in the gin variety, if you have it."

"Ah, of course," she smiled at Roman. "Perhaps you'd fancy a gin and rossenberry tonic?"

"What is rossenberry?" Roman looked at the woman and back at Tanager, confused.

"He's recently arrived from Earth," Tanager explained.

"Ah, I see." Her red eyes grew wide. "I've always wanted to go there. I've heard it's lovely in the winter…is it?"

"Is it what?" Roman was distracted.

"Is Earth lovely in the winter?" Roman likened this question to "I know a guy who lives in New York. Maybe you know him?" He was more interested in the gin and rossenberry tonic and knew of one sure way to get it. "It certainly is." He flashed a smile. She blushed a little. "Tell me, my dear…what is your name?"

"Marcy," she turned redder.

"Marcy," he smiled, calling up a memory. "I knew a Marcy on Earth. A lot like you, but her hair was a little lighter. Lovely woman." If Tanager knew how to roll his eyes, he would have. Instead, he sat and watched the exchange with the curiosity of a small puppy. "Tell me, Marcy. What *is* a rossenberry?"

"Oh, it's like your cranberries only sweeter and more aromatic."

"Well, that would be just fine."

"Marcy," Tanager asked. Marcy's face fell when she pulled her gaze from Roman. *Really,* Tanager thought, *I just don't get it.* "Could we have one of your succulent meat pies to go with it?"

"Ah, certainly," she smiled proudly. They were her specialty. "Back in a jiffy…as you Earthlings would say." She darted back into the cafe, leaving Roman and Tanager to return to light conversation and people-watching.

"Meat pies," Roman inquired. "Isn't that…wrong, here…somehow?"

"Clean meats," Tanager explained. "Same protein, vitamins and health benefits but healthier and without killing anything…more like growing a plant, really."

"Is it any good?" Roman wanted to know.

"Prepare to be amazed," Tanager boasted as Marcy set the plates before them, another male server right behind with the beverages.

"Made 'em fresh this morning," she waited, expectantly for Roman to take a bite.

"Delicious," Tanager offered. She ignored him, continuing to eye Roman attentively. He took a hesitant bite, and then his eyes grew wide.

"Amazing," he offered, as the server poured Tanager's tea. Roman kept chewing slowly until she'd walked away. "Okay," he leaned in to whisper, "it's not bad, I'll give you that, but it's not...."

"Bacon?" the young server offered with a smirk, winking at Roman.

"Exactly," Roman winked back. "Good, but not bacon." The server grabbed a tray and wandered off to help another patron.

"You remind me of a mermaid I once knew," Tanager said flatly.

"How so?" Roman asked.

"Never mind," Tanager took a bite of his pie, followed by a sip of tea. "We have to discuss your research."

Roman was sipping his gin when he caught sight of someone with a monk-like robe in his periphery, peering at Roman from in front of a bookstore window on the corner. Roman's face went paler than anyone thought possible.

"What is it...what's the matter?" Tanager looked at him, concerned.

"Far," Roman answered.

"What about him?" Tanager asked, but Roman was already on his feet, making his way toward the robed figure who had already disappeared into the bookshop.

"He's here."

"Uh...Cepheus," Tanager said aloud, to the air. A few passers-by looked at him quizzically but said nothing. "I'm still working on this mental communication thing. So far, I can only connect with Lucene. But, if you can hear me, I may be a few minutes late to the agricultural section. Roman's just run off." He trotted off in a slow-run toward the bookstore (Tanager was not the most athletic of individuals). "Will meet you in a while."

From several miles away, on an inspection visit to the rural areas of the Western Cross, Cepheus nodded to himself. *You're learning,* he praised, unconvinced that his friend could hear him. After all, while both men were genetically modified Data Collectors, Tanager's training was cut dramatically short when Cepheus went under Watch and Tanager suddenly had to replace his friend as lead instructor at TARA—and then later, when the men had to return to Earth to rescue Lucene, they had made progress during their long flight home and Tanager was very skilled. But there was still more that Cepheus needed to teach him.

Like someone learning a new language, Cepheus suggested Tanager refrain from using his communication watch unless absolutely necessary when they spoke. The pathways of empathic dialogue had to be cultivated, person to person. So, while they could pick up bits and pieces from random individuals, emotions and a few phrases, the connections between specific people had to be trained. This was a tricky agreement as Tanager was still responsible for monitoring the whereabouts of Cepheus and Roman—both of whom were under Watch until further psych-evaluation deemed them safe to society and themselves. The fact that Cepheus was still allowed to train Tanager and resume most of his day-to-day responsibilities at TARA was somewhat questionable. However, Erde was a small planet with limited resources, so inhabitants often had to find creative ways to fulfill many roles.

Cepheus felt as if he were mostly cured…maybe 80%? That was his unscientific findings. What he did know was that he hadn't had to have any antipsychotic medications since their long journey from Earth and that when he felt himself slipping, he was fairly good at recognizing the signs and bringing himself back.

"Cepheus, old boy, good to see you," a portly man in coveralls startled him out of his reverie. The man vaguely reminded him of Ivan, but without the accent and about twice the girth.

"Abe, it's nice to see you. I saw the work you've done at Tanager's new high-home…impressive."

"Well, thank you very much. It was not easy given Tanager's odd specs, but me and the missus are happy with the way it turned out." Abe was carrying several long wooden beams in his arms as if they were weightless. Behind him, a thick woman wearing jeans and a flannel shirt stood by an electric truck. When she saw Cepheus, she waved pleasantly. "Just making the rounds, are you?" Abe asked, quizzically.

"Yes," Cepheus answered. "Just…making the rounds."

"Any word on…you know…relocation?" From a distance, Abe's wife shot him an *oh no, you just didn't* look. "We love it here, but a few of the non-natives appear…restless."

"I wish I could be more optimistic, Abe," Cepheus admitted. He was torn. He didn't want to lie, but he also didn't want to give people false hope. "But thus far, none of the endangered planets appear to be ready for re-occupation just yet."

"I understand," Abe said. "Will you inform the village at the next town meeting, or shall I?"

"It's probably best if it comes from someone at TARA," Cepheus answered. "We have a young woman in the research department who's recently relocated from Earth. She could help validate what she's seen on her planet. Have you heard about Lucene?"

"Have not had the pleasure."

"Well, once she's out of quarantine, we'll be sure to bring her around to meet everyone."

Abe noticed his wife tapping her foot. "The missus is getting impatient. I best be going."

"Good to see you, friend."

"You too, champ."

With that, Abe stacked the beams onto the back of the truck as his wife climbed into the driver's seat. Moments later, the two drove off. Most non-laborers used public transport to get to neighboring towns, or they paid a premium to borrow common cars from a public lot if they wanted to go on a road trip. But for those who had jobs requiring the transporting of heavy materials, such as Abe and his wife, who owned a construction and remodeling business, the government made special exceptions provided they filed for a laborer's license.

Cepheus continued along the dirt path toward some of the local farms, pleased to inhale the fresh country air and flat planes. He could see the mountains in the distance. Like Earth, the rural regions of the Western Cross preserve had hundreds of miles of farmland for growing plant-based foods of every variety. They also had cows, oxen, deer, chickens and horses, but none were for slaughter. They milked the cows and ate the eggs from chickens, but only after asking them for permission first. The oxen and deer were subject to small skin cell scrapings periodically in order to grow clean meats. For their acts of service, these animals were treated like royalty, given as much food, space and comforts as an animal would want, which, admittedly, wasn't much.

A small cottage on a modest plot of land caught Cepheus's eye. *That is odd,* he thought to himself. *When was that built?* The cottage was painted a deep purple with Ivy vines on the roof flowing down the sides. The stained-glass windows had grape designs on them. *A vineyard,* he observed. He hadn't seen one in the Western Cross before and was puzzled. He wrapped his cape around him tighter as the wind picked up and made his way to the cottage.

He passed through the property gate and made his way to the front door, knocking lightly on it. There was no answer. He didn't want to be impolite, but curiosity got the better of him. Cepheus walked to the side of the house and attempted to peer through one of the grape-stained windows.

"You there," someone poked him in the ribs with a stick. He turned to witness a small but athletically built woman wearing what appeared to be burlap pants with a brown linen short-sleeved blouse.

"Any reason you feel the need to be looking in my window?" She scowled at him, furrowing her eyebrows. The pupils in her yellow eyes began to stretch and grow.

Cepheus was taken aback. "Are you a..." he couldn't bring himself to say it.

"A Royal?" she finished. "By birth, yes. In spirit, no." She held the stick out as if she were dowsing for water. Once her aggression waned, she realized something. "Oh, so are you," she stated, not asked, momentary lowering the stick before remembering something and snapping it back up again, holding the tip of the branch against his throat. "Are you here to try and bring me back because I claimed sanctuary and..."

"No, no, no," Cepheus held up his thin hands in surrender and tried to explain. "I am one of the lead instructors at TARA and a former negotiator for the Intergalactic Peace Project. I am only here to check on the preserves and make sure everything is okay. TARA is partially funded by the statecraft, so I have to file quarterly reports."

"I see," she dropped the stick. "And what, may I ask, do you have to report on that requires you looking through my cottage window?"

"I apologize," Cepheus's eyes welled up in what she could only interpret as allergies or possibly...tears? "My wife...my late wife ... she was a winemaker. I was just surprised to see a vineyard in the Western Cross. She was the only person able to grow grapes in this region..." He observed the rows of blue, purple and pearlized grapes. "Until now, it would seem."

"Yeah," the woman answered. "The Eastern Cross would have been more ideal. But I just happen to like the landscape here."

Cepheus smiled. "My wife felt the same way."

"I'm sorry about your wife," she replied, taking a moment to untie her black hair, adjust it, and then tie it back up again, forming a tiny knot on her head. "I'm Moksha." She then saluted, like a Royal. Cepheus offered his hand in return. Moksha paused for a moment before lowering her arm and shaking his hand in return. "Old habit." She glanced awkwardly at the ground.

"I'm sorry to pry," Cepheus apologized. After an awkward pause, he asked, "Why are you here?"

"I could ask the same of you."

"I ran away from home as a child and ended up here."

"Same here…except, as you can see, I'm not a child." Cepheus could see that. As far as Royals were concerned, Moksha would have been considered quite beautiful among the nomads. "Not the normal Royal stomping grounds, is it?" She laughed awkwardly, breaking the momentary silence. "Maybe a short chat over a cup of wine?"

Normally, Cepheus would not drink while on duty, but he was intrigued. "Perhaps just one," he replied. She unlocked the cottage, something Cepheus found to be odd since no one on any of the preserves typically felt the need to "lock up." Lucene was the only other person he'd encountered who did that.

He followed her inside and was ushered to a small table in the kitchen. "Sorry," she apologized, "it's too small for a proper dining area."

"No, it's…just fine." Cepheus felt his eyes glazing over slightly.

"Hey, are you okay?" she asked, tapping him on the chin with her fingers, peering into his eyes.

"Yes, sorry." He regained composure. "I was just, remembering."

Her face fell, sympathetic. She remembered herself and reached for two clay wine cups, pouring a glass of rossenberry wine for them both. Moksha raised her cup in a tribute. "To new friends," she offered. He tapped his cup to hers and took a sip. It was just as he remembered.

"You seem very sympathetic for…"

"A Royal?" she finished. "I could say the same about you."

"Perhaps because I escaped while I was still very young," Cepheus explained. "When Erdelings took me in and gave me sanctuary, I couldn't have been more than a teenager…I can't remember exactly."

"Just a moment…" Moksha suddenly realized. "You are not

Cepheus Baruch, are you?" Her eyes grew wide as if someone splashed her face with cold water.

"Unfortunately, yes."

"My Sovereign," she began to kneel before catching herself and then stood up again. After a moment of awkwardness, she flopped into a chair, embarrassed.

"Old habits are hard to break," Cepheus replied generously. "And, of course, you don't need to do that. I renounced the throne a long time ago."

A long pause ensued as they sipped their wine. Both seemed lost in thought, but for very different reasons. For Cepheus, Petrichor's wine had been earthier in flavor, somehow. Moksha's was a little thinner and sweeter, but equally good. Cepheus tried to connect with her using his thoughts, but of course, that wouldn't work. She was a Royal, not a Data Collector, untrained, and not known for compassion. And yet…

"What is it?" Moksha asked, fidgeting nervously with one of the small turquoise earrings that wrapped around her ear and dangled about an inch below her lobe.

"Forgive me for saying this," Cepheus began cautiously, "but you seem far too kind to be a Royal. What was your station?"

"This ought to be good for a laugh." She smiled. She had a nice smile, Cepheus noticed, and then caught himself. "I was…"

"Yes?"

"Um…an assassin?" She bit her lip.

"Is that a question?"

"No, that's it. I was an assassin."

"No," Cepheus laughed. "Tell me, really."

Moksha let out a sigh before guzzling the rest of the wine in her cup and refilling it moments later. She offered Cepheus a second glass, but he waved his hand away in decline.

"Okay, so you know how on Earth they have dog fights using pit bulls?"

"Unfortunately, yes."

"Well, you know how, no matter how much they try to train them to fight, there are ones who are peaceful and don't really want to hurt anyone or anything?"

"Yes?"

"Well, that was me." She furrowed her brows and dropped her gaze to the floor.

Cepheus let out a laugh.

"What's so funny?" Moksha demanded.

Cepheus smiled broadly. "It appears we have something in common."

Tanager flew through the bookstore doors with such force that several traditional magazines blew open and fell from the shelves. An older woman at the counter looked up in surprise. "Electronic or print?" she asked cautiously.

"Wha…" Tanager slowed down and thought for a moment. On the second floor, he spotted Roman darting between two columns of books. "Print," he answered. "Thank you!" He didn't wait for further instruction. After finding a spiral staircase, he bound up them, two at a time.

The older woman seemed perplexed but wasn't interested enough to pursue it further. She dropped her gaze back toward the electronic romance novel she was reading on a small device. The Navy SEAL from Earth had just met the half-android and half-human woman in a freak mishap on Mars and the bookstore attendant was dying to find out what happened next. After all, how could a wild seal and a person make such a relationship work? She didn't even think seals had legs…confusing.

Meanwhile, Tanager peered around a selection of intergalactic travel books. He witnessed Roman giving the frail man he had been chasing after an affectionate kiss and thought it best not to interrupt. Instead, he grabbed the first manual he could find, a heavy textbook outlining all the known galaxies by sections. Given the age of the book, he estimated that it was off by about 15 billion galaxies, ones that were housed in three newly discovered sections. He tried not to eavesdrop, but he really couldn't help it. After all, he was Roman's guardian while he was under Watch, was he not?

"My darling, how long have you been here?" Tanager heard Roman ask as Roman wrapped his arms around Far, hugging him to his chest. Had Roman not been overcome with emotion, he might have noticed Far's body bristle, just slightly, at the embrace before relaxing his body and lightly wrapping his arms around Roman's waist. For a moment, Far softened at the familiar feel of Roman's chest and the scent of his skin before remembering himself and regaining composure.

"About five minutes ago?"

"What? From where?"

"I escaped," he thought carefully for a moment, adopting a well-timed contorted look of pain as Roman gazed at him lovingly. "From the Royal Training Grounds. I have been a prisoner there since I fled Earth looking for a cure."

"My darling, I can't believe what has happened to you," Roman fought back a tear. You must be exhausted. Let me get you back to my high-home in the city."

"High-home?" Far used the question as an opportunity to pull away.

"Yes," Roman laughed. "Erde's term for an apartment or condo. It's on loan for now, but once I begin teaching at TARA, that's their Terrestrial Academy of Research and Awareness, I'll begin paying for it, a little at a time." Roman wrapped an arm around him. Let's get you home, so you can have a bath and something to eat, and time to rest and recharge.

"That would be…lovely," Far answered softly.

"I'm so glad you found me," Roman's heart opened wide with the belief that as soon as Far could escape, he returned to him as if his heart were a beacon. He wondered about Far's health as his survival projections had not been good several years ago on Earth. *Well,* he reasoned. *There's time for that discussion later.* "So glad you found me," he repeated.

"Yes," Far answered hesitantly, as the two men passed Tanager, who went unnoticed as they descended the spiral steps. "Me, as well."

7

THE COSTUME SHOP

SEPTEMBER. FOUR MONTHS BEFORE THE NEW ASSEMBLY.

It was still early when Lucene ventured out of her little cottage at the Eastern Cross. Having just arrived three weeks earlier, she was only now permitted out of quarantine, but it was still requested that she not leave the Eastern Cross region until the beginning of October, just to be on the safe side. She'd gone through a strange battery of remote tests with Dr. Wilah, who was presently aboard a vessel heading to a way station between Erde and Earth, followed by a remote consultation with Dr. Ennis on Earth and an odd series of psychological questioning administered mainly by Cepheus. Tanager was included after it was deemed that she was mostly back to "normal."

She couldn't really explain why she'd gotten so temperamental around Tanager, but since he seemed to be an emotional trigger for her, they thought it best to give her a little time before the two resumed moderate communication. Cepheus explained to her that it had to do with some disconnect between the emotional centers of her brain and the logical ones, a bridge normally helped by meditation. But for some reason, in her case, it was as if her emotions suddenly enveloped her entire thought process, and until she'd actually worn herself out (time on the Vessel's treadmill seemed to help), there was no reasoning with her.

Once they'd awakened her from deep sleep and introduced her to Erde and her new home, they anticipated aggravation by the change — reactions that did not come. She seemed to be calmer, more receptive to what was happening around her. So instead, in what would seem a counterintuitive approach, they requested she take a break from meditation and do, essentially, whatever she felt she needed to do in order to adapt, providing she stay within the Eastern Cross. At least, remain there until they could gauge her physical and emotional reactions to her environment, as well as the environment's reaction to her. Townspeople were alerted that there was a new inhabitant, something of which they had become quite accustomed to over that past few years.

For Lucene, this was her first taste of freedom in a long time. She was no longer running from some unseen and unknown aggressor, nor was she trapped on a small spaceship for months. She tried to remember the last time she was able to move about so freely without feeling apprehensive…five years old? Six? She really wasn't sure.

The truth was, she needed clothes and groceries. She'd managed to procure a few of the essentials at a local mart, though there was some confusion about what they considered fruits and vegetables versus what she believed. But they were kind, asking what part of Earth she had been from and trying diligently to match her request with what they knew of Earth and her preferences. She didn't have the heart to tell them that, the truth of the matter was, she was an unskilled cook. And, in the end, it made no difference what they gave her. Her goal became pretty simple, "Sell me foods that I can boil or pan fry in twenty minutes or less that are reasonably good for me."

The attendant at the grocery store nodded enthusiastically. "That," he told her with a smile, "we can do."

Now, as Lucene peered down at the threadbare one-size-fits-all dress that had been at the way station, the one that she was now wearing, she couldn't help but think that she needed…well…help.

She set her cloth bag of groceries on the sidewalk and pulled the watch Tanager had given her out of her pocket. She was still not comfortable wearing it, but she promised to keep it with her so they could track her if needed, and she could phone someone if she needed help. It also had this handy app that managed her money for her. She'd been given a small stipend from TARA and use of the cottage, provided she work with the students on whatever research projects they needed. In this case, *she* was the project. The agreement was for three months, and they could re-visit that plan in the new year to discuss the next steps. Surprisingly, Lucene wasn't at all worried about what she would do about food and lodging after those months had passed. There was a strange sense of peace and the trust that Cepheus and Tanager would somehow make sure things were okay for her. Not unlike her friendships with Rev. Isabella, Fatima, and Ivan, this brought her contentment. And while she had grown to appreciate Roman and value his friendship, she didn't necessarily trust in his ability to be a source of support, even with his extensive knowledge of human behavior.

She opened the bank app…not a whole lot left until the next deposit, but perhaps enough for one or two new simple outfits? Across the street was a sign, Mallory's Costume Shop. Except, the window displayed a mix of contemporary Earth garb, pant suits and jackets, jeans, dress shirts and sweaters, along with an array of odd-looking garments that included triangle-shaped silver hats and striped unitards that looked like adult-sized onesies.

Lucene grabbed her groceries and made her way across the street. As she peered through the darkened window, she let out a disappointed sigh. The sign on the window said, "Closed." About to give up and head home, a hand reached toward the sign and flipped it to "Open." A face smiled from inside the window—difficult to make out with the glare from the sun. Suddenly, the lights sprang to life as the shape motioned a hand for her to come inside.

"Welcome! Welcome," said the very large and colorful man behind the counter. "Welcome to Mallory's Costume Shop, here to serve all your pre-made and custom wardrobe needs." He surveyed her dress, distastefully. "And, from the look of it, you have needs."

Normally, Lucene would have countered with a snarky comment, but she was won over by his exaggerated overtures. He wasn't finished with his assessment.

"Did you just step off a boat that had been lost at sea? What happened to you, child?"

"Close, but it was a spacecraft coming from Earth. This was all that they had for me to wear."

The man's eyes flew open wide to reveal pupils that sparkled like tiny cut gemstones. Prisms actually flowed from them, leaving reflections of light on the floor. He touched his hand to his mouth. "Oh, my goodness…tell me you're not Lucene, born of Xan and Dora…two Data Collectors." He gave an exuberant little bounce… very little. His large frame didn't allow for much movement.

"Okay, I'm not Lucene," she answered, flatly.

He paused for a moment, eyeing her deadpan expression before letting out a chortle and waving a hand at her. "Oh, you got me. And let me just say, it's an honor to serve you. I am Mallory, owner of this establishment." Lucene paused for a moment, mainly because she kept getting distracted by the array of glittering garments that were displayed on the wall. "What, were you expecting, a woman? Don't feel bad, so was my mother." He laughed again.

"No, I'm just…confused."

"Oh, aren't we all, dear?"

Lucene began wandering between the racks displaying clothing tightly packed together and separated by size. "You're a costume shop…?"

"Yes, we are a quick study, aren't we?"

"But some of this looks like stuff I would wear day-to-day."

"And where are we from?"

Lucene got his point. Earth clothes, at least some of them, were costumes to those on Erde. "So, if I wanted something basic, something everybody wears on Erde, what would I buy?"

"Well," Mallory leaned a hairy arm on the counter and rested his chin in his palm. "I would argue that I don't sell *basic*, but what I can tell you is that my store caters to a wide variety of styles, some more traditional and then also the non-traditional." He walked from behind the counter and eyed her up and down. "Casual or dressy?"

"Casual…something I can wear to TARA and blend in with students but could also wear day-to-day."

"Maybe something like Earth, so it's not too dramatic a switch, but something we also wear here…like your jeans and sweater variety?"

"Yes," Lucene smiled. "Exactly."

"Budget?"

"Cheap."

Mallory tsk-ed at her. Lucene wasn't entirely sure anyone had ever tsk-ed at her before. "Well, Mallory doesn't do cheap, but I believe we can find something suitable. But first, how about we put your grocery bag in my refrigerator, or those poor pomegranates are going to taste like ass by the time you get home."

"Oh." Lucene glanced down at her bag and the pomegranates sitting on top. "Sure, thanks."

"Follow me," Mallory slid a glittery prom gown aside that was hanging on the wall, revealing a plain brown door, opening to what was presumably the back room. There, he led her down a narrow hallway that he seemed to barely fit through. They passed another room, one with a row of sewing machines with chairs on alternate sides of a long table, spaced out in a zig-zag.

"That's the sewing room," he explained. "I have several workers who help me with custom fittings and designs. I find when I space the chairs out, it enables them to converse with one another without straining their necks while giving them room to work, helps morale and productivity."

"I see," Lucene answered. But, she really didn't. They passed another room, where the edge of a bed and a long, ornate dresser could be seen. "Do you live here, too?"

"Yup. The shop is my life. Couldn't see myself anywhere else." At the end of the hallway, and by contrast to the large bedroom, was a tiny efficiency kitchen that appeared to have been constructed in the 1930s, complete with a small monitor-top refrigerator, tub sink and porcelain gas-range stove. Even the backsplash was covered in a floral print wallpaper. Mallory popped open the refrigerator which revealed a few paper cartons of what appeared to be last night's take-out, along with a glass bottle of carbonated water. Having pulled one of the metal shelves out and laying it, lopsided, in the sink, he pushed the cartons aside enabling him to shove the entire grocery bag in and shut the door without pressing too much to get it all to fit inside. "Voila!" He seemed proud of himself. "Now, on to more important things. Follow me."

Instead of going back through the hallway, he led the way into his bedroom, which alarmed Lucene until she realized that there was yet another door that opened directly back into the shop. The two emerged behind the counter as another patron walked through the front doors.

"Ah, Mrs. Glazor, how nice to see you again," Mallory gushed. The woman was wearing a wide-brimmed hat, boatneck dress and white gloves. Her smile turned to a look of pity as she surveyed Lucene behind the counter.

"My latest project," Mallory held a hand up as if letting Mrs. Glazor in on a secret. He winked and she smiled back with a nod. "I have your garments right here." Hanging in front of the door from which they'd just emerged was a long white satin gown.

"Just beautiful," the Glazor woman gushed. "What do I owe you?"

"Well, let's see." Mallory plunked a few keys on a retro cash register that had a strange brass handle on the side. "Custom dress… fittings…fabric…oh, let's just say, an even 4,000 units."

Lucene's face dropped. She wasn't sure what the dollar equivalent to a unit was, but since her account had about 3,925 less of them, she was pretty sure she couldn't afford whatever Mallory had to sell.

"A bargain, if you ask me," Ms. Glazor smiled gleefully. She plugged a few numbers into her watch, and the cash register lit up. Apparently, it only looked retro. Mallory cranked the handle, which quickly caused the woman's watch to light up. It was, presumably, to send her a receipt. "Thank you, Mallory. You will be hearing from me again…probably for…mmm…baby clothes!" She winked at him. "Ta ta!"

Lucene felt like she'd stumbled into a 1940s American sitcom, and she couldn't get out. After Mrs. Glazor left, Mallory's face turned sour. "Horrible woman," he confessed before turning his attention back to Lucene.

"Arms out," he ordered, pulling out a vinyl tape measure. Lucene was confused until Mallory demonstrated by outstretching his arms, parallel to the floor, in a T shape. She followed as Mallory measured her from wrist to shoulder and across her back. "Skinny thing," he commented.

"Listen, Mallory," Lucene began. "While I appreciate your help, I'm realizing now that I probably don't have enough money to pay for whatever clothing you can provide for me."

Mallory stopped and glared at her, offended. "Did I ask you for money?"

"Well, not yet, but…"

"Well, don't shoot me down before you hear my offer!" He let out a boisterous laugh. "I'm not going to design you a custom dress, so relax. I'm just getting a sense of your overall size to fit you for something ready-to-wear. For example…" He moved across the floor and flipped through the clothing racks, beginning with pants. "I'm thinking…this." He thrust his hand out and shook the denim jeans, indicating Lucene should take them. She did. "And this." He handed her a second pair of dress-casual pants. "And this." He'd moved over to a shelf full of sweaters, pulling out a simple solid blue, short-sleeved cotton one. "And finally…this." It was a long-sleeved burgundy cardigan coupled with a button-down white blouse, which Lucene would never have given a second glance to, but on third glance, she decided, it wasn't half bad.

"Okay," she acquiesced. "Should I try them on?"

He paused for far too long, as if she were a small child uttering her first words, giggling to himself. "No, child. You can try them on at home. I assure you; these are a perfect fit for you."

She laid them on the counter and surveyed the selection…pretty neutral and basic. Lucene was okay with this. "How much?"

"Don't be gauche," he chastised. Lucene was confused. How come when Mrs. Glazor asked, it was perfectly acceptable. But when she asked, it was gauche? "Let's see," he thought a moment. Lucene did too. She had about 40 units she was willing to spend, leaving her just enough for emergency food until her next deposit. *Please be less than 40 units. In fact, 35 would be ideal.* "How about 35 units…oh, my word, I can't believe I just said that. Yes, 35 units. Take it now before I change my mind."

"I'll take it," Lucene announced enthusiastically, pulling her watch from her pocket. She held it up and plunked a few buttons as she'd done for the grocer. The cash register lit up…success.

As Mallory was putting her selections in a paper-like bag, she spotted a mannequin in the corner. She wandered over to it. It was wearing a black-flared skirt with a striped sweater. Something about it intrigued her. "That's from our French designs," Mallory explained. "One of my clothiers works part time in the French district and loves the style."

Maybe next time, Lucene thought. "Just for future reference… how much is it for the sweater and skirt?"

Mallory thought for a moment. "Well, it's a package deal." He walked over to the mannequin. "It's the only one we have in stock, so you'd have to wear the display. Fortunately, she's as waif-like as you are, and the fabric is clingy, so it will adjust to your shape. But you can't get the top and skirt without these…" For a large man, he moved easily throughout the aisle. He stopped at an accessory shelf, pulling down a red beret and matching scarf. Without asking, he plunked the beret sideways on her head and wrapped the cravat around her neck. That, along with her worn-out dress, was a sight to behold. "There you go," he said, pleased.

"I've given you everything I can afford. I don't suppose you do layaway?"

"Laya—" this sent Mallory into a tizzy. "There you go, being gauche again. Tell you what, you agree to burn that awful dress you're wearing when you get home, and you can have the entire ensemble for 20 units, payable in…say, one month? Oh," he added. "And I want the pomegranates from your grocery bag."

"It's a deal!"

Mallory packaged up Lucene's new wardrobe and gathered her grocery bag from the refrigerator. She carried the clothing bag on one arm, groceries on the other. It was a bit of a struggle, but she didn't have far to go. Mallory considered offering to lend her a hand cart but then thought better of it. *For an itty-bitty thing, she has the muscle tone. She'll be fine,* he reasoned.

"Thank you, Mallory. It has been a pleasure."

"The pleasure's all mine." Mallory opened the shop door for her as she exited. Then he added, "You are an accomplished young woman, I can tell."

"Really," she seemed unconvinced. "But I haven't done anything yet."

"Oh," he nodded in understanding. "But you will."

8

ALLIANCE

OCTOBER. THREE MONTHS BEFORE THE NEW ASSEMBLY.

"Commander Royce, it's an honor to finally meet you," the Vitruvian representative bowed his head politely to the head of Erde's Planetary Defense League or PDL for short.

"Likewise, Representative Dallen," Commander Royce acknowledged, offering a slight bow in return.

Neither was what the other expected. Dallen had bright golden hair and equally brilliant blue eyes, uncustomary attributes for most Vitruvians. Had they been any less striking and embellished, he could have passed for a human. Commander Royce, by contrast, was a small, athletically built woman with walnut hair that had thin gray streaks in it and coal-colored eyes decorated by several deep-set wrinkles on her face.

"Please be seated," Commander Royce motioned toward one of the throne-like, high-backed chairs that wrapped around a large round meeting table. The League's Negotiation Room was ornate with flowing red and gray tapestries that hung from the walls, along with potted vines blooming with orange, red and yellow Cosmos flowers. There were no windows, but the glass domed ceiling revealed the cloudy sky, which was constructed so that they could see out but no one flying overhead could see in. Dallen took a seat and was quickly offered a glass of water from one of the commander's attendants, who set the beverage next to him on the table. Dallen didn't seem to notice. Instead, his eyes lit up when the Negotiation Room doors opened.

In walked Lucene wearing a yellow sundress and brown ankle boots that were completely out of place for her surroundings. Had her new friend Mallory seen her selection, which were left-over remnants from her wardrobe on the Vessel, he would have cringed. Yet, she couldn't quite bring herself to wear her newly acquired clothing out in public—yet. *Little by little,* she reminded herself. *There are only so many changes a person can adapt to at once, aren't there?* Plus, her appearance was, in some small way, a point of protest, though Lucene wasn't entirely sure what she was protesting.

It had now been eight months since she left Earth with her traveling companions, Cepheus, Tanager and Roman, after being rescued from the Royals. She'd only been on Erde for one month and still felt completely out of place in her new home. Her hair was a visible testament to her adaptation, with several inches of blonde hair growing in and replacing the brown bottom half that had been dyed to conceal her identity. To Dallen, however, she was stunning. He wouldn't have even noticed Cepheus, dressed in a pair of black pants and a tan button-down shirt or Tanager, wearing a dull brown suit jacket and matching slacks, had Commander Royce not acknowledged them.

"Welcome, scholars," she announced with pride, motioning for them to take a seat, eyeing Lucene's wardrobe curiously.

"Our apologies for the delay, Commander Royce," Tanager pulled out a chair for Lucene, who took a seat first before Tanager settled into the chair next to her. Dallen eyed this gesture with great interest. He was not familiar with this Earth custom and even more confused as to why it would be practiced on Erde.

"We came directly from class and ran into a small situation on our way," Cepheus added, taking a seat beside Dallen.

"Nothing serious, I hope." The Commander glanced between the three newcomers. Lucene shifted nervously in her seat, knowing full well that she was, at least in part, the reason for the delay. The small cottage she had been offered at the Eastern Cross was a preserve where the landscape was most like the terrain she left on Earth—the West Coast of Florida. It had palm-like trees and was near the ocean. Even the seabirds resembled seagulls and sandpipers, but it was still obvious that she was on a different planet surrounded by people she didn't know and couldn't easily escape from.

She hadn't realized before her journey how much her friend Fatima had protected her when she grew anxious, from too many people and too much energy. Even as housemates, Fatima could sense when Lucene needed a break and would either offer to retreat to her own room or simply suggest that everyone take a "silence break," where no one spoke, and the house was quiet until that time that Lucene felt like talking again. She realized now, more than ever, how much she had under-appreciated her friend.

"Nothing serious," Tanager assured her, sending Cepheus a knowing look.

"Good," the Commander paused as an attendant set cool water beside each of them. "Then, may I present Representative Dallen from Vitruvia." Dallen nodded his head and gave a slight wave of his hand, a customary greeting, when all were seated. There was a strange chill in the air. "And may I also present two lead professors and well-respected Earth scholars, Cepheus Baruch and Tanager Blackletter." They nodded in return, cautiously. There was a brief but awkward pause before Tanager realized that it was his turn to speak.

"Oh, and…Commander Royce and Representative Dallen," Tanager offered, "may I please present Lucene Jones. Lucene has recently arrived from Earth…seven months of travel on the Vessel and only one month on Erde."

Why does it sound as if he's making excuses for me? Lucene wondered to herself.

"Hi," Lucene waved, splaying her fingers in what was not at all customary. Dallen couldn't take his eyes off her, smiling at her odd mannerisms. She began nervously tapping her fingers on her lap under the table, fidgeting uncomfortably. Tanager reached under the table and took her hand in his and held it discreetly out of view from the other attendees. She squeezed it, appreciatively, in return, and settled into her seat.

Cepheus smiled with a somewhat exaggerated sense of pride, adding, "Our instructor in training, Roman Aurelius—also from Earth—was supposed to be joining this discussion today, but he appears to be absent." His deep voice made the situation sound graver than he intended and didn't match his smile.

"Absent?" Commander Royce was concerned.

Tanager intervened. "Since he is new here also, we suspect he's either gotten lost or hasn't adapted to our system of time yet," he laughed heartily to cover up his own awkwardness at the situation. "But Lucene, as they say on Earth, stepped up to the plate, and is standing in on Mr. Aurelius's behalf." Tanager couldn't help but smile at his correct use of the idiom. He still found Earth slang fascinating.

"We are deeply grateful," Commander Royce acknowledged. "Thank you for being present."

"Sure," Lucene bit the side of her lip and shifted in her seat. She really didn't think she stepped up to the plate at all. In fact, she threw what some might call a mini-tantrum at having to stand in for Roman because he was off with who knows who doing who knows what. Cepheus and Tanager finally convinced her to drag herself out of bed and at least throw on a dress and comb her hair and join them.

Commander Royce feigned more confidence than she actually felt. She had been in charge of the PDL for the past forty years, overseeing the Erde military divisions for both local (within the Erde atmosphere) and non-local (outside planets) protection, as well as heading up Erde's membership to the IPP. Compared to Earth, Erde was a much smaller planet, roughly the size of the United States, Canada and Mexico combined. It had enjoyed planet-wide peace for more than a hundred years, leaving her with little to do on the local front. As for the non-local department, Erde was overlooked by many species living in Sections 2, 3, 4 and 5, so the army would "train and maintain" but had little to do in terms of establishing new defense tactics. Thus far, membership with the Intergalactic Peace Project (IPP) had taken up the bulk of her attention, establishing the Data Collector training with TARA, working with the IPP to help other planets reach their level of peace, and helping Earth recover and evolve given its current climate.

It was only within the last year that it came to light that there were other Earth-like planets in need of support. And, in all likelihood, there were many more. This put a strain on their resources. To make matters worse, their efforts in helping Earth did not go unnoticed by those that would harm them. In fact, their Data Collection work had become so successful that it put them on the radar of those living in far regions of the universe. With their general location known, Erde was no longer as safe as it once was, and she considered her efforts with TARA and the IPP to be both her greatest triumph and her worst failure.

"Representative Dallen," Commander Royce shared, "has graciously offered to meet with us on behalf of the Vitruvian people. He is sympathetic to our current situation, and their people would like to help. We will, of course, be conducting more comprehensive meetings with our Defense League and its leadership, but I thought it beneficial for him to meet with you regarding what next steps TARA might take on the Data Collection initiative. Representative Dallen, I turn the conversation over to you." With that, Commander Royce took a seat.

Dallen stood, knowing full well what everyone in the room was thinking, feeling the full weight of their distrust in spite of their amicable gestures. He indulged in one more glance in Lucene's direction before standing and addressing the group as a whole. His garb was almost as striking as his features, wearing a white tunic with a gold-striped ribbon that ran from his left shoulder, across his chest and down to his right hip. His pants were made of a thick silver material that appeared to have bits of metal in them, possibly for protection.

"I know," he began, "that you are well aware of the previous agreement Vitruvia had with the Royals, something which my people have come to regret."

Tanager shifted uncomfortably in his seat but said nothing. Cepheus's eyes bored into the middle-aged man's head as if trying to pry information loose from it, but Dallen was well guarded. Lucene, on the other hand, didn't feel much of anything, for once. Instead, she was distracted by Dallen's shiny golden hair that seemed to catch light like sun on a mirror—enhanced by the fact that the sun was actually shining through the dome at that moment and bouncing off his head—causing a prism-like effect on the curtains.

"At that time," he continued, "our goal was to not interfere with anything pertaining to Earth or surrounding planets, but merely to be available should Earth become…shall we say, *available*? If that happened, naturally, we felt it would be safer in our hands than the Royals."

"Then," Commander Royce interrupted, "why make an arrangement with the Royals at all? To the outside observer, this gives the impression that your people were siding with them. And they are not known to be the most compassionate of species."

"We know that now, Commander," he dismissed the comment with a flick of his wrist and repeated softly, "we know that now. We assumed that the Royals would no doubt take a large portion of Earth and hoped that we could salvage what remained. We promise you; we had no intention of hurting Earthlings nor forcing them out."

"Then, what would you have done with them?" Tanager asked pointedly.

"Well…we would wait and see."

Tanager was not prone to anger, and yet he felt his unoccupied hand beginning to make a fist under the table. Lucene noticed the unusual reaction and gave his other hand, the one she had been holding, a squeeze. It was her turn to be supportive. He felt it and took a deep breath.

"Wait and see what? Wait and see if Earthlings died and then take over the space like new landlords?" Tanager asked. Lucene was surprised. Tanager was usually much more cautious with his words.

"We meant no harm," Dallen explained calmly. "We just don't believe in interfering. We simply act according to what is, it is our culture. It is our way."

"We understand and respect that, Representative Dallen," Commander Royce interjected, shooting a warning glance at Tanager. "Perhaps you could share with our scholars why it is that Virtruvia is offering to work with the Erde people at this time?"

"Quite simply," Dallen explained, "we have since learned that not only did the Royals breach our contract, but they made a separate deal with the Null—the Singulari worshippers in Section 4."

"The void dwellers?" Cepheus sat upright. "They are real?"

"Unfortunately, yes. And, as violent as the Royals are, the Singulari make the nomads in Section 3 look like small children at play in a sandbox."

Lucene suddenly had that mental glitch, the one where she was on the verge of remembering something important from her past but couldn't. It was that all-too-familiar feeling of an itch she couldn't scratch. It had to do with her brief time on the Royal ship when they tried to kidnap her. *Aha!* Suddenly, she sat upright, causing everyone to turn and look at her in surprise.

"What is it?" Tanager asked, releasing her hand and giving her back a light rub for encouragement, another gesture that confused Dallen…and bothered him a little. *Why?*

"I was heavily sedated, mind you," Lucene fought to remember. "But they were dressed for a meeting—Hamish and Sabrina. They were taking me and going to meet someone…I think they were going to hand me over to them. But then, when you rescued me," she touched Tanager and Cepheus each on the arm, "well, I guess they couldn't keep up their end of the bargain."

Cepheus fell silent for a moment. Until then, it hadn't occurred to him that when Hamish, his father, had killed Sabrina, his mother, and let him go, he was doing more than freeing him and helping Lucene. His actions likely sealed his death, and that of the Royals, as a species. It was a far greater sacrifice than he had appreciated at the time.

"I don't know the current state of the alliance between the Royals and the Null," Dallen confessed, "but I do know that they are both very dangerous. If Vitruvia and Erde work together and share our resources, perhaps we can get you re-instated into the IPP and enlist the help of all species living in Sections 0, Sections 2, and even Silva and the surrounding planets in Section 5. We can save Earth…and each other."

Tanager thought a moment. He knew his empathic skills were not as advanced as Cepheus's, nor as rich in potential as Lucene's, but he couldn't escape the gnawing sensation in his belly. "So, it is now in your best interest to help Earth…as a bargaining chip to get us to work with you and share our knowledge," he answered sourly. "Lucky Earthlings."

Commander Royce was about to object, but Dallen quickly flicked his wrist again and smiled. "I understand your hesitation and your lack of trust," he acknowledged. "Believe me, your reaction is much more temperate than that which I've faced from your military personnel thus far." There was a long pause. It felt as if all the air had been sucked out of the room.

Lucene took a sip of her water. *Just say it,* she thought. *Just say that you recognize that Vitruvia has made many mistakes. That they may not be as compassionate as the Peace-Keepers, but they are honest and speak the truth.*

Dallen looked up with a start, eyes focusing directly on Lucene's until she dropped her gaze uncomfortably. He returned his attention to the group. "I recognize that Vitruvia has made many mistakes," he began. *What the—?* Lucene thought. "We may not be as compassionate as your people, but we are honest. I speak the truth."

Close enough, Lucene thought, wondering if she passed those thoughts on to him to share or if he reached into her head and grabbed them. If the latter, she didn't like it.

Tanager looked at Cepheus, and the room fell silent as the two seemed to have a split-second private conversation without either of them opening their mouths. As the elder of the two, Cepheus spoke, "We understand, and we appreciate your honesty. What do you need from us?"

"Wonderful," Commander Royce smiled broadly, breathing for what appeared to be the first time all day. "What are our next steps?"

"Well," Dallen grinned, glancing around the room, taking an extra moment when he zeroed in on Lucene. "As a start, I would love a tour of the Academy. In particular, I've heard wonderful things about your Makerspace."

9

THE WITCHES OF FRANCE
OCTOBER. THREE MONTHS BEFORE THE NEW ASSEMBLY.

"Come here often?" Odessa asked Reverend Isabella, sliding next to her as the older woman was peering closely at a rare heliographic photograph preserved beneath shatter-proof glass and hanging on a wall at the Parrish museum. They were running a special exhibit on the witches of France throughout history.

"Tell me, Odessa," Isabella answered, never taking her eyes from the image. "Is there anything that you *won't* hit on?"

Odessa thought for a moment. "Earthworms," she finally replied. She stood beside Isabella, wearing a red flared skirt with black stockings, a yellow blouse, and her head covered in butterfly barrettes. Her usual Northern Lights blue-green skin was now a shade of pale peach, something the shapeshifter had most likely adopted to avoid drawing attention to the fact that she was not human. On this, she had an internal battle. She loved the attention but knew it could be risky. Therefore, she constantly had this, "look at me, no, don't look at me" angst about her.

"Earthworms," Isabella responded curtly, trying to understand how this was where Odessa drew the line.

"Well, yes," Odessa explained. "They eat dead organic matter which is gross. And have you seen their castings?"

"Enough." Isabella held up her hand. "Forget that I asked." Isabella stood regally in a brown and yellow tunic top with matching palazzo pants.

Odessa stretched to peer over Isabella's shoulder. "Ah," she nodded. "One of the first photographs ever." She thought a moment. "Northern France, 1830."

"Yes," Isabella answered quietly, pushing back a memory.

"Wasn't that when the townspeople took it upon themselves to burn a witch, even though it was technically no longer a crime?" Odessa searched Isabella's face for a reaction.

"What is it that you want?"

Odessa sighed. "I want to enlist your help."

"*My* help," Isabella was surprised. "Doing what?"

"I'm not sure if you're aware of this, but six years ago, Vitruvians, Erdelings and Royals were all banned from the Intergalactic Peace Project."

"Believe me," Isabella instinctively held one hand over her belly, where she had been shot in her Sanctuary earlier in the year, by the double-dealing Drake Cushing. "I am aware."

"Well, I think you should petition to become a member of the new IPP."

"Me?" Isabella looked down at the small-framed Vitruvian. "I have absolutely no qualifications to join the Earth IPP."

"No," Odessa furrowed her lips as if considering this. "But," she placed a hand on Isabella's shoulder. "If I recommended you as a Vitruvian IPP member, well, I suppose that might make a difference. While *you* may find me distasteful, I am somewhat influential with my superiors despite being among the lower caste. What do you think, Bella?"

Isabella glanced over her right shoulder, eyeing the hand before shrugging it away. "It's Reverend Isabella."

Odessa removed her hand, appearing hurt at the snub. "Why don't you like me?" Odessa whined. "I helped heal you." She stood, pouting.

Isabella let out a sigh. "I don't dislike you," she finally conceded. "I just disapprove of you wantonly throwing your sexuality around when so many of us have worked so hard for so long on this planet to make ourselves be seen beyond our gender."

Odessa thought for a moment. "Yes," she nodded "and, some longer than others."

"What is that supposed to mean?"

"Take a walk with me Bel—Reverend Isabella." She resisted the urge to circle her arm around Isabella's waist and lead her. She motioned for Isabella to follow her. She darted around several tourists taking flash photograhs before a security guard asked them to turn their flashes off. Isabella gracefully kept pace.

"See this?" She pointed at a timeline on the wall, set at the start of the exhibit. Her finger hovered above a date. "1245 in southern France. A woman convinced her inquisitor that she had no magical powers, and the inquisitor let her go."

"And?" Isabella eyed Odessa curiously.

"The inquisitor that year murdered 346 women and two men accused of being witches. This was the only person he let go, despite protests from many accusers."

"Fascinating," Isabella sounded unconvinced.

"And here," she pointed to another date, "1308 in Paris. A concubine was burned at the stake after being accused by a lord's wife of practicing sorcery."

"Ah, yes," Isabella replied thoughtfully. "Jealousy."

Odessa noticed a spark of recognition.

"And over here," Odessa took Isabella by the arm and tugged her.

"How much more of this is there?" Isabella wanted to know.

"Not much more," Odessa reassured her, dragging her to the opposite wall in the exhibit. "Here," she pointed. They stood before a large oil on canvas depicting the execution of witches by hanging in 1718 in a small village in southwestern France.

"Know what happened here?" She waited for Isabella's reply, holding her breath.

"Many of the women on trial were accused of seducing the men in the village by casting spells. In reality, most of them were raped against their will, and their accusers were the men trying to cover up their own crimes." Her violet eyes seemed to grow darker as she pinched her lips together. Odessa looked down and noticed both of Isabella's hands were balled into tight fists.

"Pretty awful," Odessa remarked.

Isabella looked at her young friend, incredulously. "Pretty awful?" She paused. "Is that how you would describe it? Pretty awful?" She gestured toward the painting. "This is exactly what I'm talking about when you throw yourself at everything on two legs— sometimes four—with no respect for your body or that people may only be interested in you because of your appearance. Many of us died trying to be seen as more than objects, being punished if men couldn't control themselves around us."

Odessa dropped her eyes, hurt. Then, she had a thought. "I hear what you're saying—I also notice that you referred to 'us' twice in that sentence."

Isabella seemed startled for a moment, as if piecing together Odessa's agenda—which was becoming clearer by the minute. She turned her back on Odessa and made her way toward the next exhibit room.

"Hold on." Odessa ran in front of her. "Hear me out." Isabella stopped. "I understand where you are coming from. But the flip-side of this argument is two-fold. First, I am not human. I am a shapeshifter. I can be male or female. I just prefer being female." Isabella threw her hands in the air, exasperated. "And second," she continued, "you fought for religious freedom and equality for more than 700 years. It is because of your efforts that women today— misguided by your estimation, or not—have the freedom to flaunt their sexuality if they choose to do so."

Isabella considered this for a moment. Odessa had a valid point. Who was she to judge how Odessa behaved? Then, as if it suddenly occurred to her, "What do you mean, 700 years?"

"Ah," Odessa smiled, happy that she and Isabella were finally on the same page. "Shall we return to the only photographic evidence we have in this exhibit of the 1830 version of Isabella?" This time, the two walked side-by-side, waiting impatiently as several other visitors gathered around the picture. One eyed Isabella curiously but said nothing.

Finally, the heliographic image was free. "Look here," Odessa leaned in close so that her breath almost clouded the glass. "The image is not super fabulous, but who does that beautiful creature about to be hanged look like?" There, stood the old Isabella. Her skin was lighter, and she appeared a bit heavier, but the resemblance was uncanny.

"How is it that you live so long and have escaped death so easily?" Odessa asked. "That's what I still haven't figured out."

"You are more clever than I gave you credit for."

Odessa perked up. "Why, thank you, Reverend Isabella!"

"Isabella is fine," the older woman said. "No need to call me Reverend outside of ceremony. I was just being irritable."

"Is it witchcraft?" Odessa continued, and the spark of admiration Isabella had for Odessa went out as quickly as it was lit.

"No," Isabella was adamant. "I no longer practice the occult, nor do I claim any one religion."

"Why'd you stop?" Odessa leaned against the wall, until a guard made her way toward Odessa and motioned her to move. "Sorry," Odessa mouthed and stepped away from the wall. "I'm kidding. I get it. But your skills are valuable to us."

"Who is *us*?"

"The Vitruvians, silly. And the Erdelings. You have great wisdom and negotiating powers."

"You can see how well my powers of negotiation worked there," Isabella joked. Then, after noticing several more visitors eyeing the two and the bits of conversation they overheard with odd fascination, she added, "Perhaps we should continue this conversation elsewhere."

Odessa nodded, and the two proceeded to exit through one of the museum's side doors that led to a small patio area, which was empty at present. There was a small fountain at the center depicting an image of a Native American man on horseback. They sat at the edge of the fountain. Odessa began to take her shoes off so she could dip her toes in the water, but Isabella shook her head. Odessa dropped her head like a small child being chastised. She had been away from the water for nearly six hours now, and she missed it.

"The point is," Odessa continued, "you learned through trial and error how to reach people who are unreachable. You understand the inner workings of politics and the human thought process better than anyone. And most of all, you have influence."

"Influence?"

"You think I don't know that your little Sanctuary is one of many that you set up here and throughout Europe? You have an underground following. They can help us on our mission."

"What mission would that be?"

"We need to save this planet, for one thing. And to do that, we need to keep the Royals and the Null people away from it."

"The Null people? The black hole dwellers in Section 4? I thought they were a myth."

"Afraid not," Odessa eyed the drops of water in the fountain lovingly. "And they are after more than just Earth. They'll go after all planets in Sections 0, 1 and 2. That includes Erde as well." She gauged Isabella's reaction.

Isabella nodded. *Lucene,* she thought. Isabella was almost positive that Lucene had been relocated to the sanctuary planet, but until that moment, hadn't been sure.

A long silence ensued. Finally, Isabella answered, "What would I need to do?"

10

THE NEW CONTRACT

AUGUST. FIVE MONTHS BEFORE THE NEW ASSEMBLY.

Jasper Set rolled into the Royal palace in his usual, tornado-like fashion, pausing to purposefully knock down a few Cyrtostachys renda palms that Sabrina had collected on one of her final visits to Earth before her untimely death. He watched gleefully as they fell like a stack of dominoes until they, at last, reached what appeared to be a shrine with Sabrina's image molded in a ten-foot tungsten sculpture. The tree fronds slapped the late sovereign in the face as they found their final resting place. Despite all that Jasper knew of the multiverse, he still could not be certain what happened to a being after it died.

It is a myth that all demons are from the underworld and ruled by the devil and that there was simply heaven, hell, and purgatory. Jasper, for example, being of the Null, lived in the upper world. He didn't believe in the all-powerful Segue and wasn't too sure about the afterlife. This lack of understanding only served to infuriate him further.

"Jasper, your Excellence," Hamish bowed politely once the demon had swirled into the main meeting room. Hamish was in his usual place, standing by the long glass window, somberly overlooking the remains of his once-great city. Something he had done, almost constantly, for the past 25 years.

Likewise, Fredo stood guard, as he has always done. This time, however, he was saddened. He loved his former sovereign, and now his child was to be raised by Hamish, a Royal he was sworn to protect, even though he felt that Hamish did not entirely deserve his loyalty. Still, he knew that his child would enjoy a much better life as a leader versus a lesser Royal—a member of the military class, as he was. Yes, his child could one day come to have what he had imagined for himself—absolute power.

"What am I exc-c-c-cellent at?" Jasper asked.

"Well, it's just—"

Jasper let out a bellowing laugh. "Hah! I am jus-s-s-s-t kidding. I know all of the ways in which I am exc-c-c-cellent." Fredo stood behind Hamish, at the respectful distance, grinding his teeth so hard that it could be heard from the next room over and probably down the hall. "Fredo, my good man. Nic-c-c-ce to s-s-s-see you again. My, my…have you los-s-s-st weight?"

While many Earthlings like it when someone accuses them of losing weight (as if they were enormous to start with), for Fredo, this was the height of shame. He ground his teeth even more forcefully, refraining from a response.

"Hamish," Jasper admired, scanning the sovereign from head to toe. Hamish was dressed in a long purple robe laced with golden threads and diamonds. "You're looking as regal as ever in an unas-s-s-suming, 'how the hell did I get here' s-s-s-sort of way."

Hamish smiled knowingly. Twenty-five years had made him smarter, and he refused to fall into Jasper's trap. Jasper liked a show, so he was fully prepared to entertain the demon.

"And where is the lovely wife?" Jasper scanned the room, up and down, back and forth, even peeping beneath what used to be her throne, just in case.

"She's dead," Hamish said curtly, without feeling.

"Oh my," Jasper feigned surprise. "How did she die?"

Hamish thought momentarily to lie—after all, the confession could affect their original contract. Instead, in a moment of bravado that bubbled up from the ground and now coursed through his veins, he answered, "I strangled her to death in a fit of rage because she disgusted me."

A long pause ensued before Jasper let out another of his boisterous laughs.

"Frankly, my good man," Jasper confessed. "I didn't think you had it in you." Hamish was not sure how to respond, so he said nothing. "Can't s-s-s-say I'm s-s-s-surprised though. She was a feisty one, though, wasn't she?" Jasper thought a moment. "I think I will miss-s-s her."

Hamish did not share the sentiment. "The reason I asked you here…" Hamish began.

"Yes-s--s-s," Jasper floated over to Hamish, standing at an overly personal inch from his face, so that the spray from his "sss" covered parts of Hamish's face. It didn't help that his breath smelled like eggs that had been left out in the sun. Hamish stood adamant, refusing to react. "Why did you as-s-sk me here?"

"There's the matter of our contract," Hamish reminded him.

"Ah," Jasper put his hands behind his back, pacing back and forth with his spindly legs hovering in mid-air, his short wings doing the brunt of the work to keep him afloat. "What about our contract? You're not breaking our agreement, are you?"

"Certainly not," Hamish reassured. "It's just that, the original contract was between you, Sabrina and me. With her gone, I wanted to be sure it was still…valid."

Jasper thought about this. If the contract were null and void (forgive the pun), he could have his people roll right over the Royals—but then he'd never have the girl. On the other hand, five more years seemed like an eternity. And, if Hamish failed, as he had successfully done for the past 25 years, then the results would be the same. Why wait?

"This is tricky," Jasper acknowledged. "This could technically be cons-s-idered a breach of contract, wouldn't you s-s-say?"

Hamish felt his face grow hot as little beads of sweat formed around his brow. "I didn't anticipate losing one of our co-signers, Jasper. It's an unfortunate event, not a breach of contract."

"No," Jasper corrected. "An accidental drowning is an unfortunate event. Death by s-s-strangling is very much on purpos-s-se."

Hamish thought a moment. "What if I sweetened the deal by offering you a new and better contract?"

"Go on," Jasper leaned in with interest.

"We promised you a Data Collector with special powers, where, once identified, might prove to be useful to you. What if we upped the ante, so to speak?"

"How so?"

No prolonged "s" there, Hamish noticed. *Did he voluntarily turn it off and on for effect?*

"Not only can we give you the girl," Hamish continued, "but we can provide a beacon of light that will lead you to the entire Peace-Keeper planet, where all the empaths live. Now, instead of having one all-powerful minion to do your bidding, you could have dozens…thousands even." Honestly, Hamish had no idea how many, if any, were still left. According to Far's recent accounts from his visit, there weren't that many. Hamish decided to leave that part out. "The point is, we have someone living on Erde that can act as a light-house, guiding you toward them, something you simply cannot seem to do on your own."

"You're forgetting one important thing, Hamish," Jasper laughed. "Now that I know he's out there, what's to stop me from finding him on my own? Your beacon is not all goodness and light. I can find the planet without you…or should I say, *her*?"

Hamish was not a braggart, but he knew when he had the upper hand, and this was it. He smiled. Jasper really didn't know.

"*Her*, you say?"

"You are referring to Moksha, are you not?" Jasper was bluffing. But he was certain he was convincing.

"With all due respect, your Excellence," Hamish replied. "If you could have found her, you would have already. The fact that I'm still alive and that the Training Grounds are still here is proof that you still need me."

"I don't need anyone!" Jasper hissed, his face aglow with fire and anger as he once again shoved it in front of Hamish, touching nose-to-nose.

"The truth is," Hamish touched two fingers to Jasper's chest and pushed him away as if pushing away a helium balloon. Jasper floated backward. "Moksha is either too good, and you cannot see her, or the planet, as a whole, has so much positive energy that it's protecting her. Either way, in spite of your protests, you do need me. Agree to a new contract, and I will make sure you have the girl and a direct route to Erde and…" Hamish paused for dramatic effect.

"And what?" Jasper was impatient.

"A mole to help corrupt the lot of them."

"I don't unders-s-stand," Jasper began flitting around the room like an annoying fly trying to find its way out, buzzing by the windows, the upper corners of the ceiling and finally to the carefully arranged food table that was always made available to him when he visited. This time, he noticed to his delight, they added a plate full of crispy roasted roaches salted just the way he liked them. He couldn't resist pausing to crunch on a few, nervously.

"What if I told you that I had a plan to help you break down their resistance? Lose enough of that good energy for you to worm your way through the barriers that prevent you from penetrating their planet and wreaking havoc? What would that be worth to you?"

"And there it is-s-s," Jasper pointed a long finger in Hamish's direction. "It wasn't just that you were worried about my cons-s-sidering the first contract void. You want s-s-s-omething else. What is it?"

"It seems the Earthlings are more resilient than we first anticipated," Hamish confessed. "And my superiors are growing impatient with the Royal military clan."

"You want me to wipe out an entire s-s-species so that you can take over? Without giving them a s-s-s-porting chance? Where's the fun in that? Bes-s-sides, even if I were to agree to s-s-something so dramatic, the s-s-simplest thing would be to have my family roll over Earth. But then there'd be nothing left but a black hole. It would be us-s-seless-s to you."

"You misunderstand my intentions," Hamish explained. "I'm not asking you to roll over Earth. I'm asking you to roll over my superiors."

Fredo's spine arched as he listened in shock at what his Sovereign was suggesting. He was sworn to loyalty toward Hamish and was bound to protect him. But he was also loyal toward his people. What Hamish was suggesting was out-and-out mutiny. He couldn't allow this. He stared at Hamish with such force that Hamish could not help but feel it. But his Sovereign didn't seem fearful at all. Instead, he peered back gently, with those tired but knowing eyes— and smiled out of the corner of his mouth.

Fredo shrank. Of course, he would follow along with this for plan the baby. As the son of his Sovereign, his child would inherit the Earth and a better life than what he could provide as a ruler, not a warrior. But if he went to Hamish's superiors, something that was just not done by a member of his caste, not only would they be unlikely to listen, but he feared what his Sovereign might do to the baby. And at this point in his life, the child was the only thing Fredo could point to that actually had meaning to him.

"You devious son of a gun," Jasper bounced joyfully. The "sss" was gone again, Hamish noticed. "I give you credit, Hamish," Jasper continued. I didn't think you had it in you. But I do believe you may be worse than Sabrina. She couldn't contain herself, but you bottle up all that negativity and deceptiveness into a bulky little unas- suming package of a lizard." Jasper floated over to Hamish and poked him in the chest in praise. "Now, I understand why Sabrina picked you. You were more alike than different."

"I know you mean that as a compliment," Hamish answered lazily. "But, you're wrong. That's not why she chose me."

Jasper furrowed his brows. He prided himself on understanding how other beings thought, but he seemed to be having a number of misfires today. Instead, he returned his attention to the conversation at hand.

"What did you have in mind?" Jasper asked.

"Keep the Null away from the Training Grounds and Earth but direct them to several nomadic hubs in the universe where the bulk of the Royal Almighty live. It will give me the time and space I need to occupy Earth and grow a new breed of Royals with myself at the helm."

"S-s-such poise, S-s-such grandeur." Jasper shook his head. "And in return, you deliver the girl you have been promis-s-sing, along with these other do-gooders for me to play with. S-s-s-eems like an unbalanced trade, if you ask me." He paused to search Hamish's face. "But wait, there's more, isn't there?" Jasper suddenly spouted, gleefully, like a gameshow host. "What is it?"

"The mole I spoke of isn't Moksha. His name is Far. In addition to the gift of prophecy, he can also transport himself between worlds. Can you imagine what would happen if you had Lucene's time-space manipulation and Far's multiverse-jumping skills?"

Jasper's eyes grew wide. The possibilities were endless. His mind began reeling. Where would he begin? First, he would follow the original plan to see what his doppelgängers in varied realms were doing. Then, they would devise a plan to grow their powers. What then? *Oh, well, I guess that will become more obvious when I match wits with my other selves.* But the larger question remained, how had he not been aware of a non-Peace— bleh, he still couldn't bring himself to even think the name… How had an anomaly of energy in the universe escaped his attention? Was the power of positive energy really strong enough to shield them? "How much time do you need to deliver Lucene and Far to me?" he choked on their names. *Funny,* he thought. *I can barely bring myself to say their names, either.*

"Not long," Hamish answered. "But to be clear, this new contract would be an amendment to the old one. We have five years remaining on that contract."

"That long?"

"You've waited 25 years, what is five more?"

"Done. I'll draft a new version…"

"That's not all," Hamish continued. "This means that the Null will no longer come after me or my military clan. They will steer clear of Section 0 and Section 3 indefinitely. And—"

"There's an *and?!*" Jasper was indignant.

"Imagine," Hamish reminded him. "No longer being bound to a single universe, discovering what else exists if not the Mighty Segue…having all the answers at your disposal, and powerful beings to support you."

Jasper sighed. *That would be nice.*

"And?" Jasper motioned for Hamish to continue.

"Do whatever you wish to the Peace-Keepers, but do not hurt my son Cepheus, unless absolutely necessary."

"Aww," Jasper mocked. "What a proud papa."

"And—"

"Seriously, if there are so many amendments to the contract, and these are supposed all-powerful beings, then why not keep them for yourself?" Jasper was growing increasingly suspicious.

"Because," Hamish was blunt. "I have neither the time, the patience, nor your skill to convince them to use their powers for my bidding. I see you as having no such obstacles."

Hamish had successfully appealed to Jasper's ego.

"Go on," Jasper smiled, proudly. "And?"

"I want Sabrina's name removed from the contract. And, in the event that anything happens to me, I want a new name added as my successor."

Fredo's eyes grew hopeful.

"Really?" Jasper looked back and forth between Hamish and his guard. "What name?"

"It will be in the contract," Hamish answered simply. "We don't say it aloud."

75 Years Ago. When the Training Grounds Were New.

"How many men are you currently training, Fredo?" A then-young Sabrina peered from the top of the open-air overlook where she watched the military practice drills below with a mixture of curiosity and boredom. Broken out into groups, some were practicing hand-to-hand combat while others were using primitive staffs and materials that could be procured in nature within a moment's notice. A few were learning remote weaponry using more advanced technology, which was incredibly dull to watch as it largely involved a group of rugged men and women gathered around holographic fish simulations.

"Currently, we have 132 men and women, my Sovereign. But we are expecting at least two dozen more recruits within the next month."

"I didn't ask you about the women, Fredo," Sabrina clarified. "How many men? More specifically, how many men who are mature enough to provide me with an heir?"

Fredo was taken aback. It had been only a few weeks since Sabrina lost her husband during a routine exploratory mission to a nearby planet. It was assumed that he contracted a rare disease in the unmarked territory, and he was dead within three days of becoming ill. His body had only been retrieved and buried on the Training Grounds one week prior.

Fredo approached his Sovereign cautiously. "At least fifty or more men would fit that criteria, my Sovereign." He stood beside her, shoulder-to-shoulder. This was generally too close for a lower-level Royal to stand when in the presence of a superior, but the line of questioning had him almost—hopeful. "But, why would someone of your caliber even entertain the idea of these unworthy lessers?"

"Not that it's any of your business, Fredo," she snapped back but then let out a coy smile. "Alright, I'll tell you anyway." She stepped away from the ledge and made her way gracefully along a stone path toward the palace, still under construction, with the main throne room and several meeting rooms not yet under shelter from the harsh weather. She motioned for him to follow. "If I don't find a replacement husband soon, then my parents will find one for me. And, I shudder to think who they'll expect me to spend the next 150 or more years with. No, I need to marry, and quickly, before they have a chance to interfere."

Fredo followed Sabrina like a lost puppy at her heels, even though he was more than a foot taller than her. "If you are in need of a husband, I would be honored to fill that role," Fredo boldly offered. "Protecting you would still be my primary concern, of course, but—"

"Stop!" Sabrina commanded. Fredo obeyed, his normally red face appearing pinker. She eyed him for what seemed like an eternity. In truth, she found Fredo to be all brute and no brain, and the last thing she needed was an emotionally overgrown child for a mate. Furthermore, she shuddered to think about the intellectual capacity of whatever spawned from their coupling. No, she decided to herself after pondering for several minutes while Fredo stood, motionless, beside her. Fredo might be good for an occasional rendezvous, but he wasn't Sovereign material. She also needed him to protect her with his life and emotions had a way of getting in the way of all that. "No," she told him, pausing while he let out a heavy sigh. "While I'm certain you would provide a mighty heir for me, you're much too valuable as my protector for me to ask such a sacrifice of you."

"But I wouldn't consider it—"

"No, Fredo." His face fell. She wasn't the sentimental sort, but she did need him to stay focused. "I am honored by your chivalry," she complimented. Softness was not her forte, and it felt forced. "But we must find someone more suitable."

Fredo shoved his feelings to a place in the back of his mind not likely to resurface anytime soon and nodded in understanding. "Very well, my Sovereign. What did you have in mind?"

"I'd like you to give me a tour of the Training Grounds and introduce me to the men. Don't tell them why I am there, though. Do you understand?"

"Yes, my Sovereign."

"We'll just tell them that I am there to see how training is progressing so I can make my report."

"I understand."

The two walked in silence down a long and winding dirt and rock staircase that had been cut into the side of the mountain. There were flimsy rails that had yet to be fastened properly. But since Sabrina and her late husband rarely felt the need to leave the palace grounds, and the only ones who typically used this entrance and exit were their guards, they were in no rush to fix this, as the palace was still under vast amounts of construction.

Fredo stopped to gather his chief guards, explaining that Sovereign Sabrina wanted to watch the troops and possibly ask some questions. They bowed, without question, offering to line their respective training teams up as Sabrina passed.

For the next several hours, Sabrina moved throughout the Training Grounds, soldiers snapping to attention upon her arrival. To avoid suspicion, she occasionally threw a question toward a female trainee, how long have they been there? Who was their family? What was their primary skill? That sort of thing. Along the way, she passed several soldiers who Fredo suspected would be suitable for her needs —handsome and skilled soldiers who would no doubt produce a fine heir, but she seemed disinterested.

"That's all for today," she finally told Fredo. "Escort me back to the palace."

"Of course, my—"

Sabrina stopped, mid-step. In the distance there was a young frumpy man carefully watering a sad looking palm tree protruding forlornly out from between some rocks. The man appeared to be…*singing* to it.

"Young man, what are you doing?"

Hamish put his small watering can down in surprise.

"Kneel before your Sovereign, you insolent boy!" Fredo yelled, about to deliver a physical assault. "Why aren't you with your troop?"

Sabrina touched Fredo's arm. "That's enough, Fredo. I can handle this." To the young man who appeared to be several years younger than she, she asked again. "What are you doing to that palm tree?"

"I'm giving it water. It was almost all dried out."

"Aren't there more suitable servants for this purpose?"

"One would think so, my Sovereign. But they must have missed this one. Another day and this Cyrtostachys renda might have died."

"A Cyrtosta—what?" She was confused.

"A Cyrtostachys renda palm. They are very regal, don't you think?" Sabrina thought for a moment. She'd never considered a plant to be regal, but she did concur that it was an attractive little tree.

"Why do you care what happens to this tree? It's just a plant. There are others."

"Not like this one," Hamish observed. "You see, this one is growing between the rocks when it shouldn't. It's resilient. And look at the way its root system has adapted by—"

"That's fine," Sabrina interrupted him. "What's your name, young soldier?"

"Hamish," he answered calmly, looking at her deeply as if he actually saw her. She tugged her blouse tightly to her chest with one hand. "Come with me, young man," she motioned.

"But, my Sovereign," Fredo whispered in protest. "I know this boy, he's among the worst of our fighters. And look at him. He's shaped like a plump pear!"

"Yes," Sabrina smiled. She couldn't articulate what it was about Hamish, exactly. Their language had no word for compassion, and yet she could feel the deep emotion he seemed to have for this silly little green thing growing in the dirt. "He's perfect."

Fredo looked at Hamish and back at Sabrina. Hamish was, admittedly, a little frightened. *Was she planning on killing him? Feeding him to one of her exotic pets?* He couldn't be sure, but he followed blindly. It was his duty.

"Meet us back at the palace, Fredo. This young soldier will escort me." She turned and remembered something. "Oh, and when you do return—bring the little tree with you."

11

THE MAKERSPACE

OCTOBER. THREE MONTHS BEFORE THE NEW ASSEMBLY.

The Makerspace was something to behold. Unfortunately, a good portion of it was lost on Lucene. At that moment, she wished her friend and former neighbor Ivan were there to explain some of the equipment and technology to her. But she reminded herself, he and Fatima would be there soon. Of course, then her concerns about the Royals, the IPP and adjusting to her new life on Erde were replaced with another one, *would Ivan and Fatima make it there safely?* She trusted Ivan's mechanical abilities, but like it as not, the two left Earth in a hurry with the first working prototype Ivan had created…well, the second if you count his adaptations to the Vessel.

Dallen snapped his fingers in front of Lucene, interrupting her daydream. "Hello," he smiled broadly, "are you there?" She bit back a snarky reply, but only because she was immediately distracted by the people mover they were now boarding (at least, that's what she named it in her head). And Lucene had to watch her step, particularly since she was still wearing boots that were slightly too large for her. Tanager went to offer his hand, but Dallen had already taken Lucene's elbow and was escorting her onto the mover and promptly shouldering Tanager out of the way. Tanager clenched one of his fists, annoyed. Cepheus shook his head at his friend. *It's not worth it,* he thought. Tanager nodded and calmed down. After he, Cepheus, Lucene, and Dallen were safely inside the small open-aired elevator-like contraption, their guide, Renenet, closed the metal side gate and locked it. "I would advise that you hold onto the guardrails or take a seat," she said with authority. "This transporter moves in all directions."

Renenet was a broad woman with a large and muscular frame. Her hair looked like that of a lion's mane, her face the shape of a feline, complete with soft patches of fur, but with a human mouth and almond-shaped eyes that resembled fire agate. She was the director of the Makerspace, a responsibility she did not take lightly. After all, while Erdelings as a species were somewhat behind other populations when it came to military tactics and defense, discipline and containment centers, as well as gaps in their development of health and social services departments, when it came to technology, transportation, energy conservation, agriculture, and education, few could match them. TARA's Makerspace was so large and well-equipped that many businesses in Achel contributed to its growth and had a working agreement to pool resources with one another in exchange for the ability to rent out sections of the space as needed.

As Lucene and the others took a seat on one of the fold-down plastic-like chairs, Renenet hit a few levers and the transporter began to ascend. Both Lucene and Dallen craned their necks to peer over the railing of the glass box as it moved. Tanager smiled and kept glancing at Lucene to gauge her reaction.

Soon, they had an aerial view of the Makerspace. Renenet paused the transporter and waited, expectantly. Without thinking, Lucene and Dallen both stood in unison by the guardrails and peered down. From this view, the entire Makerspace looked like a Fibonacci nautilus shell, with each compartment representing a room dedicated to a specific purpose.

There was a Hot Room where people could be seen glass blowing and working with metals, a giant kiln in one corner. A few rooms down was a machining area. The next, someone could be spotted sanding a large piece of wood. Still, further down the spiral, robotics of varied shapes and sizes could be witnessed in various stages of development—some in disassembled chunks on a lab table, others skirting under the feet of those working there, and a few actually participating in helping their creators construct new versions of themselves. From their vantage point, it was as if they were watching a well-orchestrated ant farm at work.

"What's that?" Lucene pointed, seeing a shadow spiraling in circles from the central ground floor through the vein of the shell, stopping in what appeared to be a textile and sewing room.

"It is a transporter like this one," Renenet explained, "That one is slightly larger and better equipped to move machinery to and from the loading dock. All shared tools, such as your lathes, band saws, welders, routers and such, are kept on the ground floor near the commissary. They can be easily moved from their central location to anywhere in the Makerspace."

"Easily moved?" Dallen was surprised. "But some of those industrial machines must weigh at least sixteen thousand units!" To Lucene, he explained, "that's around a thousand pounds where you come from."

"Perhaps it's easier if I show you," Renenet offered. "Please take a seat."

Lucene and Dallen sat beside Cepheus and Tanager, who were watching the couple as if they were parents taking their kids to their first amusement park, or to see the ocean for the first time. Tanager even forgot for a moment, his growing dislike of Dallen.

The transporter began moving again at Renenet's command. But this time, instead of going straight down, like an elevator, it revolved 90 degrees and made its way toward a wide-mouth opening that looked like a cave. The group began a slow spiral, like blood moving through a vein. Each room they passed, larger than the last. "Here's a good place to stop," Renenet decided. The transporter spun to face the front of what appeared to be an auto-repair shop. There were vehicle stalls on each side, messy shelving cluttered with tubes hanging off the sides, hand drills, toolboxes and spare tires. Lucene even spotted the occasional odd-shaped car door and windowpane.

"Looks like Ivan's workshop," Lucene commented. "Is he here?" she joked.

Cepheus let out what Lucene had come to determine was a laugh, except it sounded more like a purr that got trapped in a cat's belly, never to quite make it out of its mouth.

"Not yet," Tanager smiled. "But no doubt he'll feel quite at home when he gets here." Cepheus nodded.

"Who is Ivan?" Dallen enquired.

"Ivan the Tinkerer," Lucene explained, "was my next-door neighbor back on Earth. He's invented all manner of contraptions, including transportation technology that got us home faster."

Tanager perked up slightly at Lucene's reference to Erde as "home." Maybe she was beginning to settle in, after all.

The transporter set off a beep, and those scurrying around the room paused to look up before resuming their work, disinterested in whomever it was in the transporter. One tall man in overalls, carrying a large plastic box, skipped across the conveyor at the center of the room and hurried out of the way. The transporter followed the conveyor track, until they had turned to face a large, saucer-shaped vehicle.

"I thought this was a car shop, but it's not, is it?" Lucene's face grew wide as she peered at a smaller prototype for the very Vessel that she, Roman, Tanager and Cepheus had arrived on not a month earlier.

"It's a multi-purpose transportation room," Renenet explained. "As you can see, this would be quite a large object to move under normal circumstances, but watch."

Renenent moved closer to the vessel and barked a series of voice commands. The transporter buzzed as two large metal arms forked out on each side of it, adapting their width to the size of the spacecraft. Meanwhile, the vessel began to move. The platform on which it sat lifted, and a thin square tile disconnected itself from the floor, allowing itself to be hooked onto their transporter and easily pulled onto the conveyor.

"How much does that weigh?" Dallen was surprised.

"It's a pretty compact prototype," Renenet dropped her mouth in a thoughtful frown. "Probably only around seven thousand pounds or one-hundred and twelve thousand units."

"And what powers this transporter?" Dallen questioned as Renenet finalized moving the vessel to the conveyor and pulling it as the transporter backed toward the vein in which they had come through.

Renenet squinted her eyes and let out what could best be described as a low growl. "That's proprietary," she murmured.

"But if I am to work with your people, I need to know what resources I—" he corrected himself, "we have at our disposal."

"All you need to know is that it works," Renenet shot an annoyed glance at Cepheus.

"Representative Dallen," Cepheus explained calmly. "We are happy to share any and all of our resources, technology and blueprints where necessary—after we are reinstated to the IPP and have solidified our agreement with the Vitruvians. Until then...you understand."

"Quite," Dallen answered curtly, pouting.

Tanager balled his fists again, but after witnessing a questioning look from Lucene, released them.

"Hey," a large man in orange overalls suddenly called. "Renni, where are you going with that?"

"Don't worry," she reassured him. "I'll bring it right back. I'm conducting a demonstration."

"Oh, okay," he scratched his head. "But wouldn't it be easier to use the..." Renenet shot him a warning glance, her eyes like daggers. "Er, never mind," he went back to minding his own business.

Dallen missed the exchange as he was busy surveying the room as if taking mental pictures of everything he saw. In fact, every once in a while, his eyes blinked rapidly like the shutter on a camera. More interesting was when he tilted his head to one side before a quick blink.

"Is something in your eye?" Lucene tilted her head in front of his face. He was annoyed at first, but then when he caught sight of her quizzical expression and pursed lips, he couldn't help but smile. She was exquisite. He didn't even mind that a few strands of her hair fell in her eye. Normally, that would be something he would have corrected by helpfully pushing it behind her ear. But somehow, *disheveled* was a good look for Lucene.

From the corner of the room, Lucene caught sight of a small woman with red hair and bright blue eyes. Unlike the others working nearby, she was clad in very Earth-like jeans and a simple green t-shirt. She wasn't working with heavy machinery, though. She appeared to be painting tiny miniatures of the larger prototypes on the main floor and putting them in a small model spread out on a long table in front of her. The only thing missing from the miniatures was a classic model train. The woman's eyes suddenly looked up, piercing their way past her to someone else…Tanager. Tanager momentarily returned the gaze.

"Who's that?" Lucene leaned in and whispered to him, cautiously.

"A mistake." Tanager clenched his teeth.

"Now's a good time to take a seat," Renenet advised, missing these exchanges. The transporter, now with a small vessel in tow, backed fully into the vein, but instead of continuing its spiral path, it began dropping. Lucene grabbed her stomach as it lurched.

"Sorry," Tanager touched her hand, suddenly remembering she was there. "I should have warned you. But the drop is quick."

"Good to know," Lucene felt a little queasy. From the look of it, so was Dallen. But Tanager didn't care about him.

Renenet explained that for general use, the spiral was adequate, but for large machinery that needed to be relocated to and from the docking area, the central unit was most efficient. The group watched as the doors to the loading dock opened, and they were suddenly in an outdoor covered space, surrounded by flying contraptions, land vehicles, a few dome-shaped boats and even sections of what appeared to be a part of the SpeedCircuit under reconstruction. When Lucene looked up, she witnessed several aircrafts being suspended from the ceiling, as if they were waiting in the queue to be tinkered with. "Before we go back, maybe Lucene would like to see the research and performance spaces," Tanager offered.

"Good idea," Cepheus nodded. "That will give her a sense of how the Makerspace and the rest of TARA are interconnected."

Renenet's face dropped. Clearly the performance space, which housed the music, theater and dance area, and the research space which included a library, chemistry lab, and medical lab, did not interest her nearly as much.

Apparently, it didn't interest Dallen much, either. He was about to protest and ask to return to some of the other more interesting spaces, such as the robotics or prototyping rooms until he saw Lucene's face light up. The Makerspace, while beautifully archi-tected, was too much technology and far too many computers in one space. She was better than she had been now that she knew exactly who had been after her (the Royals) and that she was safe. Still, a music area with instruments and a dance floor went beyond just feeling safe. That sounded much more interesting.

He smiled at Lucene. "I think we should definitely see your performance area. I am rather fond of the theater." Dallen made a mental note of the rooms he planned to revisit at another time — a necessary detour, from his perspective.

Renenet deposited the vessel into a free space, and the tile sank into the floor. One of the ground-floor attendants dressed in denim pants and a rough burlap shirt was confused. Renenet let out a sigh, "Just a demonstration," she explained again. "I'll come back for it as soon as I'm done giving a tour."

"We give tours," the attendant was surprised.

"Apparently," Renenet mumbled under her breath, quickly recovering when Cepheus shot her a warning glance.

"Yes," he answered softly. "Commander Royce and the PDL requested we give Representative Dallen from Vitruvia a tour of our Makerspace."

"I see," the attendant turned to look at Dallen. He really didn't. Not sure how he was supposed to respond to dignitaries visiting, he did the only thing he could think of, he curtsied. Tanager was perplexed. *And I thought I was confused by extraterrestrial customs.*

Renenet guided the transporter down a long hallway, stopping at the main cafeteria and lounge on the ground floor of TARA's educational department. "I'm afraid that this is where I make my exit." Renenet seemed a little too happy to be relieved of her duties. Frankly, she had more important work to do.

"Thank you, Director Renenet," Dallen flashed a pearly white smile and bowed slightly. Renenet perked up for a moment and broke into a smile. At least she had been acknowledged by this visitor.

"Yes, thank you," Lucene chimed in. Renenet's smile dropped as she turned her gaze from Dallen to Lucene. She seemed almost… angry at Lucene, for some reason. *Don't you shoot those dagger eyes at me,* Lucene thought. Suddenly, Renenet relaxed her expression. "You're welcome," she answered, pleasantly enough before retreating with the transporter.

They had now been delivered to the entranceway in which they had arrived after having spent the last hour exploring the expansive performance and research spaces. Tanager paused to show Lucene the room where they would meet in the morning to begin their work, then the four retreated through the glass doors out into the world.

Cepheus was prepared to escort Dallen back to his temporary

living quarters on Achel, while Tanager ensured that Lucene was comfortable finding her way home from the SpeedCircuit.

"May I have a moment?" Dallen asked Cepheus quietly.

"Of course," Cepheus stepped back as if Dallen had something confidential to share.

"No, not with you," Dallen explained, motioning toward Lucene. "May I have a moment to speak with Lucene?"

"Why are you asking me?" There was a long pause.

Finally, Dallen understood and broke the silence. "Lucene," he redirected his question, "may I speak with you for a moment?" He took long strides over to her. "Alone," he added as he sidled his way between Lucene and Tanager. Tanager didn't move as he watched and waited for Lucene's reply.

"Sure," she answered awkwardly, and Tanager reluctantly retreated to join Cepheus by an outdoor fountain, the two men engaging in a private mental conversation about the day's events. Occasionally, Cepheus had to fill in what Tanager missed through actual words, but they were purposefully cryptic, and few and far between.

"I would like to escort you to dinner tomorrow evening," Dallen announced.

Lucene searched his eyes for a moment. "Is that a question or a command?"

"It's more of a request," Dallen was taken aback. Lucene glanced in Tanager's direction, not quite sure how to respond. "Do you need his permission?"

"Of course not," Lucene shot back before catching herself. She couldn't be certain whether or not Dallen was being sarcastic or serious. "Dinner would be lovely," she finally answered calmly. This was different from how she felt on the inside. In fact, her stomach felt a bit like the lurch from when the transporter dropped them to the ground floor. Only this one felt worse. *What was that?* She asked herself. *Nerves,* she thought finally. After all, aside from the makeshift date nights Tanager attempted to clumsily plan for them aboard the Vessel, she really couldn't remember the last time she had been on a proper date. She searched her memory but gave up once she had retreated back more than a decade ago when she was still living in New York. *Surely, she dated...someone.*

Dallen snapped his fingers in front of her face. "Are you there?" he asked. Lucene was beginning to hate that. "So, I will see you tomorrow night then," he added, "that was a question."

"Yes," Lucene smiled uncertainly. "Tomorrow night."

12

TEST RESULTS

OCTOBER. THREE MONTHS BEFORE THE NEW ASSEMBLY.

"Class," Tanager addressed his students, twenty-one in total, as they eyed Lucene with a mixture of curiosity and fascination. She pulled the sides of her cardigan sweater together uncomfortably, as if she had been standing there naked the entire time. *Why are they looking at me like that? And why did I let Mallory pick out this ridiculous outfit for me? I'm not cardigan material.* "As you have no doubt figured out, this is the Lucene you've waited more than a year to meet. Please make her feel welcome."

The students, all of varied age, size and skin tone lined up, one behind the other. One by one, they stepped in front of her, gave a polite bow and offered quietly, "Welcome, friend," before stating their name. Most were odd-sounding: Xeni, Cluseladek, Neroni, and so on. Lucene wasn't sure how to respond, so she gave a slight nod of her head in return, looking to Tanager for guidance. He nodded back, reassuring her that this was the appropriate response. So, she nodded her head in acknowledgment, one at a time, before the students returned to their seats. Except, they weren't seats, exactly. They were tall stools with the tops tilted at a sharp angle and adjustable to each student's height so that the class was half standing and half seated at the same time. There were no back supports, and she noted with some surprise that they all had remarkably good posture. There were two crescent moon-shaped lab tables, one in front of the other, facing the teacher's desk and what appeared to be a clear glass screen where she would have expected a chalkboard or whiteboard to be. Granted, it had been a while since she'd gone to college, but she suspected the technology was slightly more evolved than on Earth. From the side, the tables appeared to be comprised of stacked glass, as if they were a series of layered microscope slides. The tops of the desks were a neutral pearl, matching the chairs.

"Please open Lab Resource Test Book Number One. We will begin by reviewing the summary." Lucene watched as they tapped the table and text appeared in front of them, scrawled neatly before each student.

"Are you sure you're ready for this?" Tanager asked Lucene quietly, touching her shoulder lightly. Although they had begun to rebuild an empathic connection over the past month, he was still finding it challenging understanding her emotional state from moment to moment, as it still felt a little…queasy. That was the only word that he could think of to describe it.

"I'm ready," Lucene was determined. "The sooner we can figure this thing out—" She caught herself. "The sooner we can figure *me* out, the better." He smiled weakly. His motives for wanting to understand her better went well beyond his interest in her as a research subject for the Data Collectors, and he was self-aware enough to recognize that.

Both Lucene and the class had been prepped prior to this meeting. Each student in the class, along with both Tanager and Cepheus, had the genetic splicing that was designed to enhance empathy prior to training. There was a fresh batch of students, seventeen in all, who applied for the Data Collector training path, in spite of the violence that had been reported on Earth years prior. The new idea from the school's governing bodies was that perhaps the same training could be tailored to a different purpose, one that might be useful on Erde and in negotiations with neighboring planets. But following a review of Dr. Ennis's work back on Earth, there was now concern over the possibility of the genetic modification being dangerous to a student's mental health. Therefore, all new students were added to a future waitlist, or they opted to join a different learning path at TARA.

Of the students that remained, those that were now semi-seated in front of Lucene, all agreed to undergo voluntary psychological testing paid for by TARA.

"Everyone here has already gone through the screenings we're going to begin today with you, Lucene," Tanager explained. "And they repeat these screenings every four months, following subsequent training. Please, have a seat." Tanager directed her to one of two chairs in the room that actually looked like armchairs, situated next to his desk, side-by-side. Lucene sat, sinking into what was a remarkably comfortable cushion. Tanager sat beside her. "There are thirteen tests in all, designed to get a baseline marker as to where you are right now. Unfortunately, we didn't have the advantage of testing you at an early age, so our baseline is really somewhere in the middle. While these students," Tanager motioned to the class, "were tested as soon as splicing was complete. And, they were all adults at the time. Which is why you are particularly unique." *Not the only reason you are unique,* Tanager thought. Lucene looked up in surprise, blinking twice but saying nothing. *Did he say that last part,* she wondered. Tanager continued, "Genetically born with this mutation and having had it develop, admittedly with some rocky starts and stops, has us all curious about what we're going to find."

The class nodded eagerly, whispering to themselves. At least, Lucene thought they were whispering. Except, their mouths weren't moving. She was used to her, Cepheus and Tanager occasionally sharing thoughts and emotions, but it was disconcerting being in a class that seemed to be talking with one another in their heads. As if on cue, they all fell silent in uniform politeness so as not to make her uncomfortable. She looked up in surprise, and the young girl called Xeni smiled encouragingly at her, giving her a proud thumb's up.

Lucene smiled back. It seemed as if Xeni was testing out her knowledge of Earth customs.

"We don't want to overwhelm you, so over the next week, I'll be having you meet with no more than three students at a time, specifically trained to administer a baseline test in a particular area. Then, you and I will meet to discuss the results before we all re-convene as a class." Tanager paused. "Does that sound okay with you?"

Lucene nodded.

"Good." Tanager was satisfied. "Do you remember the thirteen areas we'll be testing, or would you like a refresher?"

Lucene thought a moment, but only a handful of tests came to mind. *Stupid, fuzzy mind,* she thought, immediately looking around to see who else heard that, but no one reacted. It was as if they followed some code of ethics and realized that in her current state, it would be construed as an intrusion. "A refresher, please," she requested.

Tanager turned to address an exceptionally tall student at the back of the class. The young man was wearing a toga-like sheet, and his pale skin with bleached blonde hair, coupled with a commanding presence, gave him the appearance of an ancient Etruscan male that had stepped straight out of a history book. "Cluseladek." Tanager asked, "Since you consistently register high marks in memory, could you please remind everyone in the class what we're testing for—without looking at your book?" As he finished his last statement, the text that was scrawled across the desk in front of Cluseladek disappeared.

Cluseladek smiled proudly. He was up to the challenge. As if standing at a lecture, he addressed the class, being careful to strategically make eye contact with each person in the room several times. "I would be happy to, Professor Tanager," he answered.

Lucene giggled at the title. Tanager wrinkled his brow and shot her a *what was that for,* look. She suddenly had a flashback of Tanager back on Earth wearing a goofy fishing hat and Salt Life shirt and was having a difficult time seeing him as a professor.

Then she had another thought, and her face dropped. She'd have to remember to have the costume shop re-create that stupid hat that he loved so much, the one she ripped apart in anger on their trek home.

Cluseladek interrupted her thoughts. "The thirteen tests we use are designed to assess our strength levels in the following areas: overall physical health, intelligence, memory, cognitive balance, telepathy, ethical mind control, telekinesis or psychokinesis, empathy levels, healing ability, precognition, psychometry and remote viewing."

"Holy crap," Lucene blurted out. Tanager turned slightly red, but the class laughed, clearly finding her lingo amusing. "I can do all that?"

"Well, not entirely," Tanager responded. "Most students have varying levels of skill in many of these areas, not necessarily all. We're not completely certain yet why, say one person excels in memory, as with Cluseladek, while another is an expert psychometrist, like Xeni, or has a proficiency in precognition with a minor strength in remote viewing, like Neroni."

Lucene tried to remember which one Neroni was, and then a slightly larger than average-sized woman with an olive complexion and red-green hair waved in her direction. Lucene nodded, noting with some level of surprise how striking Neroni's hair looked against her skin, something she would not have guessed. *Olive, red and green should not go together,* Lucene reasoned. *And yet, on her, somehow, they do.*

Tanager noticed that he'd once again lost Lucene's attention and raised his voice slightly. "Well done, Cluseladek," Tanager praised. "But you missed one."

"No, I didn't, Professor Tanager," the boy answered smugly. "The final test is the one that no one has successfully scored on and is still a working hypothesis."

"And, that would be?" Tanager raised an eyebrow.

"Time and space manipulation."

"Very good, Cluseladek. You may sit down." As he sat, the text from his book reemerged on his desk.

"Did you do that?" Lucene pointed to the desk. "How did you do that?"

"Easily," Tanager answered. "And I only have an average level of telekinetic powers; which, I might add, were all but useless on Earth. I'm still trying to figure out why." Tanager wrinkled his mouth and forehead at the puzzle.

For the remainder of class, Tanager reviewed each of the thirteen testing areas, what the tests involved and how they were administered and measured. He then divided students up into respective categories for Lucene's week-long process. They were beginning tomorrow with cognitive balance. Tanager, along with three students, would be conducting a series of assessments.

Lucene didn't have to ask why they were starting with a test that monitored mental health and screened for potential disorders first. She knew they had to make sure she wasn't batshit crazy before they continued.

Xeni didn't look like a person, exactly. More like an animated cartoon come to life. She had large pink eyes that were out of proportion with the rest of her face, a short blue-black pixie cut for hair, a heart-shaped face and a small mouth. She could best be described as boisterous. Much younger than Fatima, at least in demeanor, Xeni reminded Lucene of her best friend if Fatima were manic and perpetually overly caffeinated.

When Lucene arrived at the TARA psychology lab the next morning, it was Xeni who greeted her first. "Hi, Lucene! OMG, I'm super excited to be working with you today!"

It had come to Lucene's attention that Xeni was going to cycle through every Earth phrase she knew for practice. But, unlike Tanager,

Xeni seemed slightly more current, but only by about a century. Though to be fair, Tanager was progressing the longer she and he spent time together…when they weren't arguing, of course. That was progressing too, she realized. Lucene also came to understand that most of their communicative misfires had more to do with some of the strange ways her brain had been interpreting their interactions. While not one to pile on the self-blame, she at least had enough self-awareness to recognize that she had been more off kilter than usual ever since the trek to Erde.

"It's nice to see you again…"

"Xeni," the young girl finished as Lucene was going through the class roster in her brain, trying to remember her name.

"Xeni," Lucene repeated back to her and nodded. She wasn't sure if she was supposed to nod after every interaction, but it seemed appropriate yesterday, so she maintained the custom.

Tanager looked up from the clipboard with information that he was sharing with Cluseladek. Except, the clipboard appeared to be that same translucent glass that made up the lab tables, and the information hovered above it as if the notes jumped off the page. They consisted of a series of charts and an odd language that was lost on Lucene.

Moments later, Neroni arrived, carting in a tray filled with a large metal canister and a plate of pastries. "I know we don't typically eat in class," she explained, "but today is a special occasion." She smiled at Lucene with a calm warmth. "We don't always have such an honored guest."

It was only at that moment that it sank in. Lucene wasn't just some Earthling that came to visit. Not an experimental prototype to study. They legitimately valued her. She felt it like a wave running through her. It struck her with an unquestionable knowing. They appreciated her abilities and admired the life tragedies that she'd had to overcome. It was an odd feeling—being respected like that. Lucene fought back a tear—another surprise, as the last time she was moved to tears was the moment on Earth when she thought Tanager was dead. This was far less traumatic than that. *Perhaps I'm becoming more sensitive,* Lucene thought.

"Thank you, Neroni," Tanager acknowledged. "Lucene, please help yourself. Unfortunately, the coffee is non-hyper-inducing, and the pastries have no artificial sugar; but I think you might enjoy them anyway. We just couldn't give you any sedative or stimulant that might alter the results of today's tests."

"I see," Lucene replied. Back on Earth, caffeine and sugar were her go-to's, but after seven months on the Vessel with limited food supplies, her diet had since become better. This was the first time she realized that she didn't crave either of those things. "Thank you…"

"Neroni," the woman supplied. If Lucene had to guess, Neroni had a good fifteen years on Xeni. However, given that Erdelings age much slower than humans and matured at a different rate, that may have been closer to thirty years.

Tanager and all three of his students waited for Lucene to pour herself a beverage and snatch a pastry before they partook themselves.

"I should explain," Tanager said between bites of a swirled piece of bread that resembled a cinnamon bun. "Xeni, Cluseladek and Neroni are the senior students in class. In fact, when Cepheus and I traveled to Earth to retrieve you, we had no other qualified staff to be on the receiving end of our messages back home, nor anyone to substitute teach some of our classes. These three did a remarkable job of stepping into leadership roles and supporting us remotely. I'm very proud of them." Xeni moved her head and shoulders side-to-side as if doing a strange victory dance. Cluseladek raised his chin proudly and puffed his chest out like a peacock. Neroni, the most modest of the lot, merely smiled and lowered her eyes to the floor.

"Uh, good work…" Lucene responded awkwardly, once again fighting back the odd tear. "If it weren't for you, I might not be here today. I mean, literally. I could be dead right now. So, thank you."

"'Aint nothin' but a chicken wing," Xeni chortled. Lucene made a mental note to discuss idioms with Xeni at some point in the future, before the young girl drove her crazy…well, craz*ier*.

Clusaladek and Tanager began unpacking instruments that had been tucked away inside the cabinets that lined the room. Xeni, eager to help, all but tripped Cluseladek as he turned to place something on a lab table, only to find the young girl underfoot. "Perhaps," he suggested thoughtfully, "you can help us by warming up the wave machine."

"Sure, I can do that," she responded enthusiastically.

Neroni took Lucene by the elbow and said quietly, "I know you're new here and still getting settled. I don't know if you need it or not, but I happened to stumble across an old dress in my closet this morning. It doesn't fit me anymore, but I suspect it might be perfect for you. I left it hanging in the public bath at the end of the hallway if you want to try it on."

"Oh, okay," Lucene replied. *That was nice of her.* "Thanks—I'll take a look." Neroni nodded before pushing the pastry cart into the corner of the room and out of the way.

For the next three hours, with a break after each hour, they ran tests. Some were simply asking her questions and taking notes. Others involved having her sit under what she could only describe as an old-fashioned hair drying seat, like the one you'd find in salons. Only, instead of heat, these tiny silver, pen-like cylinders were positioned all around her head as brain graphs registered colors and forms in holographic shapes in front of her, while the four testers in the room took notes. Occasionally, Tanager would point to something of interest, and they would nod. Lucene sucked in her breath, remembered she wasn't breathing, and then tried utilizing a relaxing mindfulness tool Cepheus had once taught her. She took a deep breath. *You are safe. Computers are not the enemy.* Lucene opened her eyes and smiled, an encouraging sign to Tanager that she was okay.

At one point, she was asked to meditate, as well as possible, with everything that was happening around her. She closed her eyes again and focused, and somehow, in her mind's eye, she could suddenly see Tanager's surprised expression looking down at her as if her eyes were open. She could also see the reason for his surprise. Even with her eyes closed, the hologram in front of her, coming from her mind, was an exact moving replica of what was happening in the room around her, registering in her brain.

After an exhausting regimen filled with more questions, more brain scans, interpreting drawings, creating some rudimentary drawings herself, and some other odd balance-type exercises, they concluded for the day.

"Thank you, everyone. I think that's enough for today," Tanager announced. To Lucene, he asked, "We covered a lot of ground. Are you okay?"

Lucene nodded, but she was tired. She'd heard the expression "bone-tired" before but never understood it until this moment. She could feel exhaustion all the way deep into her body.

"Professor Tanager," Xeni chirped, "if Lucene is tired, I can accompany her home."

"Thank you, Xeni. But that won't be necessary." Neroni adopted a knowing smirk as she glanced from her professor to Lucene but said nothing.

"Have a good rest of the day, everyone," Neroni waved, as she and Cluseladek made their exit. "C'mon Xeni," she tugged at the young girl's sleeve. "Maybe the three of us can stop at the common area for dinner before heading home. My husband is watching the kids today, so I have time to be social. What do you say?" Both she and Cluseladek agreed and after saying final goodbyes to Lucene, they left.

"So," Lucene asked, after everyone had left. "Tell me the truth. Am I crazy?"

Tanager's heart sank a little. "Of course not," he replied softly. "Why would you think that?"

"Oh, I dunno, maybe because I killed your fishing hat on the Vessel and have periodically been snarky and horrid to you ever since." She found her eyes getting a little red as she fought back tears. *What the heck was up with all of this emotion lately?*

A stray piece of hair fell from where Lucene had it pulled back, falling over one eye. Lucene blinked as it tickled her eyelid. Without thinking, Tanager brushed it behind her ear. "You have been under a great deal of stress. The test today indicates heavy trauma, but nothing that would lead us to conclude that you are anything but…normal."

She let out a sigh of relief. Somehow, hearing the words "normal" put her at ease.

"If you give me a few moments to wrap up here, perhaps I can accompany you back to the SpeedCircuit? We can even stop for a drink and some dinner first if you're up for it?" *A proper date night,* he thought. One that didn't involve being stuck on the Vessel with Cepheus and Roman hiding out. He laid his clipboard on the desk and then proceeded to cross and uncross his arms as if trying to figure out what to do with them now that they were unoccupied.

"Oh," Lucene was surprised. This was awkward. "I would…but I sort of have a date tonight."

Tanager was both surprised and disappointed and was somewhat unsuccessful at hiding both emotions. "Really? May I be so bold as to ask with whom?"

"Dallen asked me to accompany him to the animal lab this evening after we had dinner." Somehow, she could feel Tanager's stomach all jumbled up. It surprised her because she had assumed that following how she had behaved lately and aboard the Vessel, that any thought of romance between them was clearly off the table. "But, some other time?" she offered.

"Of course," he forced a smile. There was something else that bothered him beyond jealousy. He didn't exactly trust Dallen but wasn't sure if it was because Dallen was Vitruvian if he was merely concerned over Lucene's safety, or something else. "Have a good time. And remember, we went through a lot of tests today. If you have questions or don't feel well over the weekend, please call me."

This was Tanager's way of letting her know that if something went amiss in her date with Dallen, he was just a phone alert away. He looked down at her wrist, sighing when he noticed she wasn't wearing her watch.

"I will," Lucene promised. "Don't worry, it's in my bag." She smiled. She still didn't entirely trust phones and computers but had conceded to carrying the alert watch with her at Tanager's constant reminders. She still couldn't get used to wearing it, though, for more than an hour or two at a time before it irritated her, and she had to remove it.

At that moment, she was overcome with emotion again. Without thinking, she rushed over to Tanager and wrapped her arms around his torso and hugged him, resting her head on his chest, just under his chin. He paused for a moment in surprise, his arms dangling until he figured out what to do with them. Eventually, he wrapped his arms around her, hugging her back, and a strange energy passed between them heart-to-heart.

At that moment, there were sounds from the hallway outside, and they quickly broke from their embrace. Lucene haphazardly gathered her belongings and left without another word, leaving Tanager to watch her go, more confused than ever.

13

MARZIPAN AND THE EMBASSY CLUB
OCTOBER. THREE MONTHS BEFORE THE NEW ASSEMBLY.

Lucene had little time to prepare for her date with Dallen and quickly darted into one of the school's private bathrooms to freshen up. Cursing herself for not having the foresight to bring a change of clothes, she dug through her large black backpack, searching for a comb and face powder. It wasn't until she leaned over the sink to splash cool water on her cheeks that she noticed a knit red dress in the mirror, hanging on the door of one of the private stalls. It was Neroni's dress. She glanced down at her own white blouse and burgundy cardigan sweater. *Guess it couldn't hurt to try it on.*

Minutes later, she emerged from one of the stalls, the long-sleeved dress forming snuggly around her arms and hips, accentuating her shape and stopping just at her calf. It was not her usual style, but she had to admit that it fit her well. Her eyes fell to her unfortunate black slip-on flats. *Ah well,* she thought. *They'll have to do. At least they are a step above boots.*

She stuffed her blouse, cardigan, and jeans into her oversized backpack, quickly combed her hair straight, and dabbed some neutral powder on her nose. Not ten minutes later, she emerged from the bathroom transformed into dinner attire, slinging her backpack over her shoulder. Lucene thought perhaps she should leave it at the school to retrieve tomorrow morning before the next round of exams, but then remembering that she needed her pass for the SpeedCircuit and the key to her cottage, she opted to drag it with her instead.

Dallen was waiting for her at the end of the stairs as she descended from the labs on the second floor. He looked up with a mix of pleasant surprise and confusion, both at the same time.

"You look beautiful," he said, reaching over to comb a few bits of stray hair on her head and patting them down awkwardly. She was surprised by the gesture and put her own hand on her head after he was done as if to assess the damage. "Not to worry. It's better now." He smiled.

Somehow, she expected him to look less formal; but there he stood in a similar suit as what he had worn at both the meeting at the League and on their visit to the Makerspace earlier that week. The only difference is that this one was a washed-out navy, and instead of a formal sash, he wore a gold medallion pinned on front of his left shoulder. She assumed it was either an award or a sign of rank but did not question him about it.

"You seem tired," he observed, taking her hand and guiding her toward the front doors that led out to the street. This also surprised her, but since she knew nothing about his customs nor that of Erde's yet, she closed her hand around his politely. "Your eyes have these unpleasant dark circles under them."

Lucene let out a sigh, "I am tired. I was the test subject in a long series of examinations today, and I didn't expect it to take so much out of me."

Dallen paused for a moment and nodded in understanding. "Do you want me to escort you home?" he asked.

"Oh, no," she forced a smile. "I'll be fine. I probably just need to get some food in me, and I'll wake back up." In truth, going straight home and climbing under the covers seemed preferable to her right now, but she didn't want to be rude. Not only that, but it had been so long since she'd actually gone out on a proper date that she'd almost forgotten what it was like. There was still that huge memory gap from New York to the time Tanager arrived to rescue her when her utility vehicle broke down in front of the grocery store, in what now seemed like a lifetime ago. She remembered the New Moon celebration some eight months ago when they were still on Earth. But that wasn't really a date, was it? She shuddered at the memory as a chill tickled her arms. Before that, however, she couldn't remember when she'd dated anyone else. *That just couldn't be,* she reasoned. But she'd been hard-pressed to come up with any name at all.

"I have just the place in mind," he led the way, interrupting her thoughts. "It's only two blocks away. They serve a rice and vegetable dish much like we have back on Vitruvia. You will love it."

In truth, she felt more like a burger, but not just any burger. The kind that Fatima used to make with lamb and eggplant. Lucene didn't even think she liked eggplant, but Fatima had a way of sneaking vegetables into her food without her noticing. "Here we are," Dallen pulled her attention back from Fatima's burger, just as she began to imagine the taste of fontina cheese being melted over the top of it. She held back a sigh as she looked up.

They were standing in front of the Embassy Club. Unlike the understated buildings along the rest of the street, the embassy stood out like a beacon of red brick with gold-trimmed windows and doors. She wasn't entirely sure what this place was, but it looked expensive.

And, unlike many of the other buildings she'd been in lately, this one did not have automatic doors, and someone dressed in a red uniform with large black buttons down the front and a top hat on his head opened an ornate gold door for them as they approached. The doorman averted his gaze so as not to make eye contact. The whole image felt wrong, somehow. Dallen dropped Lucene's hand, turning his back on her as he walked in first. She paused for a moment, confused, but then followed once he glanced back, wondering why she had not followed him. "Thanks," she said to the guard, who said nothing.

In the lobby, there was an actual cloakroom with a young woman checking people's capes, jackets and purses. At least, Lucene assumed she was female. She was very slender with an unusually long neck and face, and a nose that was rounded like an aardvark. Her skin had a blue hue to it, and she had bits of black hairs that protruded out around her ears and chin. Dallen stopped there, eyeing Lucene's backpack distastefully. She had no idea what he expected until the woman behind the counter offered, "May I register your purse for you, Earth woman?"

"Sure," Lucene answered, reluctantly handing her backpack to the woman. She knew that Erde was supposed to be a peaceful planet with little to no crime, but old habits die hard and she still found it difficult handing over her possessions to a stranger. "What gave me away?" she asked.

"I do not understand," the woman answered. "Please explain."

"How did you know I was from Earth?"

"Oh," she nodded in understanding. "Your smell," she smiled.

"What do I smell like?" Lucene had to know.

"Earth skin smells slightly sweeter than people from Erde. Erde people are more citrusy." She smiled proudly. "But don't worry," she reassured Lucene. "After a few months, your chemistry will change, and no one will be able to tell the difference." She tapped her nose, knowingly. "Enjoy your refection."

"Uh, thanks," Lucene answered as Dallen, somewhat impatiently, let out a loud sigh before beckoning her to follow him into the dining area.

The main dining room was unlike anything Lucene had ever seen in real life, the main floor resplendent with high-backed, thrown-like mustard-colored chairs curved like private cocoons surrounding gold-trimmed ebony carved tables with protective glass tops in place of tablecloths. At the center of each table were vases that were at least three feet tall, slender at the bottom to avoid obstructing the diner's views from one another and branching out at the top. Each one was filled with tall yellow and white elderflowers. At least, that's what Lucene assumed they were, but she couldn't be sure as she didn't detect a scent. *Maybe I should ask scent-girl at the front to tell me,* she thought.

As they walked through the high arched entrance, Lucene noticed that there were two balconies surrounding the main room with private dining areas overlooking the main floor. A man with golden hair almost as bright as Dallen's quickly rushed toward him, stopping three feet in front of him and just off-center, presumably not to block his path. He averted his eyes as the guard had done. "Representative Dallen," the man greeted him. He was wearing a similarly uncomfortable-looking red uniform, slightly more form-fitting than that of the guard, and minus the hat. "We are honored to welcome you again. Would you prefer your usual seat?" Dallen didn't answer, merely flicked two fingers at him. It seemed very rude to Lucene, but she admitted she wasn't entirely sure of the customs here. The man nodded and led the way toward a small glass elevator that led to the second balcony. Unlike Dallen, who repeatedly walked in front of Lucene, the host put out an arm indicating that Lucene should enter the lift first. The man followed suit and cranked an old lever that closed the doors and began its short ascent to the second level.

"Cute," Lucene commented. It was as if she stepped back in time —Earth in the 1920s, if you had enough money and the right sort of connections. Dallen cleared his throat but said nothing. The host smiled politely and seemed embarrassed for her.

Once at their table, one female server pulled the chair out for Dallen, another put a cloth dinner napkin on his lap, while a third poured him a glass of water. Once they were assured that he was settled in place, the servers repeated the ritual for Lucene, who grabbed the napkin before it could be placed on her lap. "I've got it," she told the young waitress, "thanks."

The women retreated. It was only after they left that Dallen finally spoke for the first time since they had walked into the restaurant. "Do you like it?" He gestured in a way that suggested he already knew the answer.

"It's beautiful," Lucene acknowledged. "It seems very…fancy." Dallen let out a chortle.

"Yes, I suppose it is," he answered. "The Embassy Club was built several years ago as the central meeting place for dignitaries visiting Erde. There are separate conversation rooms and lounges, and, of course, this common area."

"Common area?"

"Anyone may dine here provided they are accompanied by a member of the club, but the other rooms are for members only."

"Seems rather exclusive for a club that's supposed to be inclusive."

"What do you mean?"

"I mean, if it's a meeting place for people from visiting planets, you would think it would feel slightly more…welcoming."

"It works for most of us," he answered simply, and not without a hint of annoyance. He continued, "It has evolved within the last year as Erde is difficult to reach and doesn't have many visitors. Vitruvia and Earth are the closest neighbors and your people don't have the technology to get here. Therefore, this club mainly caters to Vitruvian dignitaries."

It was only then that Lucene noticed that everyone appeared, well, human-like. There were no blue butterflies or mermaids. "Is there a shapeshifting code, kinda like a dress code?" Lucene wanted to know.

"You confuse me," Dallen eyed her with curiosity as a server brought over a pungent tea, pouring a small resin cup, first for him and then Lucene.

"Thanks," she told the server as the server set it down in front of Lucene. Lucene went to lift the cup to her nose to smell it when the server's eyes grew wide, and she shook her head, motioning toward Dallen. He, in turn, took a sip, nodded thoughtfully, and set it back down without a word. It was only then that the server nodded toward Lucene's cup. Apparently, the rules here were pretty straightforward. Dallen walks in first, gets seated first, drinks first, and does not speak to the staff. "What I was saying is that I've met two other Vitruvians." She recalled her brief interactions with Odessa and Morphinae. "They seemed to take on different forms, but everyone here seems pretty, well, human."

"We're nothing like humans," Dallen was quick to point out. It was funny, his tone was eloquent and soft-spoken, his demeanor calm, and yet she could almost feel every nuance of his emotions. And, to be honest, they lacked depth. She assumed that she simply wasn't used to the cultural differences and that he was harder to read beyond anything but surface-level emotions. This one was easy, however, *disdain*.

"You don't like humans?" Lucene questioned as the servers returned, this time with bowls of rice, vegetables, salts and sauces that they laid out very specifically on the table. Dallen stopped talking. Lucene followed suit. It was only after the servers left the private area that she added, "I don't remember ordering anything." She went to reach over to lift the lid on one of the sauces to see what was inside but noticed his disapproving glance. *Oh, right. He goes first. Was this a man thing or a dignitary thing?*

"I like humans, but you must be aware that they are distinctly more primitive than Vitruvians."

"Do I?" Lucene made it a point to never answer a question with a question, but somehow it popped out of her mouth before she could stop it.

"And, to answer your other questions, in the order asked, shapeshifters are a very limited race on our planet, and few rise to the order of a dignitary."

"Being able to shape-shift doesn't seem limiting," Lucene blurted out. She was tired and couldn't seem to put the brakes on her comments.

"I meant, in other ways," he replied curtly. "I like to think that what we true Vitruvians lack in morphing abilities, we make up for in intellect."

Lucene forgot her second question and was about to ask what he meant by "true Vitruvians" when Dallen started dipping into the various rice and vegetables on the table. Lucene counted three different types of rice, as many sauces, and at least four varieties of vegetables, none of which she had ever seen before. Once he had filled his plate, he did that finger flick, as he had done to the host, indicating that she was free to fill her plate as well. Suddenly, she wasn't feeling very hungry but politely took a modest sample of everything, laying it out in the same way Dallen did.

"To your second question," he answered between bites, "it's Friday evening."

"I'm afraid you've lost me."

"Whenever I am on Erde, I dine here. The staff knows my preferences. I always eat this very dish on Fridays." He smiled proudly as if this were something to be proud of.

An announcement over a loudspeaker prohibited Lucene from answering, *but what if I wanted a burger?*

Lucene was too short to see over the balcony, so she peered between the balcony rails at the host below, who now stood in the center of the room, commanding everyone's attention. The round platform in which he stood suddenly lifted, not only bringing him into greater view but revealing an entire orchestra of men and women that were one level below him. They were circled around him with a variety of brass, string and other instruments—similar to those on Earth, but their shapes and styles were different, some having a combination of metal, strings and mouthpieces as if they were three instruments in one. All in all, there were about twelve members of the band, the entirety dressed in that red uniform, like the host. The only difference was that the host had a different sort of pin on his shoulder. She hadn't noticed it before. Unlike Dallen's, the host's pin was round and silver. The ones that the band members wore were boxlike and light blue.

The host, who now appeared to be the emcee, welcomed everyone in attendance. Lucene didn't notice a microphone, and yet, she could hear him clearly. His presentation was brief. After introducing the orchestra, his platform descended while theirs remained in place, and he quickly exited the center of the room. Without thinking, Lucene began to clap. Dallen shot her a look, shaking his head vigorously. She stopped clapping, but not before several people looked in her direction. She expected a lot of whispering, but no one seemed to say anything at all, returning to their meals as the band played what seemed to be an awfully somber and somewhat off-key melody. Dallen leaned back in his chair and smiled. "Just like home," he said.

"I have a question for you," Lucene asked between bites, jolting him out of his reverie. Even that seemed to unnerve Dallen as he gazed at her hand. It was then that she realized from watching him that she had to finish her bite of food and actually put her spatula-like utensil down before continuing. This dinner appeared to have a lot of rules of which she was unaware. He flicked his fingers for her to continue. She resisted the urge to fling some rice at his forehead. "If you're visiting someone else's world for such a brief period of time, wouldn't you want to experience something other than what you would find on your planet?"

"What a silly question," he chided as if she were a small child. "Why would I want to experience anything less than perfection?"

And yet, she thought. *You are on a date with me. How did that happen?*

She was saved from further comment when the server returned to replace the tea with a cold beverage in a tall flute-shaped glass. It was only then that she realized that he'd finished his tea. She had not, but the server took hers away anyway. Lucene made a mental note to eat and drink faster, just in case. It seemed when he was done eating, everyone was done eating.

"I'm curious," he said. He seemed curious about a lot of things where she was concerned. He kept eyeing her like she was a strange puzzle he was trying to solve. "What powers do you have?"

And here, I thought he was interested in my winning personality.

"We don't know yet," Lucene answered honestly. "That's what

today was about. I've got tests over the next couple of weeks to figure that out."

"But surely you have a clue?"

Perhaps it was the cool drink or the food, but somehow her mental filter returned, and she quickly sorted through how much she should say and how much she should keep to herself. There was something…a thought in the back of her brain…that reminded her of someone on Earth. *No,* she told herself firmly. *He's not at all like Drake Cushing. You just get nervous around attractive men in authority, and you feel out of place in this environment.* Still, she finished her thought, it was probably best to exercise caution.

He peered at her, impatiently, over his beverage. At least, he felt impatient to her, even though he appeared very calm on the outside. "I am a little bit empathic," she finally answered simply.

"What does that mean?" he demanded, quickly sitting back in silence as the servers approached. He motioned for them to clear the table, and they all but forced the spatula out of Lucene's hand, eyeing at her offending utensil so she that she put it on her plate so they could take it away. One server looked at her almost apologetically. *I'm sorry,* Lucene read her thoughts. She pushed them away. She wasn't going to open any floodgates accidentally during dinner and embarrass herself any further than she already appeared to have done.

"It means I'm just a little more sensitive to the feelings of others."

"How is that a superpower?"

"I've been asking myself that for months," she joked.

Suddenly, he burst out laughing. An honest laugh. She had done something right, it seemed.

"You're delightful," he decided. "Come, let's skip dessert and visit the animal lab before it gets too late."

Lucene eyed the dessert tray lovingly, but she felt too out of place and fatigued to argue. Plus, she had it in her mind that the animal lab would be like a visit to the zoo and was secretly hoping to discover some adorable alien animals. She got up and followed him to the elevation platform, being careful to stay several paces behind him and refrain from talking to, or making eye contact with, anyone. *Less is more,* she told herself.

Once through the archway, the coat check woman made a loud "hmmm," clearing her throat. Lucene was relieved. Apparently, past the archway was when women were allowed to speak again without permission.

"Oh, yes." Lucene remembered her backpack. "I almost forgot."

The woman set a forced smile at Dallen, the kind that didn't reach one's eyes, as she handed Lucene her backpack. She leaned in quietly, lifting her chin as if sniffing the air and letting Lucene in on secret, "Smells a little briny on the inside, don't you think?"

"I hadn't noticed," Lucene was confused. *What was the matter with her bag?* The woman held her gaze a moment longer. "Thank you," Lucene replied. She knew she was trying to tell her something, but she had no idea what. Dallen handed the woman a gold coin. She bowed her head and retreated into the back of the coatroom, glancing over her shoulder once more as Lucene and Dallen exited the Embassy Club.

Once outside, Dallen took her hand again. *Oh, we're back to the hand-holding thing again.*

The lab was closed for the evening, but the overnight attendant had been apprised of his visit. "Representative Dallen," the small round man acknowledged pleasantly. "Nice to meet you. Name's Mateo, but you can call me Mati. Hey…Lucene, right?" He pointed at her as if to confirm his guess.

"Right," Lucene smiled. *Thank God, a person whose external expression matched their internal feelings.* This man, whatever his name, was actually happy to see them.

"Would you like a tour?"

"This late?" Lucene was surprised.

"Aww, I don't mind. My night shift is jest gettin' started," he answered in a thick accent. His "started" sounded more like "stawted." She thought he might be from New York but quickly retracted that thought when she noticed a long rat-like tail waving out the back of his uniform. There was actually a hole for it. He lumbered to a section labeled Area 1. "Follow me." She waited for Dallen to go first, but apparently, those rules only apply at the Embassy Club. Here, he actually held onto her hand as the main doors slid open and what's-his-name led the way.

"Thank you—" *He just said his name!* Lucene tapped the side of her temple, annoyed with herself.

"Mateo," he reminded her. "Don't worry," he winked at Lucene. "It's an odd name. Just cawl me Mati, like the way my hair is always matted down on my head," he patted the top of his head for reference. He was right, his tightly wound hair stuck closely to his head as if afraid of abandonment. She smiled back, gratefully.

"Thanks, Mati," she smiled. *I like him. He's nice…and authentic.*

They made their way through Area 1, visiting habitat to habitat. Some were very large and expansive, others small and condensed. Several appeared to have snow on the ground, and the windows were frosted over, while others appeared barren, with the glass enclosure steamed over. Like Earth, not all animals here appeared to have the same needs.

Lucene stopped abruptly in front of one habitat, a ten by ten room that looked like someone's living room from the 1950s, complete with a green velvet couch, floral wallpaper and rotary phone sitting on top of a chrome-legged end table.

"What is it?" Dallen asked.

"It's a cat," she pointed to a thick tabby curled up on the couch. The room was closed off with a plexiglass shield poked full of small holes.

"Of course, it's a cat," Mati laughed. "What else would it be?"

"But, don't they just live….you know, in houses, here?"

"Well, technically, they are an invasive species," Mati explained. "People need permits to have one in their homes."

"Has this one not been adopted yet?"

"Oh, she has a home," Mati explained. The cat's ears suddenly perked up as she lifted her head, sniffed the air, yawned, stretched and repositioned herself on the couch. She quickly fell back to sleep. "She's under quarantine for another couple of weeks before we can release her into our environment. I sneak a scratch behind her ears on occasion, but I always wear a glove and mask when I do. Can't be too careful."

Lucene couldn't see the harm in a simple house cat, but then, she reasoned, she didn't know what other species were here yet and how their presence might affect them. She, herself, had to go through a rigorous decontamination routine upon arrival.

"My friend, Fatima, is on her way to Erde," Lucene offered happily. "She's bringing our cat Bagheera from Earth. I suppose he'll have to spend a little time here when he arrives."

"At least two weeks, for sure, unless they approve him quarantining along with your friends. Though, usually, if something is up, we know within the first few days." Mati thought a minute. "Hmmm, but maybe he can become a breedin' cat. My gal Tabby," he pointed to the cat behind the glass, "is rare here. If it works out, maybe your boy cat can get together with our girl cat—if her caretakers agree—of course. They are kinda cute as home companions."

"Well," Lucene lamented, "sadly, our boy cat is in no position to bring kittens in the world." Mati paused for a moment, confused, before breaking out into a thunderous laugh. "Oh, I get it now. Poor fella. C'mon, let's hit Area 2. There are some pretty unique creatures in there."

Unique was an understatement. There were mammals that were a cross between koalas and sloths that slept upside down in trees and only ventured out at night, aquatic creatures that were a hybrid between a squid and an octopus, worm-like invertebrates the size of a five-foot snake, and even a cuddly marsupial wombat that made its way into the mix, alongside the very average house cat named Tabby, which wasn't so average on Erde.

For someone not big on trying cuisine that wasn't from his home planet, by contrast, Dallen seemed overly enthusiastic about the unique animal collection at the lab.

"Tell me, Mateo," he asked. "Do you have any special animals here?"

Mati looked horrified and somewhat offended. "They are awl special," he proclaimed.

"Yes, of course they are," Dallen backpedaled. "But, I mean, do any possess any unique talents?"

"Talents?"

"Yes, like having a special poison that paralyzes people, or ones that can glide through treetops, that sort of thing. I'm fascinated by odd creatures." Lucene felt a strange bitterness in the pit of her stomach. *Must have been that weird vegetable sauce,* she reasoned. *A burger wouldn't have done that.* She found herself pulling her hand away from Dallen, who released it without seeming to care.

Mati thought for a moment. "Oh, not so much here," he explained. "Most of our collection houses either ones in quarantine or ones that need our help because they can't make do on our planet —temporarily or permanently."

"I see," Dallen was visibly disappointed.

After about an hour, they had reached the end of their tour, having circled back to the entrance. But, as they did so, Lucene heard a strange sound…almost like a small voice that was humming.

They passed a room with a small wooden door that was partially open to reveal what Lucene at first thought was an aquarium. Then she saw a small cot in the corner, a desk and a tiny screen that may have been their version of a television. Something in the aquarium fluttered.

"What's in here?" she asked.

"This is just my office and rest area when I'm working," Mati explained. "Though, to tell ya the trute (truth), I spend more time here than I do at home." He laughed. "I got eight little ones runnin' around the house at home and hanging from the rafters, and they're not as quiet as those we got here in the animal lab."

"Wow, that's quite a…collection," Lucene acknowledged. *And it sounds horrifying.*

"That's nothin'," he replied. "My wife's sister has fifteen. The missus wants to keep pace, but I've told her eight is plenty."

"Hi," a little voice called from the aquarium. Lucene looked closely to see a small figure that had fluttered to the front of his small glass tank.

"Hi," Lucene answered curiously, pushing the wooden door open slightly wider. "May I?" she asked Mati.

"Aw, sure," Mati agreed, motioning for her to enter. "Go right ahead. That's my best buddy over there."

There, in what appeared to be a miniature wooded area within the aquarium, a small insect with a human-like face pressed his nose and two arched, furry legs against the glass. His face was round and pale green, his neck was skin toned and formed like layers of rolled dough. His round back was the shape of a ladybug's, and dark blue with little black dots. His wings were a luminescent turquoise like that of a butterfly, with six legs to match—the front two being shorter, working more like arms. He couldn't have been more than four inches tall and wide, and he was gorgeous.

Lucene leaned toward the glass. "You can talk!" she seemed surprised.

"Why wouldn't I be able to talk?" he answered, curiously.

"My goodness," Mati chimed in. "Does he ever talk! You can't shut him up."

"What's your name, little one?" Dallen finally spoke up.

"Marzipan!" The little bug puffed his chest up proudly.

"You're named after food? That seems odd," Dallen answered.

"Marzipan is a noble name," the little bug defended. "What's your name?"

"I am Representative Dallen," he replied, as if this should have meaning to Marzipan.

"And you think my name is odd," Marzipan leaped around his habitat, miniature tree stumps to branches, flittering through the leaves and dipping his hind legs in a tiny pond at its center. He seemed quite content in his little grotto.

"Oh, you mentioned scary animals earlier. Well, that's how Marzipan and I became buddies," Mati offered. "I found him in the Southern Cross on expedition and rescued him from a desert glider."

"A desert glider," Dallen was intrigued.

"Mean suckers, if you ask me," Mati answered. "They are about a foot long with the body of a gray lizard, but when they're irritated, their wings open up and fan out in every direction, and they have a lot of 'em. They have three sets of wings that span more than a foot high. They're like peacock feathers, except dark brown, flag-shaped, and not nearly as pretty." Mati opened his arms wide to illustrate.

"Yeah, if Mati hadn't found me, I would have been his dinner," Marzipan added.

"So, where did you come from, originally?" Dallen asked.

"Not sure," Marzipan rubbed his chin. "As far as I know, I'm the only one of my kind here. I used to have an old caretaker. He was kind of a hermit and very lonely. He used to say that he imagined me to life because he needed someone to talk to." Marzipan thought a minute. "That was before the preserves and before Erde was populated like it is today. At least, that's what I'm told from Mati and the World Viewer."

"He means like your TV," Mati whispered to Lucene. She nodded, understanding.

"Even as Erde grew, my caretaker insisted on staying in the Southern Cross anyway, even though it's a very isolated and undeveloped terrain. He's gone now," Marzipan crinkled his lips, deep in thought.

"I'm sorry," Lucene felt his sadness.

"Aw, it's alright. He was very old. But he was the one that used to make me homemade marzipan. And boy, was that delicious!"

"Marzipan has to stay in his habitat because the ratio of carbon dioxide, nitrogen and oxygen is different in his home. He can't be out for more than an hour or two at a time."

"Yeah," Marzipan laughed. "Found that one out the hard way." Marzipan told the tale of his previous caretaker's death. It was simple, really. He sat down at the kitchen table one morning, nodded off and didn't wake up. Marzipan tried to go get help, and almost ended up a desert glider's lunch.

"How long have you lived here with Mati?" Lucene asked.

"Oh, about four years now," he looked at his larger friend for confirmation.

"Don't you get lonely? I mean, being the only one and stuck in a glass cage."

"It's not a cage," Marzipan defended. "It's my home, and I love it."

"Marzipan is the most easygoing buddy a guy could have," Mati nodded. "We talk about everything together."

"Yeah," the little bug added, "and some days, I ask to be relocated to a shelf in different parts of the lab so I can talk to my other roommates and visitors."

"Wait, they can talk too?" Lucene was surprised.

"Of course, they can talk," Marzipan put his fuzzy claw hands on his thick body, tipping his shell backward and standing on his hind four legs. "You just haven't learned to listen…yet."

"Yet?"

"You're Lucene, aren't you?" Marzipan asked. Lucene looked to Mati, surprised. "Oh, I've heard enough about you from the TARA students talking to be able to figure out who you are. They haven't learned to understand my housemates yet. But maybe someday, you'll figure it out."

"Perhaps you will help me," Lucene smiled.

Marzipan thought a moment. "Maybe… I like you," he decided, before fluttering off to an intricate Weaver bird nest, letting out a yawn. "Night, night."

"Goodnight, Marzipan," Lucene answered.

"He's not subtle," Mati laughed. "When he's done talking to ya, he's just done."

"Well, I can take a hint," Lucene yawned herself, remembering, once again how exhausted she was. Her second wind had passed, and her energy was quickly fading. "It's time I made my way home, anyway. Thank you, Mati. I appreciate the tour."

"No problem at all, Lucy… Can I call you Lucy?" Lucene cringed when she heard the name but didn't want to be rude.

"Sure."

Mati showed the two out and they said their goodbyes.

The crisp air was noticeably colder than the lab. Lucene shivered slightly. Dallen took it as his cue to wrap an arm around her; the weight of his arm, coupled with the weight of her backpack, suddenly made her shoulders feel very heavy. "Let me see you to the SpeedCircuit," he offered.

Lucene had mixed feelings about Dallen. A part of him was intelligent and thoughtful. He seemed well-cultured and had this Adonis vibe about him and a chiseled chin that she suspected most Earth women would find attractive. On the other hand, he acted superior, expecting her to understand customs that were foreign to her and fall in line as if she were somehow the lesser of the two. Even sensing this, she had this strange need to prove herself to him and felt insecure in his presence. At that moment, she felt a spark of energy between them when he wrapped his arm around her, and she allowed herself to settle into the comfort of his chest as they walked.

They reached the SpeedCircuit, and Lucene directed them to the platform that led to the Eastern Cross. Oddly, it was dark and nearly barren without any trains, while the platforms leading to the Northern and Western Crosses were bustling.

"Excuse me," Lucene asked one of the attendants standing nearby. "Why is the train not running to the Eastern Cross?"

"I'm not sure," the man answered, apologetically. "I received notification about an hour ago to shut down all connections to the Eastern Cross, including remote locations traveling from the other Crosses back to the Eastern Cross. No one is allowed in or out until further notice."

"Then, how am I supposed to get home?"

"I'm sorry," the man began before a tiny red light flashed near his ear. He was receiving an alert that transferred into a small ear pod that looked like a hearing aid with an extended wire that wrapped around his cheek as if stuck to his skin. "Excuse me for a moment." He touched his ear, instinctively, and listened to the person on the other side for the next few minutes. Dallen tapped his foot impatiently while Lucene folded her arms tighter. It was getting colder out. There were a few more people gathered, waiting for information.

"I understand," he said finally, before signing off. He turned his attention back to Lucene and Dallen. "Well, you're not going to like this," he told them, including his address to the small group that had gathered near them. "The Circuit to the Eastern Cross is not reopening until morning."

"What? Why?" people protested. The attendant raised his hand, motioning for silence.

"I am not permitted to say more at this time, other than to inform you that if you have friends in the city or at one of the other crosses, you may want to stay with them this evening. If you have any pets or people you need to check on at home, I can have a local constable check in on your residence."

"What if someone has no place to go?" Lucene wanted to know. The attendant looked at her oddly, as if it were a strange thing to say. Why wouldn't someone have friends with whom they could stay with in an emergency? Lucene had only been on Erde for a little over a month, and most of that was in quarantine, followed by self-isolation. She hadn't done a great job at connecting with anyone aside from occasional visits from Roman or check-ins from Cepheus and Tanager. "Oh, are you a visiting ambassador staying with a host family in the Eastern Cross, because maybe I can see if we can put you up in a hotel here until morning?"

"That won't be necessary," Dallen replied on Lucene's behalf. "Thank you, sir. I'm sure we can make other arrangements." The attendant wiped his brow and nodded, turning his attention to the other travelers who seemed disturbed by the news. *The SpeedCircuit has never shut down before. Why was this happening?*

Dallen steered Lucene back toward the main road. "My hotel is only a few blocks away, and my suite, while small, has an extra fold-out, efficiency bed. You can stay with me."

"Oh, I couldn't do that," Lucene protested. "Maybe I can phone Tanager, and he can open the school's lounge. I could sleep on the couch there, or something." Lucene removed her backpack and set it on the ground. Leaning over, she began to rifle through it. "That's weird. I can't find my watch. Hmmm, maybe I left it at home?"

"Don't be silly, Lucene," Dallen took her arm, gently pulling her to stand. "It's late. Why wake him to have to come down here and open the school? And, why sleep on an uncomfortable couch in a public lounge when I have a perfectly good arrangement for you?"

She eyed him uncomfortably.

"I promise you," he flashed an Adonis smile. "I will be a perfect gentleman."

14

DEATH AT THE EASTERN CROSS
OCTOBER. BEFORE THE NEW ASSEMBLY.

Lucene finally arrived home at the Earth equivalent of 9 o'clock the next morning, having returned to wearing yesterday's jeans and white blouse. Neroni's dress was wrapped neatly and stored in her backpack, which was now bulging and threatening to burst. She was surprised to find Tanager there, pacing back and forth the length of her cottage. His eyes looked red, and his curly hair was a disheveled mop as if he hadn't slept all night. When he saw her, his eyes grew wide. "Lucene," was all he said, throwing his arms around her and hugging her tight to his chest. Lucene was baffled, but enjoyed the hug, so she wrapped her arms around his waist and hugged back, the side of her face being ever-so-slightly squished between his shoulder and cheek. She didn't mind.

Finally, he took her by the shoulders, pushing her at arm's length to get a good look at her. "What happened to you? Are you okay? I tried phoning you a thousand times."

"I'm fine," she responded calmly. "The SpeedCircuit shut down last night, and I couldn't get home."

"Why didn't you call me?"

"I couldn't. I thought I had my communication watch in my bag, but it wasn't there when I went to look for it. I must have left it home."

"This is why you should wear it at all times." He drew his thumb and forefinger to his forehead in frustration. "Why don't you ever listen?"

"I'm not a child, Tanager. And everything worked out fine."

"If you couldn't get home, where did you sleep last night?"

"I stayed in Dallen's hotel room." She could both see and feel his frazzled reaction. "I slept on a fold-out couch. Geez! Not that it's any of your business."

"You're right," he answered, with growing annoyance. "It is none of my business where you sleep."

"Well, that was rude."

Tanager wasn't finished complaining. "It's also none of my business if you're safe or not, who you date, where you go at night. None of it is my business."

"Could we get back to the part where you were hugging me? I liked you better then." He resumed pacing. "Don't you think you're over-reacting, just a little?"

"A man was murdered at the Eastern Cross last night." He stopped pacing, waiting for her reaction.

"What? Who? But how is that possible? I thought you were the Peace-Keepers…100 years of no conflict, and all that?"

"Well, somehow, that's changed." He eyed her, cautiously. "Mallory, the costume maker was found stabbed to death in his shop right before closing last night."

Lucene paused for a moment as she let the news sink in. "What? No! That's awful!" Lucene furrowed her brow and fought back tears. She didn't know him well but had become fond of him during their brief interaction. "I was just there last week. I can't believe it." It was only then that she became aware that Tanager was staring at her. "Why are you looking at me like that?"

"The only thing that's changed in the past month is our arrival from Earth with you and Roman."

"Wait, you think I had something to do with this?"

"No, I don't. But others might."

"Listen, I'm really, *really* exhausted," Lucene complained. "I didn't sleep well last night—" Tanager raised an eyebrow. "On the couch!" she reminded him. "I'd really just like to take a bath and nap for an hour. Can I have a little time to process this and maybe get some rest?"

As he was speaking, Neroni, Cluseladek and Xeni arrived.

Cluseladek's toga-like garb was replaced with brown linen pants and a burlap-sack-like top. The sun was coming up, and even in the winter, it was relatively temperate. He wiped a bit of perspiration from his brow. "Good morning, Lucene."

Xeni was dressed in a brown trench coat and hat and had a notepad and pencil clearly tucked in her pocket. The coat was long and dragged slightly on the ground as she walked, kicking up dust. Neroni was the only one dressed sensibly, it seemed, wearing cargo pants and a cotton t-shirt with the sleeves rolled up to her elbows. They all stood a respectful distance away as Tanager and Lucene talked.

"Okay, why are *they* here?" Lucene started walking toward her front door, swinging her backpack down to fish through it, before remembering something. "Oh, great, how am I supposed to unlock the door without that stupid watch?"

"Oh, here," Tanager moved his fingers in front of the door as if inserting an invisible key. She heard it unlatch, and the door swung open.

"What's the point of having a lock, then?" She pushed past him with Tanager close at her heels. He paused momentarily to give a nod to the three standing outside, and they knowingly hung back.

"Well, to my knowledge, you're the only one who actually uses a lock on Erde. No one else has felt the need for one."

"Yeah, tell that to Mallory." Tanager looked pained. "So, what do I need to do to get you, the three musketeers outside, and the police to leave me alone?"

Tanager was exhausted, and even through his own sleep depriva-
tion, he could feel that she, too, was burnt out.

"Why don't I take the team to the Western Cross for investigations while you get some rest. Perhaps we could come back later this
afternoon to speak with you?"

"Investigation?" Lucene's interest was piqued. "Doesn't your
military and police have guys for that?"

"We have constables, not police. As for our military, they haven't
had much to do over the years except monitor for potential outside
threats. And, until Erde started trying to help Earth, their jobs were
pretty uneventful."

"So, what you're saying is, they have no training or experience
investigating a murder?"

"I'm afraid not. The one woman we had with this level of skill
died last year at the age of 152. We have some of her recorded tech-
niques for inquiry, but that's all."

A lightbulb went off in Lucene's brain. "Did one of the constables from the crosses ask your A-team to use their Data Collection
superpowers to see what they could figure out?"

It took Tanager a moment to process what she had said. "Uh, as a
matter of fact, yes."

"This is surreal."

"How so?"

"Well, you are so much more advanced than Earth in some ways,
and yet so primitive in others."

"Lucene," Tanager responded calmly. "You may not be aware of
this, but at one point in our species' history, one-third of our population was wiped out by a pandemic. Even more were lost when they
were unable to adapt to a changing climate. Erde, as a planet, is
much smaller than Earth, still undeveloped in many areas and with
far fewer people. We've lost a lot over the past century, which is why
we work so hard to preserve what we have."

"Is that why you were so interested in helping Earth?" Lucene responded groggily, feeling a little guilty about her cranky responses. "You saw us following your same trajectory?"

"Exactly, and—if I'm being honest—some of it was self-serving. We help Earth in the hopes that some of the skills we've lost on our planet could be re-learned."

Lucene paused for a moment before unfolding her arms, making her way to her front door. "C'mon in," she motioned to Xeni, Cluse-ladek and Neroni. "Do what you need to do."

"Are you sure?" Tanager touched her sleeve.

"I'm sure."

"We won't be very long," Xeni assured her, shivering as she bounced through the threshold.

"Are you cold?" Lucene asked. "I can turn the heat up."

"It's not that," Xeni's eyes grew wide.

"What is it then?"

"Someone else has been in here while you were gone."

⁂

Constable Melokuhle had questioned every possible witness and suspect in the Eastern Cross. So far, Lucene was the only odd one out, as she was one of the last people to see Mallory alive. She remained a suspect. Witnesses also reported seeing a strange man wearing a monk's robe wandering in the shadows of Achel. This same monk had also been spotted at the Western, Eastern and Northern Crosses. At least, it was assumed that it was the same monk. Even in the city, the population was small, and yet, no one could identify the young man. Those in the crosses reported that he always appeared to be lurking around corners, but when they turned to get a closer look, or even to speak to him, he was gone. Curious, Constable Melokuhle traced him back to Roman's high-home near TARA. This was no easy feat, as the man moved like a ghost.

For the first time in the history of his career, he was hesitant to knock on someone's door unarmed, particularly someone who was new to Achel and no one seemed to know very well. All he knew about Roman was that he was studying up on Erde culture and humans from other Earth-like planets, so he could competently teach incoming students anthropology blended with sociology as it related to other species.

"Can I help you?" Roman stood at the door wearing a white terry cloth bathrobe and nothing else. He gazed at the constable with visible discontent. Roman was typically a more affable man, but he'd had enough run-ins with investigators back on Earth that he immediately had his guard up. That, and he and Far had been enjoying breakfast together on the veranda overlooking the city.

"Uh, yeah," Constable Melokuhle took off his hat and tucked it under his arm. "I apologize for the interruption. It's just that we had an unfortunate incident last night, and we're just doing some routine questioning, is all."

"And the human was at the top of your list, is that it?"

"Well, even though you are new to arrive here and are still relatively unknown, you already have a good reputation among students and faculty at TARA." For a moment, Roman's expression brightened. "Actually, it's him I need to talk to," he pointed a finger toward Far, who had crept up behind Roman and was now peering over his shoulder, wearing his usual brown robe.

"Why? What cause do you have to come here and accost my partner in our home?" Roman's mood dropped as quickly as it had begun to rise.

Far touched his arm. "It's okay," he said gently, barely above a whisper. "You should invite him in."

Roman stepped back and flung the door open wider than what was probably needed, gesturing a welcoming (but not really) arm for the constable to enter. Constable Melokuhle slid past him, somewhat sheepishly. This was difficult to do, as the constable was not a small man. In fact, he would have been considered intimidating if he didn't slink around in such a mild way. It was as if he were trying to minimize his presence. This whole confrontation made him entirely uncomfortable. When the constable came within close proximity to Far, the constable backed away slightly. The man seemed so frail that the constable was worried that if he so much as breathed on him too hard, Far would actually fall over.

"How can we be of service, honorable sir," Far whispered as if it were an effort to speak.

"We have had the misfortune of discovering a death at the Eastern Cross," Constable Melokuhle paused to gauge their reactions.

"Might I assume from the fact that you have recently arrived on our doorstep that this death was not accidental or of natural causes?"

"No. Not accidental," the constable confirmed. "Murder."

Roman let out a sigh that sounded as if a car tire had been punctured. It was a sigh that was mixed with both relief and frustration. *On the one hand*, he thought to himself, *I've had no communication with anyone at the Eastern Cross except for Lucene. On the other hand, here we are again with rude questioning as a result of my close proximity to Data Collectors.* He then had another thought, a disturbing thought.

"Who was it?" Roman's eyes grew wide. *Please don't say 'Lucene.'*

"Mallory, the costume designer."

Roman let out a nervous laugh.

"Is something funny, Mr. Aurelius?"

"Not at all," Roman regained composure. "While I'm sorry to hear about this woman's death, I'm relieved that it wasn't someone I knew personally. I know, that sounds terrible."

Constable Melokuhle paused for a moment, adjusting his hat to fit under his arm, as it had shifted during their conversation. He chose not to correct Roman's assumption that Mallory was a woman but made a mental note of it.

"Would you care to sit down, honorable sir," Far asked, motioning toward the couch. Roman cringed. He didn't want this man in their home any longer than was absolutely necessary.

"That won't be necessary, and" he turned his attention to Roman, "you don't sound like a terrible person. Sadly, I did know Mallory, and am saddened by the news." The constable paused to size up Far. Since no one seemed to have gotten a very good look at him, he was taking advantage of the close proximity—thin blonde hair that appeared to have been self-cut and the palest green eyes he'd ever seen on another person. If he weighed more than 100 pounds, the constable would have been surprised. Roman appeared to tower over him, but then, Roman was on the tall side. So, Far was probably about average height. "So," the constable continued, turning back toward Far. "We're a pretty small community, and I've not had the pleasure of meeting you. What's your name?"

"Far," the frail man answered.

"Far," the constable repeated. "Is that your first or last name?

"It's my only name," he replied simply.

"I see," Constable Melokuhle regretted not having a notepad and pen with him. In his research into investigative inquiry, that was one of the first things he found. *If you're not a Data Collector able to transmit information easily back to a scribe ready to document observations, always have a notepad and pen with you.*

That was investigation 101. But then, this was the first time the constable had ever had to actually investigate anything. Unless you count the one time a pet walleye went missing from his neighbor's pond, only to be later discovered (it's bones, anyway) sticking to the side of a gum tree. Presumably, it jumped too far and landed in the tree and later became a condor's dinner. At least, that was the best conclusion he could come up with. His neighbors were confident that this was, in fact, what happened, and provided a simple but important ritual burial for their walleye.

"You mentioned 'our home,'" the constable pointed out. "Far, with all due respect, no one around here knows you. At what point did you come to reside here?"

"What does that have to do with anything?" Roman wanted to know.

"It's okay, my love," Far touched his arm. Constable Melokuhle cringed inadvertently at the touch. "One month ago," Far answered.

"Where did you live prior?"

"Elsewhere," Far answered simply.

"I'm afraid I'm going to need a bit more information than that."

"I was a prisoner in Section 3, near the Royal Training Grounds." Roman put his arm around Far in support.

"I'm sorry to hear that," the constable acknowledged. "How did you escape?"

"What makes you think I escaped?" Far was confused.

"Because you're standing here in front of me," the constable reasoned. "The Royals are not known for mercy. I can assume that they did not actually *let* you go." Constable Melokuhle raised an eyebrow.

Far thought a moment. "You are correct. They did not let me go. Someone helped me."

"Who?"

"Does it matter?"

"You tell me."

Far was quiet for a moment more. "No," he answered finally. "That doesn't matter. But the point of the matter is, I am here." Looking at Far, it appeared as if he were sifting through his mind, trying to determine the right thing to say among lots of options. Finally, he settled on, "…with my love." Roman's face crumbled as he fought back tears, while Far seemed to have adopted a neutral expression.

"Mister…Far," the constable continued, awkwardly. "You have been spotted in all of the occupied Crosses: the Northern, Eastern and Western regions of our planet. If the Southern Cross wasn't so barren and underpopulated, I suspect you might have been seen there, too."

"What are you suggesting, constable?" Roman demanded.

"I'm not suggesting anything. There's just one more curious thing that keeps bugging me, on top of all that."

"And what is that?" Far asked, calmly.

"How is it that you were spotted in most of the Crosses, but I don't recall your name, or any unknown name, for that matter, showing up in the SpeedCircuit registry? If you didn't use the Speed-Circuit, how did you travel?"

Far turned to Roman for support. His partner picked up the cue immediately.

"As you know," Roman replied, "we can retain the rental of hover cars in emergencies and for official business, yes?"

"Yes, and what of it?"

"Well, as a new professor at TARA, as well as a new resident of Erde, I am required to research the culture and behaviors of all inhabitants here."

The constable was busy connecting the dots. It didn't take him long. "And, is there a reason your research requires the use of hover car versus the use of our highly equipped and efficient SpeedCircuit?"

"Constable, is it not a fact that the Circuit was down last night?"

"Yes, but that is very rare."

"But still. Some of us have little time to get up to speed on Erde culture. So, the use of a faster transportation system in order to research the Crosses was essential to me. Far often accompanies me, so I'm assuming that when people spotted him in their town, he was merely exploring while I was doing my appointed research."

"I see," the constable was unconvinced. "And, do you have records of your hover car rentals?"

Roman grit his teeth. His words were half-truths. He did, in fact, make use of the rentals, but he thus far had only re-visited the Western Cross. *Would they be able to map where he'd actually gone with the rental car?* He wasn't sure. "Of course," Roman flashed a confident smile. "I don't have them handy, but I can request the receipts I submitted to TARA for reimbursement. I'm afraid I neglected to retain my own copies after that."

"Well, if you can get those for me, I would appreciate it,"

Constable Melokuhle's face began to take on a reddish hue, and his face felt hot.

"Of course," Roman spat out his reply, becoming increasingly agitated. After an uncomfortably long pause, Roman asked, "May I ask you a question, Constable?"

"Certainly, Mr. Aurelius. What is it?"

"You seem to be uncomfortable with, well, us." He pointed back and forth between he and Far. Far remained silent. "Is there a problem?"

"No," the constable adjusted his collar nervously before repositioning his hat on his head. "It's just that…"

"Yes," Roman persisted.

"I'm an old-fashioned man."

"And—" Roman's agitation grew.

"I'm just surprised that two men are, well…"

"Well, what? Living together?"

"No, that's not it."

Roman was taken aback. "From different planets?" He was confused.

"No, I'm used to seeing inter-species relationships all the time. It's just that…" Constable Melokuhle was clearly at odds with himself.

"Just that, what?" Roman couldn't let it go.

"Well, as I said, I'm a little more old fashioned. You said you lived together. With no disrespect, but Far here appears to be a monk. So, I'm guessing you two are not married?"

"Married?" Roman's face broke into a big smile. "That's what you're worried about?" Far also let out a small laugh.

"I know. I know." the constable held his hands up. "It's just the way I was raised."

"Well, honorable sir," Far spoke up, clasping Roman's hand for emphasis. "It just so happens that we *are* married."

"Really?" The constable was surprised.

"Yes," Far explained. "On my planet, Macar, monks marry all the time. Roman and I are in a committed relationship, so you needn't worry." Far reached around his neck and produced a small pendant attached to a cord hanging from his neck. Likewise, Roman lifted his arm to display a chord with the same circular pendent that he had wrapped around his wrist.

"Oh, well. I get it," the constable was too embarrassed to remember that he was conducting an investigation. "I didn't mean to offend."

"No offense taken," Roman assured him. *Except that you seem awful judgy,* he thought. "And, if that will be all?"

"Yes," Constable Melokuhle backed away. "Nothing more from me. You enjoy your weekend."

With that, the constable left. Roman slowly closed the door behind him, relieved. Far watched everything with an oddly smug satisfaction.

HOUSE ARREST

OCTOBER. BEFORE THE NEW ASSEMBLY.

Cepheus was, once again, making the rounds at the Crosses. Typically, he did this bi-monthly. But given his recent return to Erde, he thought it prudent to be extra attentive to the humans who were currently living on the preserves and that they were sworn to protect. It wasn't an excuse to see Moksha again. He was far too practical for that. At least, that's what he told himself.

He arrived at her purple cottage in time to see Commander Royce and two of her military guards surrounding Moksha. One was placing a tracking band around the Moksha's exposed ankle.

"What is going on here?" he asked, baffled.

"Isn't it obvious?" Moksha's expression was sour. "I'm a former Royal assassin. So, clearly, I was the one responsible."

It took Cepheus a moment to make the connection.

Moments later, Neroni appeared from around the side of Moksha's vineyard, along with Xeni, Cluseladeck and Tanager. Neroni hung her head in a combination of shame and confusion. Cepheus looked to Tanager and thought, *what is happening here?*

Mallory, Tanager answered simply. Cepheus shook his head. This couldn't be.

"Neroni was able to use her remote viewing skills to witness

Moksha at the costume shop the night of Mallory's murder. She was even able to confirm the location of the weapon used to kill him. It was stashed in his refrigerator, no blood or fingerprints, but the blade marks match those found…" Commander Royce let out a cough. Talking about blood and murder left her queasy.

"Neroni," Cepheus asked quietly. "Is this true?"

Neroni couldn't bring herself to look at him or Moksha allowing her eyes to drop toward the ground, instead. "It is, but…"

"But what?"

"Can I speak with you and Professor Tanager privately for a moment?" Her eyes were pleading. Cepheus glanced at Commander Royce, who nodded in reply.

"Of course," he answered. He, Tanager and Neroni began walking the dirt trail leading back into town. When they were out of earshot, she spoke. "I don't understand it," she confessed. "I didn't pick up any images in the costume shop, and yet, when doing a routine scan of the Western Cross, I suddenly had a strong but vivid image of Moksha. She was…" Neroni hugged herself, her eyes welling up. "I didn't want to see that. It was awful!" Cepheus touched her shoulder. While his heart was in the right place, he no longer knew quite how to offer comfort. But she was empathic enough to understand. "Thank you," she said quietly.

"Here's the really odd thing," Tanager added. "Xeni reported feeling a cold, ghost-like energy both at the costume shop and again at Lucene's cottage, but nothing in Moksha's home. And Cluseladek scanned the crime scene in its entirety. He claims that there was nothing in the refrigerator except a half of a pomegranate. And yet, the constable later retrieved a knife. I think it was a set-up."

"Set-up?"

"Sorry, it's an Earth term Xeni recently taught me. It means that someone is trying to make it look like Moksha is guilty." Neroni wrapped her arms around herself as if to self-soothe.

"And what do you think, Neroni?" Neroni looked up timidly and whispered, "I only know what I saw."

Cepheus's chest tightened. He trusted both Neroni's skills and honesty. His mood darkened. Perhaps he was foolish to entertain the ideas that a former Royal assassin could actually be a good person. The ground swayed momentarily as he lost focus.

"No, not, not this…not now," Tanager grabbed his one elbow, Neroni the other. Cepheus pulled back from the episode.

"Perhaps we should rejoin the group," Cepheus suggested in a voice that sounded not quite like his own. Tanager and Neroni exchanged looks and nodded.

When they did, Commander Royce was busy giving Moksha strict orders. She was not to leave the borders of her small property until further notice. A constable would be stationed at the Western Cross at all times, making the rounds throughout the day, while military guards would be assigned to watch the house at varying intervals —day and night, in the event she attempted to leave.

"Nice going, Neroni," Clusaledek muttered under his breath, once she had rejoined the group. She gazed up at him, surprised at the comment.

"Whatever do you mean?"

"Nothing you saw matches what Xeni and I saw—just an observation."

"I'm not making it up," Neroni defended, but in her heart, even she had doubts about her own abilities.

"Hmmm," was all Cluseladek said. Xeni peered up at him and then back at Neroni but said nothing. She didn't remember Cluseladek ever being snarky before. This whole thing had everyone on edge.

"So, I've left one home, only to become a prisoner in another," Moksha became indignant. "How then am I to get supplies for my vineyard and food and staples for myself?"

"Should have thought of that before you murdered Mallory," an angry voice called from the road. There stood Abe and his wife, and at least two dozen people living in the Western Cross. Many were holding shovels, brooms and pitchforks in what could only be assumed was a pathetic protest with feeble weapons—pitchforks aside.

"Stand down, Abe," Commander Royce stood in front of the man —an odd sight given her size compared to his. "We don't know for certain that Moksha had anything to do with his death. That's why we conduct investigations."

"This is bullshit," Abe raised an arm overhead in an odd show of protest. There were several cheers and "here, here's" behind him. "Where I come from, we don't stand for outsiders coming in and hurting one of our own."

"May I remind you, all of you," Commander Royce's voice increased in volume, seeming completely out of proportion with the rest of her small frame, "that we were once all outsiders."

There was a mumbling amid the crowd as Cluseladek glared at Neroni, as if to say, "see what you did?"

Cepheus had come to a decision. He snuck up, snakelike, beside Moksha so quietly no one noticed, no one except an assassin trained to notice everything. "Do not be alarmed," he whispered. "I will make certain that you have whatever you need."

16

CONGREGATION

OCTOBER. THREE WEEKS AFTER THE DEATH AT THE EASTERN
CROSS.

Odessa was not exaggerating when she spoke of Reverend Isabella's ability to build a congregation and bring people together. In the three short weeks since Odessa first approached Isabella at the museum, the priestess had managed to pack her Sanctuary with followers and even set up two new satellite churches, one in France and one in Germany. They now joined Dallen on a remote call from the negotiation room at the PDL on Erde. Dallen was joined by Commander Royce, Cepheus, Tanager, and the ever-reluctant Lucene. Once again, Lucene was to stand in place of Roman as the official Earth representative on Erde. Roman had been promptly uninvited given his connection to Far. Lucene had been cleared, for now at least, as no evidence was found to suggest that she had a connection to Mallory's death. Though, given the strange energy that Xeni felt in Lucene's home, there was still some concern about her safety, mostly from Tanager, who had taken to checking in on her, either by calling or stopping in almost daily. Lucene didn't mind the gesture. Dallen did.

"Before I introduce our esteemed Representative Dallen," Isabella addressed the crowd, the amphitheater-styled Sanctuary filled, as she spoke from the small podium at its center. "I would like to remind us of why we are here." Her larger-than-life holographic image hung in the center of the theater, providing a clearer view to those tuning in from remote locations. She was dressed in her formal ceremonial garb, a long white robe with a string of flowers that formed a stole that was wrapped around her neck and hung down each side of her robe. On her feet were simple tan sandals with little material.

Members leaned in with bated breath, hanging onto Isabella's every word. Odessa watched from one of the stained-glass windows near the ceiling, fluttering at the light, in her orange butterfly form, smiling to herself. Suddenly aware of how she might appear to onlookers, she relaxed her wings, glancing at Morphinae, who was in the window at the opposite end of the Sanctuary. Even though he also was in a blue butterfly state (and difficult to see), she could sense his usual lack of emotional commitment to the entire exchange. She wondered to herself if there were some way to make her butterfly form larger, more noticeable, perhaps. But she dared not attempt it today of all days, in case she goofed and enlarged herself into a human butterfly size.

"We are here because we love our planet." There were cheers from the audience. "We are here because Earth is our home." More cheers. "We are here because our voices need to be heard." The crowd erupted while Isabella surveyed the room, nodding. After a moment, she patted her hand in the air, and the crowd settled.

From the Negotiation room, Lucene sent a message to Cepheus. *How come we don't have a crowd of Erde supporters here?* she wanted to know.

Well, Cepheus answered, *we don't really do that.*

Why not?

Because we don't have to.

Lucene was not entirely sure she understood this answer. She leaned over toward Dallen and whispered, "Why are there no Vitruvian supporters present?"

"Oh," he whispered back, "there are."

"Really, but…"

"Please, Lucene. This isn't the time. And, you should not even be addressing a Vitruvian Ambassador so informally in meetings such as this."

Tanager overheard the exchange but said nothing.

Lucene sat back, deflated. They had been dating for several weeks now, and she still hadn't gotten a handle on how she was "supposed" to behave. It seemed to her that in formal settings or when at the Embassy Club (the only place they ever seemed to dine), she was expected to follow Vitruvian protocol, whatever that was; but when visiting places such as art galleries, outdoor botanical gardens or simple sightseeing, she could be herself, sort of. The only sign that she could see that made the true distinction was whether or not they were alone or interacting with other people. Having little dating experience, and only having Fatima's misguided relationships to go by, Lucene assumed that this was normal. She thought that maybe she could ask Neroni about this, but given the current murder investigation, and the fact that she really didn't know the woman all that well, she dismissed the idea.

"Please join me," Isabella finished her speech, "in welcoming Representative Dallen from Vitruvia in Section 2 as he shares with us his bold initiative for uniting Earth, Vitruvia and Erde for the good of our world." Whatever Isabella had said or done over the past few weeks to win over Earth supporters, it had clearly worked because everyone cheered and clapped in unison, without hesitation.

Dallen was pleased, shooting Lucene a smug, "this is just as it should be" look. She smiled back encouragingly, but something twisted in her stomach.

"Thank you, Reverend Isabella," Dallen acknowledged. "As you know, we are on a very important mission, one that few Earthlings are worthy of supporting."

Worthy? Cepheus, Tanager and Lucene exchanged looks.

"You are the chosen…" Dallen continued.

Had Commander Royce and Reverend Isabella been in the same

room (on the same planet, even), people would have observed an identical, manufactured expression. Without words, they shared a mutual understanding that sometimes you have to play along with the facade in order to support the greater good. They both adopted a small smile that included nodding, encouragingly, at strategic moments and glancing around the room to gauge the acceptance of the message.

"Sadly," Dallen puffed his chest, his hologram now taking center stage on three locations on Earth. "Virtruvia and Erde are prohibited from the International Peace Project's Assembly, ironically, in spite of their attempts to help Earth."

Tanager let out a nervous cough. Dallen peered at him with disapproval. Tanager waved a slight apology. Until recently, he wasn't aware that he had any nervous behaviors. The discovery annoyed him.

"What we are proposing," Dallen continued, "is re-uniting Virtruvia and Erde with the Assembly, explaining our position of peace, reconciliation and mutual respect." Dallen paused in all the right places, speaking between applause. "But there's an even more pressing matter than that." The crowd grew silent. "The Earth is in grave danger." There were murmurs in the crowd. "I'm sure you have heard of the Royals…" There were frightened nods from the crowd. "And the Null…" A gasp could be heard. "Then you under-stand that unless we work together alongside the IPP, the Royals will send the Null to destroy us all—Earth, Vitruvia and Erde."

Something about this didn't sit quite right with Lucene. The knot in her stomach grew tighter. Tanager was also confused, but for a different reason. *That's not accurate.* He directed his energy and emotion toward Cepheus. *Our intelligence suggests that Royals want the Null to avoid Earth so that they can claim it as their new Training Grounds. Is it possible that if the Null avoids Earth, then the Royals plan to offer up Virtruvia and Erde as 'consolation' prizes?"*

I'm not sure, Cepheus replied in thought, *but I don't think so.*

What is he up to? Tanager thought, without thinking. Then, when he realized what he had just said, he was, momentarily, proud of his newly developed Earth lexicon. Somehow, it seemed appropriate at a time like this.

Once again, Cepheus replied, ignoring Tanager's misplaced pride, *I'm not sure.*

"You may be asking yourself," Dallen finished his speech, "what can I do? I'm just a mere mortal." Lucene had to admit that she asked herself this very question quite regularly. "But I assure you, you are much more than that. You are the chosen."

As if on cue, Isabella asked, "Honorable Ambassador Dallen, what can we do to support your mission?"

"I like to think of it as *our* mission," Dallen smiled. The knot in Lucene's stomach now felt like a rock. At the same time, Tanager put his hand on his belly. *Must have been something I ate,* he thought to himself, reciting, yet another Earth phrase he'd learned from a recent movie. "Our voices need to be heard. And for that to happen, you need to protest the Assembly's removal of Vitruvia and Erde from the IPP."

"But, why now," Isabella followed the script. "Why so many years later?"

"What a great question, Reverend Isabella. That's a great question," Dallen flashed a pearly smile. "Our intelligence has learned that there is a contract in play, in which the Royals plan to overtake Sections 0, Sections 1 and Sections 2 this year, with the help of the Null." The hologram could be seen walking back and forth. Interesting, as Dallen remained seated at the table in the Negotiation Room, although his mouth and head moved in unison in reality and as a projection. "If you proclaim the injustice, Earth leaders will hear you and vote in favor of our reinstatement. Only then can we help you."

"What do you say, chosen ones?" Isabella raised her arms overhead in a natural yet rehearsed manner. The crowd erupted in cheers and applause.

"Just one more thing," Dallen added, as the sound died down.

"What is that, Representative Dallen?"

"We believe there is a baby."

"A baby?" Isabella's eyes flew open in feigned surprise.

"Yes," Dallen shook his head forlornly. "We have reason to believe that there is a baby, a hybrid between the Royals and the Null, a spawn of pure evil."

What the hell is he talking about?! Lucene wanted to know.

Nulls and Royals can't produce a baby, can they? Tanager asked.

No, Cepheus answered abruptly. *This makes no sense.*

"And what will happen if we don't act now?" Isabella's eyes widened.

"Then, the baby will grow up to represent evil in its purest form and destroy the entire universe. And we are the only ones who can stop it. Who is with me?" From all corners of the Earth where Isabella's influence reached, the congregations stood in unison, cheering, yelling affirmations of support, clapping, and even weeping hysterically. Dallen held his fist to his chest in what could only be assumed was a strange symbol of unity.

Commander Royce stood and held her fist over her heart, glaring at Lucene, Tanager and Cepheus that they should rise and do the same. Instead, Lucene folded her arms, Tanager clasped his hands together and rested them on the desk in front of him, and Cepheus held the sides of his chair, trying not to fall into a dizzy spell. Fortunately, one of Commander Royce's attendants was quick to react, turning off the single camera that put them in view of Earth attendees. Instead, all cameras pointed to Dallen, who waved and smiled regally to the masses. But in the back of everyone's mind in the Negotiation Room (save for Dallen's) was the incessant question: *what baby?*

"What the hell was that about?" Lucene demanded when they were outside, crossing the bridge to the SpeedCircuit. Dallen peered around him, embarrassed by her outburst, especially considering he was still in uniform.

Tanager and Cepheus stayed behind to speak with Commander Royce, while Lucene angrily followed Dallen—at his insistence—after the call.

"You need to calm down," Dallen demanded. "Your manner is not befitting the companion of an Ambassador."

"Hate to break it to you, Ambassador," Lucene spat angrily, "but I don't give a rat's ass about how I appear to others or to you!" Lucene marched across the bridge, fists balled, taking fierce little steps. He followed her with a mix of arrogance, curiosity and a small bit of amusement.

"Clearly," he answered, offhandedly. This only made Lucene angrier.

"And furthermore," Lucene spat, "while you may be *an* ambassador, you're not *my* ambassador. In case you hadn't noticed, I'm not Vitruvian."

"Again," Dallen answered calmly, "clearly."

Lucene stopped in her tracks. "What's that supposed to mean?"

Dallen smiled, knowing he had won.

"It means," Dallen took her by the arms and drew her in closer, "that I recognize that you are a strong, independent hybrid."

"Hybrid?"

"Yes, an Erdeling with special powers having grown up on Earth. I can't imagine that had been easy on you," Dallen offered sympathetically.

"No," Lucene was suspicious. "But why are you suddenly being nice to me?"

Dallen looked offended. "Have I not been nice to you?"

"Intermittently."

Dallen pulled her into his chest and hugged her, as he'd imagine Tanager would have done if he had the opportunity. "I will do better," he promised, kissing her gently on the top of her head, noticing her mix of blonde and brown hair with some disappointment. "So, what made you so angry at me today?"

"Well," Lucene confessed. "I may not know politics very well, but I know bullshit when I hear it."

"And, what 'bullshit' did you hear?"

"All that about being worthy, and chosen, and the Royals destroying Earth?" That didn't seem quite right.

Dallen let out a sigh. "My dear Lucene, while you are a very smart girl, you are right—you don't understand the intricate inner workings of politics. Sometimes, you have to—as you would say on Earth—fudge the truth a little for the greater good."

Lucene's mind went back to that time in New York, sitting in the office of Drake Cushing, her boss and sometimes crush, where he spoke about 'forces at work.' Somehow, this felt wrong, in the same way that it had back then.

"But, Isabella…"

"She's been around for centuries. She understands."

"What are you talking about? Earthlings don't live for centuries," Lucene chuckled. "What you know about politics is on par with what you *don't* know about human lifespan," Lucene was amused.

Dallen chuckled. "Of course, you are right." They walked in silence for a few minutes, hand-in-hand (something that Lucene had only recently become accustomed to). "Forgive me?"

"I suppose." Lucene smiled to herself. "So, what have you got planned for us this afternoon?"

"Well," Dallen was cautious about his words. "Your hair."

"What about it?" Lucene grew defensive again.

"It's beautiful," he lied. "I just thought it would be nice to treat you to a…'spa day.'"

"I don't know what you mean." It was true. Lucene had heard about spa days and shopping days and gal's nights out, but these were all just fun ideas in her head.

"You've always dyed your hair brown to protect your identity, correct?"

"I guess. I didn't really know that at the time, though."

"Well, what if you picked one?"

"One what?"

"One color, Lucene." Dallen sighed. "Don't be daft."

"I thought you were going to be nicer to me."

"I'm sorry."

"You don't like the brown with blonde roots look?"

"It's not that," Dallen sighed again. "It's just that…and, please don't take this the wrong way, but, if you are to be on the arm of a Vitruvian Ambassador, there are certain…expectations."

"Such as?"

"Your hair, for one, should be one color. I'm flexible about which one."

"Well, thank you for your flexibility," Lucene answered sarcastically.

"Try to think of things from my culture and my perspective," he pleaded. "Virtruvia is not as…relaxed as Earth…specifically, where you come from."

"Thanks for being specific."

"What I mean is, there are certain standards."

"Which I don't meet."

"But you could…with a little work."

Lucene thought about this a moment. How much was this relationship worth to her? How important was it to fit in? And, most important, in her mind, what was she willing to sacrifice? After all, when all is said and done, he lives on Vitruvia, and she now lives on Erde. "What do I need to do," she asked, finally.

As Lucene would come to find out, meeting certain standards turned out to be more superficial than she expected. It involved dying her hair all brown, which Dallen paid for. He'd wondered why she hadn't picked blonde since that was actually her natural color. "I guess I'm just not quite ready to be me yet," she explained.

She'd also been forced to give up the wardrobe that Mallory had picked out for her in favor of uncomfortable attire, not unlike 'business casual' on Earth. It was constricting and did little to make her feel attractive. The wardrobe included close-toed shoes with pointy heels, ugly and stiff polyester-like pants with a matching blazer (a blazer!), and a long-sleeved starched shirt. Lucene hated it. Dallen seemed pleased.

By the end of the day, Dallen had created the perfect companion, and Lucene had convinced herself that all was as it should be, and the reality of this made her perfectly miserable.

17

B-612

NOVEMBER. BEFORE THE NEW ASSEMBLY.

"I am sorry I could not be there to meet you in person, my friends," Cepheus's hologram floated in the air in front of a flat communication screen. "But I have matters of urgency to attend to here, and—" he paused, "I am still under watch."

"Ahh, think nothing of it," Ivan sucked in his breath. The air was a bit thinner on B-612, but he was adapting well, provided he didn't move or speak too rapidly. The gravity also felt mildly off. That, or he had lost an awful lot of weight in a short period of time without actually appearing any thinner. He felt physically unstable, but not abnormally so. "I am jest grateful fer yer assistance."

Ivan and Fatima arrived at the way station between Earth and Erde just a few days prior after a somewhat harrowing journey. Neither had any experience with space travel nor had they time to actually test their human-made vessel before takeoff. To make matters worse, Fatima had been having more regular episodes, where her heart would beat abnormally, causing dizziness and a weird cramping in her belly and mid-back. They have been traveling for three months, mostly alone, save for semi-regular communications with Cepheus, on what they hoped was a private connection.

The attendants who met them on B-612 were three third-year

nursing students from TARA, accompanied by one flight surgeon and two pilots. Rescuing refugees from Earth was not unusual for them. Still, sending a team out by special request from a lead professor to gather up Earth-traveling, non-astronaut humans, was.

The humor was not lost on the well-read Ivan. B-612 was the asteroid that the famed *Little Prince* lived on in Antoine de Saint-Exupéry's children's tale. Erdelings had a funny sense of humor, he decided, since they named their small and relatively new planet the German word for "Earth" (Erde), and the way station after asteroid B-612. *Adult humans are not the only ones who are funny,* Ivan thought.

"Did you both arrive safely, without incident?"

"Er," Ivan scratched his ear. "Not entirely without incident, no. But we are here, and your team has been jest grrrreat."

"I am glad. Communication has been spotty today, but I do want to hear more details once your vessel is back on track and closer to Erde."

"Aye," Ivan answered. "We have much to catch up on."

"Hi, Cepheus!" Fatima called from her sleep station in the next portal over. "We can't wait to see you, and Tanager and my favorite gal pal, Lucene!" She was courteous enough to leave Roman off that list, and while Ivan liked to think their relationship had moved past any cause for jealousy, he still had to admit that hearing Roman's name set off a weird flame-like reaction in his head. Then she added, "We love you!"

Cepheus's abnormal pallor turned pink. It wasn't that he didn't feel warmth and affection—in truth, he felt it more deeply than most. But since he'd lost his family due to the Royals waging a personal war against him, he had trouble expressing and accepting it, even in its most innocent form. Ivan, who started out as not the most empathic of people, began to pick up cues from his time spent with Fatima. "Don't ye worry, me friend," he confided, "we understand."

Cepheus and Ivan ended their conversation with Cepheus's image floating back into the screen and vanishing. An attendant quickly silenced the connection. "Can't be too careful as to who's listening," she explained.

"Aye," Ivan nodded solemnly. Sometimes, he wished for the days when he could hole up in his garage, work on his inventions, and not talk to a soul for nearly a week. But he had to admit, the tradeoff had been worth it. Life was decidedly better with Fatima in it then not. For her, it was worth the sacrifice.

"Everything okay?" Fatima smiled up at Ivan when he entered her portal. She was under ordered bed rest while they monitored her condition closely. Ivan leaned over to give her a kiss.

"Aye," he answered. "Everything is jest fine." They still had nearly two to three months of travel to get to Erde, but Fatima had to be cleared first.

"Excuse me," the flight surgeon stood in the doorway. She was unusually small by human standards, less than four feet tall and incredibly thin. Her skin was glossy with an energetic glow about it. "May I enter?"

"Of course, Dr. Wilah," Fatima smiled. "I wish Earth doctors were as polite as you are."

Wilah smiled shyly. "I am only here to serve," she answered, "and you don't need to call me 'doctor.' Wilah is just fine." She scanned Fatima's resting body with what looked like the check-out scanner at a supermarket. "Vitals are good for you and—" she paused.

"And what, doc—er, Wilah?" Ivan asked, concerned.

Wilah took a careful breath. "Vitals are good for you and…your baby."

"Say what now?" Ivan's ears were burning. He must have misheard.

"Your baby," Wilah repeated calmly. Fatima looked as if someone just slapped her in the face. "Were you not trying to conceive?"

"Well," Ivan stammered. Discussing this with someone other than Fatima made him rather uncomfortable. "We weren't exactly trying, but we weren't exactly *not* trying, either. How the hell did this happen?" Wilah eyed him curiously. "I mean," he continued to trip over his words, "I know how it happens, as it were, but we're jest, uh…"

"Pleasantly surprised," Fatima's face glowed. "I believe the words my partner is looking for is "pleasantly surprised."

Ivan looked at Fatima with concern. "I'm sorry, Fatima," he apologized. "I wouldn't have dragged ye out here on some crazy scheme and put yer life in danger had I known ye were…ya know—"

"Actually," Wilah hooked a small monitor to the scanner so she could read the results more clearly. "This is fairly new." She slid her finger over the monitor carefully. "From what I can see, Fatima has been pregnant for nearly two months."

Ivan's face turned red. "Well, we were alone in space fer quite some time." He tugged at his ear nervously.

"There's no need to explain yourself to me, Ivan," Wilah offered. "I'm just happy that Fatima and the baby are healthy."

"So, the weird pains?"

"More related to the pregnancy than your heart condition," Wilah validated. "That said, I'd like to monitor you for a day or two more before clearing you to continue your journey to Erde. In fact," she gave a knowing glance toward two of her students. "Given this new information, it may be prudent if we hitch our two vessels together and accompany you the rest of the way home—if you are amenable to that?"

"Of course," Fatima was overcome with emotion. "But we don't want to put you out."

"We have to travel home, regardless," Wilah explained. "I will confirm with our pilots to make certain, but I suspect that with a few modifications to our vessel, we should be able to travel in tandem."

"Aye, and I am happy to help yer crew as well," Ivan offered.

Wilah nodded. "For now, I'll leave the two of you to," she paused, "process what I've just told you." With that, Wilah left the portal, closing the thin sliding panel that served as a privacy door.

Ivan's head began racing. *A child? Really? I mean, I guess I sorta thought it could happen someday, but I'm not exactly young. And, I don't know the first thing about children, let alone raising one on a foreign planet. Hell, I don't even know yet how I'll support us. And...*"

"Hey," Fatima reached out and took Ivan's hand in hers. He stood over her, smiling sheepishly with a mix of overwhelm, love and confusion. "Don't worry," she told him, "we've got this."

TESTS GONE BAD

NOVEMBER. BEFORE THE NEW ASSEMBLY.

Lucene was already in a bad mood when she arrived at TARA that Wednesday for a class gathering, and she didn't know why. It just felt as if her skin were alive, and she was aware of every tiny sensation. The latest outfit that Dallen picked out for her was not helping. It was a combination of a stiff, high-collared course blouse and equally restrictive polyester-like pants. She reflected again on how the clothes Mallory had chosen turned out to have been much more comfortable. Hopefully, Lucene thought, they were still in her closet, and Dallen hadn't had one of his attendants get rid of them. Lucene paused for a moment of reflection about Mallory, saddened by the loss of someone she had hoped would have become a new friend. Her eyes welled up slightly before she pushed the thought away.

"Are you okay?" Xeni asked in her typical, wide-eyed fashion. She was so focused on Lucene that she almost deleted the entire virtual genetic coding that she was creating on her computer. She frantically adjusted the image using eye movements, averting them away and back again as she virtually commanded the screen to move.

Tanager looked up from his desk, saw Lucene's demeanor, and

promptly dropped the paperback book he was reading. He'd seen this before on the Vessel, and he knew the signs.

Lucene tossed her backpack on the floor. "I'm fine," she answered abruptly, plopping into her seat at the head of the class. "Why wouldn't I be?"

"No reason," Xeni replied in a whisper and drew her attention back to her project.

Neroni was next to arrive, along with several other classmates. She opened her mouth to speak, saw Lucene's expression, and closed it again. She took her seat, silently. The person sitting next to Neroni moved over a few inches as if her visions were contagious. Or, perhaps, they thought, she had made them up for some reason.

"*Lucene*," Tanager sent her a mental message. "*If you are not up to today, we can reschedule.*"

"I'm fine; stay out of my head," she answered rather loudly. The class fell silent. "Could we just get started already?" *The only thing worse than being in a bad mood is everyone around you making it evident that they are aware that you are in a bad mood.*

Tanager thought a moment. He was aware of the efforts involved in running today's experiments—not to mention the money TARA invested in the project and in covering Lucene's expenses. Granted, some of the money came from a trust left behind from her parents, but that had long since run out in the efforts of bringing Lucene home.

In spite of his otherwise best judgement, he decided to press on. A few students appeared visibly surprised at Lucene's seeming lack of respect for their teacher, but many could clearly feel the energy she was kicking off. For Cluseladek's part, he silently performed a kindness meditation, sending positive energy in Lucene's direction and attempting to mentally ask students on a similar wavelength to do the same. Given that Lucene's arms were crossed, and she slumped down in her seat like a spoiled brat, he assumed she wasn't feeling it. He continued, nonetheless.

Tanager called the class to attention. Today's first experiment was to re-test the levels of Lucene's telekinetic powers and see how modifications might dial up her powers in this area. The initial baseline tests revealed that this was an area of potential for her. Yet, she presently exhibited little to no skill at moving objects with her mind.

With several objects of varying weights and sizes in place, carefully lined up across the workspace that had been set up in front of Tanager's desk, they began.

First, Lucene sat in front of the table and was asked to focus her attention on the smallest of objects—a vanadium coin that was poised on the edge of the table. Then, Tanager handed her a blindfold and asked her to tie it around her eyes.

"I'd like you to imagine you are still seeing the coin in front of you," Tanager instructed. "Try to knock it off the table and onto the floor by mentally imagining you were moving it with your mind."

Blindfolded? Mentally commanding the coin to move? It seemed rudimentary and outright silly. She tried. Nothing happened.

"Try again, imagining you are actually pushing it with your hand."

Still nothing.

After several more attempts, Tanager asked her to remove the blindfold and rest for a moment. Finally, they continued. "Why don't we try again without the blindfold? How about tracking its intended movement with your eyes?"

At one point, the other objects on the table began to move: a sharpened pencil, a glass of water, a stone, a ceramic plate—but the coin remained adamantly stuck. Tanager recommended she attempt to funnel her energy in one direction.

Lucene let out a loud sigh. *What a ridiculous waste of time.*

This is when the class was called in to assist, with those rated high in telekinesis offering tips that worked for them, to include asking the coin politely to move, blowing in its direction (like a strong wind), and pushing outward with the palm of her hand and imagining energy was pouring out of it and rushing toward the small coin.

"Parlor tricks," Lucene crossed her arms angrily.

"What?" Tanager asked.

"There is no purpose to this. You're just asking me to perform parlor tricks."

Tanager didn't understand.

At that moment, the door burst open as two young children rushed toward Neroni in a loud frenzy. The little boy had a tangle of coiled black hair, while the girl had a long, blue-green mane that ran the length of her back. Both wrapped their arms around their mother, seated at the back of the classroom.

"I'm so sorry, Professor Tanager," Neroni's husband stood at the door. "I only meant to bring my wife her lunch today." He held up a small container as evidence. "She forgot it. But the kids were beside themselves—worried about their mother and insisting on coming along."

"I see," Tanager wrinkled his forehead. "Why were they worried?"

Neroni shook her head toward her husband and he fell silent.

"Because they think she made that stuff up about the wine lady just for attention," the little boy supplied.

"Shhh, hush now," Neroni told her son.

"Who are 'they'?" Tanager wanted to know.

Neroni let out a sigh, "I'm not sure," she confessed. "We've gotten a few notes, threatening me, saying that I am prejudiced against a Royal living among us, even though the leader of TARA is a..." She stopped herself, knowing full well that Cepheus renounced his lineage a long time ago. "But there were other messages coming in on my phone, calling me a hero for drawing out 'the outsider,' their words, and uncovering a killer."

There were murmurs across the class.

"Neroni, this is terrible," Tanager sympathized. "Have you contacted your local constable?"

"No," she hugged herself as her little boy continued to hang on her arm. Her husband now stood behind her, rubbing her shoulders lightly in support. "I didn't want to cause any more trouble."

"Too late for that," Cluseladek chimed in, while several other classmates let out a chortle.

"That was inappropriate," Tanager chastised. "In this class, we will treat one another with respect."

Cluseladek fell silent, a scornful frown replacing the earlier serenity that had accompanied his kindness meditation. Even he was having an internal battle with his emotions, and he was typically one of the most balanced among them.

The scene had distracted Lucene, who failed to notice that Neroni's little girl was now standing beside her. Even with Lucene sitting, the girl, at full height, barely reached her chin. The girl tugged at Lucene's sleeve. "Hey," she whispered.

Lucene smiled in spite of her souring mood. "What is it?"

"I know how you can make that little coin move," she offered.

"Really? How?" Lucene was amused. *Maybe she can take my place, and I can go home.*

"It's easy. You just have to pretend you *are* the coin and ask yourself why you might want to fall on the floor."

"Hmmm," Lucene was skeptical. "I suppose it's worth a try."

While the class was busy discussing Neroni's dilemma, Lucene focused on the coin. Then, she pretended she was the coin—feeling heavy, lethargic, and very warm. There was an uncomfortableness of laying halfway on the table and halfway in mid-air in such a precarious way. The floor, she reasoned, was cool and comfortable. So why not just—"

The coin fell to the floor and rolled toward Xeni's foot. Everyone fell silent at the clatter.

"See, I told you," Neroni's daughter beamed proudly.

"Well done," Lucene whispered, tweaking the girl's nose playfully.

"Your daughter has more skill than any of us," Cluseladek

observed. "I thought we weren't supposed to teach anyone else unless under the supervision of TARA."

"My daughter is just naturally curious," Neroni grit her teeth.

"This is very strange," Xeni commented, furrowing her brows as she picked up the coin.

"What is?" Lucene asked.

"This coin," Xeni closed her palm around it and stared into the distance. "It came from the cash register at Mallory's costume shop. How did it get here?"

"I read that his store was robbed," one student offered. "Is that one of the stolen coins?"

"Maybe," Xeni replied. "I'm not sure."

"Some psychometrist you are," another student commented.

"I'm still learning," Xeni pouted.

"Students, please be still," Tanager attempted in vain to regain control of his classroom, but the students wouldn't be silenced.

Neroni motioned to her daughter, who immediately left Lucene's side to join her mother. Neroni quickly gathered up her children as she and her husband attempted to make a rapid exit through the open classroom door.

"What's the hurry?" another student asked, lifting his arm in the air and motioning toward the door, laughing as it slammed wildly in the family's face. To Lucene, he smiled. "Child's play."

"I said, be still!" Tanager called out angrily. A few students fell silent, never having seen their teacher visibly lose his temper before.

Neroni fought with the door, but her classmate held it shut through sheer will.

"That's enough, Louis. Release the door."

Louis was having too much fun now and called for two of his classmates to force Neroni and her family back to their seats for "questioning."

"Yeah," a young woman in class with a misshapen head, chimed in. "It seems like quite a coincidence that Neroni happened to see that wine lady at the preserve, and now money from Mallory's shop turns up here!"

Lucene caught a glimpse of Neroni's face as she hugged her kids to her. She was afraid. *What is she seeing?*

Lucene didn't have to wonder for long as the pencil, water glass, stone and plate went flying through the air as students either jumped to avoid getting struck or attempted to re-direct them away from other classmates. The water glass shattered against the wall, the plate against the floor. The pencil made a rapid beeline toward Tanager's left eye, but he managed to deflect it. The stone was nearly at Neroni's head when Lucene mentally connected with the stone, calling to mind the lake outside that the stone came from (and longed to go back to), which, coincidentally, happened to be right behind the window where Louis now stood.

What Lucene hadn't realized was just how sentient the stone was. It not only wanted to return to the lake, but it also felt Lucene's anger. After all, Neroni had always been kind to her, and now this arrogant student was threatening her, her family, and other class-mates and convincing others to join his battle. She glanced down at her arms, briefly. For the first time ever, the tree-like patterns on her arm were glowing a blood red, and she could actually feel the heat coming from the thin lines as if they were tiny embers burning through coal.

Before she could reign the energy back in, the stone turned, making a beeline for Louis's head, striking the boy so hard that blood spilled as he fell to the floor. The stone dropped with a loud thud, cracking one of the floor tiles. Somehow, all that Lucene could feel was the stone's desperation to escape after it realized what it had done. Lucene lunged for the stone, throwing it through the window. Glass fragments flew. Wasting no time, Lucene climbed through the window, feeling shards of glass as they embedded into her hands and knees. Outside, she found the blood-covered stone and rescued it from a tangle of grass on the ground. She leaned over to grab the rock, hugging it to her chest as she turned to see the commotion behind her as several students watched from the window. The sounds of an ambulance could be heard.

"Lucene, wait!" someone called, but the voice sounded a million miles away.

Without a moment's thought, she, and the stone, descended into the lake.

SECTION TWO

"I want you to send me to another dimension, where I can hide out for a bit, see how my other selves are doing. S-s-ee what chaos we can s-s-tir up... The multiverse is a petri dish of possibilities."

19

THE OTHER FOUNDLING

57 YEARS AGO. BEFORE EVERYTHING.

Tanager Blackletter had been left on the steps of the Dragoste healing center in Achel when he was no more than a month old, with no information other than a note that read, *My name is Tanager Blackletter. My mother loves me very much but is not in the right emotional place right now to care for a child. Please find me a good home. I'm a good baby. I hardly ever cry. Lentils and split-pea formulas are my favorite.* Tanager's mother, Wren, accidentally signed her name to the note before catching her mistake, scribbling out the name and writing "Tanager" overtop of it, drawing the outline of a bird next it.

Neither his mother nor father could be found, and with traffic to and from Erde being heavy that week on account of the approaching Peacock Spider holiday, it was assumed that she visited from a neighboring planet in Section 1 merely for the purpose of dropping him off.

In later years, Tanager would always be left with that subtle feeling of unworthiness mixed with abandonment, coupled with doubt. After all, the Peace-Keepers on Erde would naturally feel it their duty to look after a foundling, but did they truly love him or was it obligation?

"Are you still working, my love? It's late," Petrichor greeted Cepheus at his office door at TARA while wearing a jumpsuit with strawberry patterns all over it. She was carrying a basket. "I brought you dinner, just in case."

Cepheus looked up from his schematics with a look of wonder and surprise. It wasn't as if Petrichor never brought him dinner when he was working late. In fact, she did so quite often, usually when he forgot to meet her at their favorite restaurant on "date night." It's just that he often became so engrossed in his work that he momentarily forgot there were other people in the world; therefore, each time she arrived with a basket of food, it was as if he were seeing her for the first time. This was why she never got angry sitting alone at a table for two sipping blackberry wine and counting the minutes until she knew that he had officially forgotten—again. It was all worth it for that look.

Cepheus glanced at his watch. "Petrichor, I am so sorry." He stood from his desk, moving toward the door. He took her by the shoulders and planted a soft kiss on her lips. "How is it that you put up with me?"

As was custom, Cepheus abandoned his work, and the two walked hand-in-hand to the university's outdoor dining area. They had been dating for a year, and while they were considered very young by Erde standards, both were convinced that they were meant to be together. This was not without a few raised eyebrows as he was technically a nomadic Royal while she was born on Erde. They weren't even sure if they could have children should they wish to marry and start a family—an answer they would get some eighteen years later.

Petrichor set the basket on the table furthest from the school but closest to the stars, and pulled out a canteen of soup, a cold vegetable salad, bread and a chilled container of tea. Cepheus reached in and retrieved cups, bowls and dinnerware.

Petrichor poured him a cup of tea. "Dandelion tea," she explained. "I assume you are still working?"

Cepheus nodded. "I am very close to discovering something," he paused. "I'm just not sure what it is."

"Well, that sounds intriguing," Petrichor acknowledged, setting a bowl of beet and turmeric soup out for each of them.

"Yes, I will have to spend a good bit of time at the Makerspace this weekend." Petrichor raised an eyebrow. Cepheus reached out and took her hand. "I will make it up to you, I promise."

"Hmmph," Petrichor wrinkled her nose at him, taking a sip of the soup. "Guess I'll just have to find another date for the festival this weekend."

"You wouldn't dare."

"Wouldn't I, though?" She wiggled a shoulder seductively. "You're right." She dropped her shoulder. "I wouldn't. Guess I'll have to drag my sister instead."

"I won't be working the entire time. Maybe I can sneak away for a few hours and join you."

"I suppose that would be all right," Petrichor teased. The two sat in silence for a few minutes while they ate. It had been a challenge adapting to Petrichor's mostly-vegetable diet, coming from a more carnivorous species by nature. Petrichor tried to meet him halfway by occasionally adding bits of beef to his dinner plate when he came to her apartment for dinner. When he thought she wasn't looking, he would add a bit more. "I heard something that might interest you today."

"What is it?" Cepheus was curious.

"They discovered a baby boy on the steps of the healing center today."

"Really? Was he okay?"

"He's fine. Chubby little thing from what I've seen in the news."

"Who would abandon their own child? Particularly since it is within every new mother's right to surrender their newborn, without repercussions, if they do so in person."

"Someone unfamiliar with our laws and very overwhelmed, it would seem."

Cepheus's eyes grew dark for a minute, "He's better off." Petrichor took his hand once again.

"I didn't mean to upset you," she replied. "I just thought you would find it interesting since that's where they found you as a young child."

"But I fled my family of my own volition. I wasn't abandoned."

"True. And they could have sent you back."

"But they didn't."

"I'm glad for that."

"As am I," Cepheus put a hand over Petrichor's. "As am I."

31 Years Ago. In the Underground Prisons.

Cepheus awoke from his dream of Petrichor, remembering where he was. And, with a sunken heart, he also remembered how violently the Royals had attacked, killing his wife and three children and dragging him back to the Royal Training Grounds for sentencing. He was deemed a traitor for abandoning his throne years earlier and then in establishing the Data Collectors on Erde to help save Earth.

So, there he laid in a fragile heap, perched up against a stone wall, barely breathing and trying to keep warm under a small tattered cloth blanket. It became abundantly clear that he wasn't going to divulge anything that went on at TARA, nor how many Data Collectors were currently on Earth and where they were located. It also became clear to him that he was going to die, if not from cold and starvation, and not from the wounds of torture, then his parents would have him killed. Therefore, when he heard a gentle breathing outside of his cell, he didn't bother to move. He assumed it was his time. He didn't care.

"Get up, vermin," a young female voice yelled from outside the door.

He lifted his head slightly, in a haze of exhaustion and confusion. *Why were they yelling at him from outside the door?*

Moments later, the cell swung open, and in walked a woman dressed in all black, wheeling a small cart. "That's right, on your feet!" She slammed the door behind her.

What was right? He hadn't even moved.

Suddenly, her voice was in his ear. "I'm sorry, my Sovereign. I would never normally speak to you this way."

Cepheus rolled over, peering up at the small but formidable-looking young woman, with a shaved head and rugged arms who was now down on one knee looking at him almost sympathetically.

"Aren't you an assassin?"

"I am," she whispered back.

"Are you here to kill me?"

"I'm supposed to kill you. But what I'm actually going to do, is set you free. But you need to do exactly as I say."

The assassin helped Cepheus to his feet, with her doing most of the lifting. She half-dragged him to the cart, which should have contained shelving filled with an assortment of fun tools of the trade under a curtain. It was empty. "In here," she explained hastily. "Curl up as small as you can."

Cepheus obeyed, not knowing if she spoke the truth or if this was the most sadistic form of torture yet. His skin was battered and torn, and every muscle ached as he folded his tall frame into the cart's hub. She quickly covered him up beneath the curtain.

With that, she wheeled him down a long hallway, the cart bumping up and down along the uneven floor. His cell door remained open.

"That him?" A guard caught her off guard, motioning to the bulging curtain. Cepheus held his already tight breath and tried not to move.

"Pieces of him," the assassin answered, smirking.

"Can I see?" He went to life the curtain.

"Back off," she barked, blocking his arm and delivering a non-lethal under-the-chin strike to the side of his neck. The guard choked and took a few steps back. He let out a few expletives.

"What was that for?"

"I doubt you have the stomach for what's under here. Back away and let me finish disposing of this traitor."

The guard, while twice her size, backed down. He lacked both the skill and the rank. And, if he were being honest with himself, he wasn't sure he had the stomach for what he imagined was underneath the cart, either.

The guard watched her, curiously, as she made a left-hand turn at the end of the hall. "Where are you going?" he asked. "The river's that way," he pointed. She was new to her post. Perhaps she didn't know that.

"I'm well aware of that," she answered sternly. "This one is getting sent, special delivery, back to where he came from."

The guard laughed. What a fine warning that would be, indeed, the bloody remains of Cepheus Baruch being sent, special delivery, back to Erde. He gagged a little as he imagined exactly what the recipient would see when they opened a single-pod vessel to find their favorite professor in a dismembered heap across the control panel.

The assassin had little time left. Once she reached the launch site, she lifted the curtain and helped him stand, and then half-dragged him to a small pod. "The coordinates are set," she said as she lifted the hatch. "Once you're out of the atmosphere, it will put you in auto-hibernation. Let's hope your Erdeling brethren can lock in on you and pull you in once you reach Section 1."

"Let's hope I don't die first," Cepheus half-joked.

"Yes, let's hope that," she answered. Someone was coming. She hit the launch codes and ran from the site before Cepheus could thank her.

The assassin dove behind an armored defense shield and covered her head. When the thunder of the vessel finally died down, she realized that someone was crouched behind the shield with her, and he was not happy.

"Moksha, what have you done," her father asked angrily.

"I sent the traitor back to his planet in pieces, as a warning to all who dare get in our way," she declared with false bravado.

"Those weren't our orders," he stood, motioning for her to do the same. "And besides, no one will believe that you, of all people, took the initiative to do something so violent yourself."

"Why not? We're assassins. Isn't that what we do?"

"That's what *I* do. That's what your mother does. That's even what your brother does. But you, Moksha? You're about as intimidating as a house plant."

"Then why did Sovereign Hamish send me to kill his son?"

"Sovereign Sabrina probably demanded it, and Sovereign Hamish, not really wanting to see his son die, sent the weakest among us in the hopes that what just happened…happened!"

"So, will you turn me in and have them imprison and kill me next?"

"No," Moksha's father thought a minute. "Time to craft a different story." She looked at him questioningly. "Cepheus overtook you, tried to murder you with one of your own tools. He succeeded in rendering you unconscious. I found him trying to escape in one of our pods. Thinking he had killed you, I ripped him limb from limb in a fit of rage, shooting him off into space as a message to those who would betray us. I wasn't thinking of protocol. I was angry."

Moksha nodded. This could work. "But if they don't believe you, then you will suffer my fate."

"Moksha, you are my daughter. I trained you. I will be blamed, regardless." Her heart sank. She hadn't considered how her insubordination would impact her family. "Quickly, we must make this look convincing." She understood.

Her father proceeded to go on the attack, slamming his young daughter in the armored shield and making non-lethal stabs with her own blade under her rib cage and arm. She cried out in pain but did little to fight back. He delivered a blow to her stomach and kidneys, making the movements seem uncalibrated. After all, Cepheus was a Royal, not a member of the military. It had to appear organic. Finally, he grabbed her by the neck, squeezing until he rendered her unconscious, where he dropped her unceremoniously to the ground.

20

COLLAPSE OF REASON

NOVEMBER. BEFORE THE NEW ASSEMBLY. LUCENE'S COTTAGE.

"May I come in?" Tanager knocked softly on the door. When there was no response, he thought, *please, Lucene, don't shut me out.*

"Stay out of my head," Lucene groused back. But then relented with a sigh, "yes, you can come in."

Tanager tentatively opened the door, somewhat afraid of what he might find. His heart sank a little. Lucene was still in her white linen pajamas, curled up in a ball on her bed, arms covering her head as if protecting herself from falling matter.

He scanned the room. She had taken great pains to move all potted plants and other greenery to one corner of the room, piling them haphazardly under a window, as if they offended her in some way but she didn't want to kill them. Therefore, she still offered them light. On the other side of the room, a closet door was bulging, half-open, where he presumed Lucene had stuffed all trinkets and belongings. In front of the closet, she had managed to push a heavy dresser, stacking the now-empty drawers on top of it. The only evidence remaining that this room was used at all was the small bed in which she was laying and a green nightstand. Its drawer had also been removed and now lived with the other drawers in front of the closet.

"Close the door," she mumbled. "The whole world doesn't need to see the mess that I've become."

Tanager's forehead wrinkled in pain. Even when feeling her emotions deeply, he still wasn't sure what to do. As requested, he shut the door.

"Bet you're sorry you took all that time to journey to Earth for your protege, only to be later disappointed for the wasted effort."

"You are not a wasted effort," Tanager replied. "And my only disappointment is in myself. I should have recognized that you were stressed and canceled class the other day."

"You are not responsible for shielding me from myself," Lucene answered miserably.

Tanager let out a sigh. "If only I could make you see how special you are."

"Special?" Lucene rolled over, allowing him to see her with pink, tear-stained eyes. Her hair on one side of her head wrapped in a tangled mess around her neck, the other side chopped short from when she'd attempted to cut it earlier that day with a pair of nail scissors, the only sharp objects they'd left in her home. "I'm following the same pattern as all the children born of genetically altered Data Collectors, aren't I? We start off appearing as some rare breed with unique gifts. And then, after enough time has passed, we begin to unravel…slowly at first…and then it snowballs. Isn't that what happened to Jim Sparks, Cluseladek and many of the others?"

"This whole process is new," Tanager tried to explain. "We gave you extreme empathy without ensuring that your biological makeup could handle the change. We are to blame."

"You didn't give me anything," Lucene interrupted. "I was an accident. My parents didn't plan on me."

"But they were grateful for you."

"A lot of good that did for any of us," Lucene sat up, staring at Tanager directly in the eyes, daring him to disagree with her. Tanager put his hand over one of Lucene's. She quickly pulled it away, holding it with her other hand as if it burned. Tanager's heart sank a little more. "My energy made them worse, didn't it? The class short-circuited because I shifted the vibration in the room."

"What happened today…wasn't your fault."

"I almost killed one of your students."

"It was an accident."

"That almost resulted in death."

"Louis will be fine," Tanager reassured her. "Turns out, he has a very thick skull. Several students joined me at the hospital to perform an energy healing on him after the doctors had finished treating him." He paused for a reaction that didn't come. He tried again. "He and all our students understand the risks involved with their training."

"Their risks should be the Royals! The outsiders…the enemies… not one of their own. Not someone sent to teach them."

"It wasn't your fault."

"I am a liability." With that, Lucene flopped back on her pillow and pulled the blankets up over her head.

"You know, there were more people in the room than just you."

"What is that supposed to mean?"

"It means that Louis, and several other students, were acting out in anger. They would have likely hurt Neroni and her family, myself and others had you not intervened. While your energy was misdirected, your intention was to help Neroni. Therefore, I refuse to believe that your vibration caused any of this." Tanager thought about this for a moment. "In fact, I don't know what caused this. It was something…something else."

Lucene replayed the part of the story where she struck Louis with the stone, continuing until she was deep in the lake. It was Xeni that ran and called to her, and Tanager, who after handing Louis off to the medical team, dove in and fished her out of the lake. In no part of her story was she in any way a hero. "Please leave now."

"Just one moment more…please?"

Lucene let out a sigh. "What do you want?"

In spite of her resistance, in spite of her pain, he could feel her reaching toward him. How was it possible for him to be so close to someone and so far at the same time?

"It's about Dallen…"

"What about him? You don't like him, do you?" Lucene got defensive. *Is it because he's a Vitruvian? Is that why you hate him?*

"I don't hate him," Tanager replied.

"Stay out of my head," Lucene mumbled.

"Sorry," Tanager sat on the edge of her bed. She recoiled a little but didn't stop him. Instead, she moved her legs aside so that he would have room.

"I'm concerned about the way he treats you."

"The way he *treats* me. What the hell is that supposed to mean?"

Tanager bristled at the thought of Dallen. "On the rare times I've seen you two together, I've witnessed him chastise you publicly and diminish your ideas, calling them childish," Tanager was on a proverbial role. "He dismantles your creativity—"

"He's just being honest…that's the Vitruvian way."

"Brashness and honesty are not the same thing." Tanager was beginning to feel slightly unhinged and couldn't stop himself. "In fact, whenever it is that you are your most brilliant, he manages to put out the flame as if smothering it with a damp sponge."

Lucene paused and then looked at Tanager with renewed understanding.

"I know what's going on here," she whispered.

"What?" Tanager tugged uncomfortably at the hem of his shirt. He waited for the words: *jealousy, envy, possessiveness, resentment…*

"You're worried that his honesty will further damage me," Lucene was matter of fact.

Tanager's face dropped as his heart sank even deeper. He didn't that was possible.

"No, Lucene," Tanager brushed a stray piece of her hair away from her eye. This time, Lucene didn't flinch. She didn't even move, only gazed back at him. "There is nothing wrong with you."

"Hah—" Lucene laughed, her eyes dropping to her bed…to the entire scene.

"Lucene," he called her attention back. He took her face in his hands and looked directly into her eyes. She didn't resist. "There is nothing wrong with you. And when you come to realize that, you may also realize that Dallen is not what you deserve."

"And what do I deserve?" Lucene asked, her voice clipped.

Tanager could feel the skin on his cheeks become hot. Lucene's face contorted, confused. "I feel that you are somehow punishing yourself by courting someone who knowingly mistreats you. You deserve someone who treasures all that you are."

"And, who would that be?" Lucene's voice challenged.

Instead of answering, Tanager moved toward her. Lucene braced herself for a kiss. At least, if it were Dallen, that's what she could expect. Instead, Tanager pressed his forehead to hers—a sign of respect, and one that says, *we are one.*

Lucene sucked in her breath.

"Thank you," she whispered, biting back more tears. "But I don't deserve your kindness. And I certainly don't deserve you. Please leave."

21

FAR'S MEETING WITH JASPER

AUGUST. BEFORE THE DEATH AT THE EASTERN CROSS.

"**B**y Segue, you were a difficult bastard to find," Jasper Set landed, butt-first on the hard ground. "Ouch, that smarts," he rubbed his hip. He'd never had trouble with varying gravities before, and Jasper couldn't fathom why his entrance had been anything less than stellar.

Far looked up from his fire in surprise. He had been roasting two dessert lizards on a stick when the demon decided to join him. It seemed that Jasper wasn't the only one who had missed his mark. Far was supposed to land at the Western Cross and seek out Moksha, but instead, now sat in the mostly barren and undeveloped Northern Cross. He'd laid his robe temporarily across a nearby boulder and sat in his underwear, bare-chested and pale.

"Have you come to take me back to Section 3?" Far asked softly. He seemed rather indifferent to Jasper's sudden appearance, yet another anomaly in what was turning out to be a very unusual day.

"No, why would you think that?"

"I sense that you know Sovereign Hamish and have some business with him."

"Ah, yes. The prophet. Tell me," Jasper fluttered his wings and stood with some difficulty, "how did you end up way out here?"

"I'm not sure," Far answered quietly. "There's something odd about the energy here. It took me several tries just to make it to Erde at all. I will attempt to move again after I've had something to eat and a little rest." Far offered his stick up to Jasper. "Want some?"

"Nah, you go ahead," Jasper waved his hand. "I've a Data Collector to eat for lunch if the day goes as planned. Wouldn't want to waste my appetite."

Far was silent for a moment as he sized up Jasper. Finally, it clicked. "What is it that you want, demon?"

Jasper circled the frail man several times, in part to try and figure out the best approach but also to adjust to the gravity of this unusual planet. "Hamish sent me to help you reach your objective," Jasper said.

"How can you know my objective when I'm not even sure what it is?" Far asked, innocently.

"Well, tell me what you know, and I'll fill in the rest," Jasper offered.

"Could you stop circling around me," Far requested. "You're making me dizzy."

Jasper let out a laugh. He was amused by the fact that this monk knew he was a demon and yet seemed completely unafraid or disturbed by him. *The Royals must have done a number on him,* he reasoned. He plopped on a tree stump near the fire and watched as Far took a bite of crispy lizard and chewed vigorously. Jasper wondered if the boy were starving or if he simply didn't absorb the food he'd actually eaten. "Certainly," Jasper replied. "Go on, then."

"My instructions are to reunite with Moksha and get her to trust me. Find out what she knows about the Data Collectors. Discover any additional weaknesses the people of Erde might have and return home with intel."

"Interesting," Jasper reflected. "Collecting data on the Data Collectors."

"Did you not already know this?" Far asked, guardedly.

"Course I did," he mocked. "It just sounds funny when you say it out loud."

Far thought for a moment and nodded. It did.

"But Sovereign Hamish didn't tell me how much data to collect, how long to stay, and when I should return."

A light went off in Jasper's scheming little mind.

"Well, you're in luck. That's why I'm here! Hamish sent me to guide you, and guide you, I shall."

"Why would my Sovereign send a demon?"

"A *reformed* demon," Jasper offered. "We're not all what people make us out to be."

"I hope that's true," Far answered, peering at him as if staring into his soul deeply. "Because it doesn't look good for you if you are not."

"Eh, not what?" Jasper had already lost the train of thought.

"Reformed."

"Oh, I see."

"Now, about guidance," Far asked, "what am I to do next?"

"Well," Jasper thought a moment. "Slight change of plan. It is no longer advisable for you to seek out Moksha."

"No?"

"No."

"What, then?"

"Well," Jasper formed his words carefully and with feigned remorse. "Unfortunately, my dear boy. We're gonna need you to kill someone for us."

22

FUGITIVE

NOVEMBER. BEFORE THE NEW ASSEMBLY.

"I can't help but notice my love," Roman commented, handing Far the book he'd requested, which was, curiously enough, about the art of rhetoric. "That you seem more—"

"More what?" Far had his legs folded beneath him on the couch with several notepads and books strewn around him. He held a simple pencil and journal in his lap.

Roman looked around his typically pristine living quarters. Now there were signs of Far everywhere. For a monk with few worldly possessions, he sure seemed to leave scattered belongings every-where. One issue at a time, Roman thought.

"More distant, somehow, than before," Roman confessed, sitting on the arm of a chair. Far looked at him, hurt almost. "I'm not complaining, mind you. Just wondering what happened to you…to us, really."

Far thought for a moment, calculating his options. After what felt like a painful silence for Roman, Far reached a handout to him. "Come here, my beloved."

Roman took it, gratefully. Maybe things were okay, after all. He took a seat beside Far on the couch as Far wrapped an arm around him.

"It has been a stressful few years," Far began.

"I know, and I don't mean to pressure you."

"Shhh. Hush," Far patted Roman's shoulder. "There are some things I should tell you."

Roman was relieved. He didn't want to pressure Far to share with him what has happened over the past couple of years, particularly since he wasn't terribly eager to share how he'd lost his mind for a time and thought he was a womanizing Data Collector sent to Earth on a special mission. But Far had been home for several weeks now, and both seemed to be avoiding discussing anything more serious than, "You drink your tea without sugar, now? Me too."

Ever since Constable Melokuhle's visit, Roman had questions he was afraid to ask, lest his partner decide to run again. And, he didn't want that.

"What is it?" Roman asked, hopefully.

Far paused, thoughtfully. "The Assembly, members of the IPP, have got it all wrong," he began.

"What do you mean?"

Far chose his words carefully. "They make the Royals out to be terrible, violent people, but that's not the case at all. A recent encounter made me realize that."

"What are you talking about?" Roman was aghast. "They tortured Cepheus and killed his family. They were responsible for the deaths of an untold number of Data Collectors, and they held you prisoner."

"How do you know they actually tortured Cepheus and killed his family?"

"How do I—" Roman was confused. "Cepheus told us. Tanager was there!"

"Were they?"

"What are you suggesting?"

"Have you ever seen the records of the supposed 'missing' Data Collectors? You would think if they were so important, there would be records somewhere."

"I'm sure that there are," Roman was flustered.

"And as for me, they cured me."

"Did you not tell me upon arrival that you were a prisoner there? That you had been mistreated?"

"I did," Far confessed. "And that part was true. But what I didn't realize—" Far paused, staring off into space as if he were putting together the puzzle pieces at this very moment. "Was that it was part of my healing."

"Your healing?"

"Yes, don't you see?"

"I'm afraid I don't."

"Had they coddled me, I wouldn't have developed resilience. I am now free of cancer."

Roman peered down at his love skeptically. While Far may have been cured of cancer, there was nothing about him that screamed health and resilience.

"So, lack of food, routine beatings—that all…helped you?"

"I'm sure I was exaggerating my training."

"Oh, it was training now?"

"You're mocking me," Far was hurt.

"I'm not mocking you. I just think you may be a little —confused."

"You weren't there," Far grumbled.

"No, I wasn't," Roman put his arm on Far's knee and rubbed it affectionately.

"But this whole thing of perception has me thinking."

"About what?"

"Well, for example, the Data Collectors."

"What about them?"

"If they are trained in powers of the mind, are they more or less susceptible to conditioning than regular people?"

"Regular people?" This line of questioning had Roman very concerned.

"I mean because they are more empathic, does that make them emotionally more malleable? Or, because they spend so much time in meditation and training, their minds are stronger against outside influences? Who is easier to influence, the common man or the Data Collectors?"

Roman thought about this for a moment, remembering Dr. Ennis's concern over the mental health of a group of people being given special empathic skills without the accompanying tools to harness the newly associated emotions properly. He shared his concerns with Far. "I guess it depends on the person and the circumstance," Roman reasoned, the anthropology studies teacher surfacing. "You could argue that some have stronger mental capabilities because they've developed their higher brain to separate emotions from reason and know when to utilize which one successfully. I guess it could go either way."

"That's what I thought," Far smiled, satisfactorily.

"Why all these strange questions?"

"No reason. It just helps me settle a debate I had with a demon recently."

"A demon? What demon?"

Far stood and leaned over to kiss Roman on the forehead. "Don't worry about it, my love. I'm just being ecumenical." Far dropped his robe on the floor. "I'm in need of a bath. Be back shortly."

"I've been meaning to ask you—"

"Yes, my love." Far turned to look at him, hoping his naked form might distract Roman from his questions. For once, it didn't.

"About Constable Melokuhle's recent visit—"

"Not that, again."

"I'm just trying to understand why he would have traced Mallory's death back to you."

"As you pointed out at the time, I was the only anomaly in this town, save for you and Lucene—both of whom could be accounted for. People are afraid of outsiders. I understand that."

"I suppose you are right."

"I know that I am," Far concluded. "Enough talking for one day. After my bath, let's relax and watch a movie."

Cepheus was awakened by a gentle breath that he heard outside of his office door. Ever since his…encounter…with his parents all those years back, the one that resulted in the Royals murdering his family, sleep had been sketchy at best, and every sound sent him on high alert. Therefore, when he sensed movement in the hallway, he grabbed the only weapon he could find on such short notice—a potted plant.

There was a knock at his door. He answered, holding the plant overhead with one long, outstretched arm.

There stood Moksha, much smaller and yet, far more formidable than him. She was wearing a brown linen top that wrapped tightly around her torso and gaucho pants that were fluid. Her feet were bound with gray sandals that laced up around the ankles and calf. In her hand, she carried a teak walking stick that somehow seemed appropriate, given her attire. She glanced at the potted plant, now held ominously over her head by a cautious Cepheus, who was wearing a black pajama set of pants and a top that looked absolutely absurd on a vampire-like half-man and half-lizard.

"Are you planning on killing me with a jade plant?" she asked flatly. "May I remind you that I'm an assassin. Death by jade plant is covered on day one."

Her deadpan expression gave Cepheus cause to pause before he conceded to lower his weapon.

"Moksha," he whispered, leaning past her to scan the hallway for other people, silly since it was in the middle of the night on a week-end. "Why are you here? You are under house arrest. If anyone catches you…"

"Might be easier if you let me in for a moment."

Cepheus backed away from the door, permitting Moksha to enter his den. She paused to survey the room. His office was about the size of single-car garage and consisted of a wooden desk and chair, both covered with books and stacks of paper. Floor space was limited, as books covered nearly all of its surface, and walking through the room was like skipping rocks in a lake. Model planes and other contraptions hung from the ceiling. Against the side wall was a long, thinly cushioned bench covered with a single wool blanket and thin pillow.

Moksha had no psychic skills, and yet it was relatively easy for her to put two and two together. "You live here," she stated. It was not a question.

"For now," Cepheus wrinkled his brow uncomfortably. He set the jade plant on his desk.

Moksha didn't need to ask what happened to Cepheus's home and family. She already knew. What surprised her was that, this many years later, he chose to live in his work office at TARA.

"May I ask," Moksha inquired, "where you eat and shower?"

"TARA has a fully equipped kitchen, including several large refrigerators and stoves. There are also bathrooms with showers on-premises because of the athletic classes we offer." Cepheus stared at her. "But you didn't come here to discuss my living quarters, did you?"

"No," she looked up at him painfully. "I did not."

"Why, then?"

"They burned my house to the ground."

"What? Who?" Cepheus took her hands in his, concerned. He quickly released them, however, once it occurred to him that he was touching another woman—one that was not his late wife.

"The villagers, I assume. My house is gone," she stated stoically. "My vineyard is gone." Tears started welling in her eyes. "I have nowhere to go, and if I turn myself in to the constable, I suspect they will send me to the underground prison at the Defense League, which, as you know, is worse than death itself." She looked into his eyes. Indeed, he did know all about underground prisons in isolation. While the people of Erde tried to manage their rehabilitation centers with more humanity than most, it was still a frightening proposition.

Perhaps that is why the cells had remained empty all these years—no one wanted to actually experience them.

"Who knows you are here? Wasn't there a guard stationed at your house?"

"If there was, I don't know what happened to him. All I know is that I awoke in the middle of the night with smoke and fire all around me," she paused, fighting back emotion. "They tried to kill me. I don't mean to sound pathetic, given my former profession, but I came here to seek redemption and find peace. I didn't expect this."

Cepheus thought a moment. "What would you have me do?" he asked calmly.

"Let me stay with you," she pleaded. "Just until the murder is solved, and we can catch whomever destroyed my home."

"But you are a fugitive."

"I know that," she paused. "I need you to keep my whereabouts a secret."

"How," he was confused. "You see where I work and live. How can I possibly hide you in my office, with one picnic bench that I sleep on and a communal kitchen, bathroom, and recreation area that I share with more than 200 other students?"

"They don't even give you a faculty bathroom?" Moksha was surprised.

"If you mean the tree outside my office window, then yes," Cepheus joked.

"Ah, well. I'm used to blending. What time are school hours? I can be sure to lay low during the day until the building locks up at night."

"But where will you sleep?"

She looked disappointingly at the bench. "The floor?" For an assassin, she seemed awfully sensitive, her eyes welling up with tears again.

"It's okay," Cepheus conceded to put his arms around her in an awkward hug. "They'll find who really killed Mallory and who destroyed your home."

"It's more than that," Moksha sobbed.

"What is it?"

"Don't take this the wrong way because I feel terrible that a man was murdered. But…"

"Yes?"

"I am grieving my poor rossenberry plants!" Having been married to a woman who treated her vines as carefully and with as much love, it seemed, as she did her children, he understood. In spite of himself, he found himself hugging her more tightly.

"You can stay with me. We will find a way."

23

REMOTE CALL

NOVEMBER. BEFORE THE NEW ASSEMBLY.

"You sure picked a crap-tastic time to arrive on Erde," Lucene greeted her friend after not seeing or speaking to one-another for nearly nine months. Some of that was for security reasons, but mainly it involved slowly desensitizing the recently *re-sensitized* Lucene to computers and technology.

"Well it's nice to see you, too," Fatima bubbled, her form appearing in front of Lucene. Fatima was still in bed on the ship, her belly a little larger. "Is that any way to greet your best friend? Wait, you didn't replace me with a new best friend, did you?" Fatima appeared momentarily concerned.

"That would never happen," Lucene answered from her own bed, the school laptop that Tanager lent her, balanced on her knees. "You're the only one who would ever put up with me."

"High praise from you, indeed," Fatima replied, flatly, but then brightened. "I should be there by the first week in February, at latest. I can't wait to see you!"

Lucene couldn't help but feel that Fatima would be sorely disappointed. Still, she mustered a smile. She did, in fact, miss her friend —terribly. "You're not going to try and sneak vegetables in my food again, are you? Because I'll have you know I've been eating fruits and veggies all on my own, thank you very much."

"Wow! The new world must agree with you," Fatima was impressed.

"Not too sure about that."

"What do you mean?"

Lucene got Fatima up to speed, including filling her in on Mallory's murder, Moksha's arrest and later disappearance, and the incident at TARA with a nod to the concern over her sanity. She left out any discussion about the assembly, or Dallen, as she couldn't be certain how easily it could be to intercept their conversation given Ivan and Fatima's present location in space. Her details were sketchy at best, and she replaced all names with aliases. Fortunately, Fatima was good at reading between the lines.

"Well, that's just silly," Fatima offered.

"What is?"

"Well, that part where you said that Dr—" Fatima caught herself. "That part about being concerned that the genetic modification scrambled your brain."

"Why is that silly?" Had anyone else said this to Lucene, she would have gotten defensive. But she gave Fatima lots of free passes, understanding that her friend was always coming from a place of compassion.

"Because empathy is a heart thing, not a head thing."

"There are many neurologists who might disagree with you," Lucene was skeptical.

"My point is," Fatima thought a moment, "everyone is affected by their environment, their internal and external ones. You put someone under stress, and they will react. It's that simple. So, maybe you wouldn't have been able to sling a rock at that dumbass kid. But, splicing or not, you would have jumped in to help your friend. Not your fault that in the *very first test* of your telekinetic powers, it was a little clunky."

"I ended up in a lake," Lucene reminded her.

"Congratulations on being a human, living on an alien planet, and being imbued with supernatural powers that your teachers don't even quite understand yet. I'm more annoyed with their having messed with your parents to begin with—but that's a different story. Don't get me started!"

"I won't," Lucene smiled, feeling lighter for the first time in a long time. "But listen to me babbling on while you are traveling in a new ship to a new planet, and preggers on top of it. Tell me how you are."

This time, it was Fatima's turn to catch Lucene up—the constant questioning by the government, Ivan being accused of helping "enemies of the IPP," their never-ended surveillance when they left their home, the threats. It had gotten to the point where Fatima dared not visit her family, even in secret. Ivan started seeing knock-off versions of his inventions online, but the modifications were dangerous. Those were attributed to him, giving him the reputation of not caring who got hurt in the production of one of his stolen ideas. The government began treating inventors, scientists and registered aliens as threats, with many inventors offering to willingly turn over their creations to their leader in exchange for protection for themselves and their family—forcing them to give up the rights to their products, along with the money it might garner them.

"Has the world gone insane?" Lucene asked when Fatima had finished.

"Yes, my dear," Fatima answered. "Yes, it has. So, you see what I mean? Doesn't matter who you are; people are a product of their environment."

"Perhaps you and Ivan escaped at the perfect time, after all."

"I would say so," Fatima smiled, patting her belly.

"Got a name picked out yet?" Lucene asked.

"We've got a couple we're tossing around, but we'll wait until he or she decides to tell us, in their own special way.

"How very Bohemian of you," Lucene joked. "Are you happy?"

"Very," Fatima smiled. "I may have made some questionable

choices in men early on, but it seems to have worked out in the end. And what about you and Tanager?"

"Oh, just friends."

"How is that possible?" Fatima demanded.

"It's a long story…and, I'm sorta seeing someone else."

"What?! How is it that you've waited an hour into the conversation to tell me that?" It was at that point that the connection started to go fuzzy, with the holograms becoming grainy and the audio difficult to hear. Fatima wasn't entirely sure that this was the technology and not Lucene using her powers to avoid the question.

"It's new, and it's not a big deal. Anyway, the connection is bad. We should probably reconnect another day."

"Hmmph," was all that Fatima had to say.

"What was that for?" Lucene demanded.

"A new romance that you're not shouting from the rooftops, or at least telling your closest friend? I already don't trust him."

Fatima had good reason not to trust Dallen. After the incident at the school, he did the Earth equivalent of "ghosting." There was one awkward visit where he stood the entire time, peering down at Lucene, who, to her credit, had at least made an effort to look presentable. She was dressed in an ugly blue rayon-like blouse that hugged under her arms uncomfortably, matched with a gray, straight cut pair of pants, both of which he had chosen for her during her "spa day." Her hair was now dyed a single shade of dark brown, and she'd even made an attempt at combing it and applying a ghastly shade of pink powder to her cheekbones and a peach gloss to her lips. Still, she could tell from his demeanor that he was displeased.

"You can sit down if you like," she offered from her seat at the kitchen table. A long silence ensued. "What is it?" she finally asked, uncomfortably, tugging the sleeves of her blouse to ensure that her lighting-stricken arms were covered up, something he decidedly did not like.

"I heard what happened at the school," he answered, like a disappointed parent.

"Of course, you did," Lucene bit her lip awkwardly. "Everyone did."

"Are you better?"

Lucene paused before answering. Somehow, *are you better* did not feel the same as *are you okay,* to her.

"Better than I was. I'm taking it day by day," she answered, honestly.

"Are you well enough for dinner at the Embassy Club?"

Lucene's face dropped slightly. She was sick of the Embassy Club. She hated the food, the way she was expected to behave while there, and she particularly hated pretending to be something she was not. Fortunately, she had an out.

"I can't go," she explained. "They asked me to stay here for at least another two weeks under Watch until we make sure I'm better."

"I see," he answered distastefully.

"But I can make us something to eat…or… I can order a meal delivery…" Lucene's cooking skills were nothing short of disastrous, but she could at least assemble a decent sandwich.

"That won't be necessary," Dallen answered. "Perhaps I should have thought to ask before making the journey out here." He noticed her facial expression and realized that this was not an appropriate answer. Dallen softened a little. "What I mean is, I could have had one of my attendants prepare a meal for us, and we could have had one of those picnic-things that you like so much."

"That would have been nice," Lucene smiled. "Maybe next time?"

"Yes," he answered politely, pausing for far too long. "Next time."

But there wouldn't be a next time. Dallen was too worried about his reputation and how it would appear having a mentally ill, Earth-born Erdeling on his arm. She was already a little too free-spirited for his taste, anyway. While he found her ways somewhat charming, he was forced to admit that she would never fit in with his culture. And, he simply didn't have the time to waste grooming her to become an appropriate future mate. *No,* he decided, *this will never work.*

Unfortunately, he never bothered to tell Lucene.

24

THE PRESENT

DECEMBER. TWO WEEKS BEFORE THE NEW ASSEMBLY.

"We come with good news," Cepheus announced. Even at full volume, his voice was low, but somehow, Lucene noticed, a little brighter than usual. He stood at the door wearing his traveling cape over a surprising red sweater, and…*was he wearing jeans*? Tanager had on the same trench coat and fedora that he had worn when he first met her in the grocery store parking lot on Earth earlier that year.

"For old time's sake," he smiled, referring to the coat and his growing knowledge of Earth slang. They had recently begun a monthly dinner ritual, a reunion of sorts, for the four people who traveled, for good and for bad, seven months together on their journey to Erde. Roman had only attended one of their gatherings.

"No Roman, again?"

Tanager shook his head. "He said he misses you but is busy this evening."

"Disappointing, but I get it," Lucene offered, graciously. "If I'd thought I'd lost the love of my life forever and he suddenly returned, I'd probably want to bask in the glow of just being together for a while." Tanager let out a nervous cough. Cepheus patted him on the back, encouragingly. Lucene didn't notice.

She had the table in her modest kitchen set simply for four, but quickly removed the extra setting. "Sorry, I don't have any fancy dinnerware, but I made us sandwiches."

"Oh, lovely," Tanager answered in a polite way that suggested that the idea was not at all lovely. *Why is everyone so opposed to my sandwiches,* Lucene wondered. "We've also brought nourishment." He motioned to Cepheus. With that, Cepheus produced a picnic basket from beneath his cape. In it, lived several meat and vegetable pies from Marcy's cafe in the Western Cross, as well as assorted fruit, cheeses, and crackers from the shop next door to Marcy's.

"Hmmm," Lucene sniffed approvingly as she accepted the basket. "But you shouldn't have gone through so much trouble as to travel to the Western Cross just to bring me dinner."

"Tonight isn't just about a dinner," Tanager explained, clearing his throat in nervous anticipation. "It's a special occasion." With that, he produced a bottle of wine from beneath his trench coat. It was then that she noticed he had on a green sweater and khaki pants.

"Do you two go around wearing capes and trench coats just for the great reveal?"

Tanager's face turned red. It was probably the first time ever that he understood her risqué sense of humor. "Very funny," he answered. Cepheus did not get the joke.

"Really, do tell…and sit. Sit!" Lucene ordered. "Here, give me that. I may not be able to cook worth a damn, but I can manage opening a bottle of wine." She grabbed the bottle before Tanager could protest. He was about to share that the bottle was one of the few remaining in his collection from Petrichor's old vineyard, once upon a time. He had been saving it for a special occasion. *Still as impulsive as ever,* he thought, smiling to himself.

The gentlemen removed their traveling gear, wrapping coats and capes around the backs of their chairs, and sat. Tanager, suddenly remembering, removed his hat and let it hang on the corner of his seatback. Within minutes, Lucene had filled their goblets with wine and set a plate full of dinner pies and cheeses at the center of the table. She decided to leave her sandwiches in the mini-refrigerator for now. Finally, she took her seat across from Tanager. Cepheus sat at the head of the table. "So, what's the special occasion?"

Cepheus lifted his goblet in tribute. "First, I am no longer under Watch."

Lucene gasped. Cepheus lost his family after the Royals invaded Erde nearly 31 years ago. They caught him, dragged him back to the Military Training Grounds in Section 3, tortured him and threw him in an underground prison with little to no food or water. And he was Hamish and Sabrina's son. They weren't as nice to those who weren't direct descendants. All because he helped establish the Data Collectors to save Earth inhabitants and because he abdicated his birthright and throne. The Royals didn't want to save the planet. They wanted everything to die off so they could have it for themselves. They were running out of time and needed a place to relocate. In their mind, Cepheus was a threat to their very survival. Why did he care about these weak humans more than his own people, the Royals questioned.

"That's wonderful!" Lucene and Tanager raised their goblets to tap against his.

"There's more," Cepheus continued, pausing for dramatic effect, "neither are you."

"Really," Lucene let out a disbelieving sigh. She had only been under "suggested home stay" for a little over a month, but she was starting to feel the same sense of confinement as she had both when on the Vessel and when in quarantine after arriving on Erde. She was secretly worried that the self-isolation would conflict with her recovery. Apparently, so was everyone else, as Cepheus, Roman, Tanager, Xeni and Neroni did regular check-ins on her.

Cluseladek was asked to stay away, at least for the time being. They were concerned he might set something off in her brain. For Cluseladek, this was a wise move. Even he couldn't understand his behavior and spent the last several weeks apologizing profusely to Neroni. Louis was released from the hospital with nothing but a small scar on his forehead. He, along with several other students, were expelled from TARA and were no longer permitted to study there. They exhibited no remorse. However, no formal arrests were made, probably because they still had trouble working out a punishment system on their planet.

When Cepheus returned home after escaping from the Royals that second time, all those years ago, he refused to let the Defense League take military action. In fact, he suggested the opposite. Instead of going on the offensive, he pleaded with Commander Royce to use their skills to shore up planetary borders against future attacks, but not to wage war on the Royals. He was certain that meeting anger with anger would only lead to more bloodshed.

The smell of meat pies brought Lucene out of her mind-wander. The three ate in pleasant silence for a few minutes. Finally, Tanager spoke.

"We've decided to keep the school closed until after the assembly, though students with ongoing projects in the Makerspace are free to continue their work. Perhaps, after the assembly, we can decide whether it is advisable to resume classes and our research." Tanager didn't have to be a mind reader to know what Lucene was thinking. "You passed all psychological evaluations. It is safe. And," he added, "the school will continue to cover your and Roman's housing during the break."

That last part was a lie, something Tanager had never done before. Therefore, he was surprised that it rolled off his tongue with such ease. The truth was all funding for the Data Collector program was now on hold until it could be determined if the students were experiencing distress from the genetic mutation. It also hinged on the IPP granting Erde re-entry. The human preserves, thankfully, were now self-sustaining; but Roman and Lucene had not established themselves. And, given recent events between Mallory's death and the incident at the school, they were unlikely candidates for hiring in the workforce.

Cepheus and Tanager pooled their resources to continue paying their mortgages. Cepheus had also begun working out the details for ensuring that Ivan would be able to access his funds on Earth once he and Fatima arrived. This was no easy task as Ivan was considered a threat to the government on Earth, and they had temporarily seized his funds. With his recent departure, Ivan and Cepheus had to work quickly to move Ivan's money before they realized he and Fatima had fled, or else they would have no doubt frozen his accounts a second time. And, converting Earth money in the Universal Marketplace was tricky, as is. *Still,* Tanager thought to himself, *one battle at a time.*

They had moved on to the cheeses: pule, tilsit, and raclette. While Lucene was not as food savvy as Fatima, she'd been around her friend long enough to appreciate the varied flavors and textures. The texture of these cheeses suggested "expensive," and she was not unaware that her newfound Erde family was spoiling her. For once, instead of feeling guilty about the attention, she savored it. Lucene began to feel a warm glow in her heart, something she didn't remember ever feeling before.

"There's one more thing," Cepheus told her, finally.

"More?" Lucene was pretty content with how the evening was going so far.

Cepheus produced a small box. "A little token to celebrate our return to civilization and in anticipation of a successful assembly." He pushed it across the table toward Lucene.

Curious, she opened it. Inside sat yellow-toned palladium earrings and a matching necklace. Suddenly, she was struck by a series of images—a red-haired woman, two small boys and a baby girl, smells from the kitchen and flowers from the den… She took it all in. "These belonged to Petrichor." It was not a question.

"Yes," Cepheus smiled sadly. "Remarkably, one of the few things remaining after our house was destroyed. We had originally intended to pass them on to our daughter, but…" He didn't finish the statement.

"And you're giving them to me?" Lucene's eyes began to well up as she choked out the words.

"Yes," Cepheus answered, his voice cracking a little.

After a long pause, Lucene leapt from the table and threw her arms around Cepheus in a hug. He patted her back, gently, at first, but then hugged her more tightly. Tanager was surprised. Cepheus, while a very kind soul, was not given to affection, at least not in recent years.

"Thank you," she whispered.

Outside, the men headed toward the SpeedCircuit to make their way back to Achel.

"That was a lovely gesture," Tanager remarked to Cepheus. Cepheus merely nodded and kept walking. "All around great evening, I would say." Cepheus nodded again. After a moment, Tanager asked, "Just one question."

"Yes?" Cepheus paused on the desolate and dusty trail in which they traversed. Tanager looked around to be certain no one was listening, out of habit, and then remembered and sent a thought, *why didn't you tell me about Moksha?*

Cepheus was surprised. He was being so careful to keep her whereabouts a secret. Many even assumed she'd fled the planet, a seed that he himself had planted in Commander Royce's brain.

I had to keep my mind as clear as possible, so even our students wouldn't intuit it. I didn't want you to have the responsibility of knowing. "How did you figure it out?" Cepheus asked aloud, pausing before they'd reached the SpeedCircuit platform, currently bustling with travelers.

"My skills may not be as powerful as yours, but I am observant."
You saw her?!

No, my friend, Tanager thought back. *I saw YOU. There's a lightness of being about you that I haven't observed in a very long time. And a red sweater and jeans…really?*

25

PARIS SKIES

JANUARY. ONE WEEK BEFORE THE NEW ASSEMBLY.

Tanager offered to meet Lucene at her small cottage in the Eastern Cross, but she insisted that she was fine taking the SpeedCircuit alone. He stood nervously at the edge of the Achelian version of the "Eiffel Tower," tapping one of its side anchors with a toe. "You're fine. She's fine," he told himself aloud, but the internal dialogue continued with a very different conversation.

"Who are you talking to?" Lucene asked.

Tanager looked up with a mix of embarrassment and awe. Lucene stood there wearing a blue and white horizontal striped cotton sweater top and a black flared skirt that was asymmetrical, short on one side and long on the other. It almost matched her hair, now all one color but still exhibiting short patches that stuck out in random spikes. She covered it with a lopsided red beret and had a matching silk scarf wrapped around her neck. *She's a mess,* he thought. *An adorable mess.*

He caught himself. "Stay out of my head," he teased.

"I wasn't in your head," she put her hands on her hips. "You were talking out loud."

"Oh," he realized. "Was I saying anything important?"

"I don't know," Lucene confessed. She was busy trying to shut off the random noise in her head. It was if there was a short circuit somewhere, and periodic flashes of images, lights, sounds, tastes, and smells were all vying for her attention. She looked up and noticed that Tanager was smiling at her. The noise stopped. She smiled back.

"I like your hat and neck thing," he motioned to her neck. "It's very…French…I think?"

"Yeah, one of Mallory's clothiers made it, back before—" she paused.

"I know," Tanager nodded in understanding. He, too, had recently visited the costume shop asking for something more Earth-like and current. He left with two pairs of denim jeans and a white, long-sleeved polo shirt, the latter of which he was wearing, along with one pair of faded blue jeans. The pants felt stiff, and he wasn't certain he felt entirely comfortable in them. Both wondered momentarily what would happen to that little shop now that Mallory was gone. An awkward silence ensued.

"So, how have I never noticed this before?" she pointed to the tower. "It's not exactly subtle."

"Perhaps you had other things on your mind?" Tanager suggested. He refrained from pointing out that Lucene's observation skills were low-ranking, at least, they were according to her baseline exams.

"Why?" Lucene shrugged her shoulders. "Why the Eiffel tower?"

"When we set up the preserves, we did our best to make the habitats as Earth-like as possible. One of the new residents happened to be an architect and suggested we have some of the current Earthlings suggest landmarks that reminded them of home. Most are still in production, but we have, as you can see, the Eiffel Tower in our Central area. Big Ben is on the other side of the Makerspace—"

"Are you kidding me?" Lucene blurted out, contorting her face. Tanager's expression suggested that he was not. "How did I miss that, too?" *Really, Lucene, she* told herself, *you need to get out of your head more often and look around.*

Tanager waited patiently for her to return to the conversation. No snapping of fingers like Dallen used to do.

"Sorry, I'm back," she apologized. "You were saying?"

"Well, there's the Taj Mahal under construction in the Western Cross and Pisa at the Eastern Cross. Once the Northern and Southern Crosses become slightly more habitable, we're planning a Stonehenge and a Sydney-style Opera House, but they are a ways off yet."

"Seems like an awful lot of work for a temporary living space," Lucene commented. *Maybe her observations skills aren't so bad,* Tanager thought, careful to guard them so Lucene couldn't get in. *Perhaps she only pays attention when she thinks something is important.*

"Well, for some of us, this will become a permanent home. And, we have to accept the reality of the fact that Earthlings probably only have a decade or two left on their planet to reverse climate change, evolve or…"

"Die," Lucene finished. Lucene absentmindedly kicked a stone pebble on the ground, deciding that death was probably not the best direction to go in while on a date.

"So, where to?" Lucene asked brightly, changing the subject. "Can we ride the tower to the top?" She was hopeful. It was something she'd always wanted to see back home but had never made it past the Eastern United States, much less out of the country.

"Unfortunately, not yet," he answered, watching as her face dropped slightly in disappointment. "But soon," he lifted her chin with his hand before catching himself and withdrawing it. "If you look," he offered, pointing to its center, "an elevation lift is being built. Right now, it's mainly for show, but can you see about three-quarters of the way up." She turned and looked up. Tanager stood behind her, placing one hand on her shoulder and moving his outstretched arm upward. She shuddered slightly and followed his gaze. "It's currently being used as a communications tower. Give it another six months or so, and it will be open for people to ride the elevator to the top." He rested his hand on her other shoulder, and she instinctively leaned into his chest. His chest felt warm and solid, and it was only then that she noticed he smelled faintly of orange… or was it tangerines? Either way, she smiled and decided she liked it.

"It's much nicer pretending we're in Paris than thinking about murder, and the Royals and my nervous breakdown," Lucene confessed. The noise threatened to start up again, but she quickly silenced it. She knew she had to let Tanager know about this new little quirk…but maybe some other night.

"I have a thought," Tanager answered. He stepped back and offered her his elbow like he'd seen on many boring romantic Earth movies he'd forced himself to watch, so he had a better idea as to how best to behave on a date. So far, real life, he was finding out, was not boring at all. In fact, he kind of liked how the evening was playing out so far. Grinning slightly, Lucene took his arm and let him lead the way. "How about, just for tonight, we forget about everything else and just focus on the now."

"That sounds like a great plan." They walked arm-in-arm until they reached the bridge. It was only then that Lucene clued in. She stopped abruptly. Tanager paused, scanning her face questioningly. The Beaux-Art architecture and ornate cherub lamps. "Pont Alexandre Bridge," she exclaimed, her eyes lighting up. "Geez, Lucene," she said aloud, throwing her hands in the air. "Open your eyes!"

Tanager smiled proudly. "Yes, except you can see that this one connects TARA and Achel's commerce district with residential homes and the SpeedCircuit."

The first passerby they'd encountered all evening overheard them. It was an older woman with big, curly gray hair. She wore a wool jacket and had a long, thick black scarf wrapped around her neck. "This one's better," she offered. "No tourists and smog." She let out a laugh and shuffled away.

The two laughed and continued their slow stroll across the bridge. "The French district is pretty small," Tanager admitted, "but I thought maybe we could take the open-air water taxi down to the end of the line. The last stop drops us at a small bistro on the water."

"That sounds lovely," Lucene answered. "I just wish I had Fatima's palate. I'm afraid fine dining might be wasted on me."

"Don't worry," Tanager reassured her. "No pork rinds and ginger beer, I'm afraid. But they do make an excellent crispy duck, clean, of course. Reverend Isabella would be proud. And, I was told to tell you that they have pistachio macarons, but I have no idea what those are. Are they any good?"

"Wow," Lucene was impressed. "You really did your homework." Tanager wasn't entirely sure what she meant by that but assumed it was a compliment. Lucene was trying hard not to compare her short time with Dallen to her current date, but it was easy to see the stark contrast.

To her surprise, the water taxi arrived just as they made it to the wait station platform. The small white river boat looked like one you'd find on Earth, except that it hovered over the water and was completely open on top. The side of the boat aligned with their feet, a small ramp suddenly branching out and locking onto the platform. The driver nodded. "Bonsoir," he greeted pleasantly. "That's the only French I know," he confessed, reverting to his usual Erde tongue.

"Still more than I," Lucene nodded pleasantly. Tanager stepped into the boat first, and then to Lucene's surprise, he put his hands on her waist and hoisted her over the ledge and into the boat. Lucene instinctively grabbed his shoulders for balance. She felt heavier than he'd expected. The men in the movies he'd watched seemed to have no trouble with this. Although, the women in those movies were arguably much thinner than any Earth women he'd ever met in real life. He was secretly beginning to think that they were either a special breed of human or they were aliens in disguise.

"Don't break your back on my account," Lucene sympathized, once he'd set her down. She took a seat on one of the long benches. Tanager sat beside her. There was room for about a dozen passengers total, and one other couple sat with arms wrapped around each other in the back.

"L'amour," the driver fluttered his eyes before retracting the lift and setting the boat in motion.

"That's two words you know," Lucene called to the driver. Without even thinking, Lucene folded her hands over Tanager's, resting them on his knee. A chill went up his spine. He decided it was on account of it being a cool evening.

The driver nodded pleasantly, glancing back at Lucene in the rearview mirror at his side. "So it is," he answered. "So it is."

26

THE NEW ASSEMBLY
TODAY. JANUARY.

"Order and dignity, please," Kunz Malaya addressed the crowd from his home planet in Section 5. There was a little more gray in his blue-gray fur, but otherwise, little had changed in the Monarch's appearance from when Lucene saw his hologram at the assembly in New York many years ago. He still wore the same silver uniform he had back then, appearing before them as if standing on a platform situated at the end of the table where they now sat. Empathically, Lucene could feel his mixed feelings of nostalgia, remorse and hope. He was a kind soul, she could tell, and secretly hoped she could meet him one day outside of the assembly.

Lucene arrived at the League's Negotiation Room wearing a long-sleeved green winter dress that she formalized with the yellow-toned palladium earrings and a necklace that Cepheus had given her prior to the meeting. She moved her toes freely in the open-toed sandals on her feet and smiled luxuriously to herself before deciding to pop them off altogether by scraping one foot, then the other, across the back of her heels. No one at the assembly could see her feet underneath the table, anyway. *It's nice to decide on one's own attire*, she thought.

Cepheus sat at her right, wearing his usual winter garb, a pull-over cotton sweater and black dress slacks. Tanager stood behind her, wearing his over-worn, retro-style tan tweed jacket and brown pants that she just couldn't talk him out of. Upon arrival, Dallen attempted to sit beside her, only to be blocked by Tanager, who slipped beside Lucene and not-so-discreetly offered him the seat at his side. Dallen took it, reluctantly, before Commander Royce took the next seat over, beside him. Roman sheepishly slid through the Negotiation Room doors just prior to them being closed by an attendant. The Monarch was just beginning his formal welcome. Commander Royce eyed Roman with mild annoyance but nodded for him to take a seat beside Cepheus. The right side of Roman's face was an odd purplish-red as if bruised from an altercation.

Lucene shot him a "what happened to your face" questioning look, accompanied with a physical pointing to her own face.

His downcast look suggested, "Tell you later." Lucene sat back, concerned. And yet, somehow, she had intuited it had something to do with Far. Odd, as the fragile man didn't give off the impression of being remotely violent, and yet, she wondered...

"It has been six years since the Intergalactic Peace Project has met, and I am honored and overjoyed for the privilege you've bestowed on me by allowing me to preside over today's meeting," Kunz Malaya continued. "We currently have six planets in attendance with two who are petitioning for re-entry into the IPP. As is custom, before we hear their petition, we will begin with that stating of intentions..."

Lucene tried not to cry, but in hearing the intentions—upholding peace, working for the good of all, making open communication among different species a priority—it made her heart sink. Six years later, and they seemed no closer to reaching these noble goals. There were several attendants in the Negotiation Room, each pulling the red and gray tapestries aside to reveal flat projection screens providing a window into the other five groups in attendance, including Earth. She was saddened at the sight. When last she attended, there were more than 200 other members there with her.

But now, following the explosion and the degradation of the IPP, she saw only about 30 or so members, old and new. And, she could feel their uneasiness. Given the fate of the last group that attended, she couldn't blame them.

It was then that she caught a glimpse of someone familiar —*Reverend Isabella.* As if on cue, the white-haired woman lifted her chin and smiled, seeming to look right at Lucene with her violet eyes. Overjoyed to see her Earth mentor, she was still confused at her presence, even more so when she saw who sat directly beside her— Odessa and Morphinae. *The worlds we live in are strange, indeed.*

"We will now move on to the petitions," the Monarch announced. Each party will have five minutes to speak their position. Given the unusual nature of their requests, we will hear from both parties first, and the IPP will then vote. If one or both parties are accepted, they are welcome to attend the remainder of today's proceedings and will be re-admitted into the IPP." He paused to glance around the room, making sure everyone heard and understood. "However," he continued, "if they are not, then they are to leave the premises immediately, and will not be permitted to re-apply until our next meeting, whenever that may be."

Hopefully, not another six years, Lucene thought. But, to be fair, prior to the assembly explosion all those years ago, the IPP had been meeting annually.

"It has come to my attention that both the Vitruvians and the Erdelings are working in partnership. It is uncustomary for two Sections, with varied species, to petition together. But I will allow it. It has also been brought to my attention that we have an Earthling who is attempting to register on behalf of Vitruvia versus Earth. Is this true?" He looked toward the Earth representatives for confirmation.

"It is Monarch," Isabella spoke. "I am the Earthling making such a petition."

"And, has the Earth council agreed to this most unusual request?"

Bryce Cushing stood, sitting several seats away from Isabella.

"We have, Monarch. We support Reverend Isabella's request because we believe it may be in the best interest for all parties in our peace efforts."

"If the Earth council has agreed, then I will allow it." Kunz Malaya turned his attention to the Planetary Defense League on Erde. "I also understand that you have a Vitruvian petitioning alongside of your team. Is that true?"

Dallen stood, "It is, Monarch. I represent Vitruvia and also the best interests of Erde."

"And, does the Erde council agree to this?"

Lucene could feel Tanager cringe and looked down to see him clamping two balled fists together and laying them on the table. Instinctively, she took his hand, a gesture that did not go unnoticed by Dallen. *This is for the best,* she thought. *It will be okay.* Tanager nodded slightly and released the grip on his hands, relaxing them on the table. Lucene, feeling that her gesture may be seen as inappropriate for such proceedings, quickly retracted her hand, letting them sit in her lap beneath the table. But then again, while Dallen might have minded this, Tanager did not.

"We do, Monarch," Commander Royce answered.

"Then, I will also allow this. Reverend Isabella, I grant you the floor first."

With the grace of a swan, Isabella spoke, sharing how she had gathered a team of Earth supporters willing to work with her and Vitruvia to ensure that proper measures were taken to preserve and replenish Earth's natural resources and wildlife, while also restoring air and water quality so that humans could thrive. "I also have the support of two Vitruvians currently living on Earth," she motioned to Odessa and Morphinae. They will work with both Earth and Erde, as needed, to bring these changes. We are also grateful for the support from Representative Dallen, temporarily stationed on Erde, to further support collaboration between Earth, Vitruvia, and Erde. Before I turn my remaining time over to the Erde council, I would like to remind everyone present that we have at least the required

50% of support from the Earth council, and I am sure that once they hear more, they will be more than willing to accept Vitruvia and Erde back into the IPP." Isabella turned her eyes toward the Erde council. "Representative Dallen, I yield the remainder of my time to you."

"Thank you, Reverend Isabella," Dallen bowed. "Given our brief time here, I must be abrupt. Within the last year, we have discovered that, beyond Earth, the human species has been struggling on several never-before-registered planets within Section 0 and Section 1."

"Other humans?" Kunz was surprised. "Living in places other than Earth?"

"Yes, Monarch," Dallen confirmed. "The oxygen, gravity, temperature and other elements have caused them to adapt in different ways than Earthlings—their appearances evolving over time—but they are, in fact, human."

"May I ask how you came to discover this?" Whispers and the sounds of shuffling could be heard from the varying attendees from all Sections. Some were visibly indignant.

"Actually," Commander Royce answered, standing, "they sought us out after they learned that we were working on Earth's behalf. Most were fleeing their own dying planets. So, you see, if we work together, we're saving more than just Earth and learning to ensure we don't make the same mistakes as they have in the past."

"And, there is more," Dallen looked at Royce, who nodded for him to continue. Cepheus's expression was blank, his posture as rigid as a stone-cold statue. It was the only way he could keep from having an episode at this moment. *Not now,* he told himself. *You've just been cleared and are no longer under Watch.*

"It seems that the Royals in Section 3 have a new alliance." The whispers grew louder. Lucene, Roman and Tanager peered around the room at the projection screens. Section 4 attendees stood behind Kunz Malaya, muttering to one another. One member actually tapped him on the shoulder and began emphatically asking the Monarch questions, something considered the height of impropriety during a meeting of this magnitude. Kunz put his hand up for the man to be silent but nodded that he'd heard him.

"What new alliance?" Kunz Malaya asked calmly. He knew the answer. He, and one representative from each planet, were given the opportunity to read the petitions prior to the assembly. His question was both to inform the IPP and follow assembly guidelines.

"The Royals are working with the Null of Section 4," Dallen paused while his words sank in. "The void dwellers."

The Null were the reason the IPP was first formed. While the Royals made an insincere attempt to join the IPP while continuing their pattern of destruction, the void dwellers had no interest in forming an alliance with anyone. The most violent species in the known multiverse, the void dwellers, lived and migrated through black holes. No one could catch them because no other species could follow them without getting sucked in, never to resurface. Their sole purpose was to destroy, in honor of their mighty Segue.

"We believe that this alliance will put all of us in danger of being destroyed and our planets re-populated with Royals, while we quickly go extinct thanks to the Null. The only solution is for Vitruvia and Erde to be re-admitted into the IPP and that we all form necessary defenses to protect ourselves. In summary, our goals are two-fold: one, to continue our efforts to restore the human species and Earth-like environments and two, to—"

"I am afraid you are out of time," the Monarch proclaimed suddenly. "We will hear from IPP representatives and then take a vote."

"But, Monarch," Dallen protested, surprised at his sudden abruptness. He looked at the clock. They still had two minutes to finish their petition.

"You are out of time," Kunz Malaya repeated, with a hostility in his voice that was so uncustomary that even he seemed surprised at himself. He touched his hand to his forehead. "We will now hear questions and comments from the IPP and cast our votes."

Dallen searched the faces of the team behind him, but all were as baffled as he. He caught Lucene's gaze. She knew what he was thinking simply from his expression. *Aren't you supposed to be special? Do something!*

Lucene's head began to hurt. Something was wrong.

"Reques-s-s-sting the floor next, Monarch," Jasper Set hissed from a seat behind Isabella. Isabella's eyes grew wide. She knew this dark energy but couldn't even bring herself to turn around and face him. Jasper Set had stuffed himself into a traditional suit and tie, his translucent face and red eyes popping out of the top of it. Those around him did not seem to notice that he was decidedly *not* human.

The Monarch acknowledged him, in spite of the fact that Jasper Set wasn't a registered member of the IPP, something that seemed to also escape everyone's attention. The other planets in attendance watched at a distance. They did not recognize him either, and yet, the hair on the back of Tanager's neck stood up. Lucene felt a bitter knot of discomfort in her belly, and Cepheus grew anxious, no one understanding why.

Lucene flashed back to the first assembly she had attended where Drake Cushing lost his temper, going into an angry rant that inspired the same sentiment in those around them. But this man was different. He was calm. He was quiet. He sucked the energy right out of the room.

"I have a few ques-s-stions for our would-be IPP members," his slithery voice addressed the assembly. "The first is for the Rev…the Rev…" He couldn't bring himself to say "Reverend."

"The first is for Mis-s-s-s Is-s-s-sabella S-s-s-simone." Finally, she turned to face him, as fearless as she could be, gathering up strength from the depths of her being.

I know what you are, demon. Isabella thought. She wasn't even trying. But she knew he could hear her. He smiled back. Then, he seemed to remember himself, clearing his throat and contorting and stretching his face as if doing a facial warm-up.

"These supporters you mention. Would they be your cult followers?" The exaggerated "Ssss" were gone. The audience grew restless.

Odessa looked at Morphinae, but Morphinae shook his head. It wasn't their place to interfere. Odessa crossed her arms and sat back in a huff, shooting an angry glare at her fellow Vitruvian and uncompromising Balance-Keeper.

"My supporters are fine, loving people," Isabella's violet eyes clouded over in a stormy haze.

"And these fine, loving people will escape with you to Erde to begin a new life in Shangri-La. Is that it?"

"That is *not* it, at all. As we have mentioned, Erde is a sanctuary for humans who are there of their own volition while—"

"Silence!" the Monarch growled at Isabella. "You no longer have the floor."

"But I was asked a question!" she protested.

"Silence, or your petition will be immediately denied." Tanager and Cepheus sat upright, searching the faces of those from Section 5 sitting behind the Monarch, but there were no signs that they viewed his behavior in any way inappropriate or uncustomary. They scanned the Earth audience and found nothing but a strange sense of angry camaraderie.

"How do you expect the members of the IPP to believe your intentions when you sound no more reputable than a cult leader promising to take the flock to another planet and be saved by a special alien race."

"You know as well as I do that the difference is that we have proof that Erde exists. We have records as to their actions, and—"

"Enough!" the Monarch interjected. "There will be no more from you, Rev…Rev…Isabella Simone." Her eyes grew wide. There was nothing she could do at that moment except sit down, close her eyes and pray. Jasper Set let out a chuckle.

"But I'm hogging the floor," Jasper announced pleasantly. "Perhaps someone else would care to speak?"

Odessa stood to request the floor, but Morphinae grabbed her arm —hard. "Ow," she winced. "What the hell is wrong with you?" she asked him.

"I'm not sure," he answered honestly.

He's controlling them. Lucene sent an urgent mental message to Tanager and Cepheus. *I don't think I can stop him. But maybe together we can?*

Manipulating people's thoughts is wrong, Cepheus protested. *No matter how noble the cause.*

Then why have these gifts if we're not to use them in defense? Tanager shot an angry message to Cepheus. Cepheus's eyes began to roll back in his head. His body began to lurch forward. Dallen and Commander Royce jumped to his aid.

"He's all right," Tanager snapped, searching his jacket. "I have his medication." He almost didn't bring it, given that Cepheus was cleared. Perhaps Tanager's intuition had served him well.

Jasper smiled at the screen, the entire IPP now watching the episode as Tanager delivered an anti-psychotic puff of serum into Cepheus's ear.

"Requesting the floor next, Monarch." Director Sutton stood from the Earth's council. Roman took notice. He hadn't seen him in a year, but he still remembered being grilled by Sutton and his men on several occasions about his knowledge of the Data Collectors. This couldn't be good. His presence was also somewhat surprising. It wasn't long after Hamish and his Royal fleet left Earth that the gruesome discovery was made that a casino explosion took out the last of the remaining IPP members on Earth, except for Drake Cushing, whose body washed up on the Gulf shores one day, presumably from a drowning accident. Sutton, who was saved from getting taken out by the Royals on two occasions, where at the first assembly an irritable bowel kept him from making the annual conference on time, and in the second, his ex-wife phoned and told him she'd had a change of heart. He ditched the casino meeting in favor of a possible reconciliation. The fact that he was brave enough to be present today showed either tremendous courage or a deep-seated death wish.

Kunz Malaya acknowledged him.

"Your man up there," he motioned to Cepheus. "You sure he's all right?" There was a look of genuine concern on his face before he seemed to remember that he was supposed to be confrontational.

"He will be fine," Tanager explained, removing his jacket. By now, Commander Royce and Dallen had successfully moved Cepheus to the floor. The rest of the IPP couldn't see him lying stretched out with Tanager's crumpled up jacket under his head.

"Why is he like that?" Sutton wanted to know.

"He suffered traumatic injuries," Tanager explained.

"Hmmm…" Sutton touched his finger to his chin as if in thought. "Nothing to do with the DNA splicing you're doing?"

"What?" Tanager responded. "No."

"Really? Because I have it on good authority from an expert that the Data Collectors have been having some psychotic episodes as a result of the genetic coding. Would this be such an example?"

"Unrelated," Tanager was curt.

"If I brought Dr. Archibald Ennis in here, would he share your opinion?" Tanager's face turned pale. Dr. Ennis was a good man, that he knew. But he would be honest in his assessment, even if it hurt the Data Collectors. More importantly, however, is how they knew about Dr. Ennis. He had always been good at staying under-the-radar in his assistance of the Data Collectors.

"Obviously, I cannot speak for anyone else."

"Hmm. Obviously." Director Sutton sank his chin to chest and turned his ear to one side as if hearing something. "I'm curious," he continued. "What other powers do the Data Collectors have? More specifically, what powers does *that one* have?" He pointed at the screen, and all turned their gaze to Lucene.

Uh oh, Lucene heard a voice. Except, it wasn't from Tanager or Cepheus, and it wasn't from inside her head like the way she usually received messages. This one sounded as if someone were whispering in her ear. She could even feel the breath from his voice. It sounded like…Jasper.

"The same as the others," Commander Royce intervened. "She can transmit messages without interception, a valuable tool when trying to avoid sensitive information being gathered by the Royals or the void dwellers." Commander Royce thought it prudent to leave out the running list of other skills they had recently discovered at the Terrestrial Academy of Research and Awareness (TARA).

"I see," Sutton replied, his voice becoming hollow. "No mind control or altering reality?"

Tanager appeared as if someone struck him in the face. He turned his attention to Roman, who at this moment was trying to shrivel into his chair. Tanager felt the heat rush to his head. *You told Far about our research, didn't you?"* Roman had no empathic capabilities, but it wasn't difficult to determine what Tanager's icy stare meant.

At this point, the IPP erupted, much like the assembly of the past. Multiple beings from the other neighboring planets tried to take the floor. Kunz held his hand to his head.

"Silence!" he yelled. "Order and dignity, please!"

But there was neither in that room. All he heard were accusations that the Vitruvians couldn't be trusted after their deal with the Royals and questions as to why the Data Collectors needed to move in secret if their presence was known. Shouldn't their information be public knowledge?

Jasper Set closed his eyes as if soaking in sunshine and sipping on a smooth cocktail. He took his seat, his work here nearly complete. As if on cue, the entire IPP fell silent as he settled into his chair.

Kunz rubbed his head again and wiped a small bit of drool from the side of his jaw. "We will now take our votes." He moved back, wobbling slightly. Two men behind him grabbed hold of his arms and guided him to his chair, concerned. He waved them away and took a deep breath.

Odessa reached out and took Isabella's hand on one side and Morphinae's on the other. For once, there was no flirtatiousness in her gesture. It was one of fear, comfort and solidarity. Isabella squeezed her hand back. And, to Odessa's surprise, so did Morphinae. Morphinae was still trying to make sense of what was happening, not given to emotion or confusion, he was left with an enormous feeling as if a piece of his mental processing were missing somehow.

The voting commenced, each remote location able to log in and make their decision, one to allow Virtruvia back into the IPP and the other to allow Erde in…or not. Cepheus was still unconscious. The remainder of his team, Royce, Dallen, Lucene, Roman and Tanager, waited with bated breath as the IPP votes were cast.

After what seemed like an eternity, Kunz Malaya struggled to stand. Once again, the men behind him guided him back to his podium. He peered down at the small screen in front of him.

"It would seem," he said sorrowfully, "that we have reached a decision. Overwhelmingly the consensus supports that we all adhere to our creed. That is, to uphold peace at all costs. To band together against the Royals and the Null of Sections 3 and 4 would mean that we are preparing for war, not peace. It seems that the Vitruvians and Erdelings have forgotten what the IPP stands for, as have some Earthlings," he targeted a disapproving glance at Reverend Isabella, who shook her head. She was one of the few people in the room who knew exactly what was happening, yet she lacked the power to do anything.

Wait for it, the voice whispered in Lucene's ear. She jumped in her seat, rubbing her earlobe nervously. Tanager tried to send her a message to see if she was okay. When that didn't get through, he touched her shoulder and looked into her eyes. *What's going on?* he asked. She jumped at his touch and shrugged his hand off of her. Dallen, who missed nothing, was surprised by this. *Stop it,* she yelled at the voice, forcing her attention back on the Monarch who was about to render the IPP's decision.

"Between your questionable religious practices, your irresponsible genetic modifications, the deceptive means by which you gather and manipulate data, and your warlike tendencies, it is the decision of the International Peace Project and members of this assembly that the petitions of Virtruvia and Erde are denied. You must leave this assembly immediately, along with your Earth supporter." Kunz paused for a moment as if there were an internal conflict in his head. "I'm sorry," he looked directly at Lucene, "but your team does not have the support of the IPP. I'm afraid you are on your own."

⁂

"What the hell did you tell your boyfriend?" Tanager demanded of Roman as the group, minus Commander Royce, left the Negotiation Room and was now making their way out into the bright light of day. Roman looked surprised. So did Lucene and Cepheus. Tanager was polite. He never swore. He never lost his temper. The meaning of this was lost on Dallen, who shared Tanager's frustration.

"Hear me out," Roman held up in hands as if to tell Tanager to calm down and back off.

"He means that he wants to explain what happened," Lucene supplied, assuming Tanager didn't yet know that Earth expression.

"I know what 'hear me out' means," Tanager barked.

"Look," Roman continued. "I'm sorry. The Far I met at the preserve was not the man I once knew. He was sick and under the influence of the Royals. And now he's just…confused."

"Did it not occur to you, Roman, that sharing confidential information about the IPP and the Assembly with those not working directly with TARA or the Defense League was a bad idea?"

Roman touched his black eye and winced as the group began crossing the long Pont Alexandre Bridge. He wasn't really in pain and Tanager knew it. It was merely a cry for sympathy.

"You asked me to study the culture here."

"I asked you to study *humans* here. What you may or may not have learned about the Data Collectors from our private, personal conversations among friends was just that—private and personal!"

"I don't mean to be critical," Roman defended, somewhat sheepishly, ducking his head at Tanager's glare as if it somehow packed a punch. "But back home we have non-disclosure and other privacy agreements for just this reason. I didn't realize I was giving out sensitive information any more than I realized that Far was…is… mentally ill."

"Maybe you need those agreements on your planet," Tanager complained. "But these things are typically self-explanatory here."

"How was I supposed to know the difference? The four of us are friends. We traveled together. We share information. Far is my partner…why wouldn't I share with him?"

Cepheus felt the need to intervene. "What is done is done," he spoke calmly. Tanager opened his mouth to protest, but Cepheus held up a hand. "Perhaps you and I could discuss this privately," Cepheus suggested. They had reached the midway point on the bridge, and Cepheus's soft words were difficult to hear above the water that ran rapidly beneath it. Cepheus repeated his request, mentally. Tanager shook his head as if annoyed but then reluctantly offered a slight nod.

Roman's apartment complex was closest to the water. "Probably best if I go," he bowed his head. "If and when TARA reopens, I'm available. Just let me know." He glanced furtively between Cepheus and Tanager and offered a quick nod toward Dallen and Lucene before jockeying his way between a few other pedestrians, his lanky frame making as quick an exit as possible.

Cepheus and Tanager slowed their pace. Lucene took the hint. "C'mon," she told Dallen, "walk an old friend to the SpeedCircuit?" She forced a smile that she didn't really feel. She didn't consider Dallen an old friend or even a friend at all. He disappeared without so much as a goodbye. But she wasn't thinking of him at that moment. She was trying to help Tanager.

"With pleasure," Dallen answered thoughtfully. While he may have been lighting up on the inside at escorting Lucene to the Circuit, his expression and the way in which he lengthened his neck and spine suggested that it was more of a moral duty. Lucene quickened her pace, with Dallen falling into step beside her.

"Allow me to explain my somewhat rapid departure…" Dallen said to her.

"No need," Lucene replied. "I get it."

"But don't you see?" Dallen took her arm. "You're better now, and my obligation to this pact between Vitruvia and Erde has been settled. We can be together now."

"No, it is you who do not see." She freed her arm from his grasp. "I have no interest in spending my days pretending to be someone I'm not to fulfill some cultural requirement I would need to adopt in order to be worthy of hanging on your arm." Dallen looked hurt. "Furthermore, can you honestly tell me that if I became…unwell again, that you could handle it?"

Dallen's face dropped. "But, you're fine now," he reasoned.

"And tomorrow, I could be not fine. That's the way mental illness works."

"But, you're not ill," he protested.

"We don't know that," Lucene reasoned. "I've already been abandoned by you once. I don't plan on letting that happen again."

Dallen tried to reason with her. "But I miss you," he protested. "I feel lonely without you." Frankly, it was the first emotional moment she'd ever witnessed from Dallen, and yet, it was somehow not enough.

"I'm sorry," she answered, pausing for a moment. "But I am not responsible for how you *feel*." She turned and continued on to the Speed-Circuit. "No need to accompany me if you've changed your mind."

"Have you?" Dallen stopped suddenly.

"Have I what?" Lucene was confused.

"Changed your mind?"

"You're not making any sense. About what?"

"Is it that you have grown tired of me or that you've grown fonder of someone else?"

"I have no idea what you're talking about," she retorted, tiredly. "You left me, remember?" Even as she was saying it, there was something about it that didn't ring true. And yet, she couldn't quite figure out what it was.

Meanwhile, when they were a safe distance from the others, Cepheus and Tanager resumed their conversation.

"Stay out of my head," Tanager said aloud.

"What?" Cepheus was surprised.

"Stay out of my head," he repeated. "Now, I understand why Lucene found this so irritating when we first met. It's more intrusive than I realized."

Cepheus wanted to protest. He wanted to reiterate that he wasn't attempting to read Tanager's mind and that the skill was only used when confidentiality was needed or when they were seeking to empathically understand the other person. But, in his mind's eye, he could see a red curtain drop as if to signify the end of a theater production. Cepheus was being shut out.

Representative Dallen, once again, ghosted them. He and his attendants left Erde the very next morning after the Assembly rejected their re-entry into the IPP. He put calls in to Morphinae and Odessa, alerting them that their service on Earth was no longer required, and that they were to return to Vitruvia immediately. Odessa cried in protest, begging him to reconsider. But empathy was never one of his strong suits.

"You are a Shapeshifter," he reminded her on a remote call to Earth. "And while your class has certain skills that are important to our people, let's not forget where your kind ranks."

Odessa's nostril's flared. Morphinae realized she was about to lose her temper and say something that would likely get them both killed. "We understand, your Excellence," he replied politely, in his male form—one that Dallen was more likely to respect.

"Who will explain this to Reverend Isabella?" Odessa asked,

tears running down her face in what Dallen considered to be a weak and unsavory response.

"No need to say anything," he reasoned. "She will understand when the two of you have left the Sanctuary and returned home.

That was the Vitruvian way, avoid confrontation and leave— leaving everyone else to pick up the pieces after you've gone.

27

SANCTUARY

FEBRUARY. ONE MONTH AFTER THE NEW ASSEMBLY.

"This is Moira Sugg, signing off. But, please join us at 8 CT for our special series, *Contemporary Cults: The Dangerous Underworld.*" Isabella switched off the television.

"I know it's wrong to hate, but I'm beginning to intensely dislike that woman," Isabella mumbled under her breath.

"Bad day?" Odessa flew in through the Sanctuary window accompanied by Morphinae. The two transformed from butterflies into their human form, now standing in the living room of Isabella's private quarters. Isabella grabbed her shawl and pulled it tightly around her nightgown. It was 7:34 a.m.

"We need to have a conversation one day about boundaries," Isabella shot Odessa an annoyed glance. "But yes, bad day. Bad year."

Odessa exchanged glances with Morphinae. Neither were particularly touchy-feely by nature, but Isabella was among the nicest humans they'd encountered, and after spending considerable time with her over the past few months, they had to admit that they had grown rather fond of her. Odessa felt a little pang in the center of her chest. She thought it might be compassion, but she hadn't felt it often enough to know for certain.

"Because of that stupid reporter?" Odessa motioned to the blank television screen. She followed Isabella from her quarters to the main Sanctuary, watching as Isabella began opening the shades and turning on the fountains. Trying to make himself useful, Morphinae filled a pitcher with water from the kitchen and poured it carefully into one of the fountains after noticing that in the Florida heat, some of it evaporated.

Isabella seemed surprised. "Thank you, Morphinae." Morphinae nodded slightly but said nothing.

Odessa continued, "Don't worry about her or what happened at the assembly. We'll find another way." Odessa didn't have the heart to tell her that the two of them were supposed to have returned to Vitruvia immediately following the assembly. Instead, Odessa told Dallen and her superiors what she considered to be a tiny fib—she wasn't feeling well, and it wasn't safe for her to return to Vitruvia until she could be cleared. After all, she could infect the lot of them. To her surprise, Morphinae, who was incapable of lying, backed her story. He didn't consider it a lie. Knowing how much Odessa loved Earth, he knew for a fact that she wasn't feeling well—at the thought of leaving.

Isabella stopped, interrupting Odessa's thoughts. "Don't you understand?" She searched the Vitruvian's defiant eyes. "Since the assembly, and since that news report, more than two-thirds of my congregation have left."

That Sunday following the Assembly, Moira Sugg and her camera team descended on the church as attendees were leaving services, making wild claims that Isabella was operating a cult. She drew references to the recent assembly, asking if she had plans to take the congregation to Erde or worse—to have them commit suicide in a secret alliance with the Null. It was all nonsense, but enough of her members were harassed and ridiculed that, week after week, the size of her congregation dropped. Among those loyal followers, there were several that seemed almost embarrassed to be there, making excuses to their families that they were really going someplace else that morning—anywhere but to the Sanctuary for services.

Odessa's face contorted as her lower lip began to quiver. It was almost as if she were going to cry. "We can fix this," she stammered.

Isabella was too tired to argue. She pulled the chords of the final set of blinds from one of the windows by the alter and recoiled with a start. There, with his face plastered against the window, was the grotesque Jasper Set.

"Mis-s-ss me?" he hissed, turning into a puff of smoke and permeating through the window. He reformed at the altar, wearing a white suit and red tie. Jasper walked over to one of the fountains and, ignoring Morphinae's slight shaking of his head, dipped his hands in, and proceeded to splash water on his face. "What brand of Holy water is this, again?"

"In the name of all that is Holy, I command you to leave this Sanctuary," Isabella's eyes narrowed. She pointed an outstretched arm to the door.

Jasper bowed as if defeated, unfurling his wings, which somehow protruded out from his suit jacket, and flew to the door. He swung it open as he made his dramatic exit, a strong wind slamming it behind him.

"What just happened here?" Odessa stood beside Isabella, confused.

"No unholy creature can remain in a place such as this. The same is true of your personal abode. If you ever encounter a dark energy and you command it to leave, it must obey."

"Really? Why?" Odessa was legitimately curious.

"It is the Universal law," Isabella answered, simply, explaining to Odessa the ritual of placing an energetic circle of protection around one's home and place of worship and expelling darkness. She nodded with fascination. Morphinae remained unconvinced.

The doors to the Sanctuary flew open once more. "I'm jus-s-s-st kidding!" Jasper flew back in, stopping inches from Isabella's face. "Seriously? I'm an all-powerful demon. What makes you think you can just command me to leave. Me!"

Morphinae tried to help, reciting the Lord's prayer, calling on God, Jesus, Allah, Kwan Yin, Shiva, Zeus, Jupiter, and so on. He was running out of ideas.

"Nope, try again. No. No. No!" Jasper covered his ears, his body growing visibly larger by the moment. With an angry swipe of his arm, he sent the altar crashing into the fountain, its wooden frame breaking to pieces as water from the fountain began spraying across the seats.

Morphinae, a Balance-Keeper, determined that there was an imbalance in this place, and that gave him the right to intervene. He grabbed Jasper by the throat and squeezed just enough so that the demon's eyes bulged. He lifted the demon off the ground.

"Oh, no," Jasper mocked. "What will I do?" Getting stronger by the minute, he flicked his long-nailed finger at Morphinae, and the shapeshifting Vitruvian went sailing through one of the windows, smashing through to the outside. Odessa let out a scream and ran through the front door to Morphinae's aid. "Run, little girl. Run," Jasper laughed. The swirling cloud around him grew bigger, and Isabella could make out the faintest of auras—one was anger. The other was fear. Suddenly, she had an idea.

"Wait!" She put a hand up as Morphinae (scratched, but mostly uninjured) and Odessa burst through the door and headed with full force toward Jasper. They stopped in their tracks. Even Jasper paused, looking at her with confusion.

She smiled at Jasper. "We must treat this being with compassion."

"Huh," Odessa wrinkled her nose.

"What? No, you don't," Jasper responded hastily.

Isabella began walking slowly toward the demon. "Everyone is deserving of love. Clearly, you didn't receive enough of it from the

Null. That's why you are the way you are. It isn't your fault," she smiled lovingly.

Jasper Jet began to shrink. "Stop it, witch. I'll destroy you," he yelled, but his energy felt suddenly drained.

"Odessa. Morphinae," Isabella called. "Let's send as much love in Jasper's direction as we can, shall we?"

Morphinae's eyes lit up. Why hadn't he thought of that? He took Odessa's hand gently. Odessa looked down at the hand and back up at Morphinae, confused. But she would try. She tried to think of loving thoughts. Odessa thought of the Gulf of Mexico and how those little silvery fish tickled her toes when they swam by. She loved that. She smiled as she conjured up images of a perfect sunset and the sound of dolphins. Odessa redirected that energy toward Jasper. *Maybe if he got to see a perfect sunset,"* she reasoned. *He wouldn't be so angry all the time.*

Jasper shrank a little further.

Odessa closed her eyes and called up other things she loved: The smell of the earth after it rained, the taste of brie and honey on toast, the feel of the wind on her face…an image of Morphinae suddenly floated before her eyes. *Oh shit.* The discovery hit her like a ton of bricks. She opened her eyes and threw all of that love in Jasper's direction. Isabella took her other hand, and the three stood in solidarity.

Jasper Set let out a few expletives and then vanished. Their greatest weapon wasn't strength, or anger, or calling for help from a supreme being. It was love.

⁂

Morphinae accompanied Odessa back to the docks. "Finally," Odessa sighed, transforming into her mermaid-like form and diving happily into the water. "I've missed you," she cooed at the water.

"I don't understand your obsession with water," Morphinae observed. "What is it that you admire about it so much?"

"It's not an obsession," Odessa protested. "It's just peaceful. And it feels nice on my skin." Morphinae nodded. He felt the same way as a butterfly feeling the wind as it breezed past his wings. "You should try it," Odessa encouraged, patting the water as if asking Morphinae to take a seat on a couch beside her.

"I've never been a mermaid before," Morphinae pondered.

"I'm not a mermaid," Odessa grew impatient. "Mermaids aren't real. I am…I just prefer the fishtail for swimming."

"Then why not become the whole fish?"

"Because I really like being a woman. The legs are just not practical for sea."

"So, you're a mer-fish?"

"No," Odessa explained. "I'm simply a woman with a tail."

"Oh," Morphinae did not follow the logic, but he'd come to realize that Odessa was nothing if not illogical.

"Well?"

"Well, what?"

"Are you coming in?"

Morphinae paused for a moment. "I don't really know how to swim," he confessed. He remembered trying it once during a storm and ended up clumsily treading water until he'd had to rescue Drake and Bryce Cushing as boys during a storm. It hadn't ended well.

"You'll be fine; the water's shallow," Odessa encouraged. Morphinae thought a moment before stepping into the Gulf stream. It was warmer than he remembered. Once he was waist-deep, he allowed his lower half to adopt a tail, his upper form still masculine. "Hmmm," Odessa commented.

"What, hmmm?"

"It's just that, well, I've noticed that I often take the shape of a woman, whereas you are more likely to take the shape of a man."

"So, what? We are the privileged few Vitruvian who can shapeshift. Did you know that only 10% of our kind can do that? It's rarer than being a double-jointed human."

"I am aware. I'm not stupid," Odessa put her hands on her hips, akimbo.

"I didn't say that you were."

"But you implied it."

"I think you inferred it based on what you think I meant versus what I actually said." Morphine crossed his arms in front, thrashing his tail awkwardly to stay afloat. Odessa looked at him sternly before taking her tail and splashing the water so hard that a large wave smacked Morphinae in the face. "What did you do that for?"

"You were being too male," she answered simply.

"What does *that* mean?"

Odessa let out a sigh. Morphinae was being impossible. She didn't answer, preferring instead to swim in circles around him. He observed with interest, occasionally trying to swim as well. He'd attempted to match her arm movements but found his gestures were not as smooth as hers. Most likely, he assumed, because she'd had much more practice being in the water. That, and he was convinced, her breasts helped keep her afloat. Finally, he got the hang of it, and stopped swimming, in favor of gently wading in the water, his arms and hands moving in and out and his curled-up tail helping him relax. Odessa lifted her tail up, distributing her weight across the top of the water and lying her head back. He tried it, too. *Why hadn't she led with that,* he wondered. *Floating on top of the water was much easier.*

"Can I ask you a question?" Odessa tried again.

"You just did," Morphinae observed. Odessa splashed him again. Really, he did not understand her very well.

"Do you prefer being male to female?"

Morphinae thought for a moment. "This form does feel more *me,*" he confessed. "Why?"

"Just curious," Odessa answered, thinking for a moment. "I definitely feel more me as—"

"A mermaid," Morphinae finished.

"I am not a mermaid!" Odessa whined. "I was going to say, before you interrupted me, that I feel more natural as a female."

"You look good as a female."

Odessa blushed, as much as a Vitruvian could blush with a blue-green complexion.

"Can I ask another question?"

Morphinae was about to answer again with, "You just did," but remembered that the last time he tried that, he'd gotten splashed in the eyes with brackish water. "Of course," he answered instead.

"If you were married and decided to have a baby, would you be the female carrying it, or would you be the male and let your partner give birth?"

"What kind of a question is that?" Morphinae was surprised.

"A perfectly normal one," Odessa defended. "Don't you ever think about things like that?"

"Marriage and babies?" Morphinae considered the question. "I'm a Balance-Keeper."

"So, does that mean you're not allowed to marry?"

"No, it's just that it's not often…done. We're pretty focused on, well, you know."

"Keeping the universe balanced," Odessa waved her hand tiredly. "I get it. But, it's not against your code, or whatever."

"No, it is not against our code." Morphinae stopped swimming, transforming his legs into human form and digging his bare feet into the sand beneath him, standing upright. "Why are you asking all of these unusual questions?"

Odessa stopped swimming, also transforming her tail into legs, female ones, and standing upright. She bent her knees slightly so that her breasts stayed out of sight, beneath the water. Morphinae was surprised by this since Odessa was not known for her modesty.

Odessa bit her lip and thought for a moment. "Because," she answered finally, "I like you." She paused to gauge Morphinae's reaction. It was blank. She assumed this meant that he didn't feel the same. Without waiting for a further reply, she transformed into a full fish and swam quickly away.

Morphinae watched her as she disappeared into the distance. She surprised him, and he wasn't easily surprised. Even more bewildering to him was a strange pang at the center of his chest. "I like you, too," he whispered back. But Odessa was too far away to hear him.

28

IVAN AND FATIMA'S ARRIVAL

FEBRUARY. ONE MONTH AFTER THE NEW ASSEMBLY.

Once Ivan and Fatima finally reached Erde, they, along with Wilah and the nursing students who had seen them home, were quickly put into quarantine. They were shown to one of the only remaining available cottages in any of the crosses, in the Western Cross, next door to Moksha's now-burned out residence. They were assigned an attendant who identified herself simply as Iris. However, other than a form that would mildly suggest that "she" was a female, they couldn't be sure. Iris wore a form-fitting black garment with matching gloves and a helmet that masked her face—assuming she had one. There were vents where a mouth would be.

Her voice was sympathetic but direct, and since Wilah did little more than briefly introduce Iris, they felt funny asking whether or not she was a life-form or an android. Ivan and Fatima decided to assume she was a life-form so as not to accidentally offend anyone.

As Iris prepared to escort them to their cottage, Ivan looked for clues.

"So, where are ye originally from, Iris?" he inquired. "Been doin' this work long?"

"Here and now," Iris answered simply.

"So, is that some sort of protective gear you wear because of new arrivals—while we're in quarantine, I mean," Fatima chimed in as a hover vehicle approached the steps of the Dragoste healing center, where they had originally been deposited upon arrival. It was small with a dome-shaped pod that could seat up to four. The entire top half was made of glass.

"Yes," Iris answered. Without another word, she flipped a lever on the hover craft, and the glass retracted accordion-style, opening the space into a car-like convertible. Except, this convertible flew.

"This is amazing," Ivan proclaimed as he surveyed the vehicle. "What does this run on? Hydrogen? Helium? Are those magnetic plates on the top?"

"A hybrid. No, somewhat, and yes," Iris answered. "You should not be out in the open longer than necessary. Please, climb inside."

"With pleasure," Ivan answered, with all the glee of a small child at an amusement park. He held out a hand to help the now five-month pregnant Fatima in.

"Okay, wow," she replied. "I assumed you would have forgotten all about us. I'm touched." She had taken to referring to her and their unborn baby as 'us.' Fatima patted her belly.

"Nothing could make me forget about you," he touched her belly with the palm of his hand. "Although," he added. "This hovercraft is a sweet girl," he admired.

"It is called an air transporter," Iris corrected. "And, it is not a life-form. Therefore, it is neither male nor female, androgynous, nor shape-shifting."

"My mistake," Ivan grinned, lifting the carrier that housed a very unhappy Bagheera and handing him to Iris, who settled the carrier into the passenger seat in front. He climbed into the seat beside Fatima in the back while Iris slid into the driver's seat with ease.

"Please keep arms, heads, and legs inside the vehicle," she requested just moments before hitting a button, causing the dome-like structure to close over the top of them. Some vents looked like gills in the upper sides of the pod, ensuring plenty of airflow.

Fatima tucked in her thick arms, feeling slightly claustrophobic, but she didn't want to complain.

The craft was surprisingly fast and equally quiet as it sailed effortlessly above the ground, gaining altitude at a slow and steady pace. Soon, they were just above the city of Achel and the treetops.

"I feel like Peter Pan," Fatima whispered, hugging Ivan's arm. He placed his hand lovingly on her knee. That was all the words she could manage to form as she surveyed their new world from above.

From their vantage point, they could make out the four quadrants of Achel. They could see the city skyline with greenery built into the architecture so that the buildings themselves housed birds and butter-flies and provided homes for a variety of plants and animals. They could barely make out the SpeedCircuit that connected TARA and the wellness center with the platform running to the four Crosses. The city itself was circular, with a grid system to easily link the city with suburban areas and business centers with parks and preserves. They were so well integrated that it was difficult to see where the one ended, and the other began, were it not for the fact that Fatima could have sworn she spotted several gray foxes in what she thought was a semi-urban area.

"What the—" Fatima spotted the Eiffel Tower in one quadrant and the Taj Mahal in another. "Am I seeing things?"

Iris paused for a moment. "Yes," she observed. "You are seeing things."

"No, I meant—"

Bagheera began whining from his crate in the front seat. He had finally adjusted to his new home on the vessel when they were moved again. His pitiful meows grew louder.

"It's okay, kitty," Fatima cooed. "We'll be at our new home soon."

The meows persisted. Apparently, Bagheera had asked a ques-tion, but Fatima's answer made no sense. Iris tilted her head ques-tioningly, then nodded as if figuring something out. She purred to

Bagheera in a very specific, purposeful manner. He immediately calmed down.

"What did you say to him?" Fatima was amazed.

"I told him not to worry. His mom and dad are not going to leave him, and that they love him very much."

"Why would he think that?" Ivan was surprised, more so than the fact that Iris seemed to speak cat.

"Because the last time you left in a hurry, his other mother went away," Iris explained.

Fatima's face dropped. He meant Lucene. "Can you give Bagheera a message for me?"

"Yes."

"Can you tell him that he'll get to see his other mom very soon and that she also loves him very much?"

Iris gave him the message. They heard a soft purr from the crate.

Fatima sank back in her seat, happily, while Ivan craned his neck in every direction, trying to figure out the air transporter's design technology. He didn't want to keep bombarding Iris with questions.

"May I offer you a suggestion," Iris asked in the manner of a GPS voice-assistant, as if she were saying, "In three miles, turn left on Valhalla Drive."

"Sure," Ivan answered.

"You should consider learning how to speak feline."

One Week Later...

Jasper Set viewed Ivan and Fatima's arrival with growing interest. The incident at the Sanctuary left a bad taste in the chronic bad taste that was already in Jasper's mouth. Reverend Isabella caught him off guard, and he was never caught off guard. *What's with all this love shit?* he wondered. More specifically, why was he so annoyed by it?

Somehow, the answer dropped him at Ivan and Fatima's front

door, not three weeks after their arrival on Erde. Quarantine had been hard on Fatima, as she had gone from hiding from the government on Earth, to being isolated on the vessel with Ivan, to finally being in the home stretch on a new planet far away from her family. Extroverted by nature, she was finally feeling the strain of being so close to freedom and reconnection, only to be thwarted again.

At five months pregnant, with a pre-existing heart condition and being in a high-risk group by Earth's standards based on Fatima's age, Dr. Wilah had Fatima admitted to the health center, not a week after she and Ivan had arrived at their new cottage. Because she was both high risk and under quarantine, she was left to the care of the technically helpful but otherwise seemingly unfeeling Iris and no one else. Suddenly, her new home felt, once again, like her old home—a prison.

Ivan was fit to be tied. "Why can't I see her?" His face grew as red as his beard as he yelled at Cepheus over the online visu-phone from the kitchen of his new cottage. He slammed the table with his fist.

"It is for everyone's protection," Cepheus tried to explain.

"I don't git it," Ivan retorted. "Yer supposed to be an advanced species that's used to traveling to and from Earth. Ye really think Fatima is a health threat?"

Cepheus let out a long sigh. He missed Petrichor. He missed his family, and he certainly empathized with Ivan now. "It's just for another week," Cepheus tried again. Ivan sucked in his breath. After being with Fatima, and almost exclusively with Fatima, for the past year, it suddenly felt as if someone had cut his arm off, and he had been expected to suddenly go on as usual. "Dr. Wilah is more concerned about how Fatima and the baby are adapting to this world and how the germs and viruses that live here, along with our atmosphere, might impact them. I'm telling you, my friend, it is for Fatima's safety and for that of your child."

Ivan wiped back a tear and nodded, hanging his head slightly. "I suppose," he finally whispered.

"In one more week," Cepheus tried to cheer his friend up, "we will give you a tour of the Makerspace and begin to discuss your new role in Invention and Development. Fatima will be home, and everything will be as it should be." Something began gnawing in the pit of Cepheus's stomach, but he pushed it aside. Instead, he said, "Don't lose heart, friend."

Jasper listened to the exchange from the cottage window, devising a plan. He asked himself how he could have grown so weak at Isabella's show of lovingkindness, and he had suddenly been transported here. And frankly, witnessing this Earthling's unsuppressed expression of regard for his female friend and unborn baby was sickening. *I mean, really,* Jasper said to himself. *The thing growing in her belly isn't even a person yet.* And yet, here he was, outside their door. Why?

He thought for a moment about love, but he didn't really understand it. According to the textbook definition, it had something to do with extreme affection and concern for someone or something. Those with the love emotion seemed to care about making the recipient happy. He suspected the Null loved him in their own special way, and Jasper had the sense that they, even in their destruction of the universe, were doing it out of wanting what was best for him, to protect him from a worse fate, somehow. Jasper mulled on this for a moment. *Whom do I have extreme affection and concern for? Whose best interested do I have in mind? Whom do I want to protect and make happy?*

Suddenly, an idea struck him that left him physically jiggling up and down as it sank in. In order to combat the love bombs that Isabella, Odessa and Morphinae tossed at him the other day, he had to destroy love in its purest form. To do that, the solution was simple. He had to focus on the one creature that he suspected he truly loved…himself.

29

GOING OUT WITH A BANG

FEBRUARY. ONE MONTH AFTER THE NEW ASSEMBLY.

"Well, I must s-s-s-say. This is the most fun I've had s-s-since, well, ever!" Jasper Set surveyed his work with pride. There, on the edge of the bridge just outside the main entrance to the Makerspace, the seven of them sat in a circle with legs folded beneath them: Ivan, Roman, Far, Lucene, Tanager, Moksha and Cepheus, each wrapped in a tight-fitting bomb vest, each connected to one-another by a frequency that communicated between the vests, making it deadly for anyone to leave the circle. At the center of each vest was a small red button, the detonator.

He couldn't get at Fatima, somehow, and assumed that it had to do with some strange added superpower that came with motherhood. And so, Fatima lay safety in an isolated room at the health center.

But as for the other lovebirds, it took no more than a flick of his wrist to round the group up from all the corners of Erde and bring them together. *If it was love bombs they liked to toss around,* he reasoned, *then they're gonna love this!*

"I confes-s-s-s, I'm used to using s-s-s-upernatural powers instead of antiquated contraptions. This-s-s was more fun than I thought it would be. I used a few knickknacks from your tech department. Hope you don't mind."

"I'm sorry, my love," Far whispered to Roman. Far wasn't entirely sure he meant it, but it seemed like the right thing to say in this circumstance.

"It's okay," Roman forced a smile. "You were brainwashed with that demon controlling your thoughts. It's not your fault." Roman's entire body was quivering, sweat pouring down his face. He was trying not to move. While he had been clouded by love, it didn't take long to realize that it was Far who was responsible for Mallory's death, not Moksha. An injustice he had planned on remedying when and if he got out of this situation alive.

If ever there were a time that Lucene could summon the power to shift reality, this would be it. She tried to mentally connect with Tanager and Cepheus, but fear was making it difficult to concentrate. The three sat in the circle with disjointed thoughts floating between them.

Deactivate the bombs? How? I have no idea how bombs work, Lucene answered Tanager.

Make them disappear? I tried that. I don't think I can remove energy from a space without replacing it with an equal energy, she explained to Cepheus.

How's it going, guys? Jasper Set's voice interrupted their thought circle, and just like that, their connection was broken.

"What is happening?" Moksha asked Cepheus after he opened his eyes. She'd witnessed the three of them with eyes closed, and an unresponsive Ivan, who stared directly in front of him, eyes open and fixated on a spot on the ground. He twitched, visibly distracted by her question. He tuned her out.

"Jasper has gotten into our heads," Cepheus replied, fighting back what felt like the beginning of an episode.

"That's right," Jasper smiled proudly, walking around the circle, occasionally patting one of them on the head, saying, "Duck, duck… who will be the goose?"

All this time, Jasper had been bored. Using his powers was far too easy. This required work, and he was proud that after all these centuries, his mind was still sharp. He didn't need to explain to them why he was doing this—that much was clear. They were a threat. They fell too easily under his radar for him to let them get away again. With them out of the way, the Royals would have no real opposition left, except for the Null, which he controlled.

Last chance to switch to Team Jasper, Jasper whispered in Lucene's ear. Lucene mentally gave him the finger. Disappointing. He was hoping to have a major battle with her—to see what she was truly capable of. If she were a worthy opponent, then she might actually be useful to him after all. And yet, it had been so easy to pull her in. This surprised him because, on the surface, Lucene didn't give much away, at least not where deep emotions were concerned.

"Now, it wouldn't be any fun for me to just blow you and half of Achel up without adding an element of s-s-s-us-s-s-pens-s-s-e," Jasper explained to them. It occurred to him that his stuttering was somehow lessening the impact of his artfully thought out presentation. He decided to slow his speech, carefully and controlled. Jasper took a deep breath before continuing.

"Let me briefly tell you how this works." He stopped pacing and flew up in the air and landed delicately in the center of their circle. He paused to wave at the crowds that had formed on the Pont Alexandre Bridge with Commander Royce's military barricading what they could of the commerce district on the Northern end, as well as the residential area on the Southern end. Meanwhile, the Defense League was attempting in vain to push the crowds back, not knowing exactly how big of an explosion they were in for, but also not wanting to cause massive chaos with people trampling over one another in a rapid escape. Little by little, the masses shifted further away from the bridge and the Makerspace. "Aww, they're so cute," he pressed his lips together. He seemed to remember himself. "Now, where was I…oh, yes. Each of you has a bomb strapped across your chest…obviously. If anyone leaves this circle right now, all bombs explode at once. If no one leaves the circle, time will run out, and one bomb will explode first, and the others will follow in sequence."

"So, we're dead either way," Lucene grumbled.

"Not necessarily. There is exactly one solution in which s-s-s-six of you get to live. One will die, I'm afraid. Sorry." He pulled a small revolver out of his jacket pocket. "If anyone decides they can't take the pressure and wants to end themselves early, here you go." He placed the gun at his feet, an arm's reach from everyone within the circle. "Otherwise, you have ninety-seconds to figure it out. Ready… go!" With that, Jasper vanished.

They all began chattering at once with Moksha at the helm, cycling through everything she knew about bombs and military tactics.

"If they explode in sequence, and are not connected by wires, then they are on a similar frequency," Moksha offered.

"Maybe we can change the frequency," Lucene added.

"Or break the connection?" Tanager suggested.

"Breaking the connection will just make them all go off at once," Cepheus reminded him.

Far sat in silence, holding Roman's hand. Roman was busy professing his love, having already resigned himself to death.

"What special combination of powers do we have that can work for us?"

A loud beeping erupted. No one needed an explanation as to what this meant. They were almost out of time.

Ivan's brain went into overdrive. Flashing before his eyes were seemingly random images: the compressor of a car's air-conditioning unit, crossing the finish line of a race, fifth-grade geometry class, an elephant with three blind men around it, a string of Christmas lights with one bulb missing. The others went dark. He opened his eyes.

"I've got it!" Everyone stopped chattering. He looked directly at Far and picked up the gun. "Ye have to run," he pointed the gun at Far's chest, its sight on the red detonator.

"No!" Roman protested, putting an arm instinctively in front of Far's body as if to protect him. Far pushed his arm away. Roman recoiled in surprise. Far's face turned to one of smug satisfaction. "Nope," he answered simply.

"Then, I'm sorry," Ivan replied, firing a shot. As the bullet hit, Far disappeared. Ivan sprang for the vest before it hit the ground, only to be tackled by Roman. Lucene locked in on Ivan's thoughts, grabbing the vest before it hit the ground and tossing it over the bridge into the water below. With Roman still strapped to Ivan's back as he clumsily tried a chokehold that wasn't working, his long legs flailing in every direction, Ivan turned his entire body to Moksha. "Run, that way," he pointed in the direction of Big Ben. She nodded and took off at lightning speed, transitioning into her lizard self along the way. She forced her way through the military blockade, apologizing as she shoved any bystanders who were in the way. She didn't know exactly how far she had to go; she just kept running toward the clock tower.

Cepheus also locked in as Ivan nodded a head toward the top of the Eiffel tower at the Southern end of the bridge. He took off in the opposite direction, leaping across the bridge, using the shoulders and heads of onlookers as if they were stepping stones in the middle of a stream. He climbed the tower in the same anole lizard fashion as he'd once scaled the walls of a warehouse one year ago to rescue Lucene.

"Git off of me, ye idiot!" Ivan wrestled with Roman, finally having migrated toward he edge of the bridge, flipping Roman off of him and onto the concrete. Roman let out a moan as his spine connected with the bridge floor.

"Get off the bridge," Tanager ordered them. He, too, had mentally locked in on the plan, albeit later than he would have preferred. "Now!" He grabbed Lucene's hand. With as much energy as she could muster, Lucene began to focus on holding the bridge together. *Hold together. Hold together.* She kept repeating in her mind. Tanager joined her in focusing on the bridge.

Ivan helped Roman to his feet. "C'mon, man. I'll explain later." There was a quake beneath their feet as Far's bomb vest exploded under water, followed by rumbling as the bridge's supports began to crumble.

Hold together. Hold together. Both were tired. Neither was strong enough. And yet…something happened. It was as if another power source had suddenly joined them. Lucene looked up. There, in the crowd behind Commander Royce and her League, stood Clusaladek, Xeni and Neroni, holding hands in solidarity. Calusaladek nodded. *We're here for you,* he thought.

Roman followed Ivan as they ran toward the Southern end. By this time, Commander Royce, while not knowing exactly what was happening, knew enough to clear a path for the two men as they sailed by with the bomb vests beeping wildly.

"Oye!" Ivan called to Royce, struggling to catch his breath. It had been long time since he'd had to move at that speed. "Air…" he gasped. "Support." Commander Royce watched as the bridge began to split apart, with Lucene and Tanager at its center.

"Air support for two rescues on the bridge," Commander Royce yelled above the thunder into the communication watch on her wrist.

Hold together. Hold together. They were beginning to lose footing as the floor crumbled beneath them, the rubble from each half of the bridge threatening to fall in on them as they began their descent into the icy water below.

Suddenly, Lucene and Tanager felt themselves being hoisted into the air by something that had hooked itself to the straps of the bomb vest. As they lurched forward, the beeping stopped, and the world went silent. For a moment, Lucene thought she might be dead and closed her eyes. When she re-opened them, she gazed down her vest. The detonator had turned blue momentarily before going dark.

Ivan's plan had worked.

No one was sure what to do following the day's events. After all, how does one defeat an all-powerful demon? After hours, in the

Negotiation Room at the PDL, Ivan, Roman, Tanager, Cepheus, and Lucene were all permitted to return home, each paired with two military guards from the League. Moksha, while she hadn't been officially cleared by the legal counsel, was free to leave but under Watch. And while Commander Royce was smart enough to have figured out where she had been hiding, under the circumstances, she pretended not to notice. After all, there was still the ongoing investigation to see who burned Moksha's house down. There was also the slight possibility that they had also attempted to kill her. Thus far, all signs pointed toward the townspeople. But after the mishap with Moksha the first go-around, Cluseladek, Xeni and Neroni refused to lend their powers to the investigation. They were afraid of making a mistake that would cause the chaos they had already experienced. *One emergency at a time,* Commander Royce reasoned.

Just on duty, the guards were to watch for any unnatural events, calling for backup should the need arise. Meanwhile, scholars at TARA were researching everything they could about mythology, philosophy and the occult, trying to figure out what to do about Jasper Set.

"Hey, wait up," Lucene called after Ivan as he hastily made his way toward the Dragoste Healing Center. He knew they wouldn't let him in the room with Fatima yet, but maybe he could convince them to at least let him peek through the window to her room, maybe make a few funny faces to lighten Fatima's mood?

Ivan slowed his pace, but only slightly. "Now's not the best time, Lucene," he pointed toward the center.

"Real quick, though," she stopped him. He was visibly annoyed but pushed it back. They'd all been through a lot lately.

"Okay, shoot," he said. Then he remembered the bomb and the revolver on the bridge and rubbed his beard uncomfortably. "Eh, sorry. Poor choice of words."

"Never mind that," Lucene continued. "I didn't understand what you explained to Commander Royce. How did you figure out how to disable the bombs?"

"Pretty simple, actually." It wasn't simple; Lucene would come to learn. Ivan was just very smart. "We knew they were synchronized by a signal in some way and that if one went off, the others would follow in short order. So, we had to trigger one and then break the signal before the others would go off. Since I remembered that Far had that weird power of transporting himself over long distances, I figured I could shoot his vest just as he disappeared, assuming he moved fast enough. But then some of us needed to move at great speed, something only two lizard people could do, which is why I sent Cepheus and Moksha in different directions. It would break the triangulation."

"Triangulation?"

"Aye, I figured the bomb sequence was triangulated to balance the signal, so at least three of us had to be out of range in three different directions."

"How on Earth could you possibly know about the triangulation of bombs?" Lucene was curious.

Ivan suddenly turned as red as his beard, tugging at his ear nervously. "Eh, no reason. Listen, I got to git—"

"Understood," Lucene leaned in for a quick hug. "Give Fatima one of these for me." Ivan hugged her back, pausing for an extra moment. It was then that he realized that with all that isolation, Fatima was the only other person to show him affection. He missed hugging friends and smiled at the gesture.

Tanager cleared his throat, uncomfortably, in the distance. He had been mentally trying to connect with Lucene for several minutes now so they wouldn't miss the SpeedCircuit. Beside him were four guards, two for him and two for Lucene. He insisted on accompanying Lucene home. He wasn't sure what he would do if Jasper Set returned but felt surer about his empathic powers than in the guards, who'd never been in an altercation in their life. He couldn't see them being useful at all.

Lucene made her way over to him. *Couldn't you hear me?*

Tanager thought. Lucene threw her hands up and asked. "What? Aren't you going to say something?"

I'm trying to. Tanager thought.

Nothing.

It wasn't until they had reached her cottage, and Tanager mentally attempted to unlock her door for her and couldn't, that a frightening thought crossed his mind. *Did they all short circuit on the bridge?* Their combined energies might have been enough to hold the bridge together and temporarily banish Jasper Set, but now it seemed as if their powers might be gone-altogether. He attempted to keep this thought to himself as Lucene fumbled with her communication watch to unlock the door.

What's wrong? she thought, looking at him. It was then that she noticed it—the nothingness. She had no idea how he felt nor what he was thinking. There were no glitchy flashes of sights and sounds in her head. In fact, everything was suspiciously…quiet.

30

THE WARNING

FEBRUARY. ONE MONTH AFTER THE NEW ASSEMBLY.

"They may have bailed on you, but we have not," Isabella's hologram spoke to all those who now gathered in the negotiation room: Commander Royce, Lucene, Tanager, Cepheus, Moksha, Ivan, Constable Melokuhl and a handful of other military personnel.

Fatima remained in the health center, unaware, but with growing concern at Ivan's lack of communication over the past twenty-four hours. Usually, Ivan visu-phoned Fatima every few hours but had been silent ever since his funny little visit to the center, where the two spoke through an intercom as he told her jokes and made faces at her through the glass. It was short because as soon as Iris realized he was there, she quickly escorted him out.

Now, Fatima was alarmed. *Was something wrong? Was that a goodbye of some sort?* She pushed the thought away. "No, Fatima," she told herself. "Don't worry until you're given something to worry about." She laid back and tried to get some rest. Difficult, as the baby seemed very active that day. "You better not be inventing something dangerous in there, future tinkerer," she joked, wondering if the baby would follow after her and take up cooking and steampunk cosplay. Or, if it would be more like Ivan, creating virtual engines that don't really exist.

Meanwhile, back in the negotiation room, the team was notified that Roman had been *uninvited* from the IPP meeting. Not only was he now considered a security risk, but his Watch status had now been elevated, and his teaching credentials had been temporarily revoked until he faced further evaluation. They needed to know how much Far had told him, how much he'd told his partner, and what, if anything, he was covering up.

"But there's only three of you," Commander Royce stated the obvious to the remaining members of the group. "Without the support of the IPP, Earth and Vitruvia, that leaves the people in this room and you—and you have no means by which to support us."

"Let us try," a new voice said as Odessa stepped out from behind Isabella. "We may be living on Earth—" She paused to glance at Morphinae, who was also dialed in from the Sanctuary, along with Odessa and Isabella. In truth, they didn't know how long they could stall their return. "But Morphinae and I are still Vitruvian. Let us try and use our influence to garner support…if in secret."

"In secret?" Commander Royce echoed her statement. "And what happens under your government if you are discovered helping us?"

Odessa didn't answer. Morphinae did, with his usual calmness. "They would immediately assassinate us and possibly seek vengeance on the Balance-Keepers, and your people as well."

"I see," Commander Royce turned to her team, all highly ill-equipped and completely unqualified for the task at hand. "Save for the one invasion from the Royals, where we were asked not to intervene," she glanced at Cepheus, who cleared his throat uncomfortably. Moksha touched his arm slightly in support. "There has been no other invasion from outsiders, and we've enjoyed 100 years of peace. What happens if we don't intervene?"

"Then Hamish's new order of Royals will take over Earth, killing off the human race on their planet."

"I'm beginning to think that we have overextended our support to Earthlings, and now Erdelings are getting caught in a vicious cross-fire," Commander Royce offered, but not maliciously.

"Do you think they will stop there?" Isabella asked. "Erde would be next. And if not the Royals, then what's to stop the demon from sending the Null to roll over and destroy your planet and Vitruvia? We can't be completely certain of the deal Sovereign Hamish made with Jasper Set. We can only speculate given our sources."

Commander Royce looked toward Cepheus and Moksha in hopes of some insight. "I'm sorry," Moksha understood her silent question. "I was merely a soldier and know nothing of Sovereign Hamish's plan." Her gaze fell to the floor in failure. This time, it was Cepheus who lightly touched her hand. She smiled back, gratefully.

Cepheus cleared his throat with some discomfort. "I haven't been immersed in Royal culture for some time, but it is my belief that my fa—," he caught himself. "That Sovereign Hamish is power-hungry." He paused for a moment. "No, that's not entirely fair. My mo—" he caught himself again. "The now-deceased Sovereign Sabrina was the power-hungry one. Sovereign Hamish wanted to please her and—in spite of his cruelty— actually does care about the survival of those under his guard. At least," he paused, "I *think* he does."

"What does that mean to us?" Commander Royce asked.

"It means that if he's making a deal with the Null to wipe out Earth, it's not for power but to save his own military brigade."

"That's what I don't understand," Constable Melokuhl piped up. "Begging your pardon, Commander Royce." He bowed his head in respect.

"No need," Commander Royce answered calmly. "In this space, you may speak freely."

"Thank you, Commander," Constable Melokuhl answered. "What I want to know is…" he peered closely at Cepheus and Moksha. "Who is above your Sovereign? I mean, we were all led to believe that they were in charge. But…that's not right, is it?"

Cepheus and Moksha exchanged nervous glances. Cepheus answered cautiously, "I was a young boy when I left," he explained. "But while under the tutelage of my caretakers, it was taught to me that those above my parents (the word got a little caught in his throat) were kept secret until I was of age, in the same way that the youngers are kept secret until they fulfilled their rite of passage. We did not speak the names of the elders or youngers."

"So," Constable Melokuhl tapped his fingers on the table, his mouth twisted to one corner as he thought. "You don't know."

Cepheus let out a sigh. "Correct. I do not know."

"What about you?" Constable Melokuhl addressed Moksha. "You got anything?"

Moksha seemed surprised before remembering that non-Royals would have no way of knowing the way of things. "I was a lesser Royal, high in the military, but low in our caste system. If *he* does not know," she gestured toward Cepheus. "Then I most certainly would not have been privy to that information."

"Pity," Constable Melokuhl said, then had a thought. "But if Sovereign Hamish *were* power-hungry…"

"Yes?" Commander Royce encouraged.

"Well then, maybe he wouldn't just take over Earth, but you'd think he'd want the Null to take out his superiors. Wouldn't you think?"

From lightyears away, Isabella was suddenly struck by a thought. "Representative Dallen mentioned a baby."

"What?" Commander Royce asked.

"A baby," Isabella thought a moment. "I thought it was curious, and while I know that our presentation to the congregation was… embellished…for effect, I have come to learn that someone selling a false idea will always insert a nugget of truth."

Commander Royce thought a moment before turning back to the group. "Okay, so we've got the Royals who most definitely want to take over Earth and possibly the surrounding planets, to include Erde and Vitruvia. We have a Royal Sovereign who wants to protect his military brigade and potentially overthrow his own leaders." She paused to look at Cepheus. "There's a chance that there is a new Royal baby. And, as you mentioned earlier, it would be kept secret until the rite of passage."

Cepheus shuddered at the thought. *Could his parents have had another child? A sibling?* He pushed the thought away. For the baby's sake, he hoped not.

"Okay, Let's discuss some alternate options," Commander Royce continued. "Given this new information, what happens if we *do* intervene? I need some pros and cons."

In the end, Commander Royce and the Planetary Defense League made the determination that this matter had to be escalated. It was being presented to their superiors—the Elders. This was something that hadn't happened in more than a century, and Commander Royce was not the slightest bit happy about one of her last acts as Commander before retirement: having to awaken the Elders to ask for their intervention. Even more unsettling was their calm response once she had filled them in on the situation.

The answer was clear. After one hundred years of peace, the Peace-Makers were now preparing…for war.

31

A TEAR IN SPACE

MARCH. TWO MONTHS AFTER THE ASSEMBLY.

"I have good news and bad news," Dr. Ennis shared when Tanager and Lucene were finally able to connect with him via the glitchy online account at Lucene's cottage.

"How about the bad news first?" Tanager and Lucene answered simultaneously before glancing at each other with nervous smiles. They were sitting in a makeshift living room that Lucene had partitioned off from her bedroom. It wasn't much, but the curtain made it feel as if she actually had a one-bedroom house with a proper living room and kitchen versus a studio-like apartment with everything but the bathroom in one space. The two leaned forward on the couch, peering at the small computer screen expectantly.

"The bad news is—" he paused for a moment to look back and forth at the couple, grinning nervously. "It might be permanent." He remembered himself and dropped his expression into one of supreme thoughtfulness.

The two let out a sigh. It was an understatement, they knew, but it was the most that they could muster. Decades of research, extreme financial loss, not to mention the irreplaceable lives sacrificed in the interest of helping Earth.

"It was almost as if a lightning strike blew the electrical circuits out of an entire house. Only, in this case, it was people."

In their efforts to take down Jasper Set and save their lives, the Makerspace and whomever bystanders happened to be near the bridge that day, they had managed to short circuit their abilities. It created a ripple effect, and Cepheus, Xeni, Cluseladek, Neroni and all other Data Collectors failed to have retained any of their genetically modified powers. And, from what they could tell so far, neither did Lucene. After all, she was a bit of an anomaly. For the first time in a long time, they were all...*normal.*

"Can we get some good news?" Tanager finally asked.

"Of course," Dr. Ennis brightened. "None of you appear to have any residual physical or psychological damage. I consulted with Dr. Wilah, and it appears that you and your students are..."

"Normal," Tanager and Lucene answered flatly. Somehow, this news didn't make them feel any better.

Thirty Minutes Later

Tanager took his leave, and Lucene paused a moment to survey her surroundings with an odd curiosity. Months after the odd energy that Xeni felt at Lucene's cottage, Lucene began to feel it, too. Only, she felt it in the pit of her stomach, like she'd eaten something that didn't agree with her. Sometimes it felt bitter, sometimes sour. She made a mental note to ask Tanager about it the next time she saw him. After all, it was assumed she had no special powers anymore. Of course, this wasn't taking into consideration the empathy that many species might have, all on their own. She brushed the feeling aside for the time being.

In the meantime, she'd taken to cleaning her home from top to bottom on a weekly basis, in a ritual that some would call obsessive. She just thought it was common sense. She also began smudging with white sage each week, something she used to do when she worked at the Sanctuary back on Earth. Lucene wasn't entirely sure that it worked in keeping out negative energy, but at least she knew of its antiviral properties, so that was something. And it made her house smell good.

"Ahh, what a s-s-s-weet s-s-s-mell," Jasper Set appeared suddenly behind Lucene, causing her to drop the smoking sage and abalone shell on the stone floor, sending dirty ash everywhere in a swirl of dust. Fortunately, nothing caught fire. Lucene held out the only thing still left in her hand, the feather she used to guide the smoke around the room.

"What are you doing here?" she demanded, wielding the feather like a knife. Jasper put his hands up in mock fear.

"Oh no, please don't attack me with that menacing feather," he laughed. Then sniffed the air once more, pretending to swirl an imaginary glass of wine and sniff it. "What is-s-s- that delightful aroma? Palo S-s-s-anto? No. Copal? No. Ah, white s-s-sage. I should have gues-s-s-ed it."

"What do you want, demon?" Lucene asked again. Her stomach growled with a bitterness she'd never experienced before.

"Isn't it obvious?" He looked at her like an amused puppy. He leaned in as if telling her a secret. Lucene backed away uncomfortably, only to have Jasper vanish and reappear over her shoulder. "You," he whispered in her ear.

"Then why didn't you take me at the Makerspace, instead of strapping us to bombs and making us your hostages?"

"Honestly, I wanted to see just how powerful you were," Jasper snorted. "Actually, you should probably not believe anything I say, or anyone, for that matter, who begins a sentence with 'honestly.'"

"Still waiting," Lucene's heart beat faster.

"I wanted to see your collective power."

"I don't follow."

"If I kept you and then helped Hamish fulfill his plan to overthrow the Royals currently in command, he could take over the

Earth, and contract fulfilled." He wiped his hands as if cleaning them. "I just wanted to be s-s-sure it wouldn't come back to bite me in the proverbial ass-s-s-, s-s-o to s-s-speak."

"How so?"

"My Null mamas and papas might feel betrayed if they discovered I purposely led them away from the Divine purpose of the Segue."

"Why do you only hiss sometimes, but not all the time?" Lucene asked.

"I don't s-s-e-e how that is relevant to the convers-s-s-as-ion," Jasper become flustered.

"Oh, I get it,"

"What do you get?" Jasper spat angrily as he spoke.

"You're afraid of the Null, too."

"Don't be s-s-illy, child. I'm a demon. I fear nothing." Jasper quickly recovered, making circles around Lucene until she began feeling dizzy. "That being said," he continued, "I do find it prudent of me to disappear for a while, just in case."

"Where could you go that the Null couldn't find you?"

"Aha, that is the million-dollar ques-s-tion," he shook his finger in her face. "That's what I need you for."

"Still not following."

"Another dimension, s-s-illy," he giggled as if he'd just taken a long whiff of helium. "I want you to send me to another dimension, where I can hide out for a bit, see how my other selves are doing. S-s-ee what chaos we can s-s-tir up."

"Even if I could do that, which I can't, I'm not following the logic. Say you take me with you, why even bother fulfilling the rest of your agreement with the Royals?"

"I may be a demon, but I have a code. I always keep my contracts," he seemed offended at the suggestion that he'd actually go back on his word.

"And the collective power?"

"I thought I might take one or two of you as backup. For

instance, that Cluseladek is quite powerful and easy to influence. And, Ivan, I must say, that boy s-s-urpri-s-sed me. No powers, but an awful lot of s-s-smarts. I assumed you would simply use your skills to deactivate the bombs, but it seems that thought never occurred to you… Why didn't that thought occur to you?" He paused.

"It did," she answered. "I couldn't. And if I couldn't then, I most certainly can't now."

Jasper ignored her. "Hmm, I guess I was mistaken. There were two solutions. Clever boy, that Ivan. But I digress," he circled her once more. "I'm als-s-so banking on their being another *you* on each of the planes, should I go multidimensional hopping. Maybe they have powers that even you don't, who knows?"

"Could you please stop circling me like a shark and sit down," Lucene motioned to a chair. The lunacy of a young woman offering a demon a seat at her table was not lost on Jasper, who sat with a smile, putting his tiny feet, now clad in soot-covered boots, on her kitchen table. She ignored that part.

"The multiverse is a petri dish of possibilities," Jasper smiled, his "Ssss" staying in place for once.

"Has it occurred to you that there are at least two major flaws to your theory?"

"Hypothesis," he corrected.

"What?"

"Hypothesis. Unless we have evidence to support our theory, it is merely a hypothesis."

"Whatever, the point is, all of the Data Collectors lost their powers following your little bomb experiment. We fizzled out. Second, if parallel-universe hopping is a thing, why haven't other Jasper Sets graced this planet?"

Jasper's face grew dark. "I'll s-s-tart with the latter," he spat. "I s-s-sus-s-s-pect that I am the s-s-martest, Jas-s-s-per S-s-s-et."

"Wow, when you get angry, you can't even s-s-say your own name," Lucene mocked.

Without another word, Jasper swept his arm across the table, sending it flying in Lucene's direction. The table sent her sailing backward, threatening to land on top of her. Dishes from her cupboards began flying about, smashing into tiny pieces in every direction. Lucene's mind went back to her childhood, in the back seat of a car with glass shattering all around her. She opened her mouth to scream, but nothing came out as she braced for the hard floor beneath her. Her back and spine landed first, searing pain shooting through her. Lucene attempted in vain to lift her head, but she couldn't. Just as her head was about to smack on the stone ground beneath her, she suddenly felt something soft…a hand.

Light poured in through what Lucene thought were the cottage windows, and she squinted to see. What she hadn't realized at that moment was that the light was not from the windows at all, but from outside, as Jasper, in his anger, had blown the entire roof from her cottage. Someone was kneeling over her.

"My dear," Reverend Isabella addressed Lucene, gently lifting her hand, which was still beneath Lucene's head, and guiding her to a seated position, putting her arm around Lucene's shoulders for support. "Remind me to talk to you later about not always saying the first thing that comes into your head."

"Isabella, what…how?" Lucene was shocked.

"Later," she held up a hand, releasing Lucene's shoulders only when she was certain the young woman could remain seated on her own.

Jasper was so caught up in his own commotion that he neglected to notice Isabella's presence. Outside, the sounds of townspeople could be heard coming to inspect the damage.

"Lucene!" Tanager's voice could be heard yelling in the distance. Moments later, he was at the doorway—the actual door to the kitchen having been blown off. It had flown into the distance, landing in a nearby field. Fortunately, no one besides Lucene was hurt.

"You're jus-s-s-t in time for the show," Jasper squealed gleefully. "Wait? Where did you come from?" He finally noticed Isabella.

"Irrelevant," she answered calmly, standing upright, her arms rigidly at her side.

"Oh, don't try s-s-s-ending those love bombs again," Jasper mocked. "I was caught off guard before, but I'm prepared now."

Tanager ran to Lucene's side, leaning over to help her to her feet. "Are you okay?" He brushed rubble and dust from her hair and hugged her close.

"Not sure," Lucene answered groggily. "I think I'm hallucinating. I just saw…" She stopped mid-sentence as she saw that Isabella was actually in the room.

Cepheus slinked through the doorway, as silent as a cat. "Not again," he said, seeing Jasper, now swirling triumphantly in mid-air. As he swirled, bits of furniture, utensils, and broken dinnerware began to get caught up in a funnel like a tornado. As the wind grew stronger, Tanager tucked his head and pulled Lucene's face into his chest to avoid broken glass from flying into their eyes. A few bits scratched across his back and neck, slicing through his shirt. He winced from the pain.

"You can make all this s-s-s-s-top, Luc—" Jasper had trouble saying Lucene's name. "S-s-s-send me to another dimension, and everything will be fine."

"If I do, do you promise to leave everyone here alone?" The swirling stopped and debris settled on the floor around them, some landing on their feet, weighing them down heavily as Tanager, Cepheus and Lucene attempted to step around it. Cepheus fared the best, gracefully side-stepping most of the damage. "No taking anyone else with you—just me," Lucene offered.

Jasper thought for a moment. "Take the deal," Isabella finally spoke, calmly. "It's the best you're going to get." Jasper felt the hairs on the back of his neck stand up. There was something about her that unnerved him, which was crazy, wasn't it?

"Fine," Jasper answered simply. "Hit me," he closed his eyes and held his arms out.

Lucene looked pleadingly at Isabella. That was as far as she had gotten with her bluff. She really had no idea how she was supposed to do what she promised. *You forget s-s-s-somthing, little girl,"* Jasper spoke from inside her head. *You may have lost your empathic abilities, but I have not. You're lying to me."*

"What's going on?" Tanager asked as Lucene grabbed her ears, shaking her head as if trying to shake water out of them.

"He's in her head," Cepheus replied calmly. "Leave her be, demon!" Like a flying bat, Cepheus sent himself sailing toward Jasper, tackling the demon to the floor before Jasper, in a rage, tossed Cepheus into the open air, following the front door's trajectory and landing him in the open field behind the house.

To Lucene, Jasper spat. "You're useless! How can that be?"

"I told you, I short-circuited," Lucene replied. "I wish I could give you what you want, so you'll leave us alone. But I can't!"

"Pity," Jasper answered simply. The wind began to pick up again —stronger this time, and Lucene, Tanager, and Isabella felt themselves being lifted into the air. The remainder of the cottage suddenly crumbled to the ground. A few shocked townspeople attempted to rush in to intervene, but Jasper quickly caught them in his tornado, now getting wider and wider as it pulled more in with it.

Lucene was ripped from Tanager's arms, feeling herself violently spinning as the outer pressure from the world seemed to collapse in on her body. She could no longer breathe and was becoming dizzy and lightheaded. Storm clouds gathered low to the ground, enveloping her.

In a moment of surprise, she saw something glowing, like lightning rays coming through the storm clouds. Her arms...they were glowing again, the patterns becoming a blood-red and cracking through her skin like growing and expanding embers on a log...just like that day in class when she'd almost accidentally killed someone.

"Stop, demon," Isabella commanded. "I can give you what you want."

The winds died down, Jasper setting his small feet on the floor and leaning forward eagerly. "How?" Lucene landed butt-first on the floor behind him with a thud.

"Ooof," she said, rubbing her hip as she struggled to stand. Tanager landed in the yard and awkwardly struggled to walk through what now appeared to be a war zone. He'd have to check on Cepheus later.

"Stand up straight, Lucene," Isabella commanded. "And don't move."

"How—"

"And don't talk."

For once, Lucene obeyed. Her arms hurt; they felt as if they were burning as the branches continued to grow. Isabella held her arms out, palms facing Lucene. She closed her eyes and began chanting. The branches continued to grow, and light began streaming from them like illuminated beams. Lucene let out a scream as the light enveloped her.

"Stop it! What are you doing to her?" Tanager went to grab Isabella's arms, but he was too late. Lucene vanished, and a giant red swirling doorway appeared. "Go now, demon!" Isabella commanded.

"Where am I going, exactly?" Jasper suddenly appeared nervous.

"I have no idea. It's another dimension, as promised. I have no idea which one."

"Fair enough," Jasper grinned, excitedly, swallowing his fear. "An adventure!" The doorway grew smaller.

"Go now, before it closes!"

Jasper gave one final survey of his surroundings before he took to the air like a tornado and sailed through the portal. As soon as he had, the portal began funneling inward. Lucene reappeared, falling to the floor in a heap as the branches on her arm went dark again—like a light that had gone out.

After a moment of silence, Lucene spoke. "I'm sensing a theme," she joked. This was the third time she landed on the floor in fewer than ten minutes. Tanager went to help her up but winced as he touched her hand as a shock went through him.

"Easy, lover boy," Isabella lowered her arms. "Give it a few minutes before you touch her again. She's still charged up."

"What the hell just happened?" Lucene demanded.

Isabella let out a sigh. "The demon assumed that you had the power to open up a portal to another dimension for him. But he was only half right."

"Half right?"

"Yes," she nodded. "You couldn't open the portal because…you *are* the portal."

"I'm the reason Far's powers inspired fear among the people of Macar," Isabella later explained to Lucene, Cepheus and Tanager. They were at the healing center, being tended to by Dr. Wilah and her team. Isabella had suffered no injuries, but the other three had all been examined and were in the lobby, awaiting final clearance to return to their homes. Had Tanager and Cepheus not met up to tour the preserves and check on the emotional states of the townspeople following Jasper Set's damaging mind control, they wouldn't have been there for Jasper's return.

"I too had the gift of prophecy but used it for my own gain," Isabella continued. "I was forced out because I betrayed the tribe." She shook her head, ashamed. "I am a different person now, but unfortunately, the damage was done. Even though Far was born nearly a century later, he came from my family's lineage. So naturally, they feared him."

"We didn't even know you had met Far," Lucene commented. "Does Roman know this?"

"Aside from the New Moon Celebration last year on Earth, I have had no communication with your friend, Roman. And," she added. "I have never met Far. I have only heard the rumors of his existence and," she laughed, "his terrible sense of direction."

"Fascinating," Tanager rubbed his head, thinking excitedly.

"What is the extent of your abilities? Can you teleport yourself anywhere you want to go? What about time travel? Can you truly see the future, or is it that you actually visit the future and then go back in time to report what you saw?"

Isabella eyed Tanager up and down for a moment as if sizing him up. She then glanced at Lucene and Cepheus as if making mental calculations in her mind.

"Soon, I will answer all of your questions…but not today."

32

MAYBE JUST THIS ONCE...

JUNE. FIVE MONTHS AFTER THE NEW ASSEMBLY.

"My memory is faulty," Cepheus confessed, as he walked with Moksha through her vineyard as she finally returned to assess the damage. In their anger, the townspeople had destroyed everything—her house, her property, her vineyard. Then, when they realized that she was innocent, they returned to try and fix it. They had been successful in re-building her cottage, or at least a version of it, even going so far as to replace the stained-glass windows and painting the house purple. They also cleared the rubble around her front door and added a pathway lined with multicolored chrysanthemums leading from her house to the main dirt road.

Unfortunately, few in the Western Cross knew what to do about the actual vineyard and enlisted the help of those living in the Eastern Cross and even a few remote growers in the Southern Cross. The prognosis wasn't good. It would likely be several years before the vineyard returned to what it once was if ever, leaving her with nothing. She was going to need to find a new way to support herself, and soon. But this wasn't what Cepheus was thinking about at that moment.

"I am quite aware of that," Moksha finally muttered with regards to Cepheus's comment about his memory. She let out a sigh as she gingerly touched a burnt rossenberry branch and fought back a tear. *Some warrior I turned out to be,* she thought to herself. *Crying over a few dead plants as if they were my children.*

Moksha continued to walk the rows of vines, most blackened by fire and still smelling of smoke even months later, or maybe that was just her imagination. "Did I ever tell you how it was that I escaped my family?" Cepheus lurked over her shoulder.

Moksha paused. "No," she answered cautiously. "How?" Did he know? She wondered to herself.

"A young soldier smuggled me out of the underground prisons and set me on course for Erde by hijacking one of the Royal's pilot vessels."

"Is that so?" Moksha answered with a calmness that she didn't feel. The sleeve of her blouse caught on a branch, and she paused to unhook it with one hand. Cepheus reached out and carefully unwound the threads for her, gently touching her arm as he freed her from the branch. Moksha stood there, looking up at him, curiously. He pulled his hands back once she was free, but her gaze was constant.

"You were younger then, but your voice…" He paused.

"What about my voice?" she demanded as if there were something wrong with it.

"You don't forget the voice of the person who saved your life," he touched the side of her face with several fingers, carefully. "I may have pushed that memory back for a time, but I know it was you."

"Well," she brought her hand to cover his. "You gave me shelter when I was a fugitive, so I'd say we're even."

A long silence ensued. "I'm not very good at this," Cepheus explained.

"You're doing just fine," Moksha smiled.

Cepheus cleared his throat. "There has been no one since Petrichor," he felt a lurch in his stomach as if he were somehow being unfaithful to his late wife.

"I understand," Moksha comforted. "And I'm not in any hurry.

Perhaps, when you're up to it, a day trip to some of the natural waterfalls in the Southern Cross? I promise I'll leave my staff and my sword behind," she laughed.

Cepheus thought a moment and smiled back, his saw-like teeth seeming almost normal for a change. "I've never actually been to the falls," he answered quietly, thinking. "Maybe, just this once…"

They continued ceremoniously walking through the fields, one row at a time. Cepheus reached out and touched a burnt berry, and suddenly he had a flash of Petrichor's vineyard, and then the wine at Lucene's cottage during their reunion dinner. His face lit up.

"What is it? Are you okay?" Moksha was concerned he was about to have an episode.

"I have a crazy idea," Cepheus answered.

"You? You seem far too practical to have crazy ideas."

"Tanager saved several bottles of wine that Petrichor and I had gifted him over the years—pomegranate, blackberry, rossenberry, you name it."

"Yes?"

"After Petrichor's death, a few growers tried to recreate the depth and complexity but couldn't. I wonder…"

"What?" Moksha was not the impatient sort, but curiosity was getting the better of her.

"I still own my land," Cepheus confessed. "I just haven't tended to it since…" Moksha touched his shoulder in understanding. He paused for a moment before continuing. "What if we took the DNA from a few sample bottles of wine like we do to create our clean meats?"

"Yes?" Moksha's eyes grew excited.

"We could recreate her exact grapes and grow it on the exact land she did. Her crops always succeeded even in times of great drought when others did not. And," he finished, "she loved them so much they grew in half the time. Just like you, she tended to those vines as if they were members of the family."

"What are you saying?" Moksha couldn't believe what she was hearing.

"I'm saying that while your land is recovering, you should continue making your wine on mine. It wouldn't take years, maybe only months."

It took Far several months to find his way back to the Military Training Grounds. After which, he immediately sought out Fredo to ask for a meeting with Sovereign Hamish. Normally, Fredo would have been outraged at the audacity of the request. But then, nothing was as it once was anymore. And so, he forwarded the request.

"What is it you are trying to tell me, you weak little man?" Hamish asked Far. While Far was technically taller than Hamish, he hunched his shoulders in such a way that he appeared more like a withered and shrunken vine in front of his new master.

"What I'm saying," Far answered in a whisper, as if it hurt him to speak, "is that after I escaped, I tried to return and find the demon, Jasper Set, but he was gone. I've spent months looking for him."

"Really," Hamish was unconvinced. "With your sense of direction, I thought you just kept getting lost on your return."

"Well, that was part of it," Far confessed. "But I'm telling you, the demon is gone."

Hamish thought of this for a moment, wondering what this would mean for their agreement. Would he then still be under the reign of his superiors? Would the Null still threaten to roll over his world? And, most important to him at present, would Earth ever be his to reside on and rule over? He took none of this lightly as, according to his best estimation, his planet only had a few years left before it became completely uninhabitable. At least with Earth, he stood a chance at reversing the damage.

Maybe a little bit of Jasper Set had rubbed off on Far after all because the young man was suddenly struck by an idea. "You are forgetting something very important, my Sovereign."

"And what is that?" Hamish spat impatiently, rubbing his forehead tiredly.

"I am a prophet," Far reminded him. "Even your Royal army couldn't beat that out of me."

"What are you saying?" Hamish was suddenly intrigued.

"What I'm saying is that I see you in a position of great power."

"What's that supposed to mean?" Hamish waved a hand through the air, gesturing wildly. "I'm already in a position of great power."

Far took a chance. "This?" He motioned around the room, matching Hamish's movements. "This is not power."

"Careful," Fredo stood guard at his station in front of the door to Hamish's private chambers, gritting his teeth.

"Whatever do you mean?" Hamish was in the young man's face now. Far could smell the remnants of leftover rodent from Hamish's earlier dinner.

"I see you ruling the entire Royal clan across the galaxy," and then he added for emphasis, "with the Child at your side."

Hamish's eyes lit up. *But is he telling the truth,* he asked himself.

"Is that so?"

"It is so."

"Then answer me this," Hamish challenged, "what is its name."

Far had his Sovereign exactly where he wanted him. You didn't need to be a prophet to figure that one out. Far leaned over and whispered into Hamish's ear, Fredo lurching forward as if to protect Hamish. Hamish waved Fredo away as his eyes grew wide.

"How do you recommend that we proceed, Prophet Far?"

Fredo was taken aback. Was this frail nothing of a man suddenly replacing him at his Sovereign's side? He remembered the last time that this happened to him, and he felt betrayed, yet again.

"I predict that the demon Jasper Set will return. But in the meantime, perhaps we have had our sights on the wrong planet?"

"The wrong planet?" Hamish was incredulous.

"Yes, Earth may be much larger and with more resources, but—as you have noticed—their resources are running out. Why not, as they like to say on Earth, 'go for the low-hanging fruit.'"

Hamish nodded in understanding. "Erde?"

"Erde," Far nodded back.

"How? My superiors will wonder why I am disobeying orders if we attack Erde."

"Not if it's in self-defense," Far reasoned.

Hamish let out a chortle as if it had been choked back in his throat and finally broke free. "You think they will ever believe that the Peace-Keepers will attack first?"

"Give me time, Sovereign," Far smiled. His thoughts went to Roman. "Give me time."

33

LAVENDER FIELDS

JUNE. FIVE MONTHS AFTER THE NEW ASSEMBLY.

I van arrived at their cottage at dusk. He looked down at the old pocket watch Fatima had gifted him while back on Earth at a time when they were merely neighbors and smiled. Not bad. Thanks to his upgrades, the SpeedCircuit was now transporting people from Achel to the Crosses in half the time, cutting his commute to only ten minutes each way by train, plus the ten-minute walk from the station home. He could further cut his travel time five minutes if he adopted a brisk jog, but he wasn't feeling that ambitious.

He felt the little box in his pocket to ensure he hadn't lost it en route. It hadn't moved from when he checked just two minutes prior.

Moksha and Fatima were out front planting purple salvia plants around the border of the home, the two having become fast friends and good neighbors over the course of only a few short months.

"Are ye sure ye should be doing that?" Ivan was concerned, watching a very round Fatima with a very round belly down on one knee with her hands in the soil. Moksha found Ivan's concern endearing but unnecessary. *Humans worry far too much,* she thought. Fatima leaned on her knee for support as she hoisted herself from the ground and slapped her hands together to shake the dirt off. She reached for a cup on the windowsill and took a sip. "Moksha," she praised. "I consider my pallet rather refined, and this iced dandelion tea is the best I've ever tasted."

Ivan's eyes widened, "And, are ye sure ye should be drinking *that*?" He'd never actually had dandelion tea, mind you. He was just concerned about Fatima consuming anything he deemed as not "normal" during her pregnancy.

Moksha, sensing a longer conversation coming, decided to take her leave. "Well, I'm just down the path if you need anything." Moksha took a moment to gather up a basket with a canteen of tea, some fruit bread and gardening gloves that she didn't think twice about throwing on top of the leftover bread. She turned to Ivan as she passed, "Nice to see you again, Ivan." Ivan still wasn't sure what to make of Moksha. She was difficult to read. Fatima had instantly befriended her, but that was Fatima's way. Cepheus had seemed to take a shine to her, and since he was the toughest critic of all, Ivan decided to give her a fair shake.

"Nice to see ye too, Mowk-shah." He still couldn't say her name without making it sound more like an "ouch" and an "ah" versus an "oh" and an "uh." She smirked, having long since given up on trying to correct him. Without further word, she made her way down the dirt path to her home, humming to herself.

Ivan turned his attention back to Fatima, who was now standing directly under his chin, waiting for a kiss. "Welcome home," she gave him a peck on the lips. She took her fingers and tried to smooth out the worry lines on his forehead. "Relax," she told him. "I've been following the doctor's orders. I'm supposed to keep up with physical activity as long as I don't get out of breath and keep the Talk-Sing ratio."

"What the hell is thah?" Ivan wanted to know. He didn't do well with change, and this planet has offered nothing but that since they arrived.

"C'mon inside," Fatima motioned, taking his hand as they walked toward the cottage. "I'm supposed to get my heart rate up enough where I can still talk but not sing, for just a few minutes, and then slow down. I can keep gardening as long as I can work and sing for prolonged periods of time."

"Aye," Ivan nodded. "What if yer someone who doesn't like singing?"

"Honey, I believe you're overthinking it." She paused to grab her beverage cup.

"And what does the doctor say about that?" He pointed to the cup. "I thought pregnant women weren't supposed to drink weird teas and wine and stuff."

"According to Wilah, dandelion tea has medicinal properties, like polyphenols, that are actually good for me. I'm okay having it twice a day as long as I space them out a few hours."

Ivan thought a moment, opening the door to the cottage and waiting for Fatima to enter first. She put the cup down in the kitchen sink. "Okay," he decided. "I was skeptical with the whole Talk-Sing thing, but once ye started throwing around fancy words like polyphenols, you had me."

Fatima moved toward Ivan, wrapping her arms around his waist, turning her hips to one side, so her belly wasn't in the way, and looked up at him, playfully. "I know the quickest way to your heart is when I use big fancy words like—" she released her grasp and backed away seductively, running to the other end of the kitchen table. "Para-virtualization."

"You vixen," he laughed, faking a move to the left to chase her around the table and then doubling back and catching her on the right. He planted a kiss on her lips. She pulled away slightly and whispered, "Axial compressor," and giggled so hard that she grabbed her belly to stop it from jiggling so much.

"So, uh," Ivan tugged nervously at his ear. "Unrelated to fancy words, I kinda wanted to talk to ye about something."

"Everything okay?" Fatima looked concerned.

"Everything's fine. More than fine even." He pulled a chair out for her. "I sorta have to ask ye something, and I think ye should sit down fer it."

Fatima shot him a quizzical look but sat, with some effort. Ivan made a mental note to re-design their kitchen chairs to be more ergonomically friendly.

He pulled out the chair next to her and set it across from her and sat down. He took her hands in his and looked into her eyes, letting out a deep sigh. "So, I know yer not as traditional as some, er, obviously," he eyed her large belly. Fatima stifled a laugh. "I mean, we're a bit older than some—"

"Not here," Fatima interrupted. "Some start families even into their seventies."

"Yeah, but that's here, and we're not from here. There's no guarantee we'll ever evolve to live as long as they. So, from our timeline, we're a little later to the game."

"Not too late," Fatima replied gently.

"No," Ivan agreed. "Not too late." He paused. "But we also went right from the love to the baby carriage things, which is okay if that's how you want it, but—" Ivan tripped over his words.

"Ivan?"

"Yes?"

"Are you trying to ask me to marry you?"

"Er…Maybe?"

"Maybe? Or, yes. They are two very distinct words," Fatima was adamant.

"I'm nah good at this sort of thing," Ivan complained. "You're the better communicator. Ye should ask me."

"Nah, ah," Fatima shook her head. "I'm not letting you off the hook that easily." She took time for a long, pregnant pause, laughing to herself at her mental joke.

"Ah, fine," Ivan released her hand and reached into his pocket. He pulled out a little box and opened it. Inside was an adjustable rose gold ring with a bright purple gemstone that had what appeared to be a vibrant orange flame sparkling from its center. Fatima was mesmerized by it. It was unlike anything she'd ever seen. "Fatima Fortunata, will you be my wife?" He held his breath.

"Of course, I will, silly." She giggled. "Did you really think I would set you up for failure?" She grabbed his face in her hands and kissed him. She turned her attention back to the ring. "This is so beautiful. What is it?"

"Ah," Ivan beamed proudly. "It's a combination of purple musgravite and orange clinohumite, they're pretty rare around here."

"I didn't think it was possible to have a hybrid of two gems within a single stone." She peered at it closely, watching the sparkles of light bounce off the kitchen walls.

"It isn't, at least not in nature so far," he explained. He tugged on his ear. "I made it fer ya in me new lab at the Makerspace."

Fatima was speechless, putting out her left hand so he could put it on her ring finger. Ivan slid it over her finger, and it auto-adjusted to the right size. "What the heck?" Fatima stared at it in awe.

"Yeah, it's adjustable. Figured that once you had the baby, your fingers might get smaller...not that they have to," he quickly explained.

"It's the most beautiful thing I've ever seen," she gushed.

"So far," he answered, touching her belly.

"So far," she nodded, covering her hand with his.

Two days later, Cepheus knocked on the Fortunata house's front door (Fatima insisted on naming their cottage, and since the name meant "fortunate," Ivan lobbied for her surname as the official name of their residence).

Ivan threw open the door, "Cepheus, buddy. Git in here." Ivan and Fatima hugged him as if they hadn't seen him in months, even though it had only been a few days. Fatima's zest for life and affectionate nature was slowly starting to rub off on Ivan, but only for certain people.

Cepheus was not evolving that quickly and lightly tapped them each on the back, gently. But he appreciated the sentiment.

"I come bearing good news," Cepheus explained.

"Please, sit," Ivan motioned toward the kitchen table.

Fatima moved toward the cupboard. "Can I offer you water, juice, or Moksha left us some of her dandelion tea? It's wonderful."

"I know it is; I just came from—" Cepheus stopped mid-sentence. Ivan's eyebrow shot up, but he said nothing. "I'm familiar with Moksha's teas." That didn't come out as intended, and the normally pale face of Cepheus suddenly gave off a pink glow. "Nothing for me, thank you," he finished in his deep voice.

"So, what is it, man?" Ivan took a seat. Fatima opted to stand. Her back was hurting, and she actually preferred it. She leaned into the kitchen counter for support.

"It took some time, but I was able to successfully sponsor you both as temporary residents of Erde," he paused, waiting for Ivan to pick up on its meaning, "with nearly all the benefits of citizenship."

Ivan's face lit up, hopefully, "Even the Monetary Exchange within the Universal Marketplace?"

"Exactly," Cepheus nodded.

Fatima was clueless, watching the men exchange knowing glances. All this time, Ivan had been worried. Earth had been inhospitable, but at least he'd made a decent fortune. He'd abandoned it all coming to Erde, his own funds having been temporarily frozen when Earth officials had him under investigation, leading to lots of hoop-jumping while attempting to transfer money at the Exchange. He had no clear idea how he and Fatima would support themselves, let alone a baby, if they weren't successful in petitioning to take up residency.

"What's going on? What am I missing?"

"It means that we are financially secure again, love," Ivan let out a sigh of relief. "Assuming," he continued, "that my funds aren't on lockdown again because the government has, on multiple occasions, accused me of treason."

"Ah, yes," Cepheus nodded knowingly. "That brings us to matter number two."

"What's that?" Ivan leaned an elbow on the table.

"You're technically under the protection of this preserve. We can further petition you as permanent citizens of Erde, if you are willing to renounce your Earth residency and claim Erde, and its surrounding planetary regions as your home."

"Wait," Fatima questioned. "So, we'd be giving up Earth, but we'd gain citizenship on Erde…and several other planets, too?"

"Yes," Cepheus answered. "Our domain currently consists of five planets, Erde being the youngest and smallest."

Fatima thought carefully. "Does this mean that I'd never be able to return to see my family again?" She felt a deep sorrow in her heart. She longed for her parents, siblings, and extended relatives to be able to be there for the birth of her first, and probably only, child.

"Not forever," Cepheus answered, with some doubt. "At least, I hope not. But Ivan is considered a threat. So, until his name is cleared by the current governing bodies, you won't be traveling to Earth in the foreseeable future."

Fatima's face dropped. She crinkled her face as she fought back tears. Ivan rushed to wrap his arm around her shoulder in comfort.

Cepheus suppressed the grieving in his own heart. He understood. "You don't have to decide right away, but it is the best option for your safety and security. If you are a citizen, then Erde cannot be forced to return Ivan to Earth by government order, and Earth will have no claims to his finances. He'll be able to reclaim his wealth.

"It would be a better life for us," Ivan reasoned, "if we had the money." For some time, he'd had this minute inkling of fear that Fatima may have only seen him as a good catch because of his financial security. When he'd lost that in their escape, he began to doubt himself, and his overall worth.

"Do you not know me at all?" Fatima chastised Ivan. "I don't give a rat's ass about the money. It's *you* that I'm worried about. So, if becoming citizens means you'll be safe, then that's what we'll have to do!" Ivan felt a little tug in his heart and a sense of something. *What was it? Relief?*

"Cepheus," Ivan asked, "Does Fatima have to renounce citizenship as well, seeing as she's done nothing wrong? Won't it hurt her chances of reconnecting with her family?"

"As of right now," Cepheus explained. "She considered an accomplice. So, she is in as much danger as you. It may not matter in a few years, but in dealing with the situation in front of us, the PDL believes that this is your best option."

Fatima and Ivan exchanged glances. "Then," Fatima answered, "that's what we need to do."

Cepheus reached into his jacket and pulled out a rolled document. "Here is more information. You can access the PDL database at TARA to fill out the necessary documentation. I've printed out the guidelines for you." Cepheus laid it out on the table. Ivan was about to laugh and tell Cepheus about the remote computer he had stashed in the basement and that he could tap into the PDL database for that information anytime he wanted, but then he figured it wasn't the best idea, seeing as he was still a fugitive from another planet. It might, he reasoned, hurt his chances of being made a citizen.

"Thank ye, Cepheus. We'll look it over."

"We're about to have dinner. Would you care to join us?" Fatima offered.

"You are very kind," Cepheus answered. "But I already—" The pink glow returned. Fatima sucked in a laugh and pursed her lips. "But I have to get back to Achel on other business matters." Cepheus was about to stand.

"Er," Ivan began. "Do ye have jest a minute more fer us?"

"Of course," Cepheus settled back into his chair, his long legs stretched out in front of him. Ivan made a mental note to, in addition to making the chairs ergonomically more sound, making them adjustable to accommodate varied heights as well.

"We were jest wondering—" Ivan eyed Fatima. She nodded for him to continue. "Not sure how ye feel about this, but ye have been a friend for a long time and have been so helpful to us. We were thinking that, with yer permission, of course, we could name our baby after yer baby."

Cepheus was confused. "My baby?"

"What he means to say," Fatima put a hand on Ivan's shoulder, "is that we just learned that our baby is going to be a girl," she let out a snort. "One of Dr. Wilah's nursing students accidentally let it slip."

"So much fer surprises," Ivan laughed.

"Anyway," Fatima continued. "We were hoping we might name her after your daughter—"

"Tallulah," Ivan finished. He sat at the ready, watching for any signs of Cepheus retreating into himself for an episode. Cepheus sat for a moment, deep in thought.

"No," Cepheus shook his head, to Ivan and Fatima's disappointment.

"Okay, man," Ivan acknowledged. "We understand."

"No," Cepheus repeated. "I mean, yes." The couple was understandably confused. "What I mean to say is," Cepheus paused to frame his words. "I would be honored if you would name your baby after Petrichor and my daughter, Tallulah. But," he cautioned, "you have to change the spelling of the name."

"Why?" Fatima and Ivan asked in unison.

"It's a custom," Cepheus answered. "If a child grows and leads a good life, then you honor them by naming another after them. But, if a child has a bad life, such as—" he welled up in tears. He didn't need to explain. *Such as being killed in childhood.* "If," he recovered, "the child fell on misfortune, then you don't want to pass on that misfortune. In this case, you honor them by naming a new child after them but changing the spelling."

"Like, taking one of the "l"s out of her name, for example." Fatima reasoned.

"Exactly," Cepheus agreed. "My Tallulah had three "l"s in her name. If you took out an "l" or even an "h," that would be acceptable."

"I think we can manage that," Ivan reached his hand up and touched Fatima's hand, which was still resting on his shoulder.

Cepheus's eyes turned bloodshot as he fought back tears.

"I'm not sure what to do here," Fatima's voice stammered. "May we hug you?" Cepheus nodded, and the couple wrapped their arms around him in a tight embrace.

"I am honored," Cepheus finally answered. "As are the spirits of Petrichor and little Tallulah."

"And, if we have any more kids—" Fatima socked Ivan in the arm and shot him a don't even go there look. After he thought it through, he realized she was right; it would have been inappropriate. He was going to say that if they had two more kids, boys, in particular, he would also name them after Cepheus's lost family. Ivan meant to be respectful but realized that this was one of those social oddities where he threatened to say the wrong thing. Fortunately, he now had Fatima to cover for him.

"We can't wait to introduce you to Talula, T-a-l-u-l-a, when she arrives," Fatima smiled. Cepheus looked at Fatima as if seeing her for the first time. His eyes floated back and forth between the two, and for the first time, he realized something. Like Tanager and Lucene, they were now a part of his family.

34

HOME

JULY. SIX MONTHS AFTER THE NEW ASSEMBLY.

"Go on ahead of me," Tanager advised Lucene as he held a small satchel of groceries in each arm. Lucene laughed over her shoulder as she opened the door.

"Kinda like when we first met," she smiled.

"Sorry, I don't have a window that would be reasonable to climb through," he joked, remembering her aversion to red doors, so much so that she'd sooner climb through an open window versus crossing the door's threshold.

"Very funny—" The words caught in her throat as she stepped inside. Lucene scanned the rectangular-shaped room curiously as Tanager followed behind her, setting the two bags on the kitchen counter to the left of the door, then kicking it closed with his foot.

"It looks like home…I mean, not exactly like Fatima's house, but very…"

"Suburban Earth-like?" Tanager finished. "That one was rather difficult to explain to the designer when I bought this place.

Lucene wandered through the kitchen, unable to find the words. In front of her were labradorite countertops wrapped in a rectangular shape and kitchen appliances that appeared to resemble something found in an ancient department store catalog from several decades ago aligning the wall…a stove, a dishwasher, a refrigerator…even an old-fashioned microwave. Unique to this kitchen, however, were herbs hanging from hydroponic containers above the counter.

"They look old…the appliances, I mean. It was the best they could come up with to look the part but still be functional. If you open the oven, you'll see that it's much more advanced than at first glance." Tanager quickly unpacked the food, stuffing things haphazardly into the refrigerator before slamming it shut. It didn't close right the first time. Agitated, he smacked the door a second time.

Lucene noticed this, curiously, as Tanager was typically pretty meticulous about keeping items organized. He wasn't the type to toss things into a refrigerator absentmindedly. She pushed the thought away, more interested in seeing the rest of his high-home.

Lucene moved on to the dining area where a long wooden table and chairs sat lengthwise along a wall-to-wall panel of sliding glass doors, giving the most spectacular view of the cityscape at sunset.

"It's breathtaking," she was awestruck.

"Yes, well—" Tanager tugged behind his ear nervously. "The designer was skeptical when I told him I wanted the apartment to have a suburban cottage feel, and he said, 'with this view…'" Tanager imitated the rough voice of the designer. "'Listen,'" he continued gruffly, "'I can give you urban Earth, more or less, but *Suburban* Earth in an *Urban* Achelian setting? That's a big ask.'"

"Those sound like challenging Earth colloquialisms to me," Lucene smiled.

"Yes, he's a gentleman I hired who currently lives on one of the preserves."

Lucene nodded in approval. "But he did a good job."

"I thought so…"

By then, Lucene had made her way to the sunken living room with water running down the walls, flowing into a small stream that flowed beneath them, visible through the glass tile.

"That," Tanager wrinkled his forehead, remembering Cepheus's old house, "had a slightly different inspiration."

"I see," Lucene hugged herself. "I assume the bedroom is through there," she pointed to an opening to one side of the living room.

"Ah, yes. Two bedrooms and bathrooms, actually, one that way," he pointed past the kitchen, "and the other behind this wall." He motioned to the living room. "There's also what you would refer to as a laundry room next to the bathroom and—"

"Where it was in Fatima's old house!"

"More or less. It was one of the only houses I got to actually visit while I was on Earth, and Ivan's looked more like an extension of his garage, so I knew that wouldn't work. As I said, I couldn't get it exactly right, so it's more of a hybrid."

"It's amazing, but…why?" Lucene stood by the window, watching as lights from varying hi-rise buildings began to light up in a soft multicolored glow that somehow didn't detract from the stars above. She folded her arms, taking it all in, including the view of the Eiffel Tower in the distance.

"Well," Tanager stood beside her, at first trying to lean casually on the table. That felt too conspicuous, so he adopted her crossed arms position and stood next to her, shoulder-to-shoulder. He could feel the intense buzzing of energy between them and was hoping she could figure it out without him explaining it.

"But I want you to say it," Lucene whispered.

"Hey," Tanager joked. "Stay out of my head."

"That's just it," Lucene responded quietly. "I'm not in your head. I made some assumptions based on observation."

"Really?"

"Don't act so surprised," she answered flatly. "A gal can learn."

"But, the energy," he was confused.

"Chemistry?" Lucene offered. It was disconcerting, not being sure how he felt and what he thought. What she knew of him was no longer based on some kind of other-worldly superpower; but time learning how to understand one another, what each micro expression meant and how to define a slight shift in vocal tone. "You still haven't answered my question. Why did you design your high-home in this very specific way?"

Tanager cleared his throat before making a motion in the air so that the lights in the room came on, adjusting to a dim glow. "It's getting dark, so…" He was avoiding the question.

"I see——" Lucene looked at him, then the floor, then briefly for someplace to retreat in fear. But, she discovered, she didn't really want to retreat. Instead, she moved around the table and toward the kitchen. "Perhaps I can open some wine for us?" She started rifling through the cabinets, having no idea where anything might actually be.

"I did it with you in mind, Lucene," Tanager finally blurted out. "Perhaps misguided, but I somehow thought that maybe someday… you might want to live here…with…me."

Lucene touched the countertop lightly with her fingers. "You know I can't cook worth a damn, right?" She laughed nervously.

"Yes, I am well aware," he blushed. "That's why the kitchen only looks Earth-like but is functional so that *I* can actually use it." He joined her in the kitchen, reaching under the counter for a rossen-berry sparkling port he'd been saving from a neighboring town, in the hopes he'd eventually have a reason to open it. After all, as far as he knew, it was a beverage unique to Erde. He set the bottle down when he noticed Lucene wringing her fingers and fidgeting in place, gazing at the floor.

"I'm sorry," he took her by the shoulders and tried to meet her gaze. "I'm not suggesting any of this needs to happen. It was an impulsive gesture, I understand."

After a pause that seemed like an eternity, Lucene answered, "You know, it's not that I'm opposed to learning how to cook," she glanced up at him, hopefully. "Though, truth be told, I'd do much better at repairing that glitchy light." She pointed up at one of the hanging tear-drop shaped bulbs that hung from the ceiling. Technology, she had come to learn, was not nearly as terrifying as she once thought.

"Then, I promise to leave all electrical work to you," he grinned sheepishly and took a step toward her.

Lucene leaned back slightly, only to discover the high bar-top counter at her back. There was nowhere else for her to go.

"I feel it my duty to warn you that unless you tell me not to, I'm going to kiss you right now."

"Well," she answered with more bravado than she actually felt. "It's about damn time."

Tanager touched one hand to the side of her face, wrapping it around her ear and behind her head. With his other hand, he circled her waist and pulled her toward him. Lucene instinctively wrapped her arms around him as he leaned forward to kiss her, vaguely noticing that the patterns on her arm were glowing again.

Truth be told, neither could be completely sure exactly when the kiss began, as the energy between them was so intense that it was as if both were swallowed by a burst of sunlight, and now they floated in a continuous pool of white light flowing in all directions.

35

HYSECHIA AND MARZIPAN
NOW.

Something caught the corner of Marzipan's eye from his habitat. He unrolled from a leaf he had been sleeping on with a start. There it was again, outside the door of Mati's bedroom. He could make out a low growl and a long tail. Marzipan tried to call for his caretaker but then remembered he had taken the night off to visit his family in the Eastern Cross and wouldn't be back until morning.

"Looking for me?" the tiger-like figure pressed her face up to Marzipan's case. The firefly-like boy backed up, tripping over a small pebble and landing backward into the small pond in his habitat.

"What are you?" Marzipan asked in terror. Its face was white and black striped with flecks of yellow in it, but it had a distinctly human-like mouth and eyes.

"You mean, you don't know?" The cat's paws had digits on the thumb and forefinger that allowed it to easily lift the lid on the habitat and clasp the firefly's delicate wings, lifting him out of his home. "Look again." It pulled Marzipan in so that the little insect actually swayed back and forth with the tiger's breath.

Suddenly, Marzipan's eyes grew wide. "Tabby?" It was the small house cat that had been in quarantine in the next habitat over. "But how—"

Tabby let out a laugh. "Actually, it's Hysechia," she corrected. "Tabby is such an overused name for a cat, don't you think?"

"Uh, I guess so?"

"But how did you get so…big?"

Hysechia bared her teeth in an ominous grin. "A high-protein diet," she answered, "which includes vitamins and minerals."

"Oh," Marzipan was unconvinced. "That makes sense."

"From snacking on little fireflies." Marzipan froze. Hysechia was just about to drop Marzipan in her mouth when she heard a voice.

"Put him down," Isabella commanded from the doorway.

"Well, well, well, what a surprise," Hysechia grinned. "Or what?"

"Or you'll have to answer to me," Isabella held her stance. Hysechia considered this for a moment and dropped Marzipan back into the pond with a splash. He went under water for a moment but quickly floated to the surface, choking out water and wiping it off of his wings.

The feline began pacing around Isabella, who was now fully in the room. There wasn't much space, and Isabella could feel the tail of the cat as it repeatedly circled her.

"Come to clean up your mess, bruja?" Hysechia growled.

"I am no witch," Isabella responded indignantly.

"Oh, forgive me," Hysechia purred as if she found this funny. "That's right. You're a Shaman…same difference."

"They are nothing alike," Isabella was annoyed in the same way that Odessa became irritated when she was confused for a mermaid. It wasn't that she had anything against the occult. She practiced it for many centuries. Isabella just hated labels and being confined to them. "And I claim no faith whatsoever."

"Really?" Hysechia was surprised. "You who have run religious institutions all over Earth have no allegiance?"

"My allegiance is to support those in need. That is all."

"Well, if you hadn't noticed, I am in *need* of a snack," Hysechia gestured toward Marzipan's habitat.

"How did you escape your form?" Isabella demanded.

Hysechia began her guttural laugh, pausing for a moment to lick her paw and preen the side of her ear. Finally, she answered, "I have you to thank for that."

"What are you talking about?"

"The portal, bruja." Isabella's eyes grew wide. "Aha," Hysechia continued. "Now, you get it. When you sent Jasper Set in, you let other spirits out and voila! I had the resources to remove the binds that kept me in the form of a simple house cat."

"What other spirits? I sent him to another dimension. How can this be?"

"No, bruja. You didn't." Hysechia found the whole thing entirely amusing. "Jasper Set isn't in another dimension. He's simply *between the layers*." For the first time in a long time, Isabella was afraid. Her eyes grew wide. "I see that you understand," the feline continued. "When you stuffed him in the middle world, you may have temporarily contained him, but he will get out, just like the other spirits you set free. And when he does, he's going to be sooooo cross with you! Good going, bruja."

The news of her mistake sank in deeply. Jasper Set was still here, between the layers. And, perhaps even more importantly. *What else was there? What had she let out?*

Stay tuned for *The Data Collectors Book Three, Between the Layers,* for the conclusion of this trilogy.

ABOUT THE AUTHOR

Danielle Palli is a writer, business owner, multimedia specialist, mindfulness coach, and podcast producer and co-host. She lives in Southwest Florida with her husband and far too many pets. She also finds joy in nature, travel, theater and the arts, and is known for singing and dancing around the living room at any hour of the day or night. Also, you can convince her to attend almost any event if you promise her that she can wear a themed costume. Learn more at www.birdlandmediaworks.com.